Pride Publishing books by Angel Martinez and Freddy MacKay

Lijun
Fireworks and Stolen Kisses

Pride Publishing books by Angel Martinez

Single Title
Wild Rose, Silent Snow
Boots

Offbeat Crimes
Lime Gelatin and Other Monsters
The Pill Bugs of Time
Skim Blood and Savage Verse
Feral Dust Bunnies
Jackalopes and Woofen-Poofs
All the World's an Undead Stage

Endangered Fae
Finn
Diego
Semper Fae

Anthologies
50's Mixed Tape: The Line

Lijun

TRYSTS &
BURNING EMBERS

ANGEL MARTINEZ &
FREDDY MACKAY

Trysts and Burning Embers

ISBN # 978-1-78686-385-0

©Copyright Angel Martinez and Freddy MacKay 2018

Cover Art by Emmy @studioenp ©Copyright November 2018

Interior text design by Claire Siemaszkiewicz

Pride Publishing

TRYSTS &
BURNING EMBERS

Dedication

For Diane and her ten tissues. Thank you for your
friendship and loving me the way I am
— Freddy MacKay

For my eternal Isis, the cat who helped write this
book. I miss you
— Angel Martinez

Chapter One

A New Year's Bang

"Uma! Uma!"

There was a tug on Haru's *yukata*.

"Uma! Uppie!"

Two adorable pairs of brown eyes gazed up at them. Livy and Jackson leaned against their legs, the children's chubby little arms wrapping around and hanging on tight. If the joeys weren't about to make them all fall over, Haru would've found the pleading adorable. The little cannonballs were going to break their neck if the kids kept hitting them at full speed, though. Haru stumbled, but managed to brace a hand against the wall to steady themself.

"Uppie?" they asked.

Livy's lower lip came out in full-on pout mode. Then Jackson's eyes went big and wide. The children were perfecting the art of manipulation under the guise of innocence. Haru felt pride and slight panic at how easily the joeys' little expressions of woe could sway them. When Livy's eyes watered up, Haru knew they'd been outflanked and outmaneuvered. They sighed, and two nearly identical squeals of triumph split the air at surprising decibels as Haru lifted their pups up.

"What trouble are you getting into?" they asked.

Jackson sniffled. "Nothin'."

"Uh-huh. I thought you were supposed to be with Lahi and Mindy?"

"They hafta get Amelia unstuck."

"Unstuck?" Haru paused their descent back downstairs and gave their pups a once-over. Livy and Jackson smiled openly, eyes wide, little fingers holding onto the front of their *yukata* with ease. Those expressions were not so innocent. They looked angelic, seemed perfectly cute and disarming, unless one looked closer. Livy and Jackson were hiding something. The pups were trying to distract them.

What had Lahi done?

Haru closed their eyes, took a deep, settling breath in then let it out. They'd thought if Mindy were helping to supervise the pups, fewer hijinks would occur. Apparently, Haru had been wrong. They leveled a patient but perturbed expression on their pups.

"What did your aunt do?"

Jackson rubbed his black curls against Haru's shoulder but didn't answer. Livy settled her long, dark brown tresses against their chest and started petting their *yukata*. Gods, exactly how 'stuck' was Amelia? Where was she stuck? Or, rather, what was she stuck *in*? The past couple months had proved Melia could fit into almost anything she set her heart on, unless she couldn't.

"Livy, Jackson."

Those two sets of adorable brown eyes lifted to Haru's gaze.

"My loving pups."

"Yes, Uma?" Livy replied softly.

"Where are your sister and Aunt Lahi?"

"On the roof. Kinda."

Of course they were.

"Melia's in the drainpipe."

Of course she was.

Jackson piped up. "Aunt Lahi thought she heard a pixie. She couldn't fit so she sent Melia in."

Of course. "Was there a pixie?"

"It's Jasper, but he's not stuck," Jackson replied with gusto. So certain. "But he can't get out."

Oh no. Ever since Kaho-chan had chomped on their little friend, Amelia had gotten bitey with him too. "Is he screaming?"

Livy and Jackson shook their heads in unison. Bad sign. Completely and utterly horrible sign.

When they found Lahi and Mindy, the two wayward babysitters were on the roof by one of the chimneys. It made sense. Lots of the pixies hibernated by them because of the heat. Nests dotted the roof everywhere. More than one sleepy-eyed pixie watched their group as Haru tried to contain their annoyance. They had one obviously distressed opossum squeaking frantically and a crying pixie whose wails reverberated up and down and through the gutters.

"Why would you send a three-and-a-half-year-old down a drainpipe?"

Lahi shrugged. "She fit."

"Melia also likes to chomp on pixies right now."

"She promised she wouldn't." Lahi frowned, then glanced down the pipe. "I couldn't just leave him in there."

"No, I know."

"I really thought it was a quick drop in, pull out."

Haru glanced over at Mindy, who waved her hands frantically. Lahi? Was a reasonable adult with periodic bad ideas. Mindy? Responsible to the core. Or she had been. They'd really expected better from her.

"I went inside to get some blankets," she said. "I thought Jasper would need some warming up once Lahi got him out."

No wonder. Also explained the wet blankets tossed into the hall through the window. Poor Mindy actually looked positively green around the edges. The pinched lines around her mouth only made her peregrine-type features more noticeable. The way her eyes focused on the pipe, how her head turned as she listened to the noises Amelia and Jasper made. Ten bucks said a part of her wanted to hunt the distressed pixie. The hawk part.

"Do we know how Jasper got stuck?" Haru asked slowly, working hard not to yell. They pictured the nice prawns Tally had flown in special for them.

"The pixies sometimes use the gutters and downspouts as quick transports to stay out of the wind. Probably got his wing caught."

The sobs got louder, followed by some chirp-humming. Impressed that their little girl had learned how to make the noises, Haru almost wasn't mad at the ridiculousness of the situation. Almost. The fury they'd felt climbing onto the roof had lessened, though. Scary how hearing one of their pups chitter made them calm down.

"It's okay, Jasper," Lahi called down the pipe. Several pixies crowded around the opening too. "We'll get you out." Then under her breath said, "Somehow. Amelia! Little girl, be gentle with him."

A chirp reverberated up the pipe.

All of them, lijun and pixies alike, were staring down the pipe discussing options when Tally showed up. Their Argaze slide a hand slid around Haru's waist before pulling them back against his chest. Tally didn't yell, or curse. In fact, he seemed all too calm about the situation to Haru.

"How can you not be upset?" they whispered.

"Do you know how many times I or one of my siblings got stuck in these pipes?"

Haru stared. Blinked. Then blinked again.

"Melia and Jasper will be fine."

"You are not serious, about the pipes?"

"Completely. Mom and Dad decided to install a different kind of downspout because frantic kid serpents stuck in drainpipes can get a little harrowing. Lahi's just never had to do this since she's almost the youngest." Tally let go of Haru and bent to pick up the stepladder he'd apparently dragged up without Haru noticing. Joey and pixie noises covered up a lot of sound. "Just give me a minute or two here."

With one hand, Tally lowered the stepladder so its bottom feet rested on the roof of the front porch below. His long black braid swung free on his back as he eased over the edge of the second-floor roof onto the ladder and pressed his ear to the downspout. Some of the pixies flitted about his head, offering high-pitched advice and instructions.

"Shh. I have to listen. Hush now." Tally moved his head down, knocked on the pipe and nodded to himself. The cold reddened his long fingers. Silly snake, out without his gloves. "Haru, are you watching? Just in case you need to do this at some point?"

Still flummoxed, Haru edged over to where they could observe Tally's hands. "Yes. But what are you doing? Do *not* drop Melia."

Tally shot them a grin and began to unscrew a bolt on the downspout near his knees. As the bolt loosened, Haru was able to discern the band of metal it had been holding, then the line of separation where one corrugated piece of downspout ended and another started.

Oh. It comes apart.

Tongue caught between his teeth, Tally pulled up on the top section, slowly easing it out of the joining section underneath. He moved quickly when the section came loose to put his hand beneath, then nodded to the pixies.

"Go on. See if you can get Jasper."

Two of them, one green, one orange, zipped up the pipe and Tally winced when the sobbing became a shriek. But whatever had been caught was now un-caught. Jasper thunked into Tally's hand and was immediately retrieved by a mob of pixies. One, at least, had to help keep him upright. Jasper did look like he'd been mouthed some.

Tally leaned to call up the pipe. "Melia! Do you see the light? Can you slide toward it? Usar will catch you."

With a squeak and something that sounded like the opossum version of *wheeee*, Amelia slid free and smacked into Tally's waiting grasp. He scooped their girl against his chest, scolding her quietly for chomping Jasper. She sneezed then climbed his sweater to sit on his shoulders.

"Not going to admit you tasted him, are you?"

Amelia sneezed again.

"Didn't taste good, did he?"

Amelia squeaked, essentially affirming Tally's tongue-in-cheek remark.

Jasper blew a raspberry toward her but just huffed as the pixie mob ushered him to the roof. Tally screwed the pipe back together then climbed up, pulling the ladder up after him. He winked at Haru, who was scowling at their Argaze.

"Lahi just let me panic."

Speaking of the devil... She and Mindy had mysteriously disappeared with the other pups.

"A little bit, yeah."

"*Still*, she should not have sent Melia after into the downspout after Jasper."

"We've done worse to each other as siblings. Lahi was just trying to help." Tally shrugged. "Frozen pixies are not fun to find in the spring."

Haru's stomach turned violently, but then they saw the slight upturned smile Tally wore. "Not funny."

"It's a little funny."

"They could seriously get hurt in those pipes," Haru insisted, not understanding why Tally was grinning. They shuddered. "Please tell me we will not find frozen pixies in the gutters."

"No frozen pixies. Promise."

Several of the pixies flitted around Haru, giving them pats, offering up reassurances that while pixies sometimes got caught in the gutters, the little devils were always found—just like their teary-eyed friend. Whom himself needed a thorough inspection. Luckily there wasn't much damage. More pride than anything else. Jasper's right wing was crinkled and listed to one side. While the words helped, Haru still had visions of pixie-icicles floating around in their head. Then the reassuring pats from the pixies turned into stroking their hair. Haru knew in a minute or two they'd be down a few strands if the 'comforting' continued.

"Let us get off this roof before we break something else," they said. Haru cupped Jasper, explaining to the pixie mob, "I want to have his wing checked. You go back to bed."

The mob's gaze volleyed between Haru's head and Jasper, the pixies flitting and weaving between them and Tally.

"Go on, get snuggled up in your nests. The temperature is supposed to drop tonight."

The pixies darted past, Haru and Tally both yelping as the little sneaks stole strands of hair. They really should not have mentioned the weather. Haru rubbed the back of their head then glanced over at Tally, who was chastising the pixies for not asking. Melia stood on her back paws, holding onto his head with her forepaws, squeaking right alongside him.

Haru shook their head. What a picture those two made. In fact, Haru pulled out their phone and snapped one. The pair was just too adorable for words — Usar and pup chewing out the pixies in the middle of a roof on a cold December afternoon.

Life had certainly gotten weird, but a fun weird, since moving to America and putting the murders behind them. It was sailing along smoothly. Almost too smoothly.

"Are you in *geta*?" Tally suddenly asked.

"What?"

"Are you climbing around the roof in *geta*?"

Haru glanced down then back up. What else would they wear with a *yukata*? "Yes? I needed something for my feet."

Tally's normal robust russet coloring yellowed. It almost looked like he was going to shout, but instead Tally moved next to Haru and placed a hand on their lower back. It was big, warm and insistent until they climbed back through the window. The ladder came in after Haru, followed by Tally and a smug-looking Amelia.

Could opossums look smug? Yes, it was the smile. Opossums definitely had some kind of smile. Amelia sneeze-chirped, tugging on Tally's hair until he reached up then plopped her on the ground. She took off like a shot down the hall, stopping when Jasper called out.

Amelia scurried back and Haru leaned over, holding Jasper out toward her.

"No. Eating. Pixies," they reminded her.

Jasper leaned over and gave their little girl a one-armed hug. He thanked her, then screeched when she licked him. Haru muffled a laugh, because Jasper should've seen that one coming. Amelia turned tail, running off again, most likely in search of her siblings.

"Go straight to Lahi and Mindy!" Haru called after her. "Please! You should have a bath!"

"She's fine," Tally assured him. "Normal kid stuff."

Haru studied their Argaze.

"Normal lijun kid stuff."

"You Americans have a weird definition of normal."

Tally pulled Haru close, holding them. A kiss was pressed against their temple. Perfect moments like this one made Haru afraid, so afraid of losing everything. Tally chuckled. "Tell me you never got into trouble as a kid."

"Shush, that is different."

"Mmm-hmmm." Tally kissed their temple again.

"It never involved pipes and downspouts and pixies."

"Mmmm-hmmm." Tally kissed their cheek, right next to their mouth.

Haru turned, because if Tally was going to kiss them, he should do it properly. Was there a reason he wasn't? Had their Argaze found out? Haru assessed Tally's expression nervously. No, he couldn't have. But they were running out of time to tell him. Problem was, Haru wasn't sure *how* Tally would take the news. It was...complicated. They licked their tongue over their lips, hoping to entice their Argaze into *something*. Instead, Tally swiped a thumb under their lips. Haru frowned, angling their mouth closer. Tally chuckled and gave them a chaste peck.

"Don't want to mess up your lipstick," Tally said by way of explanation when Haru scowled at him. "Or upset pixies."

"You can mess it up." Haru covered Jasper's eyes and cocked their head back.

"Weren't you getting ready?"

"Ready?"

"When you left my office you were headed upstairs to change." Tally chuckled as he took a step back, his heat leaving Haru. "For the party."

"Party, what—oh, my Gods. The Winter's New Year Ball! I am never going to be presentable in time." Haru turned tail and bolted for their suite, Jasper's protests in hand—literally—and Tally's throaty laughter following them down the hall.

Asshole.

* * * *

Entering the ballroom at the Bastille Arms was like taking a time capsule and traveling back over a hundred years to a typical opulent Victorian hotel. Haru knew it had been built at the end of the nineteenth century by Tally's great-great-grandfather, but the fanciful room surprised them. Huge arched windows lined the back wall, which looked out onto a formal garden.

Blue and gold brocade drapes accented the windows and ornately carved faux columns with curling acanthus leaf capitals decorated the dark wood between. Mirrors framed in gilded splendor lined the opposite wall, echoing the arched shapes and making the room appear even larger. Crystal chandeliers the size of compact cars hung from the ceiling, each facet and crystal drop meticulously polished. Gilded wooden dragons — *dragons!* — joined the scrollwork on cornices and around the massive doorframe, weaving sinuously along edges and lurking in the corners of the ceiling.

"Your family has a weird sense of humor, Argaze," Haru said as they studied the dragons.

"Everybody likes dragons."

"Hmmm."

Tally smiled and shook Councilwoman Howe's hand as she passed by. They had taken refuge by one of the large windows, away from the crowd. Too many people had surrounded the two of them on the dance floor, making it hard for anyone to enjoy themselves. Haru had suggested a respite and Tally had nodded grimly.

"Has the entire council shown?"

"Yes, the debates around the revitalization project have heated up and everyone is here to schmooze the clan—one way or the other."

Haru huffed. "One night, I want *one night* without the council's political jockeying."

Tally had the nerve to laugh.

"It is New Year's. All those things should be set aside for the ball."

"Upset they're spoiling your ball?" Tally laughed louder, drawing attention toward them. "You realize this is exactly the kind of event when all this stuff happens?"

"Hush, it does not mean I have to like it." Haru turned their back, attempting to ignore their Argaze. "I just wanted one night without any worrying."

The dragon really had a lot of detail. Someone had taken the time to add an enormous amount of meticulous scales. Tally sighed and wrapped an arm around Haru's waist, pulling them closer. The heat he radiated sometimes, despite being a reptile, surprised Haru. They glanced back. Okay, maybe it wasn't Tally putting off the heat, but his expression could melt ice. Or Haru. The past couple months he'd definitely been melting the walls around Haru's heart bit by bit. The affection, the simple touches where he expected nothing in return, had surprised Haru at first. Now they had begun to crave them, soaking the caresses up whenever Tally bestowed his affection.

The kisses really were addictive, too.

"I know what you mean," he said, then placed a kiss against Haru's throat. It lingered slightly longer than a kiss normally did. "It would be nice to just enjoy."

Haru hummed a little, turning into Tally's embrace. They snuggled, something Haru found the two of them did more and more often these days — without the pups between them. Being surrounded by Tally's cool embrace wasn't as suffocating as Haru remembered from their wedding night. It was…nice.

"Awww. Aren't you two nauseatingly adorable," Gunther said.

Haru looked around Tally and stuck their tongue out.

Gunther clapped Tally on the back, who in turn gave his friend a slight push — it would've been better if there had been some more force behind it — and laughed.

"Are you stag for tonight?"

"I'm off the deer. I think we all are."

Haru stared at Gunther. Had he really just said that? Out loud?

"I find them a little gamy and stringy, don't you, Haru?" Gunther smiled, chuckling at his own ridiculous jokes.

"Shhhh," Tally said between his own little spurts of coughing. "Not here, Gun. Too many ears."

"Councilwoman Howe's across the dance floor."

"Please stop," Haru said, shaking their head. "You are drunk, Curley-san."

"Not yet, but I'll certainly do my best," Gunther answered, then peeled away from them and Tally, waving away the calls from his friend.

Haru frowned. "Is he all right?"

"Dunno, he's been moody since the wedding."

"Is it me?"

Tally let out a breath, considering, which was nice because he didn't outright deny the hostilities between Haru and Gunther. "It's not *just* you." At least Tally was honest and acknowledged the issue, too. "There are problems with his mom's clan. I don't know all the details. Every time I bring it up, we somehow end up talking around it."

"I think maybe you need to not let him," Haru replied, leaning against Tally. "He is your friend, yes?"

"Since we were kids."

"Then stop worrying about my feelings and talk to your friend."

Tally kissed Haru's head and let out a sigh. "Okay. You're right. There's just been so much…stuff."

"You have been wooing me."

"Is it working?"

Haru let their head fall back, cocking it to the side and looking at Tally. "What do you think?"

"We've made it to first base. I think you like me a little."

"I suppose." Haru left a kiss under Tally's jaw and walked away from him. There were noises of protest, but Tally didn't come chasing after them. He let Haru wander off by themself. Not something they expected—being left alone when Tally so desperately wanted them together.

The snake had *some* smarts in him.

Different clan members swarmed Haru the minute they walked outside some invisible barrier between them and Tally. At about fifteen feet, people felt it was okay to mingle. Poor Tally got cornered by Councilmen Black and O'Rourke, though he shook his head when their eyes met. Okay, so no help needed.

"Uruma Bastille!" a young male voice called. "Uruma!"

"Hush, no need to shout."

One of the young lijun from the Judgment, Cody Redbone, pressed into Haru. If he teetered a little, Haru decided to let it go. In Japan, the young puma was old enough to drink. Haru doubted the staff had served the jittery young man, so there had to be a flask or something going around the kids. *That* they would confiscate, then they would scold. Not too much. Here, Cody was surrounded by clan and family and friends. Though someone definitely needed a ride home.

"Uruma," he whispered, now quiet and more contrite.

Haru gently extracted Cody's hands and pushed him back. "Everything okay, Cody?"

"The council members are talking."

"They usually do."

Cody shook his head then stopped suddenly. His cheeks puffed up. Someone was tossing his dinner before the end of the night. Haru would bet money on it.

"Nooo, I mean, saying things about you and Tally."

"Oh, yes, they would do that too." Haru forced a smile. The young man looked so worried. Was he really only six years younger than Haru? It felt like a gulf of lifetimes stretched between them. "I am sorry they upset you."

"You're not mad? I mean—" Cody burped.

Haru hooked an elbow through Cody's and started leading him out of the ballroom, doing their best to smile and nod at passersby and not to feel irritated about the loss of yummies as servers walked by with shrimp dishes on their platters.

"I mean, they weren't saying nice things."

"Clan politics."

"But they said—" Another burp. "Tally was favoring the humans and spending too much time fucking you to pay attention to clan business."

Only Haru's Satislit training kept them from not tripping over themself and attacking the idiot—they could guess—who had said such gauche things. "I can assure you, *Urusar Bastille* does not play favorites. He wishes to give the best businesses—human and lijun alike—the support they need so the town prospers. It is sound business thinking as well as species politics."

"Do you like him fucking you so much?" Cody let out a longer, echoing burp. Kid was going to vomit any minute. Almost deserved the misery that was about to befall him, too. That second question had caught the ears of too many guests.

"First, my young friend, that is none of your business." Haru waved down one of the staff. "Second, I think we need to find you a room."

"You want to go to bed with me?" Cody looked at Haru, dark eyebrows together, frowning, poor gaze utterly befuddled.

"No, he doesn't, Cody," Sammy replied as she appeared close by. She held open the door to the hotel hallway. "What Haru thinks is you're going to be sick any minute and will need to retch into a room they can clean without disturbing the guests."

"I'm not— I'm not—" Cody's cheeks puffed out again. Another burp followed. Several people, including Sammy, stepped back. Haru would have too, but Cody had a death grip on their arm. "Drunk."

"You most certainly are," Haru replied, hoping their new *kimono* was not about to get ruined. "Who brought the flask?"

"What flask?"

Cody had answered too quickly.

"There's no flask. I came, I came…like this."

Poor guy was still trying to cover for his friends.

Haru raised their head and glanced around the ballroom, observing who was paying close attention to their exit. When they met Tyler Hastings' eyes, the young boar balked, his complexion visibly turning a yellow-green. Of course it was Hasting-san's kid. Tonight just wasn't going to go easy on them. The council members were all nearby like the vultures they were, watching and listening to Haru, and when Councilman Hastings had worked out who Haru had pinned down for the flask, he stomped toward his son. Fury burned in every step.

"Tally!" Haru rudely pointed, giving their Argaze a target. Tally didn't even question why Haru called out but immediately began cutting a path through the crowd toward Tyler.

"Oh shit," Cody whispered, shaking against Haru as he pressed close. "Tyler's dad's going to lose it."

"Does his father hurt him?" Haru glanced down at the young lijun.

But Cody's focus was on his friend. They would've shaken him, but Haru was in no mood to be puked on.

"Does Hastings-san hurt Tyler-kun?"

"No, at least he says he doesn't, but his dad probably makes Tyler wish he did. Tyler'll be working at the store every hour of the day he's not in school. Mr. Hastings is gonna say stuff too."

That explained a few things Haru had observed over the past couple months, and was, in some ways, worse. Poor Tyler was on a precipice, and it could go either way for him. Tally got between him and his dad just in time. Voices rose in clipped bursts. A flask was pulled out of Tyler's jacket. Hastings-san's fists balled up.

One of these days, those fists would strike — if they hadn't already.

Tally's normally russet coloring darkened with a scarlet hue. The flask went into his hand while Hastings-san growled at his recoiling son. Cody made a noise next to Haru, a burbling sort of one that spoke and scented of acrid things to come. Their Argaze would have to get the tussle settled on his own.

Sammy grabbed one arm while Haru grabbed the other and the two of them dragged the drunken puma to an emergency room the hotel had set aside for, well, emergencies. Haru certainly felt this was one.

"See if one of the Blue Hollys could stop by?" they asked the staff hovering near the open door. "There were quite a few in the ballroom."

"Of course, Uruma Bastille. Here's a key to the room." The staff member paused. "Is there a particular Blue Holly you want?"

"Ted, if possible, but preferably one that is sober. Please."

"Right away, Uruma."

There were dozens of Blue Hollys. More than Haru knew about, and several sets of twins that still confused Haru. *One big family* didn't cover it. Keeping who were siblings and who were cousins and which kids belonged to which parents straight needed to be some sort of Olympic event—or someone needed to at least provide Haru with a family tree, one that made sense and was large enough to read.

I thought bears were supposed to be endangered.

"Uruma," Cody whined, the sound a rough purr that turned into a large burp.

Haru and Sammy shared a look over the kid's head. She cringed then said, "Bathroom. Now."

"I don't want a bath," Cody mumbled.

Instead of answering, the two of them dragged him over to the toilet. Haru managed to flip the lid just in time for a *blerg* noise and to see-slash-hear Cody lose all his stomach contents in one long and extremely loud heave.

"Oh…oh, Gods," Sammy stammered.

"Breathe through your mouth," Haru answered.

"I don't think that's going to help."

They glanced over, and sure enough, Sammy had taken on a greenish hue that did nothing for her normally lovely snow-white complexion. "How about you make sure the bed is set up, and then go see if a Blue Holly—"

"Thanks," she called out, already halfway through the door before Haru had finished.

"Uruma," Cody wheezed out, just before another volley of spew came up. "Ugh."

Haru grabbed hold of Cody's black hair—some of which was already wet—and began to rub the boy's back. Each lurch and hiccup had Cody hugging the porcelain god just a little tighter. They flushed, because it needed to happen. The smell—Gods, just no. A low yowl escaped the young lijun between burps. Poor kid was going to be in for a long night. Not to mention a very unfun morning.

"How's—ewwww," Sammy said, out of breath, still greenish.

"Poorly," Haru replied, then noticed a hefty shadow behind her as they looked up. Oh, good, Ted was with her. They gave the doctor an *eshaku*. "Tabib Blue Holly."

"Uruma Bastille." Ted slid into the bathroom and put his bag on the counter. "Cody must've drank quite a bit to be this sick."

A splashing noise was followed by a low groan from the puma in question.

Ted cringed. "Stomach acid is always rank."

Haru agreed. "His dry heaves are going to hurt."

"Do we know what he drank?"

Sammy's muffled voice came from somewhere in the room. "From the whispers, it sounds like whiskey."

Ted sighed, as did Haru.

Cody heaved again, this time nothing much coming up, except for a sob. Tears streaked down his cheeks. "Urumaaaa."

"What are we going to do with you?" Haru rubbed the boy's back, working hard at not smiling. They didn't like seeing Cody so miserable.

"I'll take care of him, Uruma. No, it's fine. I've nursed my fair share of knuckleheads. Why don't you get Sammy some fresh air? She was pretty green when I found her in the hall."

"Yes, she was." Haru shot a worried glance toward the room.

"Is she all right? I've seen her visiting with Mom a few times."

"Ah, yes, no. Sammy is fine. The smell upset her."

Ted nodded, though he had a knowing look in his eyes. "Yeah, some people aren't good with the whole vomiting thing."

"Quite."

Cody heaved again, his body tightening under Haru's hand. Poor boy gurgled and coughed but nothing came up. Both a blessing and a curse. Dry heaving made a body ache. The constant knotting of the stomach and puke factor took its toll. Ted pulled a few bottles out of his case then shooed Haru out of the bathroom.

"If you are sure?" Haru asked, craning their head to spot Cody, who hurled again.

"Yeah, please, go enjoy the ball, Uruma." Ted waved Haru back. "And send any of the other miscreants this way so I can check on them."

"Of course." Haru gathered up a decidedly green Sammy and ushered her into the hall. The same staff member from earlier was hovering not too far away. Haru scented, smelling wolf. He squinted at the nametag. "Rodriguez-kun? Yes. Could you herd any intoxicated, underage kids toward the room and Ted? We want to make sure everyone is all right."

"Yes, Uruma Bastille. Right away."

The wolf shot down the hall toward the ballroom, leaving Haru and Sammy alone, still able to hear the muffled groans and blerg noises Cody made. Sammy turned a chartreuse color that looked wrong on human skin and held her abdomen as if she could ward away the nausea. Not wanting her to join the sick with Ted, Haru led them down the hall and away from all the noise and heat. The two of them wandered through several corridors before they ended up outside on a small bench on one of the patios.

"Feeling better?"

Sammy shivered. "Mmm. Yes, the cold air helps."

"Smells clean."

"Yes, yes it does." She smiled wanly, and a few of her golden ringlets fell in front of her face. "Poor kid is probably coughing up a lung."

"Mmm-hmm."

The two of them cuddled together, watching the night sky, the silence welcome. Several clouds dotted the black expanse, hiding the white light of the stars shining overhead. Haru let out a long breath—a vapor cloud forming in front of their face. While the sting of the winter air felt good in their lungs, Haru doubted Blue Holly-*okaasan* would be pleased to find out they had let Sammy sit outside for so long.

"We should go inside before you catch cold," Haru suggested.

"Not yet. I'm finally breathing easier. A few more and I should be able to brave the ball again."

"You are shivering."

Sammy let out one of her throaty laughs Haru adored. "Then warm me up."

"I can do that," they replied, then slithered off the bench—ignoring Sammy's protest—and knelt in front of her. Haru pulled her forward, wrapping one arm around her waist while their free hand went to her abdomen. They leaned in, nuzzling. "Does this help?"

"Brat," she replied, but Haru heard the laughter in her voice.

Haru left a flood of kisses on her stomach. Kiss. Kiss. Sammy squirmed, pushed back on their shoulders and tried to wriggle back in an attempt to get free. They held her waist firmly, not wanting her to fall. No, falling would definitely be bad for all of them. Haru changed tactics and tickled her sides. Now she really laughed. Soft. Husky. It almost sounded like a purr.

One of her hands cupped their jaw as she guided their head back. She placed a kiss on their mouth, the move enough of a distraction they stopped tickling her. Mmm. Nice. They settled on the ground so their head rested on her lap. It had become one of their favorite positions since their friendship had begun, but especially these days. Haru petted the tiny bump forming on her abdomen, excited and anxious.

The cut of the dress made it hard to see, but soon Sammy's bump wouldn't be so easily hidden, not with two little pups in there. At fifteen weeks she was lucky to have gone unnoticed this far. Haru nudged closer and breathed Sammy in. Just there, underneath the perfume she had started using to hide her scent, they could smell her. Her and the pups. Blue Holly-*okaasan* said they would start moving soon.

One of Sammy's hands stroked down Haru's neck, soothing, familiar. "Have you told Tally?"

"Hmm?"

"Tally—have you told Tally about the pups yet?"

Haru glanced up, and they knew the moment Sammy realized the answer was 'no'. A storm brewed in her blue eyes.

"Haru, he *needs* to know. Some of the sharper grannies have been scenting me all night."

"I know, I know," Haru placated. They sighed and pulled Sammy closer. "It is difficult. To tell him this. Things have been so…so *nice* between us."

"You have been happier," Sammy agreed, still petting Haru.

"I have. *We* have."

"But Tally is going to find out sooner or later, and, Haru, sweetie, you can't let those bastards on the council catch him off guard."

"I know." Haru buried their face against Sammy's abdomen, scenting her and the pups one more time before pulling back. "That is the last thing I want. I just do not know how he will react. I do not want him resenting these pups. When this happened"—Haru pressed their hand against the bump—"Tally and I were in a different place."

"You were, but maybe since the two of you are in a better place he won't be upset. Surprised, but not upset. There are lijun who still go the traditional route."

"Mmm, but that is not what happened."

"No, no it was not," Sammy said softly before she trailed her fingertips along Haru's neck, almost tickling them but not quite. "Tally knows I'm an aromantic, Haru. It's part of the reason I was picked to be your Kwebabiad. Sex, yes. Romantic entanglements, no."

"You think he will remember that when he finds out?"

"You'll just have to remind him. As many times as it takes. It's you and him now."

Haru grunted.

"Oh no. You do *not* get to say you haven't been enjoying the courtship."

"I do not hate him anymore."

Sammy laughed. "That's a start."

Haru kissed her stomach again.

"You're going to get lipstick on my dress."

"Love you." Haru grinned before pressing against her stomach again. Kiss. Kiss. Pet. Pet. "And I love our pups." Kiss. Kiss. Pet. "So much."

"Love you too, Haru—*oh shit*." Sammy tensed under Haru's caresses, and not in a good way. Her eyes were glued to something behind them. Haru twisted around to see what had gotten her so upset and nearly froze themself.

"Tally," they breathed out. Dead. They were so dead.

Chapter Two

Zeroed Out

"I, uh, Ted said, um. Oh, fuck. Ted ssssaid Ssss-sammy wassssn't feeling well." Tally's russet-color skin had lost its golden glow, his cheeks a pale yellow. His chest heaved. "I wanted, um, I wanted to make sss-sure sss-she was okay."

"Sammy is much better," Haru replied, then yelped as a blow landed on their shoulder. "Ow! Woman!"

"Tally is going to run."

"I, uh, yeah." Tally was already backing away from the bench toward the hotel. "I need to go."

Sammy punched Haru's arm again.

Haru pushed to their feet. "Stop! Tally! Please."

To Haru's astonishment, Tally did. Frozen halfway between the patio and the door to the hotel. The way he held himself, shoulders back, his body one rigid line, Haru was afraid if they reached out and touched him, Tally would shatter. Tonight had really gotten turned on its head, all because of Haru and their inability to speak up.

"Thank you, Urusar." Haru found themselves in *dogeza*. *Habits really* are *hard to break.*

"It's Tally. You haven't called me Urusar once in private in the last eleven days. Not once besides lijun business functions."

The amount of hurt in Tally's voice pressed against Haru, but then their anger flared. Why should they feel guilty? Tally went and got hurt all by himself. Haru hadn't done anything wrong. *Technically.* Kwebabaids were there for a reason. They lifted their head slightly, eyeing the big snake.

"Why are you running?"

Tally glanced over his shoulder then sighed. He faced Haru, shoulders hunched, trying to make himself smaller than the humongous lijun he was. "You told Sammy you loved her." He gulped a couple times, then looked up at the sky. "And your pups."

"Of course I love her."

Tally's breath stuttered. The snake's entire body pulsed once and his tongue flicked out.

"Sammy is my Kwebabiad and my friend. Are you saying I cannot love my friend?" Haru looked down at the ground again, too mad to meet Tally's eyes. Were they not allowed to have friends? "Do you not love your friends?"

"Of course I do."

"Then why can I not love Sammy?"

"That, uh, that…" Tally sighed. "It wasn't what you said, Haru. It's *how* you said it."

"That makes no sense."

Sammy groaned, and Haru glanced back quickly, just to make sure she hadn't fallen. She had one hand on her stomach and the other covering her face.

"Are you sick?"

"No, you idiot."

"What?"

Sammy shifted on the bench. "Look, why don't I go back inside while you two talk this out?"

"But—" Haru began to protest.

"No." Sammy slid past Haru and made a beeline for the door. "I am not getting involved in this lovers' tiff. No, thank you." She stopped at the entry, though, long enough to call out, "Tally, I want to remind you I'm aro. Whole reason I volunteered."

"Right, yeah, aromantic. Bisexual aro," Tally mumbled, but he was looking at his feet with his hands shoved in his pockets. He probably had his hand around his worry stone.

Silence hung in the air, heavy like just before snow hits. Haru wasn't sure if it was better to stay in *dogeza* or to risk looking confrontational by standing. Instinct screamed at Haru to either get up and fight or stay down. Their ingrained Satislit training said to stay put, so they decided staying prostrated was better than any other stupid idea.

Beatings sucked. Urusar Akaike wouldn't have waited so long to punish Haru for their breach in protocol, because the Urusar was supposed to have first crack at pups. It could be the proverbial straw. Not that Tally had ever hit them, but fear wasn't logical. Besides, there was always a first time for everything.

Tally glanced around the patio before his gaze finally settled on Haru. His eyes widened a fraction, his nostrils flared and he pulled a face. A headshake followed the grimace.

"You don't have to bow to me."

"I know." But Haru couldn't stand either. Physically they could, yes, but what their head said was another matter. It kept them firmly planted against the cold concrete.

"Haru. Stand up."

"If it pleases you, Argaze." But Haru pressed closer to the ground. All their Satislit training said if they stood, they'd get hurt.

"Damn it, Haru! Stand!"

They shuddered, a whimper escaping them. An image of Urusar Akaike flashed in front of their eyes and Haru hunched in on themself. They turned their head slightly to watch Tally's movements.

"Damn. No. Shit!" Tally threw up his hands, turning a few times. He stopped and breathed in then took several additional slow, measured breaths. When he spoke again, his voice sounded tired and hoarse. "This was not how tonight was supposed to go!"

Haru agreed wholeheartedly.

"Look, Haru. I'm going to sit on the bench. Okay? See. I'm moving over to the bench. Shit! Cold!" Tally's soles no longer scuffed against the concrete. "Haru, I swear, I'm... Well, I *am* mad and confused and upset, but I swear I'm not going to hurt you. You know me."

They did, a little, but that didn't matter. Not to their heart.

"How about this—I promise to keep my hands flat against the bench. Okay? Look, Haru." Tally's hands were pressed against the surface of the bench. "Now, let's talk."

Haru glanced over.

"Damn it, Haru. I hate saying it."

They held in place.

Tally let out a puff of air, which was followed by a quiet, "Your gratitude pleases me."

The tension holding Haru in placed snapped. They pressed up slowly, watching Tally for any signs of movement. There was a shift in their Argaze's demeanor. One that went from on the verge of breaking apart to a softer, sadder expression.

"That hasn't happened in a while."

"No. Not for a few weeks. Maybe a month or so?" Their apology came out a mumbled, "Sorry."

"Right, Thanksgiving. Don't apologize... I... Gods. Just don't apologize."

"Yes, Argaze."

Tally patted the bench, but then glanced sideways at Haru. "Would you feel better if you had an exit?"

Embarrassment burned inside Haru's chest as they nodded.

"Okay, you stay there and I sit on the bench. Fair?"

They nodded again, unable to voice anything.

An awkward silence lingered between Tally and Haru—only the night's breeze to keep the two of them company. Tally sat with his arms on his knees, hunched forward. When he looked at Haru, his eyebrows had drawn together and his lips pressed shut before his words startled Haru.

"What did Urusar Akaike do to you?"

That was the question Tally wanted to start with? Haru had no idea how to answer, but the thought of saying anything burned at their chest. "I would rather not talk about the Akaike clan."

"But I—"

"I do not wish to talk about them!" Haru shouted. Gods. They had said that out loud. They snapped their mouth shut before they did any more damage.

"Okay, fine. Fair enough. Not now." Tally looked up at the sky. "We were supposed to be talking about Sammy and you."

"There is no Sammy and me."

"Are you sure? Because the way you were kissing her stomach, holding her… I've never seen you so happy or free."

"Free?"

"Haru, you were lit up, absolutely ecstatic… I've never seen you like that, except maybe around the kids."

"Oh."

"Yeah, 'oh'."

"Sammy is my closest friend, Tally. My confidant. My Kwebabiad. We are what we are. No more."

"Okay." Tally scuffed his foot against the concrete. "But the timing, Gods. Why now? With the joeys, Misaki's IVF treatments and the improvement plan, we already have so much on our plates."

"Yes, Argaze."

Tally let out a long breath. "I mean, you went the traditional route, right? I haven't seen any bills for the center… Don't you think it was something you should've talked to me about? Misaki and I've been trying the IVF route. You knew that. A bunch of pups at once… We—you and me—are Em'halafi. Shouldn't you have checked in with how I felt about it?"

"We did not *pick* the traditional method." Saying the words stung.

"Yet, here we are, Sammy pregnant."

"It happened because of my need for comfort."

A long stretch of silence filled the gap between the two of them. Tally stared at Haru, his dark brown eyes

36

focused intently on them. "This wasn't a planned pregnancy?"

"No."

Tally flinched. "And you're saying it happened because of *love*?"

"The love of friendship, yes."

"Haru... I'm struggling here. You need to help me understand. What's going on with you and Sammy? I thought *we* were doing better. That we could talk about these things. That we're happy." Tally fisted his hair. "Gods, what a mess."

"Sammy is fifteen weeks."

"Fifteen?" Tally's voice shook.

"Yes, it happened the night of the fireworks...when Cohen-san was murdered. I needed a friend and Sammy was there. That night was about comfort and friendship. That is all. But, and it is probably a large *but*, I am happy because my pups will know they were born from love, not some cold, clinical practice."

"Okay, okay. That's going to take me a minute. You're saying it just happened?"

"Yes, and—" They gulped then pushed back hard, just like they used to with Akaike-san. Angry. Reckless. Testing. "I will not apologize for it. She is my Kwebabiad," Haru uttered, finally finding the voice to say what they wanted to all along. "I want those pups as much as I love our joeys."

"Why didn't you say anything?" Tally's nostrils flared and he breathed out slowly.

"By the time Sammy found out...things had *changed* between us. *We* had changed. I did not know how to tell you."

"So you're saying you were worried I'd be hurt?"

"Yes," Haru agreed readily, but it was almost too quick. There was a bigger elephant and both of them knew it, but Tally didn't push it.

"Well, I am. I can't lie." Tally rubbed at his chest and Haru cringed inwardly as they realized the pain was physical. "I hardly even know how to...react to this. What to do."

"I do not think the council members should know about the spontaneity of the pregnancy."

"Gods, no. That would be disastrous." Tally buried his face in his hands and took a shuddering breath. "We have to...to sssay sssomething. Before people figure it out on their own. Haru, I wisssh... Gods. It doesn't matter."

"But it does, matter, does it not?" Haru backed toward the door, eyeing it just in case. One of these days they wouldn't hang themself where it concerned their snake. "I know I misstepped, but it was before...before there was an *us*. I was angry. Needed someone I trusted. I cannot deny it makes me happy despite the circumstances."

There was another long pause. Awkward. Painful. Maybe it would be better to rip off the Band-Aid all at once?

"Perhaps we should announce it tonight? The *obassans* are already sniffing around Sammy. I know I will be happy to tell everyone, but can you be? I—" Haru gulped again, pushing down the rising panic. "I love these pups. Can you?"

Tally lifted his head, his dark eyes wounds in his face. "Haru. Stop it. Just...stop. Don't make this about me somehow failing to love children. And pups, plural?"

"Twins," Haru said quietly. "Melia and Livy will have competition."

"Co-conspirators, probably more like." Tally ran both hands back through his hair. "You don't trust me. You *still* don't. Otherwise, you would've told me. And it would've been so much better if you had. At any point." He stood, suddenly enough that Haru jerked a step back. "We'll announce it. Yes. Of course. Not to would be foolish. At midnight. As if it was a joyous thing we're announcing *together*."

With that, he squared his shoulders and stalked off back inside.

Haru blinked, looking after their Argaze. They hadn't been able to deny the accusation about trust. Tally wasn't wrong. Yes, life was better. Tally treated Haru carefully. But getting their heart to listen to their head wasn't something they could just snap their fingers and make happen. Too many years of being in the Akaike clan had taught them trusting the short term was a fool's game.

Slowly, cautiously, Haru peeked inside the hotel. Sammy stood farther down the hallway, talking animatedly with Tally. She glanced in the door's direction, spotting them. Her gaze lingered, followed by their Argaze's. The two of them wore similar faces of annoyance, but Sammy's was defensive while Tally's seemed more subdued. Hurt.

That was what it was. Tally was hurt. Not by the babies, but by Haru.

How long would it take for Tally to decide they weren't worth the effort? Too many troubles and not enough given in return?

Tally held out his hand. "Come, we have pups to announce."

"Yes, Argaze."

"Stop that too. I can't...I won't be able to get through this if you do that. The least you can do is support me and not make me want to...to..." Tally pulled in a hitching breath. "While I do this."

"Yes, Tally." Haru almost fell into *senrei*, but they caught themself with a hand on the wall. Bowing would only upset Tally more. Something flickered across the humongous snake's face, but it quickly disappeared. When the two of them linked arms, Haru only hoped their shaking wasn't too noticeable. There was need, a compulsion, to bow. They offered a quiet, "Thank you. Very much."

Sammy glanced between the both of them. "Well, seems like life is about to get interesting."

* * * *

Probably what saved the evening from disaster was that most of the adults were drunk. Tally's gaze swept the room as they re-entered, taking stock. Tyler was nowhere in sight. Probably sent outside to shiver in the car and wait for his tyrant of a father. The Blue Hollys had clustered, a couple family members short, so some of them had probably gone to help Ted.

The smile Tally had plastered on would've fooled no one sober. At least, no one who knew him well. Mom caught his eye from across the room. She raised an eyebrow and Tally offered a wave and a nod. *Everything's fine, Mom. No problems here.*

Smile and wave. Smile. Smile. The rest of the clan wouldn't catch on that something was amiss. What he wanted to do was find a corner and uktena. After all he'd done, after all they'd been through together, still Haru couldn't trust him with something this important, then acted like Tally was going to hit him when the truth came out. The second part? Well, Tally had dealt with abuse victims in the community before. Now that he knew about Haru's old clan, the signs had been there, but Tally had been so excited to meet his Em'halafi he had missed them. Intellectually, he knew the bowing, the expectation to be hit was a hardwired reaction and nothing to do with him. Except it was *him*, the man who would gnaw off his right arm before he'd ever hit Haru.

"He couldn't trust me enough to tell me," Tally had said to Sammy. "Why couldn't you?"

Sammy had stared at him like he was an idiot. "Wasn't my place to tell you, Tal. No. They needed to do that. And you want too much. Expect too much, too soon. Stop pushing them."

He could buy Haru whatever he wanted. Give him anything his heart desired. Make a home built on his desperate outpouring of love. But he couldn't make Haru love him. He couldn't buy Haru's trust. If he still didn't have it… Tally allowed himself the smallest sigh as he ruthlessly told himself to keep smiling. He had to get through this.

"Urusar Bastille." A group of women cornered him, Haru and Sammy. Every single one of them drew in a slightly larger breath than necessary. Sarah, bless her, got pushed to the front. "It is so good to see you out tonight. Did you enjoy the cupcakes?"

"Ladies." Gods, last thing Tally wanted was small talk, but there was a nervous ripple through the group, eyes flicking down. Tally tried to pull back his energy, make himself smaller. Just because his night had gone to shit didn't mean he wanted to intimidate clan members already jittery around him. "Of course, Sarah. We all did. You know Haru is partial to your cakes."

She tittered, blushing as she glanced at her friends. "Thank you, Urusar, Uruma."

Haru tilted his head, the stones in his black hair glinting. "The decorations were particularly clever, Timms-san. How did you make the little opossums?"

"Oh, well, chocolate can be shaped many ways." The tension bled out of Sarah's shoulders as she focused on Haru. The question provided the perfect distraction for the group, the conversation quickly moving to types of chocolate and favorite jellies.

Tally was slowly herded toward the outside of the ring while Haru held court with Sammy.

Jealousy sparked as Tally watched how at ease his otter was with the women. It burned like a signal flare, just screaming through his chest instead of lighting up the sky. His head *knew*, or at least Tally thought he knew, why Haru would be more relaxed around women than men, but his heart didn't care one iota that his Em'halafi couldn't turn to him.

The two of them were supposed to be in this together, destined matches who worked through their problems instead of hiding from them. Tally met Haru's gaze over the heads of the pack of women and hissed softly when Haru flinched away.

"Oh, um, Urusar Bastille," Leona Waters said, catching his attention. "*Is* something the matter?"

"Ah, no, I—" *Was caught being a jealous husband.* "I didn't realize Sarah was having trouble with her suppliers."

It was a save picked from overheard bits of conversation. A small save, pitiful really, but a save nonetheless.

"I could make some calls if you like, cover the costs of expediting." He nodded at Sarah.

She tucked a stray strand of hair behind her ear. "No, thank you, Urusar Bastille. It's more of a delay really. No problem."

"If you insist."

"Really, Urusar, thank you, though." One of the gaggle of women hooked her arm through Sarah's and the group retreated from a sour-looking Haru.

His otter moved back in beside him, stiff and unyielding, the complete opposite of how he'd been this morning—loving, happy. Mostly. Haru carried a carefully constructed wall around him, almost at all times. Much like the armor he wore tonight—the beautiful *kimono*, dark with fireworks bursting all over. The carefully piled raven hair with jewels adorning it, smaller matching ones on his face. Always made up to perfection—

Maybe so everyone can't see how scared he is.

The thought struck a chord deep inside Tally and he needed to close his eyes. *Scared.* Haru was still running scared. He checked his watch—a Patek Phillippe and a Christmas gift from his otter.

Ten minutes to midnight. Ten eternal minutes. More time than Tally knew what to do with.

Time. Tally's brain caught onto a thought but couldn't hold it. Too mixed up to focus entirely. A watch meant many things.

Champagne was making the rounds. Tally snagged one for himself and one for Haru, though neither one of them drank. Just a prop.

"Thank you," he said to the server and sighed when the young man scurried off, nearly tripping over himself to get away from Tally.

Sammy leaned in and told Tally to stop puffing up so hard or he might end up scaring Haru. "Last thing you want is to scare them right now."

Wait...*them*? He'd been so upset that he hadn't even caught it. The pronoun Sammy used, was it a slip or something Sammy meant to say? She'd said it before, too. When he'd been confronting her about the pregnancy. Great. Wonderful. Another thing Haru had refused to trust him with. Possibly. How could he even ask? *Oh, hey, have I been misgendering you all these months?*

Gods.

Two minutes to midnight, Tally moved to the center of the room with Haru and frowned when he realized Sammy had not joined them. He gestured her over to stand beside the two of them, then raised both his glass and his voice. "Friends, family, neighbors, thank you all for making this a beautiful evening! As we tick over into the new year, I have a happy announcement."

From the back of the room, Gun bellowed, "You're giving me your car?"

Tally waited for the laughter to die away. "No, Gun. Sorry. Something better. We wanted to announce, all of us together, that Sammy is expecting, as our Kwebabiad. This summer, we will be welcoming otter twins into our family!"

There were gasps, scattered applause, a good deal of heads-close whispering, but the clock saved Tally by clicking over and chiming midnight.

"Happy New Year!" he called over the noise, and tossed his champagne back in one long, reckless swallow. *And now let the floor open and take me. Please.*

He needed space. He needed to breathe, but people were swarming them with congratulations, with questions. Tally snagged a second glass of champagne and downed that, too. A soft tug at his arm had him looking down at Haru, his otter's eyes wider than they should be, his smile strained. At his side, Sammy shot him a brief frown. All right, not a good direction to look.

Gun sent him a familiar head tilt from across the room. *You need me? You all right?* Tally gave him the sparest head-shake in response. No, no, he couldn't add Gun sniping at Haru into this boiling brew. He snagged a third glass of champagne. Someone took it away.

Cat-soft, Marnie was there, smiling sweetly at him, holding the glass out of his reach. "Congratulations, Urusar, Uruma, Sam. I know it's traditional for dads to get drunk when they announce these sorts of things, but maybe it's time to take our Tal home. There's no one here big enough to carry him, no matter what Gun says."

"Good idea," Sammy piped up, suddenly on his other arm. "He's looking a little overwhelmed. Say goodnight, Tally."

With just the barest awareness of what he said or whom he said it to, Tally said his goodnights as Haru and Sammy steered him out of the room. Just as well, since the stupid floor wouldn't eat him like he wanted.

He waved to his parents as they led him out the door, ignoring their worried expressions as something to deal with later. Preferably much, much later.

* * * *

The night—*morning*—had ended as one would expect. The kids had camped in Tally's room, awaiting their return, but Haru had felt they would be overstepping a boundary if they joined their Argaze in bed. Instead, they went to their own bed. Huge. Spacious bed that smelled a little of pups, Tally — family. The conversation had been awful. No, not as bad as it could've been, no beatings. Surprisingly. Haru still waited for the moment Tally did snap. They had been certain this faux pas would be the instance that broke his cool façade.

No, Tally had become colder. Distant. Not unexpected. They should have discussed preferring the traditional method over IVF with their Argaze. Would he have understood? Been okay with Haru taking the traditional route? Tally firmly believed the two of them were Em'halafi. He could've objected, then Haru would've been stuck. Growing up the way they had, the idea of pups being created the modern way rubbed them wrong. What happened the night of the engagement party just... didn't happen that way. It had been about *comfort*.

Friendly. Fun. Something Haru had been afraid they were going to lose getting married to an Urusar.

At the same time, there would be people who would find fault with the Uruma having pups first. That was for the Urusar. As was right. Two halves of Haru battled against each other. The one that longed for freedom, who watched the modern world around them and lamented they were confined the way they were. The other who obeyed. Taught from a young age where they belonged. Should just accept their place in the order of things.

Three a.m. The witching hour. Tossing in bed wouldn't do Haru any good. Getting up, they decided a good traditional Japanese breakfast might help start the day, and there was no time like the present. They had been planning it the last few days so they might as well follow through with the promise.

The joeys should appreciate it? Even if Tally could not.

After donning a *yukata*, Haru decided it was, in fact, cold, so they layered with a *kosode* and a *haori* over that. They really needed some *awase kimonos* for the winter months. No, asking now seemed like horrific timing. Maybe later, when Tally wasn't so mad. They could endure layering for now. It was what they had done growing up.

The cast of blue moonlight in the kitchen left a chill in the air, so Haru turned the lights on a medium setting to warm up the place. Once cooking, it wouldn't feel so cool. They tied back their sleeves and began rooting through the refrigerator and cabinets, pulling out what they would need.

The shiitake *dashi* to flavor the *kombu dashi* as the base for their *miso*. The soup had been a staple of every breakfast back home. Haru missed it and was excited that Tally had suggested it for today. The *kumbo dashi*, shiitake, tofu for the *aburaage*, enoki, spinach, green onion and the *aka miso* all came next. Haru eyed the onion. Maybe. Maybe not. Oooh, sesame seeds. Those were nice toasted. No onion.

As the combined *dashi* boiled, Haru pulled out the other necessities for their first family breakfast of the year. *Hakumai* to make *gohan*—rice being the staple of any decent meal—eggs for Tally, fresh bass fished from the lakes for Haru and the pups, *umeboshi* and some vegetables to have some *kobachi*. Somehow they'd get it pulled together. Start *something* on the right foot, even if it wasn't their relationship with Tally.

Cooking soothed their nerves. Being able to complete a task. *Do it right.* Get something out of it in the end. Food for the soul.

The different scents began to percolate and mingle in the kitchen, helping Haru relax. Chopping, measuring, mixing, watching the timing as they created their family a meal. Something to bring them together.

Their focus on the task at hand was why they picked up their phone without looking. If they had seen the number, they would've let the call go to voicemail.

"*Moshi moshi.*"

There wasn't a response. Haru glanced at the display and froze. Then they heard his voice.

"Is that how you greet your Urusar, Haru-chan?"

"Akaike-san." Haru nearly dropped the phone.

"You can't get even a simple hello right."

The anger with which their former Urusar threw those words at them cut hard.

"I should've known you couldn't satisfy even a simple American like Urusar Bastille. Your failure was inevitable."

Failure? Why was he calling? Haru snapped out of their stupor. "My Argaze is not simple. I have pleased him."

"Really? Having pups before him? Is that pleasing your Urusar? What an embarrassment. When does he plan on returning you?"

"What?"

"How else can he save face? Not that *you* can come back, but we do get the pups, so that is something. They are sure to be lovely. *Hāfu.* Of course, if you hadn't screwed up like this, we could've had a bigger payout, but it could've been much worse. I suppose if you *beg* properly, we could consider taking you back. Even secondhand, I'm sure we can find—"

"My Argaze is *not* returning me."

The silence stretched long enough for Haru to turn the fish.

When Akaike-san spoke, it came out a growl. "He's not seeking Dissolution for your mistake? Is he going to ask for a divorce?"

"No. Urusar Bastille is thrilled about the pups."

"Are you sure, Haru-kun? Truly sure that someone like Urusar Bastille is stupid enough to keep a failure like you? Someone who cannot fulfill their duties as a proper Satislit?"

"Yes." *No.* And how their voice shook. Akaike-san must've heard it too.

"Ha! I doubt that."

"Akaike-san. I think it's time I woke the pups. Thank you for the call."

"I'll be waiting, Haru-kun. There is no way Urusar Bastille will ever keep you. Just make sure you don't screw it up too much. The clan needs his money."

The line went dead before Haru could respond. It took a minute for them to compose themself, remember the food. It was going to burn. They needed to get it together. Just because Tally was within his rights to call off the contract—he wouldn't. No, he hated Akaike-san. Probably more than he disliked Haru at the moment. Tally had said he wouldn't send Haru back.

But that was before they had screwed up. Made Tally an embarrassment.

They moved the fish to a plate to drain. When searching for the rice bowls, Haru felt another presence in the kitchen. They turned, finding Tally watching them, leaning against the cabinets, hands in pockets.

"Argaze."
Haru dropped to *dogeza*.
Tally sighed.

Chapter Three

What's an Urusar to Do?

How could a frown look so intimidating? *Because it's Mom.* Tally fiddled with the worry stone in his pocket then realized what he was doing. He carefully placed his hands on his lap. "Mom, we're fine. It's fine. Having pups is what everyone expected. I'm not exactly getting younger."

"That is not what I meant and you know it, Tal."

When Mom had invited him over to pick up new sweaters for the joeys, he should've known it was a trap, but the pictures she'd sent over text had been adorable. Like Tally could say no to firefly sweaters for the kids, especially since Mom had made matching versions for all three.

"If you think you can lie about how you felt after the announcement, you must think I didn't spend over thirty-four years raising you."

"I have been a grown-up for—"

"A mom never stops raising her kids," Mom interrupted and pushed the mug of coffee toward him. "Tal-tsu'tsa, you were devastated."

"No, just...overwhelmed."

"I see."

Damn Mom for being too perceptive. No. Last thing Haru needed was his parents or the rest of the family up in their business. "We just hadn't wanted to announce it yet, but people were sniffing around. Literally. We were—" What could he say without opening up the wound further? "*I* was hoping the last round with Misaki had taken, but it hadn't."

"Oh, Tal. I'm so sorry." Mom took his hand. Her warmth, the concern in her gaze, spread to his chest, soothing the ache that had been lodged there since the party. "Are some clan members going to be jerks about your Uruma having kids first? Sure. Some people can't let go of the past. However, you don't have to be in such a rush to have *more* children. You don't."

"The clan expects me to take my position seriously."

"Ignore those self-righteous bastards whispering about your performance as Urusar. A family's built because of love, not because overbearing political busybodies say so. Snakelings with Misaki will happen, but in their own time. There are thirteen years between you and Nan for a reason."

Mom sighed but busied herself with snacks. Tally tasted the air with a flick of his tongue. Mint chocolate chunk cookies. She slid the plate toward him.

"What did you think of Urusar Akaike?" he asked after a mouthwatering bite.

"Akaike?"

Tally nodded. "I think... I think he called Haru today."

Mom frowned, dunked a cookie in her glass of milk. "We never really got to know the Akaike clan. Negotiations were...negotiations. That was all lawyers. They kept to themselves, even when they got here. I would have to say they were a bit *cold*. Hung up on rules."

"Yeah, that'ssss what I thought too."

"Why are you asking, Tal?"

"Haru seemed scared." Frightened before pulling up that veil of his when Tal walked into the kitchen.

"Then help him become less scared. Lean on each other. It's what Em'halafi do."

"I want what you and Dad had — have," he admitted. The pups seemed to be the one thing that Haru was completely open and happy about. The selfish part of Tally, the one who had fallen in love with his otter back in Tokyo, wanted to see *that* Haru all the time. The one who wasn't scared of him.

Mom didn't reply right away, studying Tally in that way that made him want to squirm. Inscrutable. She squeezed his hand.

"What your father and I built took time. *Lots* of time. Your father and I fought, not too often but we did. Little things. Big things. Sleepless nights happened." Mom circled around the counter and pulled Tally into a hug. "Council members challenged your dad. It was stressful. We had too many kids underfoot at times and I couldn't keep a clean house. Your father and I had our differences, every couple does, but we worked through them because we wanted to."

"What did you do? To fix it, I mean. Your fights?"

"We talked, of course, but we also had friends we confided in. You may love your otter, but expecting everything to be between you two, and only you two, is ridiculous. We have friends for a reason. I had Tyra. You have Gun and Marnie and the rest."

Tally huffed and took a sip of his coffee, if only to gather himself.

"Friendships are there for a *reason*. They serve a different purpose than a life partner. Offer different perspectives." Mom took a step back and combed her fingers through Tally's hair, the action calming and familiar—something she hadn't done in a long time. Okay, she knew something was up, but she wasn't going to push him.

"I hear you."

"That's all I'm asking. That, *and* to tell your brothers to come up for air. They're neck-deep in the developmental stage for Hal's new game, and who knows when they last showered."

"Ha!" Tally shook his head. "So the sweaters were a double-purpose bribe?"

"Yes—their place stinks. I'm thinking about calling a fumigation company."

Tally cringed. "Yeah, all right. It's the 'nearly dead' part of the cycle?"

Mom nodded, sipping her tea. Her eyes sparkled with a bit of mischief. "Did they tell you what they were developing this time?"

"Ahh, no, I-I don't think they did. Why?"

"It's a children's game. An app this time."

"Yeah? That's different for Hal." Tally tucked the package of sweaters under his arm and glanced toward the door. Maybe he could make a quick exit and call Gun, see if the others were up for dinner. Lahi had said she'd help with the pups tonight.

"It's an educational game where an otter has to collect yummy treats by solving basic puzzles before a snake catches it and eats it."

"Oh my Gods, *Mom*!"

* * * *

"I'll be back before the joeys' bedtime." Tally stopped in the kitchen doorway to watch Haru gathering things from the fridge.

"No need," Haru said without looking up. "Do not rush."

Tally tried to parse the words and the tone. He found he couldn't do it reliably. He'd thought he'd begun to understand Haru and the things he...they said or didn't say. He still had to have *that* conversation with Haru, too, about the pronouns. Where once he would have gone into the kitchen to steal a kiss, now he kept his distance. If Haru kept important things from him, how many other things were there?

Wallet. Keys. Worry stone. "I won't be long. Have a good evening."

Haru said something in return, though the fridge muffled his voice. The answer could've just as easily have been 'see you later' or 'fuck off'. The second was doubtful, of course. Haru was too polite and had been entirely supportive of Tally going out with his friends, saying he didn't see them enough and a man needed his friends.

Or something to that effect.

They met at Golden Pot, Lily's favorite hot pot place, where they could have a broth for the vegetarians and a broth for the carnivores. Tally was the last to arrive, unusual for him, and as he accepted hugs, he had the uncomfortable feeling they'd been talking about him.

"We ordered already," Pete said as everyone took their seats again. "Figured you wanted the same things as always."

"I need to be less predictable. I guess." Tally managed a half-smile and hoped the words didn't sound bitter.

"So, c-congratulations." Lily punched his arm playfully. "Pups on the w-w-way. Misaki, too?"

Tally shook his head as he gulped down some water. "Not yet. We might not be compatible at all, you know. It's worth a shot, but we don't know. The first attempt at the clinic didn't take."

"Early days, Tal," Marnie said slowly, carefully. "Was that Sammy and Haru's first attempt? At the clinic?"

He couldn't lie to his friends. They would know. But, damn it, some things were hard to say all the way through and he couldn't think of a good way to derail the line of questioning. "They didn't use the clinic."

"How interesting." Marnie purred. "Old school. I'd wondered." She leaned forward and Tally winced. Damn her. She always saw too much and now she was going in for the kill. "So you knew, right? Because Sammy's got to have known before New Year's. Her scent says second trimester."

"Does it?" Tally managed past the hard lump in his throat. How many people had known? Suspected? And if he hadn't seen what he had that night, when would they have told him?

"Tal, that's not an answer." Gunther's frown had turned stern and forbidding.

Tally spoke to his water glass. "No. It's not." They waited. He could practically hear them holding a collective breath. "I didn't know. Before New Year's. Maybe I'm stupid and blind, but I didn't." He held up a hand at the start of a Gunther snarl. "Don't, Gun. Don't. Haru was scared to tell me."

"Scared of *you*?" Pete put a hand on his arm. "How could he be?"

"I... I don't really know. I thought...but it doesn't matter what I thought. Whatever ground I believed I'd gained I guess doesn't even amount to a beachhead." Tally lifted his head. "Look. No, don't look at me like *that*. Gods. The bunch of you. For things to be different,

I need a time machine to change stuff in Haru's past. Unless you have one, let it go."

"He hurt you, Tal." Gun had gone from snarl to growl. "He's still hurting you. I don't care what fucked-up stuff's in his past. Why are you letting him *hurt* you?"

Tally grimaced, shaking his head. "It's...not something... I love him. I can't help that. And someday I hope he'll at least trust me not to hurt him. That's all I can tell you right now. My expectations were mine and that's what gets *me* hurt. I have to do better."

"Would be great if that otter tried to do better." Gunther sat back and held up both hands at Tally's squint. "Just putting it out there."

"Speaking of people we love hurting us the most." Marnie turned her keen eyes on Gun, much to Tally's relief. "Why are you still here, Gunther Curley?"

"What? You don't want me here?"

"Mmm. We'd all rather you came home permanently, but you're supposed to be in Colorado." Marnie stirred her White Russian and changed tactics fast enough to cause whiplash. "How's your mom?"

"Weren't we talking about Tally?" Gunther's forehead crinkled in confusion. "I thought we were here to talk about Tally."

"We did and now we're talking about you," Pete said with a bright smile.

Gunther shrugged as if he weren't at all concerned. "Tal asked me to stay for a while after the wedding. Things were weird, so I stayed."

"I appreciate it and I'm glad you've been here." Tally reached for the beer that had arrived at his elbow at some point. "But maybe it's time you told us what's happening back home."

"Yes." Lily nudged him. "Cause *you've* b-been w-weird."

"Mom said nothing's changed in the past few weeks and we *were* talking about Tally. How long have they known, Tal? I mean, second trimester means, like, more than three months, right?" Gunther's jaw jutted stubbornly.

Tally heaved a breath to steady himself. "I didn't ask how long they've known. It didn't seem… It didn't matter by then, Sammy's fifteen weeks along. Actually, sixteen now."

"Gods' sakes, Tal. Four months? And Sammy didn't tell you? Did you even *know* they were going old school?" Gunther's voice had risen until Marnie put a hand on his shoulder and shushed him.

"Sixteen weeks is almost four months, yes. Thank you for the obvious." Tally couldn't quite stop a glare across the table. *Shut up, Gun. Shut up.* "And what's not changed for your mom, Gun? Why is it every time I try to talk about what's going on out there, you brush me off?"

"Because there's nothing you can do and it gives me a headache. What's your excuse?"

"Because it's none of your business and you're just making me more miserable!" Tally stilled, realizing with a jolt that they'd both risen from their seats and were shouting in each other's faces. He reached across and patted Gun's chest. "I'm sorry. Gun, sit down, please. I'm sorry."

Gun opened his mouth, closed it, and sat hard. "Sorry, Tal. I just… I worry about you, all right?"

"Likewise," Tally allowed in his driest tone. "I'll say a little. What I'm comfortable, no, what I'm willing to say without bleeding into other people's privacy. I'm not upset that Haru has Sammy to lean on or that they can share something..." His voice cracked, giving the lie to his words. "Something Haru's not ready to share with me. Yes. All right. That hurts, but not in the way you might think."

"Sammy's aro." Marnie wrapped her fingers around Tally's. "I get that it's not the same as it might be with a romantic entanglement. But they still kept it from you."

Tally nodded, gripping her hand like a lifeline. "Haru's fears are... They're old. It's a thing I've been a little slow to piece together. It hurts like hell that he can't trust me with everything, but I can't push him. It'll just make things worse."

"How much worse does it get than your friend having casual sex with your husband and getting knocked up and not telling you?" Gunther huffed out.

"Gun," Pete broke in, his voice low, warning.

"It's not like that." Tally forced himself to speak in a calm, measured tone. "I'm glad Haru has someone he can confide in. In a way, that makes me feel a little better that he's not so alone. Yes, this, um, takes us back a few steps, but it's my own fault for thinking we were further along. It hurts, but it's not a *rational* hurt. I have to remember that."

"It's okay to be m-mad, Tal," Lily said gently. "It's okay to b-be u-u-upset. You don't want to scare him. S-sure."

"But it's okay to say you're hurt, you know, Mr. Nobility," Pete said with a gentle smile, finishing his twin's thought, as twins often did.

"Maybe. I'll try. When things aren't so...fraught," Tally finished and distracted himself by shoving some lotus root into the cauldron of broth between him and the twins.

"Did you really say *fraught*? Have you been reading Regency stories again?" Marnie chuckled. "All right, Tally went. Your turn, Gun. We love you, and that's why we ask. Just remember that."

Gunther went to push the beef into the pot for the meat and Marnie stopped him with a scowl. "Piece at a time, Gun. Or it'll all be shoe leather."

"Oh. Right." All the fight seemed to whoosh out of Gun and he let Marnie take charge of the meat. "So you guys all remember my Uncle Harley died, right?"

"Sure." Pete nodded. "They said a hunter shot him out of the sky."

"Yeah, maybe." Gunther frowned at the beef strip Marnie put on his plate as if it might have answers. "Though…sort of weird that there was a hunter there on national parkland and that he shot down a protected bird that no one would mistake for a goose."

Tally leaned forward, a hard knot pressing against his chest. "Your mom suggested it wasn't an accident?"

"No one's saying anything for sure. All the things just didn't add up, but there's no way to prove anything." Gun waved a hand, trying hard to be dismissive. "Anyway. So Harley's my only uncle on my mom's side and his wife died some years back—"

"Was that s-suspicious, too?" Lily's eyes widened on her question.

"Nobody thought it was back then. But that's when Mom went back home, since they didn't have an Uruma, when Aunt Etta died."

"I remember," Tally said softly. "And your cousin Sage was Sardu, but he was only nine, so there wasn't anyone to take Harley's place. And the clan elected Pike to act as Urusar."

Gun snorted. "*Elected* meaning he bullied them into it. Yeah. And that's when the problems started. Pike trying to change things in the charter. Trying to take out the part that guaranteed a certain bird-to-mammal ratio on the council. Trying to say predators didn't have any business leading a clan."

"That's a familiar song." Marnie rolled her eyes.

Yeah, too familiar for Tally. The last couple years had not been easy.

"Yeah. But council meetings out there aren't like here." Gun stopped to eat some of the beef Marnie had slipped onto his plate. "I mean, Tal has asshole council members to deal with, but meetings still sound pretty, you know, civilized. Businesslike. Out there, things got hairy when Urusar Pike started trying to change bylaws. Stuff the clan's followed for generations."

Tally crunched on a bit of lotus root to keep from making distressed sounds. "Things actually got violent in council?"

"Extra people started showing up to meetings. Things were getting ugly. That's when Mom called me out there as Enforcement, but it was more like being a bouncer. Someone to break up fights and walk people out who were getting too worked up." Gun pulled a frown, and Tally was hard pressed not to reach out to him. They should've talked more, visited, kept in better contact. Something. Gun sighed. "It was that way for a couple of years, that council meetings were crowded and nothing got done 'cause everyone was just yelling at each other."

"We had no idea, Gun. Crud. Why didn't you say anything?" Tally wondered if this was a pattern that the people he loved couldn't confide in him.

Gunther shrugged. "It settled down, mostly, after that. I stayed, 'cause things were still kinda rocky, but people were starting to work together a little. Sometimes."

"And n-now?" Lily asked softly.

"Now stuff has started to bubble up again. Stuff people didn't talk about. Sage is almost grown, so there are people who want him instated as Urusar, to put things back the way they were. Pike's faction says no, of course. Not only the predator thing but that my family's too tied up with the Bastilles. Too much money equals too much power potential, according to them, and Bastille clan's always been too progressive for those retro, lijun first folks."

The way Gun hunched in on himself was too obvious a tell. Tally tapped his arm. "There's more, isn't there?"

"Yeah. There's people saying Sage didn't have a chance to be trained to lead since his dad died. They want a Curley but not him." Gun slumped back in his chair. "They want me to challenge for Urusar. Can you see it, Tal? Me, trying to be all diplomatic like you? There'd be fistfights in the first ten minutes."

"I don't think you give yourself enough credit, but I can see not wanting it. Is there anything we can do?" Tally asked out of habit, even though he couldn't imagine how he could help.

Gods, this is a total mess. One more worry to add to his growing list. Whatever was happening—or not happening—between him and Haru, problems with his own council, and the state of things in Colorado worrying Gun. Why hadn't he spoken up? Was he afraid to set off Tally's own anxiety? Damn, he needed to be a better friend. Tally clutched the worry stone in his pocket.

Gun shook his head. "No. Thanks, Tal. But no. I should go back. Try to help Mom get things settled down. I make a better Enforcer than I would an Urusar. Sage is a bright kid with a head for business. I feel guilty staying. I feel guilty going. Feels like I need to be two people right now."

"You don't. You really don't. I always feel better having you here, but if your mom needs you, go." Tally waved a hand at the table. He had to push the rising panic down. Gun leaving town—that wasn't something he wanted to think about. Having his best friend back had made things easier the last few months. "I'm not alone here. Family, friends, solid allies. I'm all right. Your mom's not."

"Yeah. Okay." Gunther let out something between a snort and a sigh. "Will you think I'm being a wuss if I say I don't want to go back to that nut farm out there?"

"No, we think you're a wuss for not using enough chili sauce." Pete ducked the napkin Gun threw at him.

"You do what you have to," Tally reassured him, despite the gnawing in his own gut. "If you go, we'll always be waiting here to welcome you home."

* * * *

Melia sneezed, drawing Haru's attention to their girl. Her head and one tiny paw were under the bookcase. Several disgruntled sneeze-chirps followed as Melia tried her hardest to get stuck *under* the furniture again. Livy looked on while Jackson pressed against her bum, *helping*.

Was that Jasper?

Yes, the pixie was under the bookcase trying to pull her under. When did the two of them become conspirators? Was it a good idea to have those two in cahoots? Haru looked on, trying to decide if they should intervene. Tally had said they should let the pups be pups and play, but sometimes it was hard to know when to step in.

"Are you going to stop them?" Sammy asked, nudging Haru's rump with her foot.

They chirped back, resettling on the pillow.

"Are you going to human any time soon?"

Haru closed their eyes.

"I'll take that as a no." Sammy huffed. "You can't avoid this forever, sweetie."

Trying never hurt anyone. Haru was within their rights.

Sammy reached over, petting Haru's pelt slowly, scritching under their chin. She lowered her voice. "Did something happen with Tally?"

Haru peeked up at her.

"Ah, of course it did. You had to know he'd be upset being kept in the dark like this." Sammy placed a hand on her belly. "But I know why you didn't say anything. Come here."

Haru slid off the pillow onto her lap. She hugged him. Nose. Nose. Kiss. Kiss.

"Gah! Otter mouth!" Sammy turned away, pushing them and laughing. "Geez. All right. All right. We'll drop it for now. Probably don't want the pups hearing that conversation anyway. Maybe after they've gone to bed, if the big bad Urusar hasn't gotten back."

The light tone in her voice meant Sammy was teasing them. Tally wasn't bad. Naïve. Big. Powerful. But probably not bad. Haru just couldn't help the way they reacted sometimes. It was hard to give themself over to the person who had bought them. The look on Sammy's face said she had an idea of what was going through their head. Retreat seemed like a reasonable choice. Not that Haru was running away—though they totally were—they decided to figure out what Amelia and her siblings were up to.

They bounded off the couch over to the pups to find Jasper, Melia, Livy and Jackson all squished under the bookcase. Excited sneezes and chirps filled the space as they chittered with one another. Something held great interest for all of them. Haru poked their nose underneath, scenting.

Dust filled their nose, making them sneeze, garnering the joeys' and pixie's attention. They all gathered close, a frenzy of chattering while Jasper lugged a furry something up in his arms, needing both to lift it.

What— Haru squinted. What the hell was that? Jasper rolled the fuzz to them. Sniffing didn't help determine what the mystery item was. Smelled fruity, though. Melia came up close, nosing the furry-whatever, then chomped it.

Haru humaned, bumping their head. "Ow. No! Melia. Spit that out. *No.* Now."

Caught in a tug o'war with their daughter, Haru desperately tried pull the icky-ick out of her mouth while Melia kept her teeth firmly chomped on it. Luckily, or unluckily, she decided their hair was more interesting and climbed into it. Haru tossed the fuzzy to Sammy, who wasn't even trying to hide her laughter.

"Are you?" — snort, giggle — "Going to let her swing in there?"

"Yes. Yes. What is…whatever *it* is?"

Sammy eyed the fuzz. "Looks like an old piece of taffy."

"Little girl." Haru pulled their hair in front of them, eyeing their rambunctious daughter. "What have I said about chomping things?"

Amelia squeaked.

"Remember the tubing? Remember how much that hurt? We do not want a repeat of that."

Nose. Nose. Kiss. Kiss.

"I am not mad, but who knows how long that was under there?" Haru suppressed a shudder. Talk about gross. They shot a look over to Jasper, who was riding on Jackson's back, ignoring the showdown. "And you, do not encourage Melia's biting. Do you want her to try *you* again?"

Jasper went wide-eyed and shook his head vigorously, almost dislodging himself from Jackson. Of course, their son immediately stilled and waited for the pixie to reposition himself. The action warmed Haru's chest, the considerate display so familiar to them now. Their little boy was growing up fast and Jackson was doing his best to be the big brother. Though the pixie wasn't technically younger. If anything, Jasper was older.

Sammy joined Haru, disentangling Amelia from their hair. "Is it me or have you gained a plus one?"

"Maybe." Haru shrugged when Sammy's eyebrows rose. "Ever since the downspout incident he has not left."

"Have you tried opening a window?"

"Actually, yes, but Jasper just set up with a pillow on the sofa in my room. Sewed an entrance into it and everything."

"Huh."

"Quite."

Sammy tucked Melia against her chest. "Hey, Jasper, want to help me with bath time?"

The pixie pulled a face.

"Haru has rocks *and* bubbles."

Jasper kicked Jackson's sides and the two of them trundled up the steps, Livy close behind. Sammy leaned in for a kiss. Firm. Gentle. Amelia sniffed Haru's jaw, pawing their hair.

"I'll get the pups down," Sammy said. "You get yourself put together so you can face Tally when he gets back."

"Right."

"Oh, and you might want to be clothed for that."

"Yes, that is… Yes."

With Sammy running off to put the joeys down, Haru found their pile of clothes and pulled them back on. The warm green corduroys pushed back the slight chill in the air, while the T-shirt and warm button-detail wrap sweater helped the goosebumps go down. Haru smoothed down the sides before grabbing their thick brown belt. Presentable. As they slipped the pin into the buckle, Haru took a couple breaths to calm their nerves. They patted down their front, hoping the look would please Tally when he got back. *If* he came back tonight.

Maybe Haru needed to pull out all the stops. Do a little something with the hair. Some makeup. The jade hairpiece—just in case. *Show* they had invested in trying to make things work. Yes, that was the reason. Not that they felt Tally was going to kick them out. Take them away from the joeys and Sammy. Tally wouldn't make them leave. He had said he wouldn't.

But when their Argaze had left for dinner, there had been no kiss. No soft touch goodbye. There hadn't been any recently. Nothing. Intellectually Haru knew Tally would need time. That he was hurt, but he would, with time, get over it. Now Haru had to convince their heart that much was true.

When did I start enjoying his company? Why do I miss the kisses so much?

Panic had already set in, though, when they had sent the joeys off to bed with Sammy and Haru started putting on the finishing touches, but then Haru remembered the one thing that might help them. They dug through their jewelry drawer, a little frantic. Several rings and bracelets bounced. A favorite amber stone necklace. No. No. Still not what they wanted. They had to find it. And honestly, when had Tally bought them so many gifts? Well, no, he always had a little something for Haru at the start of every date, watching them attentively as they opened the gift. Now too many pieces of jewelry were in the way.

The last time they'd even given the bracelet half a glance was when they had packed the lacquer box away. *Ah-ha!* Finally.

Haru pulled out their prize, mixed feelings as they opened the box. This was the gift that had started everything—the gold bracelet with blue diamond chips. Haru had refused to wear it since the Imsi Tamgradat, making excuses whenever it was asked after. It had felt like shackles, a reminder that they had been sold and bought.

Still does.

Pushing the nausea down, Haru slipped the bracelet on. Gods, please don't let them throw up now.

"Haru?" Sammy stuck her head in the door and gave a whistle. "You're making an effort. Hmm. Just tread lightly, okay?" She wrapped her arms around their shoulders and nuzzled in. Kiss. Kiss. "The joeys are down and out in Tally's bed, as requested."

"Thank you."

"I think they'll probably be down for the night. Though they were very excited when you said they got to sleep in their Usar's bed. Took five books, and *Hubert* was a threepeat tonight."

"Sorry." Haru busied themself with a ribbon in their ponytail, unable to meet her gaze. Maybe a flower?

"Don't be sorry. You *sure* Tally won't mind?"

"No. He loves the pups."

"He does, and he'll love these too, just give him time. You guys will weather this bump."

Haru twisted, searching for the comfort they knew they'd find. The kiss was soft, gentle, full of affection. Everything they needed to get through the evening. Sammy understood how much they needed these little pieces of tenderness. How much they craved them. Needed the reassurance.

"Come on, walk me out." Sammy pulled Haru to their feet.

"Are you tired?" They offered her an arm. "Should I make up the guest bedroom?"

"Hm, no. I'm good." Sammy arched her back and wriggled. "Though I'm starting to see the upside of being an author."

"What is that?"

"Being able to sleep in after a long day."

"Mmm, yes," Haru agreed, chuckling with Sammy. The two of them stopped next to her car for a moment, cuddling. Nose. Nose. She was trying so hard to make them feel better. Take the weight. But it had been Haru who had refused to say anything to Tally.

Upsetting the balance so early on… Haru sighed. All they had wanted to do was find their feet. Back home in Japan they knew how things worked. Here, none of the normal rules applied. Haru had trouble knowing their head from their ass.

Nose. Nose. Kiss. Sammy nuzzled against their chest. "It's going to be all right, Haru. You're going to have so many pups who love you, filling up this house. It will be a warm and loving home."

"'Home'?"

"Yes, *home*. Tally loves you. The big, ole romantic can't help himself."

Haru grunted, patting her back.

"You're easy to love."

Haru glanced down at Sammy — eyebrows raised.

"You know what I mean. Big goof." Sammy pushed against him. "Platonic love is a thing."

"It is." Haru held Sammy closer.

Lights from a car lit up the driveway. Sammy started to pull away but Haru held onto her, needing the lifeline. She huffed, side-eyeing them, but didn't say anything. Instead, Sammy rested her head against his chest again. The car didn't pull into the garage but came to a stop behind Sammy's car, the crunch of the gravel a bit ominous to Haru's ears.

Tally's head popped out of the car. His eyes slid over to Haru and Sammy. The lines around his eyes became more pronounced as his face tightened. He didn't say anything as he jogged around to the other side of the Bentley. The door swung open, barely missing Tally. He scowled as he reached into the car and pulled Gunther out.

Who promptly proceeded to collapse in his arms like a boneless jellyfish. Gunther's head lolled back, his eyes glazed over. He noticed Haru and Sammy. A sharp *caw* escaped him.

"You twoooh don' need tooo shooove it in hisss face," Gunther slurred out.

"We are behaving how we always have," Haru responded, holding Sammy a little closer. Okay, maybe they were being a little petty.

"A Satislit should-shouldn't…"

Tally sighed and heaved Gunther into a better hold. "Shut up, Gun. Just…shut up."

"Yes, please." Sammy heaved a large sigh too before she stood on tiptoe. Haru bent down automatically so they could let her kiss their cheek. The warmth spread

70

fast, and she winked as she pulled back. "Be good, okay?"

"I try."

"I know you do."

Sammy petted their cheek one more time and walked around to her driver's side. She paused by Tally and Gunther. There was a moment where she didn't say anything before she leaned in, talking low to Tally, but it wasn't too quiet for Haru to hear her censure.

"Haru's past is messed up. All they ever had was rules. You understand what that could do to someone, right? We don't know the extent of everything because they don't talk about it, probably never will, but *you* of all people need to be patient. Need to let them know you're not going to toss them out of the house and away from the pups."

"I would never—" Tally began.

"Have you ever noticed how starved for physical touch they are? Suddenly denying them only makes them more insecure."

Gunther laughed. "That's utter shit."

Sammy shot him a dirty look. "I never said it was sexual, asshole."

"Both of you. Not helping." Tally's jaw looked tight enough to snap.

"Affection," Sammy said, rubbing her belly. "Haru needs affection. It's contradictory, but—"

"That's Haru," Tally finished with a jerky nod. "Who's standing right there."

Haru was hard pressed not to look away. Their gut roiled, but they couldn't say anything. Didn't know what to say. Though Tally putting a stop to the gossiping made them feel slightly better. Sammy ducked her head, waved and got into her car. Haru backed away, turning to watch her leave. Gunther drunkenly argued with Tally as they went inside. Remarks that dug like claws into Haru's skin. They ignored the digs, letting each pinprick bleed.

The only consolation they had about the rant was Gunther was honest about how he felt. Haru knew where they stood with him at all times. Knowing Gunther hated them actually made life easier. No guessing games. Not with the eagle.

When Haru retreated into the house, Tally was wrangling Gunther down the hall to the guest bedroom.

"But Tal—"

"Shut it. Just, I don't know. Pass out or something already." Tally's tone was possibly the most exasperated Haru had ever heard him. "Go to sleep. Don't throw up on my grandmother's quilt. On second thought..." Thumps and thuds came from the bedroom. Tally emerged with Gunther's keys and shoes in one hand and the blue-and-white quilt in the other, shaking his head.

"Should I get some aspirin and water?" Haru asked, hovering at the intersection.

"I suppose." Tally cracked his neck and sighed. "Yes, thank you. I'm annoyed enough to let him suffer, but you're right, of course. Terrible hospitality."

Haru smiled. "It can be, yes." They quickly retrieved a pitcher and a glass, plus the bottle of aspirin. Gunther would probably need it. When they turned around, Tally was watching them with an intense gaze. "Could you wait for me? I will be only a minute."

"I can bring it to him."

"No, let me. I am Uruma."

Tally opened his mouth, head tilted, like he was about to argue, but it turned into a nod. "You are that. I'll... I'll be in the kitchen."

"I have some snacks on the middle shelf if you need something," Haru said before slipping down the hall. The guest bedroom had a soft orange light glowing from the guest bathroom. A beacon in case the eagle needed the toilet.

Gunther's head hung over the edge of the bed, right over the trash bin.

"You should drink something," they said as they placed the pitcher down on the nightstand.

No response. Not a squawk.

Haru filled a glass then tapped out a couple pills. They shook Gunther's shoulder. "Open."

"Errr." He groaned. One eye popped open.

"Swallow. Drink."

Gunther opened his mouth.

"Fine." Haru helped Gunther swallow the pills and sip the water. "Okay, try to drink the water when you wake."

"Errr. You don-don't deserve himmm."

Snores quickly followed Gunther's cutting remark. The huge eagle down and out for the count. Haru gave him their back, raced out of the room and down the hall. They slowed, trying to regain some composure before turning into the kitchen.

"Everything all right?" Tally asked.

"He took some aspirin. Had a little water." Haru dove into the refrigerator, shuffling through the shelves. Not because they needed something, but it was the only place they could hide.

"Haru." Tally's voice was soft, tentative. "Would you come sit with me? Please?"

"Would you like some hummus? There are pita chips. Veggies. Or maybe some of the pickled radish?"

The sound from behind him might have been a laugh or a sob. Or both. "No. I'm not... I just came from dinner. Thank you. Please come sit with me. *Please*."

That meant Haru needed to turn around and face Tally. It did. Haru hiccupped. What would they see when they did? Had his friends convinced Tally to walk away? To ask for Dissolution like Akaike-san said he would? That had been the fear when he had left for the dinner.

"Yes, Argaze."

"Gods."

"Sorry, Tally. I—" Haru swallowed. They went over to the stools and sat, folding their hands carefully on the counter. Then remembered that was not what they were supposed to do. Urusar Akaike's voice rang in their ears and Haru put their hands out, spread, their fingers shaking.

"Haru, what are you doing?"

"I am following procedure."

There was a long pause before Tally spoke. "What procedure?"

"I have displeased. If you do not want Sammy around, I ask the joeys still get to see her." Haru let out a slow breath. Their hands no longer shook so much. They were able to hold them out evenly. "Please."

Tally glanced away, his throat working. When he finally spoke, his voice was low, cracking. A wet sheen glimmered on his dark lashes. "Haru, beyond *that* first night when I got so upset and snaked, have I ever done anything to make you afraid? Made you think I could *hit* you?"

"We have known each other how long? Four months? Maybe? No one can know anyone in that short a time."

"No. I suppose not." Fatigue suddenly clung to all the rough edges around Tally, darkening under his eyes and burdening Tally's large back as his shoulders slumped. "But I thought at least by now you would know me that well. Let me start with that then. You have my solemn promise, on all I hold holy, on all I believe good, that I will never strike you. Not in anger. Not as Punishment. Not because I'm displeased. Never."

Haru nodded but kept their hands out. It could be a test. "Okay."

"You don't believe me. Deep in your bones you don't. And I think I expected that." Tally wiped at his eyes.

"I—I apologize." What else could they say?

"You can't change instinctive reactions any more than I could shift into a rattlesnake. I just…needed to say it. And I suppose I will keep saying it until it does sink into your bones." Tally held up a hand, maybe to stave off more apologies. "Sammy's my friend, too. Maybe not like Gun or Marnie or the twins, but a friend. I'm not looking to banish her from the house or from our lives. So there's that."

"Thank you." Haru's hands started to shake again, so they clasped them together. "I do not…" They paused. The large bubble in their chest hurt so much. "I do not know how to do *this*. *Us*. There are no rules. *You* do not follow the rules. It upsets me. I do not know how to respond nor am I able to predict what will happen. It makes me uneasy."

Tally stared a moment then nodded slowly. "And I don't know the rules. Whatever rules they might be. It makes me…so unhappy to make you anxious and upset."

"Are rules wrong? Is there something wrong with me? You keep giving me things, overlooking my gaffs. I can— I can show you the books, so you know the rules. It worries me. I do not know if I am pleasing you or upsetting you. You are *always* nice."

"There's nothing *wrong* with you, my love. We're speaking the same language but...not speaking the same language at all. I see us more as partners. As equals."

"You really see us that way?" Haru interrupted then cringed.

"Yes, and when you act as Uruma, we *are*. So often in these past months, I've looked to you when things have been strange with the council. But when it's just us? You don't seem to want that anymore." Tally pulled in a huge sniff and let out a shaky laugh. "Nice. Yes, well. Look at me, Haru. I'm huge. I had to learn a long time ago that I can't have a temper. I just can't."

Haru stared at him but managed a nod. Some part of them understood the snake's reasoning. The pressure to perform made for strange behaviors. Haru understood that even better.

"So it's... I learned to talk. To negotiate. To think about how other people felt. I don't know how to yell at someone to get my way. Sometimes, sure, I get frustrated and yell. But it's not a tool in my arsenal as it is for some people." Tally scrubbed both hands over his face, his long black hair tangling. Haru wanted to smooth it out with their fingers, but such a touch would not be welcomed. Their Argaze was coiled tight. "This isn't at all what I wanted to talk about. Though I guess what I've done when I'm frustrated is worse than yelling sometimes. I was upset and, yes, angry. And I pulled away. Because I didn't know what to do or why you would...keep important things from me."

The speech overwhelmed Haru. They weren't sure how to process it all. Intellectually they understood Tally was aware of how humans and lijun saw him.

Worked hard to not fall into those stereotypes. But everyone fought. *Everyone*. Especially couples. A well of despair also rose up inside them. Tally sounded so *normal*, which meant Haru was not.

"I told you. I did not want you hurt," Haru answered quietly. "You believe in Em'halafi. That comes with expectations. First I was afraid you would change your mind if I told you, make me leave, but then we were happy. And Christmas. Christmas was fun."

Tally was wiping at his eyes again, making that strange not-laugh sound. "Yes. Christmas was great. But what did you think was going to happen? As Sammy started to show? As the grandmothers started to whisper?"

Haru shrank back, looking out of the window. "I do not know. I did not know how to handle it. I think the last week made that obvious. How much of a failure I am. I am not sorry for the pregnancy, yet all my training says I should be capitulating before you."

"I don't want that," Tally insisted.

But Haru pushed on. "Because we are courting, I should beg for forgiveness. Offer Reparation. But I do not think the pups are something I should be apologizing for. And that makes me —" Haru breathed in before mumbling, "Quite horrible."

Another shaky breath left Haru. Confusion, anger, embarrassment, sadness. It all whirled in a big ugly mess inside them. They didn't know what they should do. They wanted to protect Sammy, the pups. Instinct screamed to safeguard their pups. Protect that one piece of happy they had with her. The friendship between the two of them meant the world to Haru, but they also knew they were hurting Tally, which Haru also didn't want. The circumstances meant that any avenue Haru chose, they were screwed.

"I do mean it. I do not want you hurt. By me. Yet that is what I am doing." Haru gulped. "I have enjoyed our courting. And the kisses."

"Well…" Tally traced a slow pattern on the table, his eyes down. He always did that, avoiding Haru's gaze when he was trying to piece together something diplomatic. It stung, though they had no room to complain. At least their Argaze had finally stopped ignoring them. Tally clenched his jaw and nodded once. "Well. I'm going to be very honest here. Maybe blunt is a better word. Yes. It hurt. It hurt a lot.

"Not…so much that you've been with Sammy." A shudder went through Tally's large frame, the motion so strange to see from someone so large. It made Tally seem vulnerable. "That hurts in a strange and different way that's me being selfish and wanting things all at once. But that you and Sammy both thought it better to keep it secret. I had thought…I still think. I hope. That we're building family. Which means doing it together. Pups. They would be *our* pups. All three of us. I would like a rule."

"I like rules. I can follow rules. I can," Haru answered quickly, relieved, though Tally flinched. Why would he flinch? He was the one who'd suggested it. Haru frowned. They were trying to put it right. The last week had been so — *lonely*.

"While I don't expect you to tell me everything — no one tells their spouse *everything*. But if it's something to do with family, with the children, with someone's health, safety, something that will change the family in some way, you need to tell me. You can't exclude me to protect me."

"Understood. And what will be my Punishment if I fail to follow the rule?"

Tally flinched again, though he stared at the table, working at his lower lip. "The house will be without shellfish and crustaceans for two weeks. No food that comes from the water."

A gasp escaped Haru. That was not what they were expecting. That was just plain cruel. Tally never denied them their treats. *Though it wouldn't be a Punishment otherwise, would it?*

"I understand," Haru answered feebly. They shot a wistful glance toward the fridge. "Should— Do you want me to clean out the refrigerator? I have many treats right now."

Tally glanced up, his brow furrowed. "No, no. It's not fair to put a rule into effect retroactively. Just…in the future, please."

"Yes, Tally."

A silence fell between them. Tally's lower jaw clenched, the muscles ticking, as he stared at Haru. They fiddled with the clutter on the counter, unsure what to do next. They had dressed up hoping, well, Haru wasn't sure what they had been hoping. But they had wanted to *please* Tally when he came home.

"Haru." Tally's voice was soft again, not quite as broken but not at all sure. "I have something to ask you and I'm…I feel terribly embarrassed about it."

"Yes, Tally?" Haru straightened. Tally *wanted* something. That was the voice he always had when he was unsure about voicing something about his own desires on their dates.

But Tally looked away and shook his head. "Maybe not now. It's late." He stood slowly, as if his legs had stiffened, and walked over to Haru.

They reached out, almost instinctively grabbing onto Tally's sleeve. "I hope my appearance pleases. Does it not?"

"My beautiful otter." Tally reached hesitantly to cup Haru's cheek. "Your appearance always pleases me." He glanced at the hand on his sleeve with a hint of a smile. "You're wearing the bracelet."

Haru's throat worked. Such a torrent of emotions caused by a single piece of jewelry. It meant different things to the both of them. Haru knew that. They let out a raspy, "Yes."

Tally smiled, though it *felt* uncertain.

"It is a beautiful bracelet. With pure intentions. From you." Something to remind Haru of Tally's hopes when they had met. They just had to keep reminding themself of those strange ideals. Maybe their heart would learn it.

They angled their head back and a tremor worked through them. So many emotions whirled in those dark eyes of Tally's. The way his jaw worked meant he was desperately trying not to show his emotions. All kinds of feels swaddled up around his heart. A tattered heart Haru poked daily. Their lips parted in question, but they didn't get that far.

Suddenly they were gathered up in an embrace, Tally's mouth on theirs. It was hard and fast at first, much more possessive than most kisses Tally had given them. A small thrill worked its way up Haru's spine. Tally had lost his composure. Haru had made him break those carefully woven strings.

The kisses. The tongue and teeth. It was angry at first. Haru wasn't afraid of the anger, though. It made sense. Twisted and broken. That was what Haru was. Then the angry swipes and demands gentled, confusing Haru. The little nips became careful along their lips. The moans tugged at their heart—*sad*. Tally was sad.

Haru wrapped their arms around Tally's back and pulled the two of them together. They leaned their head against Tally's broad chest, listening to his heart, the fast *tap-tap* mirroring their own vivace tempo.

Deep down Haru knew, they *recognized* how broken they were. They had figured out that much in the last few months with the Bastilles. Part of them wanted the life Tally and his siblings had. Another, more frightened part of them wondered how long that life would last. Then another, more reasonable voice, said to run as far and as fast as they could — make a clean break for freedom. That Haru could never live in the world the Bastilles did. They lived in a state of walking contradictions, each avenue of desire battling with the other.

It made Haru sick sometimes.

The only time their training served them well was when Haru had to deal with the council. Meetings were the only time they felt like they were of some use. The rules made sense then because they understood them, but their contribution to the clan as a whole was abysmal.

Gunther wasn't wrong.

Tally deserves better than me.

Chapter Four

Holding Pattern

"We need to stipulate specifics in these quotes." Tally tapped his pen against his desk, frowning at the documents. When he glanced up, the video feed from both Berlin and Barcelona showed anxious faces watching him carefully. *Good. Let them be worried for now. This is sloppy.* "Per piece. Per pound. However they're charging. We need this broken down."

"Yes, *Herr* Bastille. Of course." Karl, his new manager in Berlin, was an interesting shade of pink now. "We will have these reworked by the end of the day."

Ambitious, since it was already mid-afternoon there, but Tally didn't call him out on it. *Impress me.* The Barcelona staff made promises for the next day and Tally let his rattled European personnel end the call.

It ate at him that he wouldn't *be* there for the opening of the new hotel in Berlin and the reopening of the newly renovated Barcelona property, directing, overseeing. When he'd been a young snake just out of school, handling new acquisitions for his dad, he would've been. Now, he *was* his dad, in a business sense, and traveling was a far less frequent thing. *Delegate*, Dad had always hammered into him. He tried. Hiring management he believed in, even if they had some rough edges.

By noon, he'd approved the flats Meli had sent him for the Barcelona re-opening marketing blitz, mediated a dispute between his Seven Pines Lodge in Maine and the Park SService, promised Misaki he would look at the regulations for new construction in Tokyo that she'd sent over, and had a conversation with Addy about when might be a good time for a vacation.

The answer was 'never'. He was starting to understand why his father had been so filled with unholy glee about retirement. Would one of the joeys be interested in the business? Maybe he should start bringing the kids to work sometimes to see if anything sparked. Though maybe not...yet. Travel with the kids and Haru, though, that might be a good idea. Expose them to new places, new cultures and languages early. Show them...

Would Haru enjoy travel?

Tally stared at his screen, annoyed with himself. He didn't know the answer to that question. So many things he needed to know. Far too many things he hadn't thought to ask. That was what it all boiled down to, didn't it? Tally's need to forge ahead, to solve things and make things right, kept those assumptions piling up. Even if they were Em'halafi, they still needed to find what worked for the two of them. It still took effort. He kept making mistakes with Haru because everything looked fine on the surface.

Did he have any illusions that it was *all* his fault? Some, yes. He knew himself that well. It was in his bones to take responsibility when something went wrong, even when he felt as if he'd been stabbed with a rusty spear. This? Finding out that Haru still thought he needed to hide things? Yeah. That was a big freaking spear with a barbed tip.

He thought he had been providing a stable environment and the whole time Haru had felt like he was walking on shifting sands. Rules. Expectations. Consistency. He insisted on it at work, so he could damn well start managing at home.

Not that he would ever be the tyrant Urusar Akaike was. Tally shuddered. *That man...* But for Haru to stop feeling so anxious, waiting for the other shoe to drop, there would be rules, and they would be consistent. Then maybe, slowly, they could start feeling like a family again instead of two people walking on sharp stones and eggshells.

But Tally couldn't concentrate on what was happening at home. There was business to take care of, and he needed to focus on that. There was a lot of money riding on the new properties. The last thing he needed was for something to go wrong because his head was filled with thoughts of his Em'halafi. Yes, the business could take a hit and keep running, but Tally's pride in what he did wouldn't let him slack off.

"Time to get with the program," Tally mumbled, scrolling through the messages from the various managers. Maybe Meli would want to take a bigger role in the Midwest developments. Though she had her littles to think of too.

A little after noon, just when Tally had most of his empire under control and no meetings for the foreseeable future, a call came in on his private line.

"Urusar?"

He pummeled his overloaded brain until it supplied a name for the quavering voice. "Sylvie?"

"Yes." Sylvie Blue Holly stopped for a shaky breath. "It's the drum heights on Blue Holly Hill, Urusar."

Tally struggled with that sentence. What could've happened? "The drum heights? I don't —"

"Please come, Urusar." Sylvie's voice broke into a jagged whisper. "Please."

"All right, Sylvie. I'm on my way."

She thanked him and Tally called Gun as soon as Sylvie hung up. Yes, Gun was at his house, and yes, he could be there in a few minutes.

"I don't know what has Sylvie so upset, but I'd feel better having you there."

"Yeah," Gun drew the word out. "I don't want to think too hard about what upset an old grandmama bear."

Not twenty minutes later, in cold weather gear rummaged from what Tally kept in his office and what was in storage, he joined Gun on a couple of the resort's snowmobiles, heading out across the hard-packed snow. Blue Holly land abutted the resort property and the gentle rise soon gave way to a steeper gradient as they approached. The Hill, in capital letters — the old ancestral Blue Holly ground with its ancient caves and its circle of giant stones at the summit. For the black bear family, it was a place of teaching and of ceremony. They named new cubs in that circle of stones, held weddings, celebrated life's milestones.

Near the foot of the hill proper, Tally and Gun parked the snowmobiles and trudged up the path to the summit that someone had shoveled. Sylvie waited for them on a rock outcropping near the top, apparently comfortable in her wool skirts and shawl while Tally shivered in his parka.

"Go on in, Urusar." She nodded to him, her eyes red-rimmed and shadowed, though she had recovered her composure. "Ted's up there. I can't look at it again."

Gun leaned in to give her a quick hug before they continued up and into the circle, a strange collection of both vertical and man-high flat rocks that could, perhaps, have been natural, but most likely were an ancient construction. Ted was there with six of his sibs and cousins, all grim-faced, and it only took a glance to see why.

Spray-painted in garish reds and blues, slogans and slurs covered the rocks. *Lijun first! Race traiters! Stop suporting burners! Wadiswan belongs to lijun!* Those and various other gems, many misspelled, met them every way they turned, along with the old lijun symbol of a crescent moon in a circle.

"Burners? Really?" Gun snorted softly.

An old-fashioned slur, it referred to times when humans executed lijun at the stake, but that didn't make the intent any less vicious. Tally pulled his business mask over his emotions. The last thing anyone needed was to see him upset by this. "Ted? Any damage beside the paint?"

"The assholes managed to push over one of the standing stones." Ted's chest heaved as he tried to control his snarl. "Sorry, Urusar. It's just…"

"Yes. No one helps the community more than your family. What a thing to do." *And why now? What's behind this?* "Any scents left behind? Tracks?"

Ted shook his head with a disgusted grunt. "Nothing. They waited until wet snow was on the way. Covered any trace."

Tally stood for a moment, hands clasped behind his back, long enough for all eyes to turn his way. "Gun, perimeter check, just in case. Ted, call the Dignans. They should be able to get that stone upright and secure again. Clara, get Addy on the line and tell her what we have. If there's a safe way to clean the paint off, she'll find it."

A few more directives, a few more terse phone calls, and Tally had work crews organized and Ted convinced that the site needed a sentry. The family was large enough to provide coverage around the clock. Gun soon returned shaking his head—nothing—and Tally said their goodbyes.

"Well that was kinda scary," Gun said as he threw a leg over the seat of his snowmobile.

"Traditionalist vandalism?"

Gun let out a little *ha*. "No. You being Urusar. It's like you're, well, someone else. Bigger, almost. Kinda chilly."

"It's still me." Tally considered. He knew he did it. He knew why. He'd just never had someone who knew regular Tally call it out before. "I can't look nervous or upset when people depend on me. It's what I have to do, Gun."

"Hmm."

"Speaking of things I have to do, as long as you're still here and undecided about staying or going back to Colorado, how do you feel about taking your old job back?"

Gun leaned back with a frown. "Tal, don't tell me you didn't assign a new head of Enforcement since I've been gone?"

"I, ah, well. Hank took it on a temporary basis. But he makes it clear whenever he can that he doesn't want it."

A little raptor squawk got away from Gun before he shook his head. "I'll take it for now, Tal. But if I decide to leave again, you gotta promise me to put someone good there."

"I do the best I can, Gun."

And I never seem to be able to get ahead of everything. Something's brewing. I just wish I knew what.

.

Chapter Five

Games

January could be bitter, bringing snow and ice storms, but it also brought bright crystalline days that could have been freed from a finely made snow globe. It was on one of these days when the winds had settled and the sun made jewels of the snow that Tally became restless. Things were still strained between him and Haru, but tiny steps. Maybe some time outside would do everyone some good.

"Haru? Do you ice skate?"

"Yes, of course."

Tally leaned back against the counter, watching as Jackson methodically speared one pre-cut pancake piece at a time and Livy and Melia made squashed messes of theirs. "I was thinking we could pick up Gun and take the kids up to Sapphire Lake. It's safely frozen by now and the staff has the skating concession set up."

The excited spark in Haru's eyes turned wary. "Curley-san?"

"Yes. He's an excellent skater. Nearly every kid up here plays hockey at some point, but Gun was more serious. Played through college and had considered it as a career." Tally frowned down at his coffee. Things in town and with the council had been tense. A niggling feeling wouldn't leave him alone. "Just in case. I want him there."

Haru let out the smallest huff. "Do they serve alcohol with the skating?"

"No. That's a scary thought. Hot chocolate, though."

"Hot chocolate!" Melia picked up on that, though she hadn't appeared to have been paying attention. "Uma, skating? Please?"

"The joeys do not have skates."

Tally smiled as the rest of the kids piled on the pleading. "There are skates for rent. Ones in all sizes."

Melia quieted and returned to her pancakes. She knew perfectly well that she had won.

"Could we ask Sammy?" Haru said in an airy tone, as if it wouldn't matter.

"I don't think that's a good idea." Tally held up a finger, stopping the protest forming on Haru's lips. "Not like that. What if she fell? The pups? Second trimester's a little far along for that to be safe."

Haru opened their mouth, closed it again, then said, "You have been researching, Argaze."

"Damn right I have," Tally muttered as he poured another cup of coffee. They were his pups, no matter what. "Too much we need to know."

He wasn't sure what that odd sideways look from Haru meant, but probably better that he pretended he didn't see it.

Taking kids skating was, of course, not as simple as picking up the car keys and throwing on a jacket. Haru had to change out of his yukata into pants, leaving Tally to wrestle the joeys into winter things. Mittens had to be found, warm socks put on six kicky little feet, scarves, hats. All of these things had to be tugged and fastened and wrapped onto excited joeys before they could set out. They took the SUV, since there were car seats and an extra adult, though Tally banished Gun to the back with the kids. He still hadn't quite forgiven the eagle for his behavior the other night.

He loved Gun fiercely but Sammy was right. Sometimes, and especially when he was drunk, he could be an asshole. Today, though, Gun was stone sober and sharp as glass shards.

"Enforcer?" Gun murmured as they stood together waiting for Haru to herd the kids to a bench for skate lacing.

"Only if it's necessary." Tally patted his shoulder, stole a look at his family and lowered his voice. "Just keep an eye on the kids and Haru especially. A frozen lake is no place to get flattened by bullies. I don't have anything specific. Haven't heard any rumors. Just…"

"Bad feeling." Gun cracked his knuckles. "Got it."

The rented skates for the kids were the old-fashioned double-bladed sort for small children, and though there had been some dismay on Livy's part that they only came in black and white, all three joeys were now completely riveted to the process of getting them on. Haru had gotten them to sing a song as he laced and tightened each skate. A little competition to see who finished first—him or the pups. Tally took the end of the next bench to pull on his well-loved hockey skates while Gun patted at Jackson's leg to get him to slide over.

"Why are yours all scuffed up, Uncle Gun?" Jackson asked, wide-eyed and earnest. He held onto legs and the bench as he carefully worked his way over to examine the skates.

"'Cause they're for hockey, kiddo." Gun grunted as he yanked the left one on. "And hockey's rough on everything."

Jackson nodded, considering. "Uma's are prettier."

Trying his best to be discreet, Tally peered over and, oh yes. Haru's skates were much prettier than Gun's, elegant figure skater ones rather than chunky old hockey skates, and a pale lilac instead of Gun's scuffed black and brown.

"I'd guess they'd have to be," Gun grumbled. "Your Uma's much prettier with everything."

"I did not realize you had noticed, Curley-san," Haru said without looking up from checking Melia's skates for the proper fit. His eyes narrowed as he pulled on the laces. "Perhaps you do notice things when you are sober."

Gun snorted. "I notice things when I'm not, too. *All* sorts of things."

"Do you intend to be today?"

The irritation rolling off Gun was hot enough to melt the ice. Tally stood and came over to offer Livy his hand and to head off any real nastiness. "There's no alcohol allowed in the skating area. And we're here for the kids."

He hoped they both heard the implications. *Gun's more responsible than that and let's not fight in front of the joeys, please.* Haru turned to get on his skates, giving both of them his back.

The tight set of Gun's jaw presaged a fight, but he surprised Tally with a shrug and an offer. "Why don't you two go do the couples thing? I'll start the kids on their first lesson."

Tally took a few steps onto the ice, gliding back and forth in front of the bench to give Haru a moment. The day's surprises kept coming when Haru finished his laces and nodded to Gun, though his expression gave nothing away.

"That is kind of you."

"It is. Thanks, Gun." Tally held out a hand and waited for Haru to skate to him, entranced as his husband skated to him with an understated, elegant confidence. He tucked Haru's hand into the crook of his elbow and pushed off at an ambling pace.

For his part, Haru took two small steps and quickly matched strides, gliding in tandem beside Tally. Greetings sailed through the bright winter air to them as people skated by—the employees who monitored the skating area, lijun of all ages and humans who knew Tally from various local projects, committees and businesses.

"Urusar, Uruma, so lovely to see you."

"Congrats on the pups, Urusar."

"Tally! Stop by for some cider before you leave. We haven't met your elusive husband yet."

There were whispers, too. Ones Tally and Haru ignored as they skated next to each other.

"They look good together."

"I hear they have a surrogate."

"How could Tally have allowed his Uruma to have children before him?"

The last comment made Haru stiffen, but Tally kept them moving around the rink, away from the cutting remark. Tally honestly didn't care which one of them had children first, though the Traditionalists were having conniptions. It just wasn't done. Of course, an uktena and an otter marrying wasn't done either, but here they were, Tally and his Em'halafi, enjoying the great outdoors together.

Enjoying? Tally glanced over, and yes, Haru wore that curved smile of his, the one right at the corner of his mouth. His eyes shone with excitement as they skated along side-by-side, and his cheeks had started to get rosy. For the first time since New Year's, Haru looked settled, and Tally's heart didn't ache so much.

They had been able to forget all the troubles at home—just for a little bit in this proverbial winter wonderland.

We'll make it. We'll figure it out. One step at a time. Because that's what Em'halafi did. Tally believed. In fact, he could believe enough for the both of them. The question was how to bring them together without causing more hurt. Tally's battered heart needed a respite. Having to lay down 'rules' tore little bits off him, but it had seemed to be the only way to get Haru to relax since the birth announcement. Maybe someday they wouldn't be necessary. Tally hoped it would be soon.

A hasty *shk-shk-shk* of skates coming up fast behind them had Tally turning his head with a frown, but it was only Justin Tripp, one of the Harris hawk brood in and around Wadiswan. "Mr. Bastille!"

"Justin? Everything all right?"

"Yes." Justin huffed to catch his breath, skating backward in front of them as he went on more softly. "Urusar, Uruma, are they still taking names? For older kids to help with the littles in the games?"

The games? Oh, Evade and Hunt, yes... "The council's still taking candidates, yes. Give Ms. Pierce a call. She's the one making the decisions on that part of things."

Red flushed Justin's face as he must have realized he'd come to the wrong person. "Oh. Okay. Thanks, Mr. Bastille!" With a wave, he raced off again, the Eberhardt girls across the lake his all too obvious goal.

"Mindy has put her name on the list," Haru said in a dry, airy tone, though his eyes were laughing with understated mirth.

Tally snickered. "Has she now? Who would've guessed?" He pulled in a deep breath, the crisp air somehow invigorating today rather than demoralizing. It helped that the sun was bright and that Haru snuggled closer. "This is nice. What a perfect day."

"It is good for the community to see you like this," Haru said with a solemn nod.

"Um. I suppose. Not really what I meant." Now the cold started to worm its way through his socks. Why did his feet always chill first?

"Ah."

Just that, and Tally knew he was in danger of damaging the fragile beauty of the day. No. It couldn't be allowed. He wrapped an arm around Haru's waist, took his right hand in his, and pointed them toward the center of the area roped-off for skating. Haru kept up with him effortlessly, even as Tally took them through a tight figure eight. *There*. There was a little smile and Tally pressed his advantage. Both hands on Haru's waist, he spun them both in a circle, took them through an arc to pick up speed, and picked Haru off the ice on the next little spin.

Haru laughed, a clear, unimpeded sound of surprised joy, and suddenly Tally's feet weren't so cold anymore.

A pure wonderful moment of togetherness on a date. A semblance of what they had before New Year's. But did Tally want what had been before then? Haru had been scared to tell him anything. Tally pulled Haru close, holding him in an awkward embrace in the middle of the rink. A curious expression flitted across Haru's eyes when he looked up.

Tally smiled. "Today's been nice. Here with you."

"It has."

Tally ran his gloved hand along Haru's jaw then smiled. "Let's get a few more turns in then check in on Gun."

"Mmm. Hopefully the pups have left him alive," Haru said and backed away, a twinkle in his dark gaze. He held out his hand and Tally took it, or tried to, but Haru pushed off with a gentle kick and evaded Tally.

The last few turns around the rink sparkled with a little bit of expectation, of excitement between the two of them. Haru teased by skating around Tally, getting close then backing away when Tally reached for him. It felt like a chase, one in which Haru was inviting Tally to hunt him. A shudder went through Tally. *That's exactly what Haru's doing.* Trying to entice Tally.

Each low laugh, each twitch of Haru's lips, were a moment Tally wanted to capture and remember dearly. Haru was trying so hard to figure out their lives together, and pure unadulterated moments like this were rare. The glimpse into what Haru could be took Tally's breath away each and every time. No matter how upset he was, his heart wanted his Em'halafi. They just had to build the bridge instead of shaking it apart.

Tally needed a way to make more of these moments happen.

"Gotcha!" Tally crowed triumphantly around the far bend. Haru's laughter rang out. They nuzzled together, but a few catcalls had Haru pushing Tally back so he allowed it. They were both out of breath, faces burning with the exertion. "Time to rescue Gun, my beautiful otter."

"Yes, of course. Before Melia bites him."

"Oh, crap." Tally took off toward the practice rink area, Haru's laughter right behind him.

"Usar!" Jackson yelled the moment he spotted Tally. He pushed away from Gun and managed to walk-skate to Tally, grabbing onto his legs to stop. "Look! Look! I skated!"

"You did." Tally ruffled Jackson's hair. "Uncle Gun has been teaching you well."

"He fell and said bad words," Melia said breezily as she inched across the ice toward Tally.

"Oh for..." Gun snapped his mouth shut and shook his head.

"Melia helped him," Jackson added matter-of-factly.

Tally looked over to Gun, who shrugged. "She went between my legs. I was crouched."

Oh.

"No permanent damage done." Gun scowled, his gaze moving behind Tally, where Haru was, holding onto the side of the rink and shaking. He wasn't even trying to hide his laughter. Gun let out a breath. Not one of pain, but he was definitely working to keep his temper in front of the kids. "Anyway, they want Usar and Uma. How about letting me sit out for a spin?"

"Sure thing, Gun."

Tally took Livy and Melia for a tiny bit of a skate, each twin clinging to one of his hands, while Haru took Jackson. The roped-off rink seemed much larger when skating with small people, each laborious push of a skate both a triumph and an effort.

"Usar, I'm tired," Livy finally declared when they reached the quarter-way around.

"Sure thing, sweets. How about hot chocolate?"

"Chocolate!" the girls chimed together before being echoed across the rink by their brother.

Tally scooped the girls up, took them back to the bench and started on their laces. Not a full day's outing, certainly, but this had been perfect. The dates he and Haru had stolen over the last months had been wonderful. These little family outings? He sometimes enjoyed them more.

* * * *

Some non-predator lijun could be as fully threatening as true predators. When angered and believing themselves cornered, boars were among those. Barry Hastings stood slowly from his chair at the council table, fists planted on the wood, his breathing resembling nothing so much as the snorting of a wild pig at bay.

"You did *what*?"

Tally sighed and tapped his papers straight to give himself a moment. He'd known going into the meeting that there would be opposition, but Barry's reaction was out of proportion to his previous statement.

"The Wadiswan business council agrees with me. Businesses that have been in residence for decades should not be forced out to make room for something newer. Harris Street needs help, yes, but shouldn't lose its character entirely."

"And this is how you do it?" Dan O'Rourke's moose was slower to anger, but not by much. "By prioritizing human concerns over lijun?"

"Assisting with loans to allow three or four human businesses to remain is hardly putting lijun concerns in jeopardy," Tally countered, keeping his voice soft and even as the voices of his opposition rose. "There will be room for growth, for entrepreneurs from both sides of the community."

Disastrous. This month's council meeting was becoming absolutely disastrous. Everyone had known going in that this was the meeting where the final plans for the Harris Street revitalization project would be put on the table. Everyone had known that they needed buy-in from the human city and business councils, that they could influence decisions, but ultimately the decisions would be out of their hands.

Except that certain lijun had thought differently. Certain lijun had still thought they would be able to snap up the available and at-risk properties to develop as they saw fit. Tally shuddered at the hints of chain stores and eateries Clement Black had brought him. Clement's motives were suspect, of course, but Tally knew he didn't lie. Barry and Dan had wanted Harris Street as their own retail empire.

Maybe his end run around them hadn't been politic, but it had been necessary.

"So who owns this property now?" Dan stabbed a finger at a prime corner spot where Harris intersected Barnes.

"I do."

Barry slammed a palm on the table. "You underhanded, selfish...*snake*! You've been buying up lots under our noses!"

"Just that one. And the ones next to Best Bakery." Tally had no illusions about them letting Jean keep the bakery if they'd gotten hold of that block. 'Lijun First' they might mouth off about until everyone was sick of hearing it, but what they really meant was their own interests first.

"I don't understand." Rose's nose twitched, emphasizing her confusion. "I thought—"

Clement patted her arm. "Never mind now. This is what we have to work with." He turned his clever, glittering eyes to Tally. "So what you're saying, in a nutshell, is that city council will be approving all new businesses for the project and, essentially, victory to the strongest?"

Tally managed a laugh, grateful for the pressure of Haru's thigh against his under the table. Even though his husband had been silent so far, the unquestioning support didn't hurt one bit. "Not quite. Any business is welcome to apply for consideration. But keep in mind that city council is looking for a balanced and varied selection of businesses. There are three properties" — everyone leaned closer to the diagram as he pointed them out — "where they will permit larger, out-of-town corporations, but, for the most part, the idea is to encourage local commerce."

"And you have their ears and you have them in your pocket, Urusar," Dan growled. "Don't think we're stupid."

"It's what you've wanted all along!" Barry waved his arms, the volume control on his voice obviously broken. "To weaken lijun interests here! To give ground to the humans! Is this why we built this town, on lijun sweat and tears? Is *this* what our founders hoped for all those years ago?"

"You have to admit, it gives the humans a lot of power over the project," Cora Miles, their elk councilwoman, tapped the paper with a dark frown. "I'm not sure it's wise, Tally."

"Now, now, Cora," Hakkon intervened. "It's not as if we don't have lijun on city council."

"His people!" Dan bellowed, pointing a finger at Tally. "Entirely his! Damn progressives with no sense of tradition, no sense of loyalty. You go too far, Bastille. You go too *far*."

Haru looked up from his notes. "The plan is in place, O'Rourke-san. Perhaps energies would be better spent working with the city council now."

"From you, we thought better." Barry gathered up his papers and stuffed them violently in his suitcase. "An Uruma from a traditional family. You should have done so much better."

With that, he stalked out. Dan followed him after a last glower. The rest of the council sat frozen, either in shock or in calculated observation, each to their own nature.

"Well, that went well," Tyra purred from Tally's left. "All things considered."

Tally sighed and looked around the table, taking in Rose's barely contained flight response, Cora's irritation, Clement's far-away thinking gaze. "As Uruma Bastille stated, the council's voted. This is what we have. Please encourage your business-minded friends and relatives to consider possibilities. The applications and proposal forms are attached with the council notes I sent this evening. Everyone gets a fair hearing."

"In business, that's never the case, Tally." Clement said it with a smile that didn't come close to reaching his eyes. "Sounding all bright-eyed and naïve just makes you look, if you'll pardon the expression, shady."

He heard the accusations loud and clear, certainly ones every Urusar in the history of lijun councils had heard. Favoritism. Cronyism. Nepotism. "Tell you what, Clement. Why don't you and Rose look over the proposals with me as they come in? We'll decide together which ones deserve championing with the city and I'll do my best to lean on them in favor of the ones we like best."

Rose surprised him, speaking up before Clement could shush her. "That sounds fair. All right. We should do that."

With a few more remarks and reminders about the upcoming Evade and Hunt games for the kids, Tally wrapped up the meeting, a little of the tension leaving his shoulders at Haru's approving nod. Some losses, small gains, which was normal for council meetings these days. Tally wondered as Haru took his arm to walk out with him if all lijun councils were like this or if somewhere in the world there existed some wonderful, fairy-tale lijun community where everyone worked together for the good of all.

Ha. Probably not.

As he and Haru walked out of the meeting, Tally's frustration bubbled over.

"I don't know why they have to be such a pain in my ass. This is supposed to help everyone. All of us. Sometimes I feel like I should just buy out the lot of them."

His otter gave him a sideways glance before stepping carefully onto the icy lot. "Sometimes it is what is needed, but your positions, the money they produce, is also why people fear you. You can use money. Use it however you like to get what you want. No matter how much good you do, they will always see you as the snake with money."

Tally paused at his car door, looking over the Bentley at his otter. Sometimes Haru knew how to twist in the knife too well.

* * * *

Silence increased the tension during the drive over to the Blue Holly Clinic. Haru had to work hard not to fidget in their seat. Last thing they wanted was for Tally to think they were nervous. He wouldn't be *wrong*, they were, but Tally wasn't the reason. Not the whole reason anyway. Today they'd be able to see the babies, and Tally would be there. To see them. With Haru and Sammy. It made the pregnancy and the situation more real.

All of it.

Wow. Haru was having babies. Well, no, technically Sammy was, but Tally and Haru were going to have *more* pups. They were already outnumbered with the joeys, and now their family was growing. Five to two. Would they survive it? And that was only if Misaki's last IVF treatment hadn't worked—because that was a thing still happening. Politics were so much fun. Their family was exploding at the seams. A lot faster than Haru had expected. Probably faster than Tally had expected.

A heavy sigh left Tally, the sound loud in the enclosed space of the Bentley. Haru sent a sideways glance toward their Argaze.

Definitely faster than Tally had expected.

"We're almost there," Tally said, his eyes focused on the road. "It's just around the next bend."

"Yes, I know." Gods save Haru from their own mouth.

Oppressive silence permeated the car again, creating a vacuum and making it hard to talk, let alone breathe.

Awkward.

Not the smart move, reminding Tally he'd been excluded. That Sammy and Haru had been going to all these appointments without him. Despite Tally saying Sammy wouldn't be excluded from their lives, the uncomfortable tension when she came over to help with the joeys was ever-present. It was also the reason they'd had Sammy meet them at the clinic instead of picking her up.

That would've been even more awkward.

Little increments. Interactions in small doses should help. Or so Haru had hoped.

"Have you gotten all the books?" Haru asked. If Tally would just learn the rules, it would make their courting so much easier.

"Books?"

"With the Satislit guidelines. For you. For me."

"Ah, yes, those. Yes, Urusar Akaike said…*many things*, but I have them."

"Good."

Tally glanced briefly in Haru's direction. "It will take some time to go through it all, but can we talk about them? The rules? Some feel rather archaic."

"That is acceptable," they answered. "We have the rule about the treats."

"We do. We do. And nothing will be implemented retroactively. Like with the pregnancy."

"As you wish, Argaze."

"I do." A shudder went through Tally, making Haru curious as to what he felt about the consequences of the breach in protocol.

They almost asked but decided it was better not to, that now wasn't the time. Haru didn't want Tally upset when they got to the clinic. It was better just to be quiet like a good Satislit.

Tally and Haru had been dancing around the pregnancy for the past month, gains and slides every which way. The family date to the lake had been a gain. The ride to the clinic? Definite slide. They knew the pups weren't the problem. Any time Tally looked at Sammy's growing belly, he got a spark in his eyes.

"Do you want to know?" Tally asked, breaking the silence as the pulled into the small paved lot.

Haru frowned. There were a lot of things that question covered.

"The pups' sexes."

"Ah, we can. If that is what you want." Haru glanced out the window. Why was that the one thing everyone wanted to know? "Healthy is all I need them to be."

"Right. Um. Right."

Walking into the clinic felt just as awkward and cramped as the car ride, despite being out in the open air. Tally stayed close but didn't hold Haru's hand. Instead, their arms brushed as they went through the entrance. Even though they only had millimeters between them, the space might as well have been as thick as an iceberg, the air absolutely frigid in the gap separating the two of them.

Tally didn't initiate touches frequently, but he had stopped avoiding Haru. It was probably the best they could hope for.

Hot and cold. That was how they ran these days.

As they entered the waiting room, Sammy hopped up from her chair and came to them, pulling Haru close. Nose. Nose. Kiss. Kiss. The two of them hugged before she angled toward Tally. His expression was hard to get a read on. A smile that seemed genuine, but the lines around his eyes were pinched, not relaxed. He pulled Sammy and Haru into a hug. Hmmm. Warm. For the first time since they'd gotten up that morning, Haru relaxed.

Tabib Blue Holly called out, breaking up their cuddle. She had a smirk when she said, "Not that the three of you aren't sickeningly adorable, but you're going to make my other patients nauseous with that sweet display."

"My apologies," Haru answered, offering a *futsuurei*. Right. Propriety must be observed. Too many eyes watching that could later share information. However, they didn't miss the look Sammy and Tally shared as they straightened. The Blue Holly matriarch wore a wry grin when they met her eyes.

"Teasing, Mr. Bastille. Teasing."

"Oh, my—uh!" Haru had started to bow, but Tally and Sammy grabbed their forearms.

Sammy laughed, petting in a downward motion. "We're obviously excited. Are we next?"

"You are!"

"Good." Sammy ushered them forward with Tally's help. "I was starting to get antsy. I *need* to pee."

Several people and lijun chuckled, the women nodding.

"Right. This way." Blue Holly led them down the corridor to exam room C. "I'm so glad you made it this time, Urusar. It's too bad your work has kept you so busy."

"Yes, well, rest assured, I don't plan on missing any more appointments, Tabib Blue Holly." And there was the frost again, though Tally managed a polite smile. The political one he pulled out whenever he was unhappy.

"Good to hear, Urusar Bastille."

Sammy climbed up onto the exam table after getting weighed. She cradled her bump, rubbing it. Then she grunted as she slid down and exposed her belly for the checkup.

"Very ladylike," Haru said.

She stuck her tongue out at them. "Not everyone is as graceful as you."

Tabib Blue Holly chuckled. "So true. Pretty lijun like Haru are a rare find."

"Thank you?" Haru was being complimented. Yes? Tone made it hard to understand sometimes. They looked at Tally, who nodded. This time the smile reached their Argaze's eyes.

As Tabib Blue Holly measured Sammy's belly, she winked at Haru. She felt around, pressing, asking Sammy questions. All Haru could do was watch, their eyes riveted on their Kwebabiad's abdomen. Haru reached out then pulled back. Tabib Blue Holly chuckled then grabbed their hand.

"Here," she said.

"Oh! Oh!" Haru pressed closer. "That is!" They looked up at Tally. "The pups! Both of them are kicking!"

Tally's hand covered Haru's. Another kick. Then another. Several beats played out against their hands. Haru grinned up at Tally.

"They are strong."

"Mmm-hmm. Like their Uma."

Haru pressed their hand against the beats, steady as a largo. Tabib Blue Holly's chuckle drew their attention. It was always so happy. How she managed with so many family members stepping over one another, they weren't sure. It had to be magic. She winked again.

"Moments like this one are why I'll never get tired of this job." She patted their hand. "Now, let's see these pups. You *do* want to see them, right?"

"Yes, yes we do," Haru answered quickly.

Her throaty chuckle had Haru ducking their head. Yes, they were excited. They couldn't help it.

Seeing the pups — so tiny and frail on the screen of the ultrasound — made Haru's breath catch.

"Just a few more measurements, but I'd say they are developing right on schedule." Tabib Blue Holly flicked her wrist, clicking buttons. "Yes, even with being twins, their growth is coming along. How is the morning sickness? Getting any better?"

"Mmm. Yes. Still sometimes after dinner, but it's not as bad as before."

"You gained weight this time. If you hadn't, I would've had you stay here to make sure you're getting all your nutrients."

Sammy rubbed a hand over her belly. "I'm getting better."

"Do not quote Monty Python to me, young lady. This is serious."

"I know."

Haru nosed her belly, grabbing her hand. All they wanted was happy, healthy pups.

After a second Sammy's hand went to Haru's head, pulling her fingers through their hair. "I'm eating. I swear I'm eating."

"We know, dear," Tabib Blue Holly replied. "It's the keeping the food down that's the problem."

Tally pressed closer and Haru sat up to give him room. His eyes had locked on the screen. "Is there anything we can do?"

"Make sure Sammy gets foods that don't upset her stomach. Don't create stress for her. Make sure she rests. Twins are not easy." Tabib started moving the wand again. "Do we want to take a reasonable guess at the babies' sexes?"

There was an awkward moment when there were two yeses and one no. Haru was the no. Why did they have to open their mouth? Foot, meet pie hole. Again. Sammy's expression was neutral while Tally's brows were drawn together, lines around his eyes.

All the while, Tabib Blue Holly clicked and took pictures. She mumbled a 'for later' as they printed off. The three of them stared at one another, the frost coming back. Haru hadn't noticed that it had disappeared until it returned. Sammy was the first to speak up.

"I thought you'd want to know how to decorate the nursery, because—" She waved a hand at him. "Of you." But then her voice trailed off. Her eyes sparked with a renewed understanding. "Right. Right."

Tally's dark gaze flicked between Haru and Sammy, the frown still prominent. Sammy shrugged. A silent little eye battle went on between her and Tally, before he turned to Tabib Blue Holly.

"On second thought, surprises are fun," he said.

"Sounds good. You can always call if you change your minds." She stood, arching up. Had to be hard to sit at such small tables for a bear like her. "But it seems everyone is healthy and hale. Here."

Oh. Wow. The pictures made Haru's heart stop. Their pups. Two precious little beans until the end of June. They hadn't gotten these moments with the joeys. Haru wished otherwise, but maybe they could share it a different way. Try to mend some of the breaks they had made.

"Tabib Blue Holly?" they said as she helped clean Sammy's abdomen up.

"Yes, Uruma?"

"May we bring the joeys next time?"

The bear glanced over, her mouth open in an 'o', but she quickly recovered. "I'm not sure. Poor kids would probably be bored."

"But I want them to know their siblings."

"Siblings?"

"What else would they be?" Haru frowned.

Tabib Blue Holly's expression softened, a warm smile replacing the confusion. "Of course. But are you ready to answer those kind of questions?"

"What kind?"

"Where babies come from, Uruma."

Haru shivered. "Would little pups really ask those questions at their age?"

"Hahaha, so innocent." Tabib Blue Holly patted their cheek. "Ready, Sammy?"

"Yup. I need to pee." She stuck out a hand and the bear helped her off the exam table. Sammy winked. "But I doubt sex education was on Haru's agenda for the joeys."

"Poor pups won't know what hit them," Tabib Blue Holly responded somberly before cracking a wry grin.

They stared at the Blue Holly matriarch as she escorted Sammy out of the exam room, the Tabib's bemused chuckling rather disconcerting. No, they hadn't been thinking about those questions. All they'd wanted was their pups sharing in the experience together. But now... Now they worried over what the pups would think and feel about the new babies.

Tally bumped Haru's shoulder. "Come on. We'll get the joeys from Mom and Dad and you can show off the pictures."

Haru glanced at the ultrasound picture. The black and white grainy photograph made their heart squeeze. "You think the pups are excited? For the babies? So much has happened. Maybe they are afraid they are getting replaced."

"Not at all." Tally gathered Haru up in a warm embrace. They sighed and snuggled closer. "Never. The joeys know how much you love them. If anything, they're impatient for the babes to get here."

"Really?"

A firm but gentle kiss pressed against their temple. "I know so. We are all excited for these pups. All of us. More to love, that's all."

And for a moment, in their Argaze's embrace, Haru could believe that.

Chapter Six

Evading Guests and Hunting Trifles

Crystal stemware chimed as a server relieved Haru and Tally of their empty drinks and gave them new glasses. The noise level was at a steady hum, but anticipation filled the dining hall. It was the good kind of energy, or Haru hoped it was, since the renewed Evade and Hunt games started tomorrow.

"This was a good idea," Tally said, leaning close.

"Pierce-san helped quite a bit. She wanted the kids to have fun, too."

Tally hugged Haru against his chest. "But you are sneaky enough to know a banquet celebrating the return of the games would get everyone on board."

"I do not sneak. I strategize."

"You're a sneaky strategist then."

Yummies on a tray caught Haru's attention, so ignoring Tally's teasing was easy. Delicately butterflied prawns with a dipping sauce, fried shrimp and *oooh*, *takoyaki*. They hummed with pleasure as they grabbed a bowl and filled it. A chuckle interrupted their pilfering. Tally was watching them, the gaze warmer than it had been in weeks.

Haru stuffed one of the balls in their mouth. "What?"

"Nothing. It's nice seeing you happy."

"Treats are always nice to have." Haru licked their finger with a hum and noticed Tally's gaze lingered on their mouth. They had a nice buzz going from the champagne so maybe they were reading into the expression.

"Yes," Tally murmured, gaze definitely on Haru's lips. "Yes, they are." He blinked as if startled and cleared his throat. "I, ah, should go over and say hello to Rose."

"Oh, yes, Argaze," Haru answered, watching Tally's back in confusion. What had happened? They pilfered a few more treats and began a circuit around the room in the other direction. Haru adjusted the sleeves on their *kimono*. Divide and conquer. That must be what Tally wanted. If their Argaze wanted to take on the skittish rabbit councilwoman—odd choice, but okay—that left the boar to Haru.

Literally.

Different clan members stopped to say hello as they worked around the room toward Councilman Hastings. They congratulated Haru about the pups and chattered on about their excitement for the games. It made Haru hopeful. The general vibe was excitement *for* the Evade and Hunt activities Saturday. Even the more resistant council members had shown up, so that meant Haru's campaign for the children was working.

Please, let it be working.

Several kiddies ran around the room, squealing and giggling as they wove through the adults—a game of tag between the older teens and the younger pups.

Haru glanced around for their own joeys. A clump of children were under the drapes looking up, pointing up with excited movements.

What in Gods...

"Melia!" Haru rushed toward the drapes over by the fountain—the loud clack of their geta drawing attention. "Do not dare!"

Then she jumped. Daring, of course Amelia dared. Her little opossum body went flying through the air then down. Down quickly. Too fast. Much too fast. They wouldn't make it in time. And she was going to miss the fountain.

"Melia!"

The other children shouted frantically too, rushing toward the fountain. No one was close enough.

Then a large, looming figure stepped out behind the pups.

"Gotcha!" The man said as he swiped Melia out of the air. She squeaked and sneezed, pawing at the hands circling her. He lifted her so they faced each other. Her little mouth chomped down on his thumb. "No biting."

"Excuse me. Ah, excuse me," Haru said as they pushed through the last of the crowd. "Melia. Let go now!"

The stranger shook his hand, grunting, and repeated as he frowned at her, "No biting."

She squeaked again, her little body puffing up as she did so. Amelia stubbornly kept her teeth embedded in her rescuer's hand, though. Then she hissed.

Whoa.

Time for damage control. "Thank you, Mister, ah? Thank you, and I am so sorry. She has been bitey lately. I apologize." Haru held out their hands as he offered a *saikeirei*. "May I take her off your hands?"

"We can try," the stranger answered tersely.

Haru petted Melia's back, the tension in her tiny body breaking as they soothed her fur down. She relaxed enough that when Haru pulled, she did let go of the man's hand. They pressed her against their chest.

"What do you think you were doing, young lady?" they murmured. Despite their anger, Haru pressed several kisses on her head. She sneezed. Of course she did. Yuck. That went in their mouth. Then Melia nuzzled into Haru's neck. "And again—" Haru bowed to the stranger. "Thank you."

"Not a problem at all. Mostly." His smile was more a baring of teeth than a friendly gesture.

"I am—"

"Uruma Bastille. You're as lovely as the rumors say."

Haru slowly raised their head. "Do we know each other?" They sniffed discreetly, scenting. Predator. But Haru couldn't place him without a more intrusive sniff. "I am, unfortunately, at a loss for your name."

The predator stuck out a hand, the smile becoming, if anything, more disturbing. "Jason Kaul. I've come in from State as an observer."

Excuse me? Haru managed not to miss a beat, despite the shock, and offered an *eshaku*. "For the games? How lovely. My Urusar has been so busy, it must have slipped his mind to mention it. I apologize for not welcoming you personally. We must make amends, especially since you saved Melia from becoming a pancake."

Said pup sneeze-chirped her disapproval.

"Actually, Councilman Hastings invited me to watch," Kaul-san replied, smile uncomfortable as ever. "The State is interested in how these games play out."

"How considerate of him." *Not*. The words pinged all of Haru's Satislit training. "We must have everyone to dinner, then."

And, as if the mention of his name summoned him, Hastings-san materialized next to this new unknown. "We need to ensure that the games are reinstated properly," the boar snorted, very near a challenge. "Jason's here to be sure traditional rules are adhered to."

"How generous of him," Haru responded, biting down their less-than-appropriate reply. A crowd of clan members had shifted toward them, pretending not to be eavesdropping. "But which of the traditional rules?"

Both men stiffened. Councilman Hastings' expression clouded. "The ones we've always used?"

"While each clan, and clans from different countries, all have their own traditions," Haru replied, then stopped for a moment to choose their next words. "Most clans have the same, if not similar, rules?"

"We'd obviously use the Bastille clan ones, Uruma."

"Really?" They petted Amelia, glancing at her. She licked their cheek. That was still not getting her out of trouble, despite its cuteness. "In the Akaike clan, the predators were allowed to draw blood on the prey if they managed a catch, no matter how old" — gasps shuddered through the crowd — "the pup."

"We have several medics on hand for any possibilities," Councilman Hastings ground out. The crowd hushed, with the exception of a pair of footfalls. Steady — familiar — steps toward them.

"A medic? No. An accident can happen, but drawing blood with ones so young could send the wrong message. Bullying is not something we want to encourage. Maybe we should review the rules? Make sure they are appropriate for *this era*." Haru nuzzled Melia and got several more licks in return. "I am not sure there is much of a need to have the little ones get hurt."

Murmurs rippled through the crowd. Good. Worried parents meant there was time to fix whatever the hell Councilman Hastings was trying to pull.

"If I remember correctly, most clans have bylaws about reviewing the rules every so often. Did we already do so? Pierce-san assured me everything was set for the games."

Hastings-san glanced toward the crowd of lijun, back to Haru, then to Kaul-san. The way his eyes widened, his cheeks ruddy with color, meant he was pissed. *Too bad, asshole.*

"Don't know how you did things back home—" Kaul-san's nostrils flared as he took a deliberate, obvious sniff of Haru. "Otter. And I don't care. State has bylaws in place for a reason, ones that supersede clan traditions. If this clan has let things slide so far that you don't know them anymore, that's not my problem."

"Unless if affects the *direct safety* of said clan," Haru replied, meeting Kaul-san's stare. "How would the parents explain gashes and stitches to their human neighbors?"

"Kids get hurt all the time," Councilman Hastings snorted out.

"With bite wounds? Clawed-up arms? Bruises? Broken bones every month?" Haru edged closer to the big boar. "I would not call those *regular* injuries. What would the clan do if a *human* teacher called in the authorities? Like they are legally obligated to do. Are you willing to risk that kind of exposure of lijun?"

A murmur rose in a tide then fell away. Something dark and violent rode behind Hastings-san's eyes, as if Haru had scored too close a hit. The footfalls had stopped. Tally's scent, strong and comforting, filled Haru's lungs. They looked up to their Argaze, whose crow's feet had crinkled — not from laughter like usual, but from the deep frown he wore. Gunther flanked Tally's left side, close, *protective*.

Haru handed a protesting Amelia to him, but Gunther immediately tucked her up against his neck and she quieted. Good girl.

"My dear Argaze, meet Kaul-san. He saved Melia from a bad fall and is here to watch the games, on Hastings-san's invitation."

"So I heard." Tally took a step forward, his presence bigger than life, an intensity Haru rarely felt. "We are so pleased Councilman Hastings took the initiative to involve State with the program's return."

"I also invited them to dinner."

There was a beat, where the room felt smaller, not a single noise from anyone. Then Councilwoman Pierce stepped forward and clapped her hands. "Excellent. We will have a chance to go over the *new* rules for the games so they're clear for everyone."

Tally nodded. "Yes, the last thing we want is for any of the children to get hurt. Don't you agree, Barry?"

"Yes, yes, of course, Urusar Bastille. We would never want any harm done to the children."

* * * *

"Do you know him?" Haru had crowded close, indicating Kaul with his chin as the two of them peered around the kitchen doorway at their guests.

Tally kissed the top of his head as if he'd only stopped there for a stolen moment of affection. He kept his head lowered to murmur, "No. And there's precious little in the database about him."

"You do not *know* the people in your state council?" Haru was giving him that *I-can't-believe-Americans* stare.

"I know the council members, my love. I helped elect them." Tally took the overloaded tray from Haru's hands and hoped his smile didn't look frozen. "It's all the people attached to State that I don't know. Clerks, accountants, aides and so on. I don't know many of those."

Haru's eyebrows tried to meld with his hairline. "I do *not* think Kaul-san is an accountant."

"No. It's a sure bet he isn't. That one's more predator than Gun."

"Careful steps, Argaze."

All expression had melted from Haru's face, a tactic Tally had come to recognize as extreme wariness. This time it wasn't directed at Tally, and warmth spread through him at the simple show of solidarity. *'Careful'*, his otter said, and meant *I've got your back* at the same time.

Part of him seethed with resentment over having these people in his home for dinner *after* already having to deal with them at the gathering for the kids and the parents. The more political bit of his brain knew perfectly well that this was necessary. "Be the arbitrator, Tal. The impetus in the background. Let them talk more than you do," Dad had often said. For the most part, Tally tried to follow his advice. Not seizing control of every conversation and issue was damnably hard sometimes, though.

Tyra leaned back against the sideboard where Tally set down his tray of cut veggies and cheese, her movements too casual to be innocent. She waved hello to Lahi across the room.

"So?" Tally murmured as he fussed with the arrangement. "Do we know him?"

"Not as a person, no." Tyra's nose wrinkled before she smoothed her features and sipped at her martini. "You smell *what* he is, don't you?"

Tally gave a tiny headshake. "I can't place it."

"Honey badger. Not a big predator, but all the attitude of a wolverine with five times the mean."

"Tyra, I'm shocked." Tally let out a soft hiss of reproof. "Stereotyping?"

"Hmmm." She made a sound halfway between a purr and a growl. "I don't know who he is, Tal. But I know the type. He's not just some bureaucrat sent to observe."

"Duly noted. I wouldn't care if State wanted to observe. It's our first Evade and Hunt in far too long. But certain council members went over my head to request this. *That's* what rankles."

Tyra patted his shoulder. "I know. But he's here. Sending him packing would be… I wouldn't advise it."

"No intention of it." Tally turned to the room with a smile. "Thank you, everyone, for joining us. Feel free to graze as you like while we review. Councilwoman Pierce has all of the particulars. Gun, let's get the map spread out, please."

Tyra took the chair at the head of the table while Tally chose to loom. He leaned in for a quick kiss on the cheek from Haru as his otter swept by to take position on the opposite side of the room. Oh, they had issues still, ones worth losing sleep over. But Haru understood these games. Gun spread out the map, using coasters to weight the corners, and claimed the doorway as a good leaning place, not openly threatening, though no one would be able to get out of the room without going through him.

"We'll be using Hastings Woods as our grounds for the games," Tyra began.

Barry's chest puffed out. "Named for one of my ancestors."

"It was," Tyra agreed at her calmest. "Though it's been Bastille land for generations, kept free of commercial concerns." It seemed to Tally that she purposefully bent over the map so she could ignore the venomous glare Barry shot her. "As you can see here, we've partitioned the woods into six sections, each for a specific age group. We'll have spotters—air and ground—to turn back any of the kids who wander out of bounds."

"The spotters will be responsible adults, I assume?" Kaul's deep voice only seemed to have two modes, snarl and growl. Tally reminded himself sternly that Gun often sounded like that, too.

Tyra shook her head. "The spotters will be the older high school and college kids. Adult volunteers will have other jobs."

"First I've heard of it," Dan snorted.

Clement leaned over to peruse the map. "If you'd attended the planning sessions..."

"Let's not go off the rails quite yet." Hakkon cleared his throat, addressing Kaul. "Tyra searched State archives for current best practices, many of which we agreed were sound. Especially those utilizing tech that didn't exist when she and I were young and hunting in the games. Each child will have a unique GPS tag. Our adult volunteers will be tracking and communicating with the spotters so no one gets lost."

"And to make sure the spotters verify and referee catches," Cora added, her expression forbidding. "Certain things are non-negotiable here."

She still doesn't trust us. Not yet. Cora had always been a staunch ally of Tally's mom, and he still hoped she might warm up to him or transfer her allegiance to Haru, but so far she had been wary and suspicious, acting as a stubborn and sometimes obstructionary advocate for the prey kids in the process of setting up the games.

Everyone had agreed that there would be some overenthusiastic catches and accidents because well, kids, but Cora had been the one to insist on flag catch rules. Tally was certain the flag issue, with each prey kid wearing one as if they were playing flag football, would cause objections. They didn't. Kaul simply nodded along to Tyra's recitation, his flat, cold eyes giving away nothing.

Finally, Tyra wound down and Kaul folded his hands atop the table. "I'll be interested to see your innovations in practice. State has no objections to the rules you've established."

Barry let out a huff and did a double take that would've been hilarious under any other circumstances. Across the room, Haru's expression hardened just a hair, confirming the direction of Tally's thoughts. They'd brought an observer from State in because they were sure there would be official objections resulting in delays and bureaucratic nonsense. Disruption of the games this late in the process would've been a terrible embarrassment for Tally, a huge blow to the community's confidence in him. That Kaul refused to play along was...interesting.

Maybe tomorrow's games would clear up motives. Then again, maybe not.

* * * *

Frost painted every leaf and blade the next morning, turning Hastings Woods into a fairy-touched Otherworld. Tally stood with the other parents in the Under Six group, cradling Jackson and Livy in possum form, while Haru stood tense and silent on his right, holding Melia.

The joeys had grasped the concept of the games quickly, as a new sort of hide and seek, and Gun had practiced with them several times so they understood how the flag concept worked.

"It's like freeze tag when you lose your flag," Jackson had declared solemnly. "Except you're done."

Tally had confided to Haru later that they should've just had Jackson explain the rules to everyone. Would've been much simpler than letting grown-ups do it. So many questions, one of which had been whether the smaller predators, like opossums, should be considered predators or prey. Haru had suggested to the parents that they let the children choose whether they wanted to seek or hide. Their three joeys had chosen the prey option, since, as Livy said, "I can't reach a moose kid flag."

Hakkon stood as the starter for their group, since only his youngest, Mason, was still eligible for the games and her mom had charge of the Fourteen and Older group. His eldest, Mindy, was already in peregrine form to serve as one of the spotters for this section, Justin beside her in his Harris hawk form. How he'd managed to get assigned to the same section as Mindy was baffling, but it wasn't as if he'd have a lot of time to make puppy eyes at Mindy anyway.

"Spotters away!" Hakkon called, and the raptor teens took to the air while the ground spotters, mostly raccoon and rabbit, raced off to their assigned spots around the perimeter. One hand raised, Hakkon stared intently at his watch. "Prey kids ready!"

"Ready?" Tally whispered to his joeys and got two nods in response. He set them on the grass, one hand on each joey's back.

"No biting," Haru admonished a squirming Amelia as he set her down.

"Set!" Hakkon called, faint echoes of his cry coming from other parts of the woods. He brought his hand down sharply. "Go!"

The little ones raced off, one moose calf, three little squirrels, a beaver kit and the joeys, Amelia outpacing them all to plunge into the underbrush. Tally found himself inexplicably wiping at his eyes.

Haru's hand slipped into his. "Are you all right, Argaze?"

"I am. Silly, I know." Tally squeezed his husband's fingers and managed a smile. "I'm just so proud of them."

"Here, proud papa." Addy handed him one of the tracking screens, because, of course, the entire family had come out as volunteers. "You can help keep up with who's where." She handed Haru a sheet of paper. "So you can tell which code on screen is which kid. We're only tracking our own sector on these."

"Predators ready!" Hakkon called and the predator parents got their quivering offspring into position.

"Livy and Jackson have already gone to ground," Tally leaned down to whisper into Haru's ear. "Melia's still on the move."

"Of course she is," Haru said with a warm chuckle.

"Go!" Hakkon called again, answered by the yip of two fox cubs and the screech of a young kestrel taking off in a flurry of wings. The one bobcat cub melted soundlessly into the woods before the others had decided on a direction.

Proud yes, but Tally's stomach also churned with worry. What if someone got hurt? What if something went wrong? What if one of the kids fell into a hole and the GPS lost the signal and they were down there for days and days before anyone found them? Tracker, worry stone, Haru, he wanted to hold all three at once and finally settled for palming the worry stone and wrapping that arm around Haru's shoulders to pull him close.

Haru gave him an odd look, and Jasper peeked out from his hiding spot in Haru's bun. Since when did his otter let the pixie hitch a ride in his hair?

"So you can see the screen with me."

"I see. Yes. The screen."

"You're laughing at me."

A little snort answered that, so yes, Haru was laughing at him, but he also leaned into Tally, his quivering telegraphing through the contact. Jasper let out a squeak of laughter but quieted when he got side-eyed and buried himself back into Haru's bun. Tally decided not to mention that Haru was just as worried as he was. Better for everyone that way.

Consulting the sheet and peering closely at the moving blips on the screen provided enough distraction to calm Tally. "Look there." He pointed to a spot near the center. "I think our beaver kit's been caught already."

"She's gonna be so upset," Mirna Schwarz, the beaver mom, said. "Katie was so sure she could hide better than a moose."

"Katie's also the youngest." Tally flashed a reassuring smile. "I'm sure she'll be running rings around everyone before long."

"Beavers don't exactly run, Tally," Mirna said with a choked laugh.

The moose calf was next, his flag plucked off by their young kestrel, and the foxes managed against all odds to herd the squirrels and capture their flags one after another. Soon the found kids started to trail back with hangdog expressions, Katie trying so hard not to cry when she humaned. Mom managed to stave off a full meltdown with snuggles and licorice, a beaver kid favorite.

2397, Livy's tag, was on the move again.

"No, no, Livy, stay hidden," Haru hissed at the moving number as if she could hear him.

"Too late," Tally murmured. 2165, the bobcat youngster, had spotted her and was closing in fast. He cringed when the two numbers collided and ceased moving. "Oops."

A few minutes later, one of the raccoon teens returned with Livy riding on his back. She humaned and let Tally wrap her in a waiting bathrobe, but her expression was thunderous.

"Kitty sneaked up on me," she grouched.

"Snuck," Haru corrected. "She only saw you when you moved."

"There was stickers under my butt," Livy protested. "I had to move."

Wordlessly, Tally held out the plastic bag of spiced grasshoppers he'd brought for just such a moment, pleased when Livy's expression cleared from near-tantrum to thinking. The foxes soon found Jackson, and Tally wondered if they needed a conversation about predators working individually. Their oldest joey was much more philosophical about it than Livy, though he was happy to accept grasshoppers of consolation as well.

"Melia's better at hiding," Jackson conceded. "She's under something, probably."

He was most likely correct. Amelia hadn't moved since she'd reached her initial hiding spot and Tally couldn't imagine what she'd managed to hide in or under. He frowned at the display, watching the kestrel circle, the bobcat stalk through one quadrant after another and the foxes scurry about, probably casting for scent. Half the time one predator or another was practically on top of Amelia, but they kept moving so they hadn't found her.

Finally, the two hours expired and all the starters blew whistles to call the kids in for praise and snacks. Amelia came galumphing in last, her little opossum mouth open in an obvious grin. Haru started forward to meet her and staggered back a moment before Tally caught whiff of the scent.

"Dear Gods, what *is* that?" Tally dropped to one knee to dig in their bag for wet wipes.

Amelia humaned, grinning proudly. "I hid in a stinky log! They couldn't find me!"

"Oh...um. That was very smart. Melia. Very. They couldn't scent you at all, could they?" Tally wiped off her face and hands but despaired over the stench. She'd obviously hidden in a recently skunk-sprayed log. How could she stand the smell?

Haru wrapped her in a bathrobe, stench notwithstanding, and took a practical view of things. "Bath when we get home, little girl. But that was clever. If you are ever in real danger, you might have to do hard things like that."

Tally swallowed hard, smile still plastered on. He wished Haru wouldn't say things like that, even if they were true. As he straightened, he realized with a start that Jason Kaul stood nearby. Tally hadn't heard him approach and certainly hadn't been able to scent him through Amelia's *eau de skunk.*

"Impressive, Urusar Bastille." Kaul nodded to him with one of his flat, unreadable expressions.

"Thank you." The response was automatic, though Tally wasn't certain what Kaul meant.

"All of this" — Kaul waved toward the woods — "was organized in a matter of weeks, wasn't it?"

"Well, since late fall, yes." Tally took a step toward the lijun from State, conscious that he placed himself between the honey badger and his family.

"The control you exert over this community *is* impressive. Quite something to watch." Kaul gave another vague wave and wandered away. "Thank you for allowing me to observe."

Tally watched him go, no longer trying to hide his frown. Why did he feel as if they had simultaneously passed and failed some test? He shivered and tried to banish his misgivings to deal with the wrap-up of the games.

Chapter Seven

A Wicked Time

Loud music piped throughout the restaurant at the Sapphire Lake Resort, making it more difficult for Haru to hear and understand the many conversations intersecting one another. Being able to follow along when this many English speakers were excited and rambling was hard when they felt this tired. Though the dinner was necessary no matter how much Haru wished otherwise. They wanted to keep the excitement over the success of the games going and continue to establish goodwill for the community project.

The circle Haru found themself stuck in was a new level of hell. The effort it took to listen to Councilwoman Howe ramble with her starts and spurts, looking over her shoulder every five minutes to stare nervously at Kaul-san then start all over was maddening, but Haru kept the smile plastered on their face and nodded when appropriate.

"The games really invigorated the kids, don't you think, Uruma?" Howe-san asked, her large eyes darting to Haru then to their shoulder. Her ears twitched in an obvious sign of nervousness. "The teachers reported back to me that our little ones seemed less distracted and jumpy in classes the past few days."

"Yes, we are quite pleased with the results."

"I must admit I was skeptical, but maybe the new Evade and Hunt games were the right thing to do."

Haru smiled. "And we all want what is best for the children, as well as the clan."

"Quite," she answered, and her ears twitched again. "And you most certainly do. The school district could've used a teacher like you."

The sharp pang in Haru's heart caught their breath, but they managed to dip their head, mimicking regret instead of the sorrow her words caused.

"I saw the reports about your performance at your old school," she continued. "Your principal and colleagues all liked you and your work. The students couldn't say enough good things about your lessons."

What reports? "Your praise is most welcome, especially coming from the school board president."

"It's too bad your duties as Uruma keep you so busy."

Councilwoman Howe really knew how to rub salt in a wound, though the poor rabbit had no idea she was doing it. She was an inadvertent sadist. But her mention of reports pinged Haru's radar hard and he needed to ferret out what she had meant without raising suspicion.

Grin and bear it. *Grin.*

"I am glad my former principal wanted to share my triumphs with you," Haru answered with a smile and tucked a piece of hair behind their ear, the bracelet catching Howe-san's attention like they wanted. It *was* sparkly.

"Oh, how beautiful," she said as she reached for it then answered distractedly. "The report was from Mr. Kaul."

Alarm skittered through Haru but they let Howe-san grab onto their wrist and pull it forward. "My betrothal gift from my Argaze."

"Urusar Bastille has always had an eye for pretty things," Councilman Black interjected as he eyed Haru, not the jewelry. "Not always practical, but pretty."

Talk about backhanded remarks, but the fox was always good for those kind of 'compliments'. Haru held their tongue, despite the urge to call the councilman some nasty names. No use in giving the sanctimonious pain in the butt more ammunition. To their surprise, it was the rabbit lijun who looked offended on their behalf.

Howe-san frowned then quietly whispered, "Urusar Bastille's eye for detail and beauty has led to many good projects for the community."

"Are you *really* taking his side, Rose?" Councilman Black's hand froze in mid-air, his drink forgotten, no doubt as shocked as Haru by the little show of assertiveness.

"I may worry about some of Urusar Bastille's methods, but his track record is speaking for itself, Clement."

"I suppose."

"Did you bother to look at the last earnings report for the clan treasury Tally submitted?" she asked, this time meeting the fox's gaze. Wonders never ceased. The bunny had backbone. Haru wondered if she realized she still had hold of their wrist.

"Well, I may not have gotten a chance to go over it in detail." The fox rolled his eyes at her glare. "Things at the hospital have been busy."

The taciturn reply hit Howe-san. Her eyes dropped again, her shoulders shook and she finally let go of Haru. Maybe she hadn't been as unaffected as they had thought. They put themself between Councilman Black and the smaller rabbit. Haru feigned adjusting their *kimono* as they gathered their thoughts. Played the wrong way and Tally would end up on the wrong side of the hospital, which would put the Blue Hollys in an awkward position.

"Is there not adequate funding for the hospital, Councilman Black?" Haru asked, subtly shifting farther in front of Howe-san.

"Excuse me?"

"I am asking if things are so busy you cannot keep up with your council duties because you are short on resources." Dig and check. Haru did not gloat. Not visibly. They cocked their head to the side, pretending to observe the fox with rapt interest. "I am sure Urusar Bastille will look into allocating funds if they are needed. We wouldn't want the nurses and doctors to be so overworked something unfortunate happens. And since profits are at a record high from Urusar Bastille's guidance, we want to make sure everyone can do their duty properly."

Between the shaking at Haru's back and the narrowed eyes focused on them, they had a moment of doubt they had done the right thing. It had felt like a victory. The question was, why hadn't the payoff happened?

Councilman Black's attention went behind Haru and he frowned, and harsh, deep crevices formed around his mouth and eyes. Worry flashed over his face for a moment. Not long, but enough to know whatever — whoever — was behind Haru upset Black-san more than Haru's pointed barb.

"Perhaps you're right, Uruma. Excuse me for speaking out of turn. I'll call to schedule a time to talk to you and our Urusar."

Haru bowed. "We look forward to it, Black-san. Say hello to your wife for me and thank her for the crayfish."

"Of course, Uruma Bastille."

The startled expression on the fox's face as he retreated had been worth exposing that little tidbit. Was Black-san really so naïve as to think Haru hadn't been around to meet the families? Or was it that his wife had kept Haru's visit from him? Either way, Haru called it a win.

The shaking behind Haru had gotten worse during the exchange and they turned to Howe-san to ask her if she was all right. Only she was focused on someone else. Well that explained things.

"Kaul-san." Haru offered an *eshaku*. Of all the people. "Your company is always a pleasure."

Coucilwoman Howe scooted behind Haru, using them as a shield. They didn't blame her one bit. Every sense Haru had pinged the other lijun as a threat and danger writ large. There was more to Kaul-san than met the eye, but Haru couldn't put their finger on what it was. The man was not just a regulations inspector.

The honey badger dipped his head, his dark brown eyes focused on Haru. "As is your beauty, Uruma Bastille. This dinner party has been most informative."

"I see." Haru offered their arm and Kaul-san instinctively took it, properly escorting them away from Councilwoman Howe. At least the nervous rabbit caught a break. The two of them began to circle the restaurant. "And what did you think of our games?"

"They were executed perfectly."

"The children enjoyed themselves."

Kaul-san chuckled easily. "Your Amelia was quite the clever little girl."

"Yes, she was." Haru stole a glance up then wished they hadn't. There was no warmth in the lijun's eyes. They were cold, flat brown disks, like dirt in the winter. No life whatsoever. "She has quite the knack for finding hidey-holes."

"But not your boy, Jackson."

What was *that* comment supposed to mean? Haru did not like how it came out. "Jackson can overthink and likes to play, but he also wants to take care of others. He is a nurturer at heart. Our son has already been through a lot in his life."

"Hmmm."

"Did Councilwoman Howe report about the improved attention of young ones at school to you?"

A little hum left Kaul-san before he glanced up. "She did. State was quite pleased with the report."

Then why did it sound like Kaul was not?

"In fact, my superiors tell me they want to implement the Bastille Model with other clans."

Bastille Model? Why did *that* sound like good and bad things at the same time? The way he sneered their surname, it was slight, but Haru had caught the ill intent behind it. Gunther came into view and his presence was the first time since Kaul showed up by Haru's side that he felt the honey badger waver. It wasn't much, tension in his arm that held theirs, but it was enough of a twitch for Haru.

Their eyes met. Gun straightened, his hands at his sides and his arms fanning out like wings.

One predator recognizing another.

"Your elegance is quite astounding, Satislit Bastille," Kaul-san said, breaking the connection. The use of their traditional title renewed the alarm in Haru. "It is surprising someone with your superior training ended up here in Wadiswan. Your assets would've been more useful to a bigger clan, one that would know how to *utilize* the skills you were given."

"I thank you for the compliment, Kaul-san. But you praise me too much. I am only a Satislit. Nothing extraordinary."

Their eyes met with the honey badger's as he stepped away and took their hand. He bowed and placed his cold lips against the back of it. "You think too little of yourself Satislit Bastille. A lijun such as yourself is a rare find. You are wasted here in the backwaters of Wisconsin."

The comment needled, and Haru was sure Kaul-san meant for it to. He would have to try a lot harder than insulting their new home to get a rise out of them. "When one meets their Em'halafi, it does not matter where they go, what matters is that they have each other."

"Em'halafi? You and th—Urusar Bastille are Em'halafi?"

"Yes."

"That is unexpected."

"So were our pups, but the Gods have their reasons. Do you not agree?" The stunned expression of Kaul-san's was the first real slip Haru had seen. Rage. Unimaginable rage lit behind his brown eyes. When he noticed Haru watching him, though, he quickly buried the emotion.

"The pups with Kwebabiad Weber are certainly worth celebrating. May you be blessed with strong sons."

Horror raced through Haru at the traditional blessing but they managed a "Thank you."

"It will be good for the clan to get *new* blood in the leadership."

Oh, Gods. "Yes. Though I am certain Jackson is more than up for the role. Empathy is a great asset for a leader."

"Jackson?" Kaul-san hummed again. "Your opossum joey?"

"Yes." Alarm bells clanged loudly but the road had no turns. Just one straight and narrow with a *do not enter* sign at the end. The honey badger was a *Traditionalist.* The kind Haru knew back home. The man was no ordinary Regulations Observer. He was too trained. Too poised.

"That is different."

"He is our oldest."

"Hmm. True. Very true." Kaul-san sniffed and cast his gaze behind Haru. It soured as his frown came back. "I will take my leave, Satislit Bastille."

"Thank you for your escort, Kaul-san. I hope we shall have a chance to speak again." Not ever if Haru could manage it. They wanted the lijun gone. Somehow they needed to shake him off and get him sent back to State.

"Nothing would please me more." The evil man bowed — Haru had no doubt he was evil — then nodded to the comforting presence behind Haru. "Urusar Bastille. Thank you for your hospitality. It has been unequaled."

"Anytime," Tally responded flatly.

Haru held back a sigh then said, "We hope we have performed admirably and to your expectations, Kaul-san."

"*You* have satisfied, Satislit Bastille."

A large, warm hand pressed against Haru's back as the honey badger beelined toward Councilmen Hastings and O'Rourke. Tally's hand was a lifeline as chaos rampaged through their mind and heart. Despite the dinner being an overall success, a black cloud of failure now rained on Haru. Being outmaneuvered without knowing what they'd been outmaneuvered for sent little spikes of anger all over, but it was nothing compared to the barely suppressed loathing rolling off Tally.

"Argaze."

"Yes, my love?" Tally pulled Haru up against him. Large. Warm. Strong. Reassuring. Haru turned into him, holding their Argaze close. To anyone else it would look like a couple having a moment. They were. Just not a fun one.

"I need a room. Any room. Now."

"Anything." Tally tucked Haru against his side and walked with purpose toward the foyer. People offered quick congratulations but did not stop their forward progress. In fact, people seemed to be parting in a wave to let Tally through. He lifted a hand and by the time they reached the door, Diane was there, iPad and all. "We need a suite. Send several dishes of prawns and lobster up. Fruits. Champagne. Sparkling Water."

"Ordered. It looks like the honeymoon suite is still available, Mr. Bastille."

They both managed to not miss a step, but the hallway certainly felt like the temperature had dropped by several degrees. Probably had, because there weren't so many people milling about. Still. A chill ran through Haru.

"What about the Blue Room?" Tally asked.

"Booked, so is the Presidential Suite, the Crystal Room and the others are all booked as well, Mr. Bastille."

"All of them?"

"Yes, sir." Diane stiffened and tapped her Pencil against the iPad. "With the dinner party running so late, and because of the drinks being served, several guests decided to take you up on the offer for accommodations. I could look into a regular room if you like, Mr. Bastille."

"No, it's fine. The honeymoon suite. Sorry, Diane." Their Argaze did his best to look smaller and less cross. He was failing at hiding his discomfort almost as much as Haru. His poor manager was obviously confused, but it wasn't like Diane was privy as to why that room wouldn't be at the top of their choices.

After letting them into the room, Diane said a server would be by with the food and drinks. She handed Tally the keycard and sped off down the hall. Not at a run, but a brisk walk certainly.

As the door clicked shut, the overwhelming sound of *nothing* filled the room. No stemware clinking. No chattering. No music. Just Haru and Tally. Their breathing. The memories of the last time they were in this room together between them.

How fitting was it that they felt a sense of foreboding again?

"Gods," Tally moaned and scrubbed his face. "This...this, what is this? What happened in The Den? One minute I'm schmoozing the business board members, the next Gun is dragging me away saying Kaul had you cornered."

A knock at the door saved them from facing their Argaze's anger. "Room service."

Haru was at the door before Tally could stop them. "This way please."

The staffer rolled in the food cart but stalled the moment he spotted Tally. "Boss."

"Hi, Benjamin, right? By the coffee table is fine."

"Sure thing," he muttered, shuffling forward. He went to take off the lids but Tally escorted him back to the door, slipping a tip into the staffer's hand.

"Thanks," he said as he pushed the small human out of the room. But Tally didn't turn around immediately. Instead he stared ahead at the closed door, shoulders hunched and arms crossed. "So you want to tell me what happened at the restaurant?"

Unable to put together what had gone so wrong so quickly, they did their best to explain, but the more they tried, the more pathetic they sounded — the less English came out. All their training and the best they could do was pit a dangerous lijun against their Argaze. Talk about failure. They couldn't do anything right. Not for Urusar Akaike, not for their Urusar now. Every single piece of praise Kaul-san had for their training been an insult, a jab at how poorly they served their Urusar.

"Haru, no. Wait." Tally pulled at their arms. "I'm not mad at *you*."

When had they gone into *dogeza*?

"I hate saying it. Please don't make me say it."

Haru trembled. "I have not pleased you, so it would not be appropriate to say."

"Then what do I say?" Tally ground out.

"That you will accept my Reparation for my failures."
Utter silence.

"Will you accept my Reparations, Urusar?"

Heavy breathing was the only response Haru got.
They pressed their forehead against the ground harder.
How had they fucked up so badly? Ever since New
Year's they had felt like they were at the end of a string
on a yo-yo. Up and down, back and forth, never able to
orient past the center point of a ball that was constantly
moving. If only Tally would follow the rules, it'd make
knowing what steps Haru needed to take easier.

Tally cleared his throat, his response raspy. "What are
Reparations? I haven't, I'm still…"

"What would please you, Urusar?"

"I have a feeling if I asked you to stand that *wouldn't*
be the correct answer."

"No."

"Damn it, Haru."

A tremor went through them despite their best
attempts not to let it.

"Fine, Gods, *fine*." Tally let out an irritated huff.
"Then what is the answer? Just tell me, Haru, and I will
say it."

They looked up from *dogeza*. They had given access to
their manuals. Managed to get the ones for their Argaze
sent over—translated into English, no less. Tally was
supposed to be learning them.

"I'm trying to do what you need here, Haru. Follow
the rules, but we are still negotiating them, remember?
I still don't *know* most of them from memory. Not like
you."

"Say you accept my Reparations," they answered,
their heart tapping out a frenzied presto.

"But what *are* they? What do *you* have to do?" Tally fisted his hair in one hand and the other had his worry stone out, tumbling between his fingers.

"They are what you want them to be. A way to show my remorse, to earn your favor back."

"You haven't lost it."

"But I have failed you."

A tic developed under Tally's jaw. "We don't know that."

"Kaul-san is a predator among lijun. I have put a target on your back."

"You believe that, you do." Tally sighed. His hair fell off his shoulders and swung in front of his face, partially obscuring Haru's view. His next words came out tired and rough. "I accept your Reparation."

"What would you have me do, Urusar?"

Another long, drawn-out sigh came and Tally turned away from Haru. "What would Urusar Akaike expect you to do?"

The presto tempo in Haru's chest broke, a sharp pain replacing it. Their breath stopped. Yes, of course. They should've—yes. That made sense. It did. This Punishment would not be in anger. Tally had promised as much. He didn't seem angry, either—more like he was tired. He had also promised to never hurt them in punishment or displeasure, but that was before the *rules.*

Slowly, Haru moved into *seiza.* Their fingers fumbled with the *obidomo* but they managed to get their *obijime* off. The *obi* and *obiage* spooled around them as they unwound the belt. Only when they had the *kimono* off their shoulders and back exposed did they look up to meet Tally's wide-eyed expression. His mouth was pulled tight and the tic was back.

"Your belt, Urusar Bastille."

Tally was up, off the couch, pacing, his expression thunderous. "I won't hit you."

"Then you do not accept my Reparation?"

"I told you I would never hit you! Never! Gods." His chest heaved as he strode to the door and back. "This — *any* of the rules — where it says to hit you, *we are not doing*. None of them. Do you understand?"

No, they did not. Tally had asked for what Urusar Akaike would do. His heavy footfalls as he paced the room sounded ominous and angry. What was Haru supposed to do if they weren't going to follow the rules?

"I won't do it, Haru. I won't. Any modifications to the rules are decided, yes, they are *approved* by me. No hitting. None. That is final."

"As you wish, Urusar Bastille."

"Gods. Argh. I can't. There has to be something else. Another way to make *Reparations*. Did Urusar Akaike have another option? There has to be."

"If it pleases, my Argaze, will you sit?"

Tally's gaze swung to Haru's. They did their best to remain calm in the face of a storm. His dark brows had drawn together. He stepped carefully over to the couch and lowered himself to it, focused intently on Haru. They gulped, unsure how the new offer of Reparations would be met, but there were only two types Akaike-san ever enforced.

They shuffled to the edge of the couch and placed their hands on Tally's thighs. No objection, though his muscles jumped under Haru's touch. They pressed down, pushing along the tension, kneading it out. A groan fell from their Argaze. His head fell back along the cushions. Good. Good. Haru moved down to the calves, working them one at a time. More pleased moans met their ministrations.

"Why didn't you start with this one? On second thought, I don't want to know."

The knot in Haru's chest lessened as they worked back up Tally's legs. They had finally done something right in their duties this evening. The rigidity within Tally melted away with each press of their palms.

Now to finish.

Haru reached out and unbuckled Tally's belt. There was a murmur above them, a question. They pulled open their Argaze's trousers and cupped his dick. In an instant, all the dispersed coiled strain within Tally was back. Two crushing hands gripped their wrists, yanking Haru up and away from Tally.

"What the hell do you think you're doing?" he yelled as he stood, pulling Haru with him.

"Pleasing my Urusar," Haru choked out. Their eyes stung. Their wrists screamed in protest.

"Gods. Fucking—Gods, *no*. Abssss-solutely *not*."

"I apologize."

"No, that'ssss not—Godssss."

Haru fought against the hold, but the more they struggled the tighter it got. They knew Tally was talking, saying things, but the words weren't making sense. Too frantic. Not unlike Haru themself. Suddenly they were pressed against Tally's chest, held so tight it was impossible to move. Ragged breathing wafted against Haru's ear.

"Damn it. One step forward, five steps back."

But the two of them weren't walking? Tally had Haru wrapped up in his arms, squeezing—constricting— them. Much like a snake would its prey. Except the fierce hold was in juxtaposition to the soft murmurs

Tally said as he rocked them, his face buried in Haru's neck.

"I hate them. I hate the Akaike clan."

Warmth, wet warmth, fell onto Haru's shoulder.

"Not you, never you, my love. But I actually hate them." Tally sounded surprised.

A shudder went through Tally and his embrace gentled, their Argaze cradling Haru against him.

"And Urusar Akaike is the worst. I hate him more than anyone."

Chapter Eight

Dinner for Two

Everything had to be perfect. The *kimono*. Their hair. Every makeup accent and stone placement. Nails redone. The pieces of jewelry chosen. Themself. If they were going out to the fanciest restaurant for Valentine's Day, then Haru had to look their best. Too many eyes were on them and their Argaze for Haru to present themself as anything less than perfect.

Not with all the whispers. Why were there so many whispers happening?

It was hard to understand *why* the date was happening. Life had been confusing since the disastrous dinner at Sapphire Lake. Tally and Haru ran hot and cold. Mostly cold. To have such a public date with how Tally felt about them seemed like a disaster waiting to happen.

But the date needed to happen. The clan needed to see Tally and Haru out—together and happy.

Haru checked their reflection in the full-length mirror Tally had installed in their walk-in closet. The *kimono* felt like the right and wrong choice at the same time.

The light blue coloring faded into white at the bottom. The stars cascading over their right shoulder to the left bottom turned into sparkling snow. The deep red *obi* popped against it.

The choice was the right one for winter, but not exactly something romantic for a Valentine's date. Haru pulled at the silver *obijime*. There wasn't time to change. The jade hairpiece was in place, perfectly complementary to the outfit. The betrothal bracelet was in its proper place too.

A tug on their sleeve drew their attention to Jasper.

"My little friend."

Jasper held up a heart-shaped blue diamond in silver inlay and pointed to Haru's eyes.

"It would be an excellent addition."

The stone *was* pretty. Haru rubbed a fingertip over it. Jasper smiled shyly then fluttered up to place the stone just under their right eye — another gift from Tally. A new one. He'd left it on the breakfast bar two days ago with the note about dinner, apologizing for having to duck out early for work.

With gentle hands, Jasper helped position the stone and made sure it stayed in place. The flutter of his wings felt nice against their face, almost tickling them. Jasper placed a small kiss on Haru's cheek then flew away, tucking himself in the jewelry box he'd turned into his second home.

"Do you want me to keep the doors open?"

A quiet 'no' came out of the box.

"Little done for the day?"

There wasn't an answer, but Haru knew the pixie was probably tuckered out from a day of helping with the joeys.

"How about we just keep the vent open? In case you want to get some snacks?"

This time Haru got a sleepy 'okay'.

They quietly made their way downstairs to the front receiving room. The murmur of people talking had been steady until they entered. All conversation stopped. Tally stood, Lahi quickly getting on her feet as well. She smiled and gave Haru a wink. They wished they had her confidence.

"Oh, I, um." Tally held a bouquet of flowers, but was frowning at it. "Um, Lahi, could you? Thanks. I'll be right back. Mindy and her sisters have the joeys downstairs."

"What—"

"Give me a minute to change," he interrupted as he patted his suit.

"But—"

"Five minutes tops."

Haru watched with Lahi as Tally skirted out of the room. "Of course, Argaze."

Lahi held the bouquet to her face, laughing into it.

"How did you know he would change?" Haru asked.

"Because when you go all out, no one wants to look bad next to you, least of all Tally." Lahi wiped her eyes. "I haven't seen his eyes bug out like that in ages. Twenty bucks says he's changing the reservation too."

"Oh, no. Tally was more than presentable."

"Not if he stood next to you."

"I should apologize." Haru turned to leave, but Lahi had grabbed their arm.

A smile, warm and open, met them. "He wants to look good for you too. Okay? Let the big lug put in a little work."

"If you say so." Haru stared at the door, unsure of their next steps.

"Let me grab the stuff. I put everything in the downstairs guest room." She dragged over a small stool and patted it. "Sit your butt down."

Trusting Lahi's orders, they sat down, arranging their *kimono*. She placed the flowers in a vase on one of the credenzas and took off, returning with their *biwa* and *bachi* from Tally, bouncing into the room with energy Haru lacked. Her dark brown eyes were lit with excitement and her russet cheeks tinged with a deep red. Lahi ran back out to get her guitar. She came back with a huge smile. Her ease did not alleviate their anxiety, though.

What if they had judged wrong? Chocolate was the normal treat. But that had felt inadequate.

"It'll be fine, Haru. Stop worrying." Lahi petted their hair and nosed them. "We've practiced plenty. Tally will like this surprise."

Kiss. Kiss. Nose. Nose.

The anxious knot in Haru's chest loosened. Their sister-in-law was really starting to pick up on otterisms, and using them against Haru. Sly snake. She settled onto the couch, perfectly relaxed, not minding Haru or their fidgeting one iota. How could she be so tranquil when their heart couldn't stop beating with such intensity?

The creak of stairs and heavy footfalls disrupted the silence. Tally rounded into the room, his braid flying over his shoulder. The end had one of the platinum hairpieces Haru had given him for Christmas. The sight of it did funny things in their chest. The custom-made burgundy suit with embroidered lapels and cuffs fit

Tally in all the right places, showing off every muscular curve. Were those snakes and otters in the stitching?

Wow.

"Sorry, took a minute longer than— What are you doing?"

Lahi dipped her head toward Haru. "Now."

The two of them began to play. A mix of Western meets East—guitar and *biwa* creating harmony together. Something Haru hoped for, if they could ever find the right balance for themself. Tally's intense gaze made it hard for Haru to concentrate as they should. They wanted to look away, hide, but there was nowhere to go. The song needed to be finished. Haru opened their mouth and sang. Their voice wobbled at first, difficult to find their footing with Tally watching them so.

Words came out. Ones Lahi had helped them write. She had had Haru write a letter in Japanese then translate it to English for her, spending hours going through what they had wanted to say. They had had to rewrite it several times before Lahi would help with the song, trying to fulfill her need for authenticity.

Would it be enough? Would Tally understand what Haru was trying to tell him?

About the loss of their life before the betrothal. The anger turned into confusion. The hope created and lost. Their uncertainty. Their need to please. How much they loved the kisses. Their desire to find a home. To make one. The pups. All of them. How frustrated they were and how they wanted to be able to be what Tally needed them to be. Happiness at all the cuddles and treats.

It was a lot to pack in one little song, but Lahi assured Haru they had done it. Haru still wasn't sure it said the right things. They hoped so. So very much.

But Haru couldn't tell if Tally was happy or angry. He held himself so still, his humongous body coiled tight. The intensity in his dark eyes hadn't wavered. Not a bit.

When the last note had been plucked, Haru froze for a moment, not sure what the next move should be. Lahi glanced at the yellow-green bruises on Haru's wrists then grabbed their *biwa* along with her guitar. She no longer looked as certain anymore either. The bluster all but gone. Haru placed their *bachi* aside.

"I hope I have pleased, Argaze." Haru knelt, moving into *senrei*.

Tally's breathing sounded strained. A hiss came out. "Your gratitude pleasss-ses me, my Satislit."

Haru rose to their feet, smiling. Oh, they had done something right. Finally. A gasp from Lahi momentarily distracted them—why did she look upset?—but Tally took hold of their hand. The gentleness sent a zip of pleasure through Haru, so they sneaked a peek. Tally looked happy? But not? The joy in his eyes fought with the stern set of Tally's mouth.

"Are you sure, Argaze?"

"Yes, very much so." Tally pulled Haru against him. "I loved it."

"Ah!"

The sudden kiss had caught them off guard. So much so they didn't kiss back initially, but then Tally wrapped his arms around Haru and held them close. Secure. There was movement—Lahi saying something—but the way Tally touched Haru made it hard to focus on anything but their Argaze. Tender kisses. Light pecks with teasing moments of tongue.

The gentleness became more frustrating with each pass. Haru didn't know what to do with it. Passion, they understood. These sweet kisses were confusing. They were in contrast to the barely held tension in Tally's body.

They broke apart, foreheads touching. Tally held Haru's jaw in one hand, petting them, while the other firmly and insistently held them against Tally's chest.

"Thank you," he said.

Tally placed a feather-light kiss on Haru's cheek.

"Thank you," he said again as he took a step back. But didn't he want more? Haru had felt the *more*. Tally moved his thumb along the underside of Haru's mouth. "How about those dinner reservations?"

"My makeup!" Haru pulled a compact out of their *kinchaku* and glowered at the smudged lipstick while simultaneously ignoring their laughing snake. Luckily it was an easy fix.

* * * *

Haru was glad they'd taken the extra minute to fix their face before going to dinner. They had not expected to be taken to The Yellow Perch. It had the finest seafood and was among the finest restaurants in Wadiswan.

Treats. Haru found themself pressed against the tanks where the prawns, crayfish and fish were displayed. So many yummies. The urge to otter out and join them in the tank was strong. They hadn't ottered much lately. The lake wasn't much fun without the joeys, and it was frozen solid, though Sammy was good company.

"Thank you for squeezing us in," Tally said behind Haru.

Look at the way their little legs move.

"It's our pleasure, Mr. Bastille."

Mmmm. Nummy. Haru wanted.

"It was a rather last-minute request, but—"

The maître d' interrupted, "Everything is set. Don't worry, Mr. Bastille. We're happy you chose to dine with us tonight. If you and your husband would follow me?"

"Haru— Just a second."

"Of course, Mr. Bastille."

"Haru."

A tap on Haru's shoulder got their attention. When they looked back Tally was smiling. "What is it?"

"Our table."

"Oh, yes, my apologies." Haru took Tally's offered elbow and followed the maître d' to the back of the restaurant—through the center of the room where they felt quite on display—but then they were led into a large private room with a small two-person table overlooking one of the lakes. "Argaze?"

"Your server will be with you in a moment," the maître d' said with a bow then quickly exited through the framed glass doors.

The room had been filled with candles, the soft orange light pushing back the darkness. Flowers flourished over the sideboards, in baskets and on windowsills. Velvety classical music was being piped in from somewhere but Haru couldn't locate the speakers. The table even had a hook for Haru's *kinchaku.* That was unexpected.

Behind one of the intricately carved chairs was Tally. His large hands were sitting across the top. A look once unfamiliar to Haru was in his eyes. They had learned it was tenderness. Tally motioned to the seat. "Care to join me?"

"This is lovely."

A smile, a real one, flickered across Tally's face as he seated Haru then joined them at the table. The intensity in his eyes had come back and he reached for Haru's hand. Their fingers meshed in a clump—awkward but tender.

"Do you like it?" Tally asked.

"It is beautiful." Took their breath away, really. All for them. It didn't make sense but Haru wasn't going to argue. At least the two of them were away from the general audience of the restaurant. There had been too many clan for them in the general seating. Too many council members. Maybe they would have a chance to relax without prying ears.

"Sirs," a person interrupted.

"Derrick, come in," Tally said and waved him in.

Or maybe not. *Clan.*

"My name is Derrick, Uruma. I'll be serving you this evening. I have the chef's recommendations for this evening here."

Or maybe they would.

Derrick went through the specials, recommended some wine, then looked at Haru, who in turn glanced at Tally—whose cheeks looked rosy. What was Haru supposed to do? Luckily Tally saved them from making the faux pas of ordering in front of clan, ordering the pasta dish from the chef's recommendation for himself and a spicy prawn dish for Haru.

"And the *sake* I asked for, to go with the appetizer and the main dishes," Tally continued.

"Let me get the order in, sirs," Derrick replied and stole out the door. As he closed it, Haru felt an uneasy sensation and looked out into the room.

They stood, unable to catch themself before their hand was on the door, and Haru found themself in a stare-down with Kaul-san and Councilman Black. What were those two doing together?

"What is it—? Oh." Tally sighed. "Haru, ignore them."

"But he—"

"I am the one who changed reservations. There was no way for either of them to know we were coming."

"As it pleases you, Urusar," Haru replied, and barely repressed a shudder when Kaul-san grinned.

"Haru, sit with me."

This time they listened to the *order*.

Tally, ever-expressive gaze pinned on Haru as they settled, said nothing as Derrick came in to pour the sake and serve the oysters and salad. On his way out, though, Tally stopped the server.

"Derrick, if you could undo the curtains?"

"Of course, Urusar Bastille."

They were a fine gauzy material that let the light through but gave a certain level of privacy. When the predators were out of view, Haru was finally able to focus on Tally properly as they should.

"I apologize."

"I know, I do." Tally took their hand again. "Please, I want you to enjoy tonight. They can't see us anymore. Not really."

It took a lot of restraint for Haru to say their Urusar shouldn't be pleading with his Satislit, but they managed to hold their tongue. Barely. Haru nodded and took a couple breaths. They could do this. The night, more than just tonight, had been going swimmingly.

"Mom is making more sweaters for the joeys," Tally said.

Oooh. "What design?"

"Water lilies."

"That will be lovely for the spring." Haru took a sip of *sake. Ooh, the flavors.* It wasn't champagne that tickled their nose, but there was something about the taste they couldn't resist. It settled the soul. He'd been smart to have it brought in for Haru instead of something showy like the bubbly wine. They noticed Tally's smile and grinned back. For the first time since New Year's, the two of them finally felt in sync again.

The conversation moved to school for Jackson. Lahi's next album. Tally skirted what kind of game Hal was working on—*hmmm,* they'd better make a call on brother dearest. Bastille-*okaasan* and *otōsan* were thinking about a trip to Germany with Addy—a partial business trip on their behalf for Tally. The stemware Klug-san had made for them was apparently a huge hit. *Mmmm.* The oysters were divine. Perfect. Yummy treats. Their conversation flowed from one friend to small matters so seamlessly that when Tally brought up the *rules,* the segue caught them off guard.

"What?" Why now? Things were going so well.

"Sorry, I just, I know the timing is a little off, but there were a few things in the guidebooks I feel can't wait."

Haru slurped the last bit of the oyster juice out of the shell and set it down. "As you wish, Argaze."

That pained smile, the one Tally had worn on and off since their dust-up at the honeymoon suite, was back.

"I think… I think I understand better why you are the way you are now. I'm not complaining, please don't think that, but these *rules* have certainly given me insight."

"I am glad they have helped you."

Tally's hand tightened around Haru's and replied quietly, "Yeah, me too."

One of their Argaze's fingers moved over the back of Haru's hand. They smiled encouragingly. Tally was in control here. Not them.

"I have some questions."

"I will do my best to answer."

Tally nodded, looked away. His free hand was tucked in his pocket, no doubt in Haru's mind it was around his worry stone. "How long have you been in training?"

"Since I was born."

"What?" Tally jerked back like Haru had slapped him. "Have all the *rules* been enforced sss-since you were-were that young?"

"No, some of them changed over time, especially when I hit puberty."

Tally flinched.

"I apologize."

"No." Tally's response came out rocky. "No, please don't. Never apologize for that. Does that mean—" A huff left Tally. "Does that mean the Reparation you tried to give me has been enforced since you were, what? Fourteen? Thirteen? Younger?"

"I do not wish to answer."

"Haru—"

They stood, pulling their hand away. "I said I do not wish to answer!"

"Okay, okay. Maybe a therapist—"

Haru growled. "I am not so weak that I need a, a *shrink*."

"No one said—" Tally pushed back his chair and stood, moving around the table. Haru moved opposite him.

"I am not weak!" Just because everyone—*Urusar Akaike*—told them as much didn't mean they were. It cut Tally thought so too. "I do my duty!"

Tally stopped opposite Haru. His eyes closed, his head dropped back. He took several deep breaths. "Yes, you do. You are a fine Satislit, Haru. More than I could ever want."

"Thank you."

"And I think I get what triggered you. All of this. What some of triggers are for you. I think."

"What is this 'triggered'?" Haru frowned. Unfamiliar terms were so bothersome. Meant they couldn't perform properly, left them at a disadvantage. Though words helped too. Haru never forgot the American websites that had helped them understand who they were when they were so confused.

"It's what sets off your need to live up to your duties."

"Any Satislit should want to please."

Tally's shoulders slumped. "I know. I read that too. Can we sit?"

"Yes, Argaze."

Why did Tally shake his head? Why were his usually jovial eyes so dull?

"Have I displeased?" They had *shouted* back. It was an infraction. Tally knew that now.

"No! We are discussing. Just discussing." Tally set his elbows on the table and plopped his head into his hands. Several minutes went by before he looked at Haru again. "Okay, okay. We're—*I'm*—changing certain protocols and Reparations."

"As is your right."

"Ugh, please, Haru. Let me finish." Tally looked frayed around the edges. Not quite all there. "Any Punishment that metes out violence or where I receive sexual favors is stricken off the rulebook. That does not foster a positive environment for you."

"Reparations for Punishment are not supposed to be positive."

"No, I know, but the Uruma is supposed to be the heart of the clan. If you cannot perform your duties, then the clan suffers. And to be honest, *some* of the Reparations are illegal. In human laws."

Tally wasn't wrong, but his tiny speech also sounded rehearsed.

"Having you upset only upsets the little ones. We want a happy home for the joeys, yes?"

"Very much so."

"Okay. Okay." Tally sat taller, looking less resigned. "Mom, Dad, Misaki and I are evaluating and rewriting the Reparations and will give you the updated books when we're done."

"They are good choices." Who Haru would've picked.

"We are also updating the rules for the Urusar —"

"But there is no reason to," Haru protested. No. Too many changes. It would be too much.

"Remember?" Tally took their hand again. "Equals. If you have rules, then it's only fair I do too."

"But —"

"This is my decision as Urusar. We are also placing some guidelines for touching. Platonic. Affectionate touching. You need to learn what positive touch is, my love."

Haru bowed their head. It was an odd add, but they weren't going to argue. "As you wish, Argaze."

A knock at the door brought the two of them dinner, giving Haru a reprieve, though their mind didn't settle immediately. What Urusar had their own Punishments? Their own Reparations? It could undermine the clan's confidence in Tally. They had to make sure he was never called on any infractions then.

"Oooh, treats." The prawns were huge. Bigger than Haru's hand. Lobster size and oh so yummy. Their only focus was working the meat out of those long, skinny claws. "Mmm."

"Those are some, uh, um, I take it you like your dish?" Tally asked.

"Yes, thank you, Tally."

There was a barely perceptible gasp.

"My Argaze?"

"No, it's nothing. I'm happy you're happy."

Haru hummed as they sucked on a claw. "Extremely."

"How about one more surprise?"

"More treats?" Haru looked expectantly at the door.

"No." Tally laughed. "But we can get more if you want. I do have a dessert ordered."

With renewed interest, Haru watched as Tally fumbled in his pockets then came out with a small box. Oh, yes, excitement burbled up inside Haru. They knew those boxes. *Those* boxes always held the prettiest stones.

"It's not as, um, comparable to your song, but I hope you like them."

Haru worked the ribbon with their nails and tore open the top. "Oh, oh, this. This."

It was perfect, and they couldn't find the words in English to say so. There was a white-gold charm necklace with five carved precious stones. Three joeys and two otters. Haru held it against their heart, looking at Tally, hoping he'd understand. The smile meant he did, didn't it? They tumbled out of their chair and knelt in front of Tally, grabbing his waist.

"Thank you, thank you. Thank you, Tally."

"I wanted something to show I want the pups."

"It does."

Tally placed a hand on Haru's head. "Something to show you, help you, believe I want them."

"I do."

Haru buried their face in Tally's lap, their fingernails digging into his thighs. They might just burst from their joy. Wouldn't that be foolish? But the stones, so carefully crafted, were filled with love. Haru *felt* it.

"I love you, Haru. Someday I hope you believe that too."

The door creaked. "Oh, sorry, Urusar Bastille. I-I will come back at a better time."

"Derrick." Tally stiffened, his gaze focusing on something behind the server. "The door."

"Yes, Sirs."

Their Argaze kept his hand on Haru's head, not allowing them to peek. Something was obviously wrong. However, only when the door shut did Tally let them up. They slid a look at the door, but the curtains had shadows against them, nothing more.

"Everything all right?" Haru asked.

"Yes, um, yes."

That sounded like a lie.

"I'm glad you like your gift, my love, my Em'halafi."

"What is for dessert?"

"I'll have Derrick bring it in. No, stay here. I'll be right back."

The kiss on Haru's cheek was soft and warm. They did not appreciate being left alone in the room, but too many clan were around to see if they made an infraction. Plus they really didn't want to see Kaul-san anyway. Better to ignore him, like Tally said.

When their Argaze came back, he had a plate balanced in one hand and another bottle of champagne in the other. He hip checked the door in Derrick's face too. Rude, but the lijun had done something. Had to have.

"Mochi!"

"A little bit of home, for you." Tally brushed their lips together.

"Perfect. Tonight has been perfect."

"That's all I wanted."

They cuddled, Tally feeding Haru bites of mochi and letting them sip the sweet champagne. For a while, all the noise of their everyday lives, the worry, the panic, the duties required of Haru, fell away. It was just them and Tally.

Going home was almost hard. They wanted to stretch out their time together even longer. Maybe steal some kisses. However Tally seemed content to just hold Haru. That was nice too.

When they did leave, almost no one was left in the restaurant, only a few lingering couples like them dotted the tables. A slight buzz left them floaty and with good feels. Tally held on to Haru's hand as the two of them drove home, though as they got to the backroads where there was ice, he had to let go.

The kiss before they got out of the car gave Haru's lips tingles. Maybe the garage wasn't such a horrible place. No need to let that idiot deer lijun taint Haru's memories. Tonight had been perfect. Just perfect.

Somehow they'd become worthy of Tally, his adoration. Haru wasn't sure *how*, but they knew they *wanted* to.

The house was quiet as they entered through the mudroom. No. There was a buzz. Something in the vents. They would have to call the heating and cooling people as soon as possible.

What was that smell? It smelled like— Haru's heart froze. That overwhelming smell tinged with copper. Gods. Why was it so strong? Haru pushed past Tally, running to the front entry. Their geta clacked hard against the wood, mimicking every heartbeat. Their Argaze called after them, swearing then yelling? Why was Tally yelling?

No.

Lahi was in the foyer, crumpled over. Ashen. Her normal rosy completion gray.

No.

"Haru, Gods dammit!"

They felt for a pulse, but her neck was slippery. Why was there so much blood?

"We don't know if someone is still in the house!"

Her stomach. *Oh no.* No. No. Her stomach. Those gashes. But then a beat was there, under Haru's fingertips. Thank the Gods. Barely, but it was there.

Haru called back for an ambulance.

"Calling!"

There was wood—splintered wood covering her wounds—but what wood?

The pups.

The door to the downstairs playroom was hanging on one hinge.

"Melia! Jackson! Mindy! Livy!" Haru hiccupped. Tally was yelling again, but the sound bounced and they couldn't understand. "Morgan? Answer me!"

Down the stairs. Two at a time.

"Mason!"

The smell. Gods the smell. And the buzz from the vents. It wasn't a buzz. It was crying. Heartbroken wailing from a pixie.

"Little girl!"

"Haru! Wait!"

"No!" Not when that smell suffused *everything.*

Something crunched at the bottom of the steps and Haru jerked their foot back. A peregrine lay, unmoving at the bottom of the stars. Stiff. Vacant eyes.

"Morgan. Oh, Gods. No! Morgan!" Haru picked her up, but she was cold. Too cold. Their throat caught. Their eyes burned. That *smell.* "My sweet girl."

The pups. There were no squeaks. No sneezes. No chirps. Just the cry of a pixie.

"Jasper?" Haru flipped the lights and immediately threw up, nearly dropping to their knees. "No. Gods, no!"

"Gunther, I need you at the house. Call Sheriff Amick. And Enforcers. Alert the Blue Hollys and my parents. Do it now!"

Another falcon lay by one of the bookcases, her neck at an angle that made Haru cry out. "Mason!"

They raced over, gathering her to their chest with her sister.

"Sorry. I am so sorry, girls." Red-hot tears stung Haru's eyes. Their voice wavered. Then they saw the paw. "Jackson, my little man."

"Haru, don't."

"Jackson! Come to Uma."

A hand pulled them back.

"No!"

"Haru, no."

"He is my pup," Haru bit out.

"I know."

"Let me go!" they yelled, pulled against the hands keeping them from their pup.

"No."

Each breath hurt. Every single one pierced their heart. "Let me go!"

They kicked back, catching a shin. Their head caught a chin. The grip loosened. "Fuck!"

Haru dropped to the floor, gently laying the hawks down and glanced under the bookcase. Why was there so much blood? They carefully pulled on the paw. But the smell. Oh Gods.

"Please, baby boy. Squeak. Tell me you are playing opossum."

Two hands took hold of their shoulders and Haru twisted, hissing. Their boy was cold and the blood. So much of it. And the smell. Haru gently placed Jackson next to the girls, shaking. They couldn't. They couldn't. Tears overwhelmed them and they just couldn't *human* any more.

They ottered. Uncontrollably. Without thought. A hand touched them as they pulled out of the cloth. They hissed, barking at the intruder, then turned to their pup. Haru nudged their boy. Nose. Nose. Kiss. Kiss.

Please. *Please* squeak.

"Stop. Just stop." Hands lifted them bodily away, the voice connected to them nearly unrecognizable in its anguish. "Stop *touching* everything. Gods. We have to know what happened. Who *did* this."

Haru bit down. Hard. How dare the intruder touch them? Take them away from the pups? They chomped harder. Swearing, incomprehensible words left the intruder. They thrashed back and forth but the hands wouldn't let go.

Another shout, from farther away, came through. "Tally! Gods. What the fuck! Tally! Haru!"

"Gunther!" The voice cracked.

Thudding, loud and ominous, came toward them. Haru didn't want to let go of the arm, but another intruder was coming. They hissed and barked. Their paws tingled. Their nose dripped.

"What the— What is… Haru?" the voice choked. "Has he gone Xus?"

"No! Check the other rooms. Look for survivors! Now! Jasper's in the vents somewhere. Mindy. The twins."

"Yes, Urusar."

They barked, clawing against the intruder holding them back. They couldn't breathe. Their chest. It hurt. It hurt so bad. Like it would never stop hurting. The spikes wouldn't stop. They were dying. Had to be.

Haru chomped down on the arm again. Black and silver dots flashed before their eyes. They couldn't breathe. The smell. Blood. Decay.

It was the smell of death and their pups. Mingled inextricably.

"If it helps, chomp on me all you want." At least the deep, broken voice had stopped yelling. "It's Tally. Haru…it's me. We have to… Melia. Livy. We need to… Gods."

Chapter Nine

The Stuff Made of Nightmares

Tally's heart had become disconnected. Somewhere off in the distance, an ocean of pain crashed and ebbed against him, but it was so far away. Here. Now. This was where he had to be. Acting, not reacting, with a white-cold rage settled into his chest where his heart should've been.

He tucked Haru, still fastened onto his arm with sharp otter teeth, close to his chest and swarmed up the stairs. *Screwdriver. Where the hell is that ambulance?* The junk drawer in the kitchen had the tool and Tally stormed back to the vent by the front door.

"Gun! Where the *fuck* are you?"

"Top floor's clear!" came the answering bellow. Gun's booted footsteps thundered down the stairs, his thudding steps starting through the first-floor rooms.

Maneuvering a screwdriver one-handed wasn't easy, but Tally managed to get the vent cover off after a soft stream of curses and a scraped knuckle. He tucked Haru closer and bent nearly in half to peer into the duct where a faint blue sheen tinted the gloom. Even harder than not trying to shake Haru off his arm was trying to lower his voice to normal levels.

"Jasper. I need you to come out. Now." Some part of Tally cringed at how cold and metallic his voice sounded in his own ears. The greater part of him couldn't find a way to care. He didn't have time to coddle anyone—not himself, not anyone else. "Now, Jasper. Don't make me snake and come after you."

Snaked... The thought skittered over Tally's brain. Someone had forced their way in. Why hadn't Lahi uktena'd and stopped them? Choking back sobs, Jasper crept from the vent, wings torn, damaged. He peered out around the corner and zipped unsteadily to Haru, half-burying himself in the fur at Haru's neck.

"What happened, Jasper? Where are my daughters? Who did this?"

"*Monster!*" Jasper squeaked. "Monster came!"

That was all Tally could decipher amidst the rest of his frantic peeps and squeaks, no matter how Tally cajoled or threatened. He stopped wasting time and surged to his feet to pace the house, calling for his daughters.

"Melia! Livy! Where you are?" Melia was an expert hider. That thought kept a flickering hope in his chest. She would've hidden and probably taken her twin with her. "It's Usar! I'm here now! You need to come out!"

While he searched behind cushions and under furniture, Tally made phone calls. To Marnie first. He needed her nose. Then to update his parents. His father took pity on him and told him in short clipped phrases they were coming. If he'd had to hear his mom's *oh, no, Tally*, he might have broken down. But he needed them now more than he wanted to admit. Lahi needed help. The twins and Mindy were missing. Someone had gotten into his *home* and k— No, he couldn't think about that yet. Couldn't do anything but bury those images yet.

"*Tal-tsu'tsa!*" Gun's frantic yell came from downstairs, his use of Tally's full name more alarming than the tone.

With Haru tucked under his arm like a football, he ran, heart slamming against his ribs. He skidded around the corner, back down to the stuff his worst dreams were made of and into Lahi's studio only to find another nightmare scene. Gun knelt bare-chested in a puddle of blood, his T-shirt tied off tight around Mindy's mangled right leg, both his hands trying to slow the bleeding from a deep gash in her side.

"The girls?"

Gun shook his head, his face pale and stricken. "Just Mindy. Claw marks on the back door, but I don't think that's how the bastard got in."

"Help's coming." Tally gripped his shoulder, one hard squeeze as he pushed himself off. Too many emergencies and only one hand. He stopped long enough to lift Haru to eye level. Hard to tell if his otter was functionally conscious or not. "Haru. You listen to me. I need you to human and I need you to do it now. The sheriff will be here soon. Melia and Livy are missing. Do you hear me? Our *daughters* are *missing* still. Human, damn you! I can't do this all myself!"

He hated himself for being so harsh when he wanted to hold Haru close and give in to the sorrow threatening behind the rage. Everything had been so perfect that evening. They had been so close to real communication that night, a real togetherness. Harsh, maybe, but the yelling worked. Tally soon found himself with an armful of limp human instead of having an otter lockjawed to his arm. Not that Haru would look at Tally. Those empty eyes wandered as Haru staggered up the stairs to the mudroom to pull on the robe he kept there for when he came in from the lake.

Still no time for comforting anyone. Tally raced back to Lahi, opening the front door before he dropped to his knees beside her. Her gashes bled, but not as fast as Mindy's had been. Putting pressure on them was impossible with all the wood wedges and splinters, so Tally focused on that one thing, picking wood off his baby sister. The world had come apart at the seams and this was a thing he could do to hold on to the threads before it unraveled further.

The hallway was suddenly full of feet, equipment and voices. Blue Hollys growled out orders. Someone tried to pull him away from Lahi. He snarled and struck out, but strong arms closed around him, his dad hissing soft and slow in his ear.

"Ssss, shh, my Tal. We're here now. You're not alone."

"Tal." Marnie was in front of him, gripping his arms. "What do you need?"

"Find them, Mar," Tally growled. "Start in the basement. Find my daughters."

A heartbeat later, a bobcat stood where Marnie had been. She flicked her ears and bounded away, big paws silent on the hardwood floors. An ambulance crew now worked on Lahi, so Tally hurried back to the studio, allowing himself some relief when he spotted the second EMS crew taking over from Gun.

Bloody, looking a little shocky himself, Gun leaned into Tally when he came close. "She keeps saying he took them. He took the girls. He took them."

"Who?" Tally spun him around and gave him a shake. "*Who* took them? My girls? Took them where?"

Gun swallowed hard. "Dunno, Tal. I couldn't get her to say. They... They did the best they could. They're just *kids*."

Tally found he had nothing to say to that and he had no comfort to offer Gun, either. He spun and left the carnage as sirens came screaming up the driveway. The sheriff's office had arrived and now he had to deal with *that*. *A monster came, Sheriff. A monster attacked my household and stole my children from me and I can't even tell you that my son is dead.* He stalked back to the front of the house where the first ambulance team was just raising the gurney with Lahi strapped to it, the circling lights from the emergency vehicles painting blood on the white sheets. He tried to go out to meet the sheriff, but Lahi caught his sleeve.

"Tal," she murmured.

He leaned down and took her hand. "I'm so —"

"Don't. Tal, I don't know. But maybe."

"Maybe what?"

"He came to the door. Said he would wait for you. I told him it was late and told him to go away." Lahi grimaced and stopped for a slow breath. "It might have been him. He probably came back. Heard a sound. Hit me before I could get the light on. Can't be sure."

"Who wasss it?" Tally hissed.

Lahi gazed up at him with narrowed eyes. "Kaul. It was Kaul who said he was looking for you."

He stumbled back as the ambulance team got the gurney moving and the hand at his elbow was Marnie's, humaned again and back in her sweats just ahead of Sheriff Amick coming up the walk.

"The girls aren't in the house, Tal," she murmured close to his ear. "There's faint traces out back, but the trail vanishes there. And the whole house stinks like a certain predator."

"*What* predator?"

Marnie's lip curled in a snarl. "Honey badger."

Every muscle in Tally's body locked. The hallway swam in his vision for a few precious seconds. Kaul had been at the restaurant. Kaul had known he wasn't home and wouldn't be for some time. The threat he'd always seemed to carry under his skin was terribly clear now, but why in the names of all Gods did he want to slaughter *children*?

"Tal?" Gun was on his other side. They were holding him up between them. "You wanna sit down?"

"Probably. Yes."

They led him to the front parlor where Haru had curled himself into a corner of the sofa, feet tucked up, arms around his legs. Tally sat rigidly beside him, but not close enough to intrude on his space, and Sheriff Amick joined them, though Tally couldn't recall whether he rose to shake the offered hand or not.

In terse, tight words, Tally ran through all he knew, which was pitifully little. Yes, Mindy had been babysitting with Lahi. Yes, he and Haru had been out to dinner. Yes, the sheriff's office should probably start in the basement.

"The intruder killed our... One of our opossums down there." The words threatened to choke Tally. *My Jackson, my baby boy, he killed my son!* "And two...two peregrines the family was rehabilitating. He attacked my sister. Tried to kill Mindy. Her sisters...my son...gone." They were dead. Torn from the clan. "My daughters are missing, too, Sheriff. I think he took my children."

Beside him, Haru let out a low moan but didn't speak. The Blue Hollys had deaths — children's deaths — to cover up. The standard there was only revealing enough to the humans to ID remains, somehow. It wouldn't be pretty, but it had to be done. They would grieve later.

"Do you know the intruder was male?"

"I…" Tally shook his head. "No. I'm making assumptions. Lahi felt it was the same man who had come to the door earlier in the evening."

Sheriff Amick rose, still scribbling in his notepad. "Did she know him, Mr. Bastille?"

"Yes." Tally's fists clenched so hard, he wondered if he might break a knuckle that way. "He's from an associated business council in Madison. His name is Jason Kaul."

"Thank you. I'll get that out on the wire and get this called in to the FBI."

"FBI?" Tally stared at him in confusion.

"Child abductions have to be reported. Better resources. It's a good thing."

Unlike the first time the sheriff had come to investigate a crime at the house, there were no suspicious glances, no hostility, no third degree. He simply patted Tally on the shoulder and strode out to join his officers in their crime scene search.

Only when he had left the room did Haru stir. He reached over and grabbed Tally's jacket lapel, yanking until Tally had turned to face him.

"Haru? What?"

The voice was hardly human at all as Haru snarled, "I want his head, Tally. On a spike. I *want* his head."

The chill around Tally's heart hardened into granite. He covered Haru's hand with his own. "So it will be, then. My only goal until you have it."

* * * *

Hakkon had never looked older. It was like he'd aged decades since Tally had made the call. His hair was a shocking white. Eighteen hours, less than a day, that was all it took. He sympathized. Tally felt the weight of the attack too. It was hard, having to sit in Dad's office, away from home.

No, away from the crime scene.

The house was closed off until forensics gave the all-clear. And the children. They couldn't mourn yet.

"When will we get them back, Tally?"

"Sheriff Amick has them in storage at the morgue."

A strangled grunt escaped Hakkon and a hand went over his heart.

"Small favors, Hakkon. One of the deputies had suggested a freezer." Tally had almost decked him too. Luckily clan had stepped in. "But reason prevailed."

"And Marnie ID'd Kaul."

"Without a doubt. Several Enforcers backed up the scenting too."

"Sheriff Amick has an APB out, though so far nothing." The chair creaked under Hakkon as he adjusted. "My sources haven't seen him since the dinner with Councilman Black at The Yellow Perch."

"Yeah, that's what mine say, too. I've activated *all* Enforcers, just in case."

"Good. That's good." Hakkon closed his eyes, new lines etched deep around his mouth.

"Hakkon, I-I have no words. I am so sorry." Mason and Morgan had fought hard, but what consolation would that be to a father? Jackson had too. Honey badger fur had been isolated from their claws, mouths... It meant nothing to Tally. Only lit the white flame of rage higher. Tally flipped the worry stone through his fingers, but it held little comfort for him. "I'm sorry."

Sharp blue eyes focused on Tally. "You couldn't have known. Not something like this."

"This attack—"

"Is unprecedented, Urusar Bastille. And you have my complete faith that you will bring justice to those who committed these crimes." Hakkon stood and moved over to the window. "You need me in your corner more than before now. I will *not* waver in my support."

"So you agree?"

"That this attack was to undermine you? Yes. Though Kaul killing children took it too far. It may actually work in your favor. Much as it pains me to say it."

"I knew the Evade and Hunt games went too smoothly." Tally sat back in the chair, staring at the ceiling. "I just never... The viciousness."

"It was without provocation, Urusar. Don't forget that." Hakkon returned to his chair. It groaned, maybe he did too, as the hawk settled. "You've done your job admirably. Almost too well. People can fear that kind of strength."

"You mean Dan and Barry."

Hakkon shrugged. "More *conservative* members of the clan."

"Barry and Dan swear they haven't seen Kaul since before the fourteenth. I don't believe either of them." Barry was lying. *Definitely* hiding something. The white-hot anger was back. "But Kaul was with Clement at the restaurant. He's not a full-blown Traditionalist. I thought he wasn't. Though, maybe we have to re-evaluate."

"No, Clement looks out for himself and the hospital, but I'll have a conversation with him."

"Be careful. I don't want you putting yourself in danger."

The barest whisper passed Hakkon's lips. "One can't always choose the dangers, Urusar Bastille."

Sadly, the clan had learned how true that was.

The door to the study opened and Haru stepped through with a tea tray. "Pardon my intrusion, Urusar, Councilman Eberhardt."

"Not at all, Uruma." Hakkon frowned at Tally.

Haru set the tray down at the desk then began serving tea. He was quiet and focused. A small tremble gave away Haru's less-than-together state. His poor otter had been inconsolable since the attack, barely humaning. More than anything, Tally wanted to wrap Haru up and hold him, but he wasn't sure it'd be welcome. Some day he hoped his otter would open up to him, be comfortable enough to confide in him instead of the different women in their lives, and mostly, for his Em'Halafi to *want* to be held in his arms. To say Tally was surprised he was up and about was inadequate, especially considering Haru's disheveled state. His otter had a faint puce glow under his lackluster tawny skin. And Haru's silky black hair. Never had Tally seen it so, so *nest*-looking. He was in no state to be serving guests.

"Haru, my love, you don't have to do this right now."

"It is my duty as Uruma."

Tally flinched at the cold response, and their friend was astute enough to notice. To pretend it hadn't affected him was easier than addressing the question Tally saw on Hakkon's face. However, when Haru dropped to *dogeza*, forehead pressed hard to the floor, Tally couldn't hide his shock.

Neither could Hakkon, who immediately tried to talk Haru up. His otter would not be swayed. Not even when Tally knelt next to him and placed a hand on his back. In fact, it seemed to make the situation worse as Haru began to talk in starts and stops.

"I failed you, Councilman Eberhardt. You trusted me with your daughters—" There was a pause. Painful. Hollow. Then Haru pushed on. "You trusted me to keep them safe and I failed you. Whatever Reparations you seek, I shall endure."

"Haru, Uruma, please." Hakkon glanced over to Tally. "This was not your fault."

"Your beautiful girls," Haru choked out. Tears flowed down his cheeks. Claws punctured through his fingertips. "Dead and maimed."

Another startled look was sent Tally's way. "The report said you found them."

"As in Haru. He found Lahi and the children. Gun found Mindy." Tally rubbed Haru's back, reminding him to breathe. "Count backwards from one hundred, by sevens—in English."

The garbled count came out rough and slow. Hakkon's brows drew together as he watched. When his piercing gaze meet Tally's, the inevitable question was on his tongue. Tally saw it and wished he wouldn't ask.

"What are Reparations?"

Too late.

Haru tensed under Tally's touch and hiccupped.

But it was another voice that explained. "Reparations are Punishment for failure to adhere to one's duty."

Mom stood behind Barry with a worried expression. She mouthed 'pushed through' to him, crossed her arms and sniffed. How dare the bastard show up and push their way into his — Dad's office? He had no right.

"How can we help you, Councilman Hastings?" Tally asked. He stood slowly, deliberately using his size and height. The old boar actually stepped back, his expression no longer so confident.

"I am here on the behalf of concerned clan members, Tally. It — "

"Urusar Bastille," Tally interrupted.

"What?" Barry's mouth twisted at the correction then he did a double-take when he saw the hawk. "Hakkon?"

"When addressing the clan father, it is proper to use his title, Councilman Hastings." Hakkon stepped in front of Haru, his purposeful shielding not lost on anyone. "I suggest you remember it. *Urusar Bastille.*"

A beat passed before Barry acquiesced. "My mistake. As I was saying, it is a matter of clan safety and I am here on behalf of concerned clan members."

"What is their concern?" Hakkon asked.

"That Tal — Urusar Bastille cannot adequately protect the clan." If Barry hadn't been smiling when he said it, then Tally might've believed it. All the boar had done was confirm the suspicions Tally and the others had.

A fucking power play. One that had cost his son and Hak's girls. The ice around Tally's heart gripped it hard.

Barry brought his hands together. "If an Urusar cannot protect his own family, how can he protect the clan?"

What a dumb, blatant, forward attack.

Hakkon's snarl surprised Tally. "Are you suggesting our Urusar is at fault for this?"

"Why else would Uruma Bastille be offering Reparations?" Barry shot back.

"Because of an Uruma's guilt and shock," Mom said. She pushed into the room and pulled Haru up into her embrace. "Any Uma worth their salt would be devastated by what happened in their own home."

"Then you don't plan to seek Reparations?"

Hakkon shook his head. "No. Why would I blame our Urusar for the act of a lone, sociopathic lijun?"

It was Barry's turn to balk. "How can you not?"

"Because no reasonable person would expect someone to break into a house full of people and kill children!" Hakkon squawked, getting right in Barry's face. "We live in the twenty-first century! What kind of bastard kills *children*? *My* children."

"I—no, that's not," Barry stammered.

Tally decided looming over the councilman was a good thing and did so. "I think any reasonable person would understand an unprovoked attack and slaughter of children were not anything we could plan for in this day and age. If your *concerned* clan members need reassurances, then let me tell you this, *councilman.*

"The Bastille homes are being reinforced with state-of-the-art security and I have recalled all Enforcers, active and inactive, to duty." Tally slid half a step closer and let his tongue fork and eyes glow. "Until the person or persons who attacked *my* family and Councilman

Eberhardt's is caught, there will be heightened security for us all."

"Yes, Urusar Bastille." Barry backed right into the wall. "Of course, Urusar."

He shot out of the study and the front door slammed quickly after his exit.

Mom shouldered Haru against her. "I'm taking this one back to bed."

"Thanks."

"Come on, sweetie. Let's go. Sammy's looking for cuddles." Mom half-led, half-carried Haru out, talking in hushed tones.

Tally huffed out a breath, letting himself unpuff. He hadn't even realized he'd done it. He sent an apologetic nod to Hakkon, who just waved him off.

"Don't. You spoke in a way Barry understood."

"I don't have to like it."

"No, but, to be honest, I'm glad you did." Hakkon sat down in his chair again and took a cup of tea. Tally joined him. They drank in silence, the world spinning so hard Tally was still running to catch up on it. The peregrine sank lower in his seat. "You know they're not going to like being blocked out of the gate."

"Yeah."

Hakkon shuddered. "I didn't think they'd be so stupid."

On that Tally agreed more emphatically. "Quite."

His head whipped around at a knock on the open office door. A man in a suit stood there, regarding them with a bland expression. Not too tall, not too short, umber skin, short cropped black hair, dark eyes. Nothing about him that would stay reliably in a person's mind. The parallels to Kaul sent a shiver up Tally's back.

"Help you?"

The man held out a badge, keeping it steady so Tally and Hakkon could read it. "Agent Kennett Firebaugh. FBI, violent crimes unit. Sheriff Amick filled me in on the basics." Now he extended a hand to shake. "I'm so sorry for your loss, Mr. Bastille. Mr. Eberhardt."

Hakkon snatched his hand back. "What do you—"

Tally put a hand on his arm. He'd caught the scent, the way the agent also sampled the air around him. "It's all right, Hak. He's one of ours. Wolf."

"Oh. Of course. Thank you." Hakkon slumped and returned to the chair by the desk. "Not that I'm complaining, but how are we lucky enough to get a lijun agent?"

Agent Firebaugh offered a wry smile, one that hinted at a wolf grin. "There are programs that work behind the programs at the Bureau. Mr. Bastille's name sent up huge waving flags from one of those and those and assigned me to the case. We have quite a few lijun agents, but I was closest and not on an active case."

"That's a relief." Tally returned to the desk chair and waved at the last empty seat for Agent Firebaugh to join them. "We lost our own law enforcement contact last year…"

Firebaugh nodded. "I heard about that. Terrible business."

You did? "So it's been difficult communicating and not communicating with our sheriff. My son…" Tally had to stop and gulp a breath, his eyes threatening tears no matter how hard he blinked.

"Take your time, sir," Firebaugh offered softly. "I have questions, of course, but only if you're ready to talk to me."

Tally managed a nod. "Thank you. My son and Hakkon's two younger daughters, they had taken their animal forms."

Firebaugh edged the chair closer to him. "That has to be hard. Telling the humans that they were pets. I'll do my best to help with the release of the remains to the families and we'll make sure everything's properly handled in the end so your kids aren't in legal limbo."

Tally had to clamp his jaws together and, though he felt guilty about it, he let Hakkon talk for a bit, answering questions about the opossums' adoption and the time since they'd come to live with Tally and Haru. He didn't ask about that night or the crime scene. Probably had all the information he needed about those things for now.

"Who was the boar I saw storming out of here as I came into the house?" Firebaugh looked up from his notes.

"That's Barry Hastings." Tally managed to gather his anger together enough to speak again.

They took it in turns, telling Firebaugh about Barry and what the boar had said when he'd come to see Tally. Hakkon finished with, "I don't think Kaul is working alone."

"Nope. Not after that display." Tally drummed his fingers on the desk, suddenly weary and aching.

Hakkon sat forward, checking his watch. No doubt restless to get back to Mindy before visiting hours were over. "They're going to get sneaky."

"Probably."

The wolf sat back, frowning. "I have to work with the agents I have on hand. Problem is I'm the only lijun. That's going to make it harder to sniff out where the girls are. It'd raise too many flags if I request certain personnel."

That was Tally's biggest fear, that those flags would alert them, because whoever *they* were had his girls. They had to. Tally had to hope the girls were still out there, somewhere, and he'd find them if he had to tear through all the bastards in his clan and the bastards at State. He didn't care how high up it went. Tally would bring his Em'halafi the head of that fucking bastard Kaul.

Firebaugh stood and produced cards that he held out for Tally and Hakkon. "Thank you, gentlemen. I have a lot of people to talk to today. Need to catch up. If the kidnappers make contact, and we'll work under the assumption that the little ones are being held, call me immediately."

"I can do that."

There was a pause, then the agent added, "There is going to be a lot of hurry up and wait now, Urusar Bastille. Kidnappings aren't an action fest chase scene like in the movies. That's not how these work. It's usually a lot of sitting around. I'll do my best to sniff out Kaul, but you're going to need to be patient."

"*That* might be harder to do, Agent Firebaugh."

* * * *

An hour after Hakkon left his office, Tally thought he might be calm enough for the phone call he had to make. That bastard honey badger had said he'd come from State and Tally hadn't questioned it at the time. Barry and Dan had *known* him and Tally had assumed they'd gone over his head to make him look bad. He should've verified, questioned…something.

Going through official channels was out. No way to know who was involved here. Not yet. If he poked too hard, asked the wrong people, he might endanger the twins. No. Instead, he called the one unassailable, unwavering ally his dad had maintained at State Council for so many years, a lijun who had been one of their own before moving to Madison. He knew he was calling at a time when the councilman would be in his office and still his heart pounded a little too hard anticipating a refusal or a rebuff to his call.

He shouldn't have worried. The call was answered after a ring and a half.

"Tally Bastille, is that really you? We haven't talked in ages."

"Morning, Rory." Tally couldn't help a little smile at the booming, friendly voice on the other end. "I *do* send reports every quarter."

"Not the same as talking to you, you little shit." Rory MacLean, a Scottish red deer lijun, might have been one of the few people on the planet who could accurately call Tally short. Everything about the man was huge, from his hands to his speech to his wild mane of salt-and-ginger hair. "I'd ask how you are, but I don't think that'd be right, considering."

"I'm managing, considering." Tally took a breath. "I need to ask you some things, Rory, and I need straight answers."

"If it's something I know and I'm at liberty to answer, you know I will."

"This first one's just independent confirmation. Is there someone working up at State called Jason Kaul?"

The slight hesitation screamed volumes. The fact that Rory kept his answers short bellowed more. "Yes. There's a Jason Kaul on staff."

"What's his job title?"

A smaller pause, then, "He's an auditor inspector."

Tally nodded to himself. So truths within the secrets, all right. "So far we're lining up. Did you know he was in Wadiswan?"

"Me? No." The answer was too short and sharp, setting Tally's alarms off. "Who sent him there?"

"That's the question, isn't it? Are there people there in Madison with the authority to send him?"

Rory cleared his throat. "I don't have to tell you that any lijun can request an auditor."

"Let me come at this a different way. Jason Kaul killed my son and Hakkon Eberhardt's daughters and kidnapped my twin girls. Toddlers, Rory. We have verification that puts him on site and witnesses who lived. We have no idea where he's keeping them and the federal agent on the case has nothing but cold leads. If he's gone rogue, I know there's not much you can do. But if he's working for someone at State…"

Tally let that hang between them, the silence so complete he could hear the heat in Rory's office kick on. "What you're implying, it's…unthinkable."

"I know." Tally wanted to say something comforting, something to take the weight of dismay he was piling on an old family friend, but his voice stayed chill and sharp. "I'd like to put my head in the sand and not think it. But I have to. Rory, if you have any information, any suspicions —"

"I'll nose around." Some of the strength had returned to Rory's voice, at least. "I can't make promises, but anything I can root out, I will."

Tally hung up after promises to call sometime without such dire need and slumped in his chair. Rory hadn't denied the possibility, hadn't laughed off Tally's fears, so the big deer had suspicions of his own.

Chilling? Yes. He might never be warm again.

Chapter Ten

Broken Pieces

The water was too warm. Smelled flowery. Haru sniffed and pawed at the bubbles. They looked up at Sammy. Why was she so big? She should be by them on the slippery rock too. Haru hummed, earning themself a scratch under the chin. Nose. Nose. Kiss. Kiss.

"Argh. Otter breath!" Sammy laughed and pushed their nose away.

Fine. They would get in the water by themself. Maybe they should make splashies, then everyone would come and play.

The pups love splashies.

A sharp pain in their center reminded them. No pups. Haru barked out a "Hah!" Only the ones in Sammy's belly. They pressed against her bump. Her arms circled Haru and she held them close.

"I know, Haru. I know. It hurts."

Nose. Nose. A bump back at them. They pressed their head against the kicks. Each one a lifeline Haru desperately needed. A squeak excited Haru until they realized it was the door. Not the joeys.

"Hah!"

"Ah, so ottering," Tally said as he stepped into the bathroom. "Hmm."

Sammy shrugged. "They saw water and ottered. I don't think it was conscious."

"That's part of the problem." Tally sat down on the toilet and held out his hand. "Sheriff Amick and Agent Firebaugh came around again."

Ooooh. Treats. Haru stole the shrimp then skittered back over to the water.

"Any news?" Sammy asked.

"Nope. Same as yesterday. The day before that. And the day before that. Like it's been all week." Tally leaned on his elbows.

"How'd today go?" she asked, prodding Haru with her foot. They swatted it away.

"The emergency meeting was hell, but it looks like I actually have the majority support. Lots of clan showed up. Hastings and O'Rourke have backed down for now. No challenge."

"That's good." Sammy poked Haru with her foot again.

Fine. They could listen. Haru used one paw on the slippery stone to balance themself and looked at the snake.

"What about the other front?"

Tally huffed. "Gun is making progress searching the archives, so is Misaki. She agrees that they're going to leverage the girls."

"Oh, Tal." Sammy pulled him in for a hug and nosed his ear. The snake let her too.

Odd. But why was it odd? Haru should remember why it was weird the two of them were getting along, but they couldn't. All the memories that hurt were one big pulsing, fuzzy red spot. They squished between Sammy and Tally, humming as they petted him. These feels were much better than the ones that stabbed their heart.

Nose. Nose. Kiss. Kiss.

Tally picked them up, cuddling close. "Sammy?"

"How about I check in with your mom about dinner?" she asked.

"Thanks."

When the door clicked behind her, Tally lifted Haru, cuddling them to his chest. He scratched behind their ears then petted down their back in nice long strokes. Haru hummed again, nipping at Tally's fingers when he stopped. The snake's chest lifted, puffing up, then shrank. Then it did it again.

Haru nibbled Tally's shirt cuff.

"Oh, Haru. What am I going to do?" His voice was listless, barely above a whisper.

They nosed his face, trying to make the snake not so sad. Instead they got a sigh and another pat.

"How about bed? We can talk there." Tally cradled Haru close. "I need…" But he stopped. Haru stretched out their toes, reaching for the warm comfy, as Tally put them down. He shed until he only had softies on his middle. "Covers or none?"

Haru pawed at the top of the warm comfy.

"In it is." Tally pulled them close once he'd settled, stroking Haru's back. He started talking, soft at first, then more assured as he went on. "I know you're in pain. I know how much the joeys meant to you. To me.

But I can't do this alone, Haru. I need my Em'halafi. I need you to human."

A shudder went through Haru at the suggestion. No, they most certainly didn't want to *human*. All the emotions were louder when they humaned. The memories burned hotter when they humaned. No. Otter was better. Their heart didn't feel so shattered.

Tally tugged on a paw. "Our girls are still out there. I have to believe that. I need you to believe it. Please, Haru. I need you. Please."

The crack on the 'please' hurt their heart. Haru nosed Tally's jaw.

"I don't want otter kisses. I want Haru. I *need* human Haru. I want his — their — arms around me. Because it is *their*, isn't it?" Tally's chest rose high again, but the ride up and down wasn't so fun this time. "Another thing we haven't gotten to talk about. I *need* my Satislit's brain. The human one. My clever Haru. Please. I feel so alone."

It was the heartbroken 'alone'. One minute Haru was all fur and paws, the next he had humaned, gathered up in Tally's embrace. Kiss. Kiss. No more hurts.

"Gods." Tally pressed Haru against his heart. A *whoosh* escaped the big snake. "Thank the Gods."

"My —" Haru coughed, their throat scratchy, tight. It took a couple swallows to get it feeling better. "My Argaze."

Tally kissed them. A demanding, insistent kiss. Firm lips captured theirs without demanding more. Their Argaze's hand held Haru's jaw, a thumb caressed their skin. The desperate need broke more bits off Haru's heart. It was so raw, unfiltered. Tally hissed each time his tongue flicked out. Whatever he needed, Haru would give, because the demands meant they didn't have to think. But the more the two of them touched, held each other close, the less frantic the kiss became. It gentled to sweeps across the mouth. The barest of movements, and it meant everything.

"I am sorry, my Argaze. I just— I could not," Haru began.

A kiss stopped them. Then another. And another. Each more gentle and tender than the last. "It's all right. It's okay," Tally murmured between kisses. "You're here now. That's all that matters. You're here with me now."

"I have left you to hurt…"

"Oh, my love." Tally's voice broke as he pulled Haru in tight. "Hakkon keeps saying it's not my fault. But you know I can't see it that way. I failed our children. I failed his. Our poor little boy…"

Warm wet fell onto Haru's face. Tally was crying then sobbing in their arms. Haru held on tight, their hold fierce and unrelenting around that broad back, their own sobs hiccupping from them. Tally had been trying so hard to hold together. He probably hadn't let himself shed a single tear. And Haru… They'd been so numb and fogged with rage and sorrow. They hadn't been able to.

It solved nothing. Fixed nothing. Brought no one back. But the two of them both needed this so that neither of them shattered any further.

"I'm sorry. I'm sorry," Tally finally managed through hitching breaths. Whether he apologized for crying or for his supposed failure, Haru didn't know.

"You must not be." Haru stroked his face, wiping some of the tears away with their thumbs. "You have a promise to keep."

Tally nodded on a hard swallow, his breathing steadying. "I do. Yes. I don't know how yet, but yes."

"You are the strength of the clan." Haru burrowed closer again, needing the warmth. The cold seeped into their bones. "You will find a way."

"I'll do my level best." Tally drew in another huge breath, stroking Haru's back in long, sure trails of both hands. "It is *they*, isn't it? The pronoun you prefer?"

Haru nodded against Tally's chest. The change in subject was both strange and comforting. They understood why Tally needed it.

"I do wish you'd have told me. Instead of letting me misgender you all this time."

"You did not ask."

"True." Tally let out a heavy sigh. "I have to stop making assumptions. About lots of things. Haru? Will you stay with me for a bit? I'm just... I'm so tired."

In answer, Haru just snuggled closer, tangling their legs with Tally's, holding on as if they could make the world stop heaving that way. Of course they would stay. Tally needed them, truly needed them, and something in Haru became less jagged at that thought. Warmth, comfort, they could offer each other that, even if it changed nothing. In that comfort, maybe Tally would be able to think better. Maybe he would take strength from it.

And from that, circumstances might change.

* * * *

Dinner was not a festive affair, even though most of the family was there. Tally had been edgy about leaving loose ends fluttering out in the world and had gathered as much of the family to him as he could. He and Haru were still staying at Mom and Dad's cottage. Sammy had the downstairs room since Tally wasn't about to let her out of their collective sight. Nan and Addy had moved in temporarily, sharing a room as they hadn't since they were little. If he could have, he would've moved *everyone* close to him onto the property, but with the big house not ready for occupation yet, they would've had to set up a tent city.

Of the local brood, only Hal and Che refused to move out of their den to assuage their big brother's nerves. Too close to the end of development, Hal had said, but they did show up for dinner every night. *For food. Imagine that.*

Still, a much-subdued Bastille family gathered around Mom's table. No yelling. No boisterous teasing. No Lahi there to interject cutting, smart remarks. No kids...

Oh, Gods. He couldn't start crying again. Not in front of everyone who looked up to him. People were already starting to think he was going loony. Gun had gotten annoyed with him about his morning rounds of phone calls to check in with everyone. Not that Gun had said he was annoyed, but he did remind Tally that despite everything, he still had a clan *and* a business to run.

Yes. He did. Business was such a distant priority, though. He hadn't been ignoring his staff. He answered the emergency requests, resolved issues, kept things going, but it was all so cursory. No engagement. No planning.

Haru took the seat beside him, not quite their usual perfectly coiffed self, but they had made an effort with corduroys and cardigan, hair pulled back in a neat ponytail. A warm, elegant hand closed over Tally's and he clung to it, grateful to have at least this much of Haru back by his side.

The family talked softly about inconsequential things. The new recipe Nan was trying for risotto. The tenants across the hall from Hal and Che. The Shafa working with the Blue Hollys to fix Jasper's wings. The bulbs Mom and Dad were thinking about ordering for the spring. A possible visit from Meli. Rehabilitation doctors for Lahi. Addy rambled about a new set of stemware from Herr Klug. It sifted around him, unacknowledged. He heard them. He even appreciated that they *did* talk about normal things, but he couldn't actively participate. When he'd tried, his agitation would rise, the rage that lived in a box, no, a trunk...a wardrobe under his heart would break free and ruin the conversation.

He ate because he needed to. He encouraged Haru to eat because that too needed to happen. Things that lay ahead of the two of them meant they both had to be strong. Sharp. They —

Thump.

"The hell was that?" Hal glanced up toward the roof. All of them had.

Thud.

Tally was out of his chair before anyone could move, ignoring his mother's calls behind him. From the umbrella stand by the front door, he seized the weighted baseball bat he'd put there a few days before and stalked outside to where he could see the roof over the dining room.

Up near the roofline perched a black vulture, a large example of the species. Tally flicked his tongue to test the air, confirming what he'd suspected. *Lijun.* It cocked an eye at him and opened its beak on a ghastly gasping hiss.

"You." Tally pointed with the bat. "Come down and identify yourself or I'll shoot you down."

The family had joined him, damn them. *This could be dangerous.*

Che tugged on his sleeve. "Tal, you don't —"

"Shh. Get back in the house. Now."

Predictably, his annoying family didn't obey him. The vulture came toward him in an ungainly waddle, something impeding the use of its right foot. It hissed at him again and let out a series of short *hru* sounds, peevish and vaguely challenging. A carrion bird, reeking of death, Tally had no doubts who had sent it.

"Are you here as a threat? Or do you have something to say?" Tally bellowed up.

The vulture spread its ebony wings and launched from the roof. Certain it was an attack, Tally shoved his mother behind him and raised the bat in both hands to smash the bird from the air. It gained altitude, though, and only circled once to drop something from its claw before it flew off over the trees.

"Asshole," Tally growled after its retreating form.

Addy bent to pick up the paper, unfolding and straightening it on her thigh. "Tal." Her voice drifted to him, soft and colorless. "You should probably…"

Tally whipped around to face his sister, her face stricken. "Nan, get me gloves. No one else touches that piece of paper. *No one!*"

Now they obeyed, everyone backing away from Addy. Nan soon came running out of the house with plastic bags for Tally's hands. Fingers shaking, Addy handed the paper over.

"Tal?"

"Hush."

"What does it say?" Haru whispered, their shaking telegraphing through the fingers they'd placed on Tally's arm.

You know what we have.
We'll keep the treasure safe as assurance for your cooperation.
What we want should not be a shock if you've been paying attention.
We'll be in touch.

Slowly, carefully, Tally turned one of the bags inside out over the note to contain it. The not-ransom note. The note that told him not one fucking cursed thing. He shook off the hands reaching for him, strode back into the front hall, put the note on the little table beside the door and slammed his fist into the wall three times. Paint cracked. Drywall crumbled. On the third punch, he hit wood and pulled back, shaking his hand out.

He turned to find his family gathered in a shocked knot nearby, staring at him with various degrees of horror. "I need to call Agent Firebaugh," he managed in a tight, low growl. "They've made contact."

* * * *

The lake's frozen expanse gleamed under the rare rays of sunlight from this time of year. It was weird, being back in his office at work. While Sheriff Amick had finally given his home the all-clear, damage control still needed to be done before Tally even considered moving the family back in. Besides, Sapphire Lake Resort was his. Conducting clan business from here felt right since he could not do so from *home*. The hotel was something Tally had nurtured and grown — and now it would be the symbol he needed it to be.

Power. A show of his power. And in light of recent events, Tally thought this might just be a permanent move.

The table in his office had several dishes spread out over it. Snack items. Drinks. Little things to make the room feel less threatening for the coming meeting. It was certainly not within Tally's means to appear less so.

A ping drew Tally's attention away from the lake. The family chat notification popped up on his phone. He swiped it open.

Meli: I'm thinking about flying in before the Quarterly meeting.

Addy: I could meet you. Send me your flight info

Nan: me too, what souvenirs are you bringing this time?

Mom: Your brother is about to have an important meeting, girls.

Hal: Aren't *all* his meetings important?

Mom: Hal...

Meli: I have a couple things I want to go over when I come home.

Tal: Could we maybe hold that thought, Meli?

Meli: K

Che: I need this contract reviewed

Nan: Wrong thread, doofus

Addy: Aren't you in the same apartment as Hal?

Lahi: I hate this physical therapist. Some1 tell her torture is not therapy >.<

Mom: Don't hurt her!

Tal: Yes, please don't

Meli: Is there anything I can get for Haru?

Tal: You can try some rocks

Nan: Do well in PT and I'll bring you my newest creation <3

Lahi: you just want a guinea pig

Hal: I'll eat it if she doesn't want it

Che: Srsly, this contract, but food is good too *holds out hands*

Meli: You 2 live in the same place, or is talking that hard for you?

Mom: I sent you home with three bags of leftovers O_O

Che and Hal: We ate them

Addy: Sparkly rocks like diamonds make Haru smile, right Lahi????

Lahi: I'm pretty sure any rock makes Haru happy — have you seen the collection he has in the studio?

Tal: Actually it's 'they'. Yes, on the rocks. Any will do. Sparkly ones get worn as accessories.

Nan and Lahi: Since when is Haru 'they' >.> ??? !!!!

Tal: Since I asked!

Nan: Where are they on the NB spectrum?

Tal: ....I don't know

Meli, Hal, Nan, Lahi, and Che: Someone has some groveling to do.

Tal: I have a meeting, can we not right now?

Meli, Hal, Nan, Lahi, and Che: But this is important o_O

Always together. Impeccable timing. While life had turned heads over tails and was completely unpredictable, his siblings remained the one solid, unchanging force in his life. There was a knock at the door and Tally checked the time. Not quite three.

Dad: Guys, this meeting is important too.

Hal: Late as always pop :P

Dad: I will make sure Mom stops packing you leftovers.

Che: OMG, no
Mom: It's with Clement so stop bugging your brother.
Meli, Hal, Nan, Lahi, and Che: Ewww. He's such a smarmy douche.
Dad: Hakkon will be there too.
Meli, Hal, Nan, Lahi, and Che: GOOD.

For once the pinging stopped. Almost frighteningly *all at once.* The *tap-tap* of a knock on his door came again. Tally wasn't worried about it, though. They could wait. He wasn't even feeling anxious over making them wait. He didn't even feel the need for his worry stone. Councilman Black could wait. Maybe Tally was being petty, but he was tired of the council pushing him around. It was time they remembered who and what he was.

Another knock came at his door. "Mr. Bastille? I have a Mr. Black and Mr. Eberhardt waiting for your three o'clock?"

"Send them in." Tally took a seat away from the table.

Clement entered first with Hakkon following close behind, almost like he was herding the fox. Tally stood and removed his jacket to hang it on the back of his chair. Suit jackets were civilizing armor. Without them, nothing hid the bunch and slide of muscle under his tailored shirts. Tally spent most of his time underplaying his size, distracting from it, dismissing it as inconsequential.

This was not one of those times.

"Clement." Tally held out a hand, indicating a chair. "Hakkon, thank you for coming."

They sat. He loomed.

"Tally, I'm pleased to meet with you on any occasion." Clement shifted in his chair, crossing his ankles, then crossing his legs and leaning back. "But your admin wasn't clear concerning the *topic* of the meeting."

Two paces to the window. Glare out over the lake. And turn. "Entirely intentional. I have questions." Tally strode back to the desk and planted both fists atop the polished oak. "You will provide answers."

The fox lijun frowned, tugging on his ear. "I can't say I like your tone…"

"What you like is irrelevant to the situation. You know what happened to our children, Hak's and mine."

A wary light entered Clement's eyes. "I'd heard, of course. I was terribly sorry to hear."

"Clement!" Tally slammed a palm against his desk. "No games! Jason Kaul broke into my house, attacked my sister, slaughtered my son and Hak's two youngest and *took my daughters*! You were with him that night. I *saw* you."

"You can't think…" Clement rose from his chair, hands shaking.

"I don't know what to think, damn it! I saw you with that murdering bastard. Do you know where my joeys are?"

Pale as frost, Clement sank back down. "No. I don't." He held up a hand to stave off Tally's next outburst. "I really don't, Tal. If I did, I would've told you long before this. I don't condone the murder of children and the kidnapping of toddlers. You can't think I do."

"Then why were you having dinner with him?" Hakkon broke his silence, his tone soft and even.

Clement let out a desperate bark of laughter. "I didn't trust him. There was something off about him, so I took him to dinner to see if I couldn't shake any information free. He saw you there, you and Haru, and he must've been all too happy to seize the opportunity, knowing you wouldn't be home for some time."

With a slow exhale, Tally backed off to lean against the windowsill, arms crossed over his chest. "What did you find out? Anything...anything at all might be helpful right now."

Clement stared at his hands, turning the carved onyx ring he always wore on his right. "I can't prove anything. Please understand that. I can only tell you my suspicions."

"What are those?" Another soft prompt from Hakkon.

"He's old blood. *Old.* I could tell from things he said. He never used the words *purity* or *separation*, but you could hear them implied. He is on State's directory. I looked him up. But he's not some bland inspector." Clement raised his head, his dark eyes troubled. "I think he's *Sisum Abser.*"

Hakkon swallowed hard. "I haven't heard that term in years."

"I...I didn't realize..." Tally reached for the worry stone in his pocket. "I didn't think State still used them. An *official* assassin, you think? State sent someone to kill our *children*?"

Clement held up both hands. "I don't know. My bets would be on this not being openly official but being sanctioned by a certain faction. Someone has Kaul's leash. Someone with the power to use him as they please."

Tally turned the worry stone over and over, a sick weight in his stomach. "Why didn't you come to me with this, Clem?"

"And tell you what, Urusar? That I had a bad feeling?" Clement waved a weary hand. "I'm sorry. In hindsight… But even after, I have no proof. Just educated guesses based on a lifetime of watching people give themselves away." The fox ran his hands back through his silvered auburn hair. "Here's the rest of it. Again, I have no proof. But I don't think him killing Jackson was in the heat of the moment. There've been too many mutterings about an orphaned opossum being groomed as Sardu."

Chapter Eleven

Punt

"It hurts!" Lahi groaned then lay back on the floor.

"You did have your stomach ripped open," Eleanor, her physical therapist, answered. "It's going to take time to heal from something like that, even for someone like us."

"I hate you," Lahi moaned again.

Haru edged closer to the mat and wiped a wet washcloth over Lahi's forehead. Her head lolled in their direction. The smile she wore dug into their heart. Her happiness at such a small act was not something they deserved. Lahi was having to put herself back together after Kaul-san's attack because Haru hadn't pushed hard enough.

"You, I like," Lahi said. "You don't make me hurt."

They froze, their lungs tight. She had been maimed because of them.

It was as if she sensed their thoughts. Lahi grabbed their hand and kissed it. "You are not the cause of my pain."

They weren't allowed a respite, to refute Lahi's claim. No wallowing. Eleanor's rules because it was her therapy room. The therapist got behind Lahi and helped her up.

"Yes, it's me. Now stretch," Eleanor said. "Those muscles need tender loving care."

"Haruuuuuuuuuuu," Lahi whined.

They wiped the sweat around her face. "I will make cake if Eleanor says you did a good job."

"What kind of cake?" Lahi's eyes turned calculating.

"Triple chocolate and berry."

"Deal." Kiss. Kiss. Nose. Nose.

Sneaky snake. But the heavy weight on their chest didn't hurt so much.

Eleanor shook her head. "Whatever motivates her to work."

Apparently cake did the trick for today because she stopped complaining and followed through with each exercise to help strengthen her abdomen without causing more damage. Little steps. Stretching. Reaching. Twisting. Each time little beads of sweat showed up, Haru was there to wipe them away, let Lahi know how well she was doing, even when Eleanor said she could do better.

Mean therapist. Couldn't she see how hard Lahi was trying?

"Now with your eyes closed," Eleanor insisted.

"What?"

"Close your eyes."

Haru frowned. The front of Lahi's shirt was wet with perspiration. Wasn't that enough? They turned their attention to the therapist, who gave Haru the barest of headshakes when their eyes met. It was the first time her eyes had softened the whole session. Then the fierce glint was back, the second Lahi dropped the resistance band.

"Five more!"

"Ugh. Yeeeeeeeeeeeeeeeessssssssssssssss, misssstress."

Haru almost snapped, except when their eyes met Eleanor's, she was mouthing *please*. Please what?

"You can do it."

"It hurts."

"Does it hurt, or is it uncomfortable? We'll stop if it's hurting, Lahi. Because it *shouldn't* hurt."

A mumble, barely audible, was her answer and Lahi picked up the band again. "Fine. For cake."

Eleanor gave Haru a wink. Oh. *Ooooh.*

So...so she *had* to push Lahi.

Hmmm. Then that meant Haru could be the *comforter* rather than rule enforcer. It *felt* nice. Not to be the one responsible. A wave of nausea rolled through Haru. The thought confusing and scary. It picked at their heart, peeling it back a vein at a time.

Ow.

A warm presence eased Haru back from the mat, and they found themself wrapped up, strong arms holding them together. Tally's scent surrounded Haru, pulling them back—from wherever they had been. Lahi and Eleanor were staring at them, similar expressions of concern on both.

Had something happened? "Is Lahi all right?"

"She's fine," Eleanor answered. "You had us worried for a minute there, but Lahi's good."

"Me?"

"We lost you for a while," Lahi said, rolling to her side then pushing up on her hands and knees. Eleanor helped her stand the rest of the way. "But Tally got you back."

Got them back? Haru's head pounded, right behind the eyes.

"We're good," Tally said, rubbing up and down Haru's side, right against their skin under their shirt and wrap-around sweater. "Everything's all good. Does Lahi have any more exercises or is she done for the day?"

"It's stoppage time."

"Yes!" Lahi wriggled in place.

Eleanor slid a wink toward them and Tally. "You still have to do the leg exercises we talked about once you get to your room."

"Booooo, hisssssss."

"Very funny. See you later, Uruma, Urusar," Eleanor said as she picked up a rag. "Time for me to get ready for the next victim."

Lahi stuck out her tongue. "Told you guys. She likes it. The torture."

"Yes, yes, evil physical therapist." Tally consoled her as he guided them out of the room.

They managed to make it back to Lahi's suite in the rehabilitation facility without busting her, though she didn't argue when Haru tucked her into bed. She only protested about the cake.

"I have to cook it first, Lahi."

"But cake."

"How about a chocolate croissant from Kits and Cupcakes Bakery to tide you over?"

Lahi managed to pluck the treat out of Tally's hand and pop it in her mouth before he could get a second out of the bag. She shrugged, held out her hand for more. It seemed food was a big incentive for *all* the Bastille children. But it was the middle of the afternoon.

What was Tally doing here and not at the resort? Haru asked as much.

"I was checking in on Mindy for Hak," Tally answered softly. "He had a court date and couldn't make it today for her physio."

"I see." Now didn't that kick?

"It's not you, Haru. It's really not," Tally said, taking their hand.

"Really? Because refusing to see me makes it feel like it is. She hates me. How could she not?"

Lahi coughed and waved her hand toward the water on her tray table. They handed it to her. She swallowed a few gulps then said, "That's what you think? That she's blaming you?"

"I would."

"Remember I don't?" Lahi answered. "Haru, Uruma. We feel like we failed *you*."

"She is just a child!"

"Who tried to save yours and *didn't*." Lahi's voice broke. The fact her pain was clear as the sky outside, etched on her face, the way her hand shook, was the only thing that stopped Haru from arguing with her. "*We* didn't, and trust me, Haru. It's really, really hard not to feel guilty about that. Mindy too."

"How do you not feel guilty?" they asked.

"By remembering it wasn't my choices that hurt our family that night. For putting the blame squarely where it belongs. Dr. Stix has to remind us about those things, but therapy with her is helping. And because I have my music to help me work it out. Something Mindy doesn't have yet. An outlet for her pain and guilt because she's still just a kid."

Sometimes Lahi amazed them — sometimes in terrifying yet later funny ways, sometimes in how much depth she had. But her empathy, the way she saw the world, was why her music was so well-loved, wasn't it?

She grabbed Haru's hand. "Give her time, *Uruma*. She's got Dr. Stix helping her to work it out. Mindy just needs time."

That they could do. Haru nodded in agreement and took a breath. They needed to remember, to not be so selfish and see that others were hurting too, not just them. The more they gave in to the pain, the more Kaul-san and the Traditionalists stole from their clan.

Lahi reached for her guitar and settled it in her lap. She began to pluck out a melody, humming along with it, the single notes drawn out like a heartstring being played—fine and sweet—with careful fingers. Sad but loving. She would have words soon. Not now, they weren't ready, but they were coming. Haru saw the way her expression changed, getting thinky.

Soon. Very soon Lahi would have a song for *everyone*.

That evening, Haru wandered their in-laws' cottage, cleaning a bit here, straightening there. They couldn't settle. Even climbing into bed and into Tally's arms hadn't helped. Tally had been holding them every night, never making demands, never initiating more than kisses. It was something *Tally* needed, something Haru enjoyed as well. They'd been through so much during all the turmoil.

Still, Haru's brain wouldn't stop spinning and they had known sleep wouldn't happen. They had waited until Tally had drifted off then waited a little longer until that broad chest rose and fell in a slow, even rhythm before climbing out of bed.

They did have a promise to Lahi to keep. That was a legitimate reason for getting up, right?

Bastille-*okaasan* had always loved to bake, the family told Haru. Probably why Nan had become a chef and definitely why Bastille-*okaasan*'s kitchen was always stocked for any baking project. Haru would make something for the family too. That was only right if they were going to use supplies and equipment. Two cakes were just as easy as one once the oven was heated.

The good baker's chocolate. Flour. Sugar. Butter — should've taken the butter out earlier. They set it by the oven to warm and soften. *Cake pans. Mixing bowl. Mixer...*

No, that would make too much noise. Haru retrieved one of the good poplar spoons from the utensil stand instead. They would have to mix by hand. Not a problem, since the extra physical activity might wear them out enough for sleep. Eventually.

Haru was just stirring the chocolate chunks into the chocolate batter when a soft sound made them turn. His long hair mussed from bed, Tally shuffled in and plopped onto one of the stools at the center island.

"I apologize. Did I wake you?"

"No. I mean, I realized you were gone, but I wake up a lot these days anyway." Tally put his arms on the counter and set his chin on top, watching Haru. "Don't mind me. I love to watch baking."

Haru fumbled the spoon once, but soon found they didn't mind. Eyes half-closed, Tally did just watch without commentary, advice or criticism. They imagined a small Tally doing this in the family kitchen, his childhood anxiety soothed by his mother's sure movements and by the warm, inviting smells. *Of course.* It was a day of social revelations. Tally needed soothing these days and Haru was happy to provide if he could.

By the time Haru had the second cake in the oven and was spreading chocolate icing on the first, they realized even the little appreciative sounds had stopped. They glanced over one shoulder to find Tally fast asleep with his head on the counter. That dragged a smile from Haru, the first real one in some days.

They would let Tally sleep until the baking and clean-up were finished. It would have been a terrible shame to wake their Argaze when he looked so peaceful. Then he could wake to the second cake. Hopefully everyone shared.

* * * *

Walking into Lahi's room the next morning nearly broke Haru's heart. They had wanted to surprise her with the cake but were knocked for a loop themself. She was up already, despite the early hour. Her head was ducked over the guitar and bedside table. Her ear down. Long, black hair veiled her face from them. Lahi was singing...and her voice. It *hurt*.

"Gardenia greets the moon
Newborn waves her hands and smiles
Dawn paints the gray-blue sky
All these have their time,
Give the world its beauty – "

Lahi stopped singing and scribbled out the words. Hard strokes. Ah, so she wasn't keeping those. But they had resonated something in Haru. Deep, quaking waves. That could be why she didn't want to keep them. They picked too much at an open wound.

"Stupid. Stupid," Lahi mumbled. "Not right – not..."

Maybe it was good time to intrude. "I have cake!"

"What?" Lahi glanced up with a dazed expression, pupils working to focus. "Oh, cake! What's in the other bag?"

"Your prize for physical therapy today. I thought it was better to come prepared this time."

Dark circles shadowed her eyes, but the small pink bag had garnered her interest.

"Did you sleep last night?" they asked as they placed the cake container and bag down on the side table.

"Bad dreams," Lahi mumbled. She sighed and put her guitar in its stand. "What time is it?"

"Breakfast time."

"Are you saying I get cake for breakfast?" Lahi sat up in bed and flinched. A hand went to her stomach. "Ooh. Yeah. No."

Haru hurried over to her side and helped Lahi sit back. They lowered the bed, despite her protests, but the pain around her eyes lessened. Her breaths came easier. Haru snagged the treat bag they'd brought and took out the apple juice.

"Here, sip this."

She obliged, taking small, slow slurps. Her dark eyes followed Haru as they moved around the room, cleaning, wiping down the tray, fixing her sheets and adjusting the blinds.

"You will hurt yourself if you do not give your body a break."

"I can't let it go, the song is right there, right underneath. I can *feel* it."

Haru took the empty juice. Nose. Nose. Kiss. Kiss.

"I *need* to finish it," she said.

"You will, but maybe your tired brain wants some rest so it can," they suggested as they pulled the comforter up higher.

"Maybe." Lahi eyed the cake.

They took her comb from the end table and began to pull it through her thick hair. "The cake will be here when you wake up. So will I."

"Promise?" She yawned, fingers popping out from under the covers

Haru hooked their pinkies. "Promise."

Lahi's smile as she drifted off was definitely worth it too. They shuffled around the room, arranging the flowers, dusting and packing her laundry to do at home. No matter how good the service, it was always the clothes that went missing. Finally, they just sat in the chair by the window, watching the world move by as Lahi slept.

White covered everything, making the ground and brush glisten under the pale yellow winter sun. A stillness entombed the landscape. Like it was waiting for the world to breathe. Or maybe that was just Haru.

The door clicking drew Haru's attention back to Lahi. Breakfast had been laid out for her on the table. Good, then she would have energy for PT. Haru was arranging the food when they noticed a small envelope with the meal. Another fan note?

When they turned it over and saw URUMA BASTILLE scrawled out on it, a chill ran through Haru.

"Mmmm." Lahi shifted under her covers. "Eeeeggggssssssss."

They pocketed the letter. "Seems you get cake and a breakfast."

Lahi rubbed her eyes but didn't open them. "Mmmmm."

"The eggs are warm and runny just like you like them." Haru wafted the smell toward her.

"Cake first."

Now she sounded like Melia. A pang struck Haru and their hand automatically went to their chest. Lahi had opened her eyes and was watching them.

"I can eat the eggs first if it means that much to you." She sighed and the gears on the bed whirred as she had it help her sit up.

"No, no, cake is what you get." Haru might not be able to pamper their little girl right now, but they were sure Lahi could use some love and support. "Here. I need to make a call to Tally. Be right back."

Haru made their way into the hall before Lahi could question them. Clacking filled the hall, their geta noisy against the tile, as they hurried to a nurse's station. The young blond man at the desk watched with piqued interest as Haru drew near.

"Call Sheriff Amick, please. And do you know who served my sister-in-law breakfast? Do you *not* have security here?"

There was a pause before the young man realized Haru was serious. Security was part of the reason Lahi and Mindy had been placed there. The staffer reached for the phone. "I need Roland at 24-C." He clicked the receiver and dialed. "Yes, it's Birch Hill Rehabilitation Center. We need the sheriff."

Oh, no, that was... There was a sharp wolf that had been put on their case by the Bureau. Agent Firebaugh, was it? Haru turned and pulled out their cell phone. They tapped and waited.

"Hey, Lahi giving you trouble already?" Tally asked.

"Yes, well, only Lahi trouble. That is not why I am calling, my Argaze." Haru pulled the letter out of their pocket. "I think the kidnappers have made contact again. There is a letter."

A loud crack came over the phone.

"My Argaze?"

"Just the desk. Don't worry."

"You broke your desk?"

More noise, doors and other voices filled the background over the phone. "I'm coming to you."

* * * *

"Agent Firebaugh?" Tally juggled phone and keys as he hurried out to the garage. "It's Tally Bastille. I've... Haru says he received another note."

The noise on the other end of the line was hollow and hissing, indicating Tally was on speaker in Firebaugh's car. "Where?"

"At the rehab facility where—"

An unmistakable squeal of tires made Tally wince. "Agent Firebaugh?"

"Sorry. Not-quite-legal U-turn. I'll meet you there."

The timing wasn't lost on Tally, nor was the placement of the delivery. One of Kaul's minions, or Gods help him, Kaul himself, had delivered the note to a building where his spouse, his sister and his friend's child were, all at a time when he hadn't been there to protect them.

He tried not to drive like a demon loosed from some hell maw, but his mind wanted to fly to Haru. His foot kept answering by growing heavier on the accelerator. The Bentley was a tank in many respects, but it could *move*. He screeched to a stop in the rehab facility's parking lot just as Agent Firebaugh's dark blue SUV screamed around the corner.

Firebaugh was out of his vehicle and jogging toward Tally almost before he'd managed to get his seatbelt off. He didn't even remember fastening his seatbelt. *Have to pull it together.*

"I have law enforcement coming to secure the principals," Firebaugh offered as he caught up and joined Tally in a jog to the door. "Let's see this note first."

Tally tried not to snarl. "Maybe we should see if everyone's all right first?"

"I've already spoken to hospital staff. Made sure that Lahi and Mindy are unharmed and that Haru isn't alone. If something had threatened them, I'd know it by now."

"You, ah..." Tally gaped for a moment before his brain restarted. "You certainly made a lot of phone calls in a short drive."

A twitch of a smile answered him. "I have a Master's in phone-fu." He nodded to the reception desk. "There's your husband."

Tally didn't have to be told twice and didn't slow his steps until he had a stiff Haru wrapped in a smothering embrace. Haru flailed for a moment before they relaxed far enough to wrap their arms around Tally's ribs.

"Gods," Tally breathed into their hair, telling himself sternly that Haru was *not* fragile. "Are you... Did you read it?"

Haru pushed back and shook their head. "I did not know if the agent would need to read it first."

"Thank you." Firebaugh came to where Haru pointed out the note on the counter. "You did touch it, Uruma Bastille?" Haru nodded, but Firebaugh didn't react beyond taking a pair of tweezers from his pocket. With them, he unfolded the note and read, a deepening frown furrowing his forehead.

"What does it say?" Tally craned to look over his shoulder.

"Here. Read. I'll take a picture and send it to you, but don't touch it any further."

The note was written on the same nondescript white paper as the first with the same self-satisfied, neat block letters.

Are you listening, oh mighty uktena? For your treasures' sakes, you need to.

This only happened because you have not listened, because you discard tradition and the old covenants. So now, listen.

The word *listen* was underlined four times.

You may keep your position, your property, the remainder of your family – we are generous. You may even earn the return of what we took if you do as you are told. You are a leader of lijun. A protector of lijun. Time to begin acting as if you were.

We will choose an emissary from your council. They will be furnished with specific instructions. The vehicle of these instructions will vary, so don't think to use the emissary as a means to find us. We will know if you fail to follow these instructions. There will be consequences.

"Fucking hell," Tally whispered.

"Just about the perfect assessment," Firebaugh murmured as he snapped pics of the letter, then placed it carefully in an evidence bag.

"What should we do now, Agent Firebaugh?" Haru vibrated beside Tally, possibly from an overload of both frustration and adrenaline.

"Do? Oh, no, no." Agent Firebaugh turned and pointed from Tally to Haru. "You two aren't going to do anything. You go about your lives. Tell me the second this emissary makes contact. If it's someone on your local council, that's a pretty short list."

Tally's own frustration grew into a ball that threatened to devour him. "What are *you* going to do?"

"I'm going to question staff here. Watch security footage. Set up surveillance at key strategic points. And other such things you don't need to know about." Another pointed finger at Tally. "Growling at me isn't going to help. Though, if it makes you feel better, I suppose I can't really object."

Growling? Oh. Um. Yes. The leftover vibration in his chest confirmed that he had been. "Sorry."

Firebaugh waved a negligent hand, the other already busy with his phone. "It's all right. I've certainly heard worse. Serious about the going about your life thing, though. There's nothing you can do looming over me. Really."

"All right." Tally scrubbed both hands over his face before he glanced over at Haru. "Has Mindy seen you?"

"No, I—"

"We'll do that, then." Tally took their hand and started them down the hall. "Good hunting, Agent Firebaugh."

Firebaugh gave them a distracted wave and Haru held tight to Tally's hand, finally speaking when they turned a corner. "Did you hurt your hand?"

"Did I...oh." Tally stared at his knuckles, realizing only now that they did hurt. "No. Not really."

"Did you break your desk?"

"I, ah, cracked it."

Haru shook his—*their*—head. "You should stop damaging property, my Argaze."

"I know. Of course." Tally squeezed their hand. "I'm so... I feel so angry. Like there's boiling tar just under my skin waiting to catch fire."

An odd sound escaped Haru, almost a chirrup. "I share this with you. It is a terrible feeling."

"But you don't break things. It just... I don't know where they are. I don't know what's happening to them. I want to bring them *home*."

Haru stroked his arm when Tally's breathing hitched. "I know." Their voice wavered when they spoke again. "Mindy does not wish to see me. She has been very clear."

"Mindy doesn't really want to see *us*," Tally corrected gently. "She allowed it briefly from me, since her dad sent me. But it's like Lahi says. It's because she drowning in guilt. We can't let her do that. Gods. If anything... Anyway, I'm her Urusar and I won't be kept away. Let me try first?"

That wasn't a comfortable expression. Haru's jaw was too tight, their eyes narrowed. Still, they nodded. "As you wish, my Argaze."

Tally stifled a sigh and patted the hand on his arm. "Give me a few moments. I'll stick my head out if she agrees."

He got a nod. Haru would most likely eavesdrop just outside the door, but what responsible Uruma wouldn't? Tally knocked at Mindy's door, poked his head in to make sure medical staff wasn't in the middle of anything and walked in without asking for permission.

Mindy was sitting up in bed, breakfast pushed to one side on its rolling tray. She let out a little *chuk* when she caught sight of him, so much like her father's sound of surprise, like an adult peregrine. She was so close to being one and she'd nearly been cut off from growing up. Like her sisters.

Don't cry, you idiot. That would really *make her feel better.* Tally managed to plaster on a smile instead. "Good morning, Mindy. How are things going?"

"Morning, Urusar." Mindy pulled a protective mantle of adolescent surliness around her, plucking at her blankets and staring at her hands. "They're going, I guess."

Tally pulled a chair up beside her bed. "Things tend to do that." He waited, letting her adjust to his presence. "I'm so sorry, Mindy. I wasn't there to protect you. To prevent all of this. I should have been there to stop it."

Her gaze shifted sideways. Her mouth pulled down. "That's stupid, Urusar. Sorry, but it is."

"Is it? Why's that?"

More blanket twisting. "Because you were out. You weren't anywhere near the house. It's not like you knew...like you had some kind of house telepathy or something. *I* was there. I was babysitting. Morgan and Mason, too, yeah. But *I'm* the oldest...*was* the oldest."

Tally's arms ached to hug her, but he didn't think it would be welcome, not right then. "You feel responsible." He waited until she nodded. "You feel that you were the one who was supposed to protect everyone else, so you're sure this is *all your fault.*" Another slower nod, though now her eyes shone with tears. "All right, then. That makes three of us. You. Me. Uruma Haru."

"Uruma Haru?"

"Yes. Blames themself for the deaths of your sisters. For the death of our son. For you and Lahi getting hurt. For our daughters being taken. They are consumed by guilt, so much so that they asked your father for punishment."

"But..." Mindy's gaze had made it to Tally's face, her eyes wide with horror. "But that's..."

"Stupid? I suppose so. All of us blaming ourselves doesn't fix anything. And it doesn't blame the man who really *is* responsible. He's a killer, Mindy. A professional. No one stood a chance against him and the fault lies only with him."

She chewed on her lower lip, anguished gaze boring into his. "But it doesn't really help, does it, Urusar? Knowing that."

"Not really. Not yet. Because you're a leader. Because you're hard on yourself and expect to be the one to protect others, it doesn't help much. We still have to push on because people depend on us. And we have to admit to ourselves that we're not alone. That we can lean on other people, too, and that other people can feel just as responsible, whether it makes sense to us or not."

"This is where you ask me to see Uruma Haru."

"It is. Please, Mindy. They blame only themself. It's important for them to be able to see you."

She wiped at her eyes, then reached for the tissue box to blow her nose. "I'll try. It's just so...aargh. I promised to keep the joeys safe and I failed *so* hard."

"I know it feels that way. I really do." He patted her shoulder and rose to stick his head around the door. "Haru, my love? She'd like to see you."

Chapter Twelve

Busy Hands

Another letter had arrived, this time with a picture of the girls in a cage and a request. Melia and Livy were opossumed but Haru could see the misery on their faces. No, Amelia looked mad and upset. Olivia looked scared and tired. Her little eyes droopy. Either way, those bastards had their daughters and deserved a slow death. One filled with agony and fear.

Haru tapped through the report and the agent's most recent findings, reading, taking notes.

Why had no demands come yet? They had taken the girls. The demands should've been swift and comprehensive. Instead, threatening notes had been sent. A request for clean clothes. What kind of murderous kidnapper asked for *clean clothes*? What was the hold-up? The necklace Tally had given them burned against their skin. A reminder of what they had lost, the girls they missed and the potential dangers yet to come.

"Uruma Bastille."

They looked over the top of the computer. "Agent Firebaugh."

"I would tell you it's illegal to go through my files but then I'd have to report you and explain how you broke into it."

"I was simply dusting when the screen came on."

The long and lean wolf chuckled. "I'm sure."

With a one-shoulder shrug they stood. "I take it by your presence you are staying for dinner?"

"At Urusar Bastille's request, yes."

"Then I shall leave you to your work."

Agent Firebaugh tracked Haru around the desk. The look in his eyes, *hmmmm*, interesting. The fact he didn't immediately start freaking out about Haru's nosing also piqued their interest. The wolf's gaze *felt* predatory but not in a way where danger lurked behind it. More like the agent was assessing Haru.

It was a quick inventory, a look Haru had seen dozens of times with respective matches, one where they were trying to decide if they were worth the trouble or not — or whether they found Haru attractive enough to be worth that trouble. Most people would've missed it. Haru used to miss it all the time, but as they got older they knew what to look for. To see it coming from the agent was...*curious.*

When Agent Firebaugh's gaze came back to Haru's, his eyes widened a fraction. He knew he'd been caught. The question was why. What was he looking for? It wasn't like the wolf didn't know Haru was Tally's.

"Were you a love match?"

The question threw Haru. *Not the one I expected.*

"The clan members say you're Em'halafi," the wolf continued. He reached out, a gentle tug on Haru's forearm. "But..." He sniffed, not just a little one, scenting. It was a lungful. "But your smell."

Talk about being invasive and rude. Haru shook their arm but the agent didn't let go. He did gentle his touch a fraction. He stood close, too close.

Was Agent Firebaugh waiting for an answer? Then he could wait all night as far as Haru was concerned. The two of them locked eyes. The silly wolf probably thought Haru was some fragile Satislit.

Considering their reaction to *that night,* it wasn't surprising.

"Is he forcing you to stay?"

Another unexpected question.

"If he is, I can help you. You don't have to stay if you don't want," Agent Firebaugh continued. A thumb rubbed back and forth over Haru's arm. "We can get you out. All of you."

They shook their arm again. This time the wolf let go. "I do not know what you are presuming, but the reason you are here is to help get my pups back."

"Of course, Uruma Bastille."

The two of them broke apart, stepping back.

"Why do you think these people took your pups?"

"To undermine my Argaze. Being a married Urusar makes him a threat to the Traditionalists in the clan. Before, they were fine working in the shadows. Now they're not."

"Why now?"

"Because Tally symbolizes everything they hate and fear." Haru shuffled toward the door. "And now that he has a family, he is more dangerous to their way of life."

"Hmm."

"I am more than my looks, Agent Firebaugh."

There was a chuckle. "You are that, Uruma. You are that. Try not to get me in trouble, okay?"

Haru flashed a smile toward the wolf. "I am confident you are looking for trouble, Agent."

A startled laugh followed behind Haru as they made their way down the hall. They wanted to make sure Bastille-*okaasan* knew more guests would be dropping in for dinner. By the smells coming from the kitchen, there would be soup and bread. And meat. Haru sniffed. Some kind of tasty meat.

"Can you hand me the ladle, Haru?"

"Yes, Bastille-*okaasan*." They dutifully handed it over and watched as she poured some of the stew, *not soup*, into a small bowl. She slurped then hummed. She handed it to Haru. They sampled as well. "Hmmm."

"It's missing a little something."

"It is."

"What do you think?"

"How many chilies did you put in?" they asked.

"The usual amount, but I did use vegetable stock, so Tally could have it."

"Mmm."

She hummed and tasted again. "Maybe a stronger flavor to make up for it?"

"Cumin?" they suggested.

"That could work. Can you check on the roast?" Bastille-*okaasan* sighed. "Agent Firebaugh will be here for dinner."

"Do I need to ask him to leave?" Haru stuck the thermometer in. Only a hundred and forty Fahrenheit. Not too much longer, though. What had the wolf done to upset her? They cocked their head to look up at her as she stirred the cumin into the stew.

"No, no. It's Tal. I'm afraid he's going to corner the poor agent."

"I see. We could seat him down by Nan?"

"It might work?"

Haru busied themself with getting the table arranged. There was a brief thought to intercept Tally and warn him off, but they had been caught *sneaking*. No need to throw stones. Besides, Haru liked their stones. No need to share.

A hand slid around Haru's waist, and they smacked it automatically.

"Ow!" The heat left their back and Tally huffed. "What was that for?"

"My Argaze. Sorry. I — sorry."

"No, no, my fault. I shouldn't have startled you." Tally waved his hand and rubbed it against his chest. "Can I help?"

"The spoons," Haru answered, their eyes down.

"Hey, none of that. You didn't do anything wrong." Tally placed a kiss against Haru's temple. "Make sure Agent Firebaugh has a place, okay?"

"Of course."

By the time the food was out and everyone settled, Tally's mood had soured with the wolf's placement away from him. However, the conversation was flowing, mainly grunts of appreciation from Hal and Che, but everyone was eating. Jasper had even made it to the table, sitting close to Haru, stealing bits of food. None of those awkward silences. People getting up and sitting back down as they needed. Conversations ebbed and flowed. It almost felt normal.

As normal as it could be with not having their pups around. Guilt surged, a cold hand constricting around Haru's heart. They pushed back from the table.

"Excuse me. The biscuits."

There were biscuits to be had, the timer counting down the last couple minutes. But Haru wouldn't have been able to hold back their anger and frustration. They leaned against the counter, desperately trying to hold themself together. How could Tally just sit there and smile? How could Bastille-*okaasan*? Or the siblings? Or Bastille-*otōusan*?

Metal scraped as someone pulled out the rack. Haru frowned at the wolf, who gave them a sheepish grin. How interesting. Was he blushing?

"The buzzer went off on my way through to the bathroom. You seem *preoccupied*."

"I see. Thank you. I can—" Haru closed their mouth as Agent Firebaugh slid the biscuits into the waiting bowl. "Thank you."

"My pleasure."

The doorbell rang as Haru floundered as to what they should do next. A guest should not be serving dinner. The bottom of a chair scraped against the wood floor in the dining room.

"I will answer!" Haru shouted and headed for the door. They tried to ignore the fact the wolf trailed a distance behind them. "Hel—Councilman Hastings. What can I do for you?"

"It's a pleasure as always, Satislit Bastille." The boar let himself in, pushing past Haru and bumping them on the shoulder. A gust of snow and cold air followed him. "I am here to discuss something with your Urusar. Fetch him."

A heavy winter coat and scarf were tossed at Haru. They caught it automatically, more from surprise than anything else, and they almost hung up the outerwear.

Almost. With a thump, the coat and scarf fell to the floor.

"Satislit Bastille. I expected better of you, with someone of your training. Maybe you need a brush up on your hospitality skills."

"You have entered my house uninvited, Councilman Hastings, demanding to see my Argaze. Right now, you are forgetting proper etiquette for requesting an audience to see your Urusar!"

Maybe if Hastings-san hadn't been standing there with such a smug smile, Haru would've been able to handle the intrusion better. It wasn't in them at the moment, though. Too raw and wound up. Why was he still smiling? The boar should be excusing himself back out of the house. Then again, he was the one who had come bursting into the office before.

A thud echoed through Haru and they stilled. The question became, because of the councilman's recent actions, why he felt so entitled. Why he thought he could just enter the former Urusar's home? He was too happy.

The moment their gaze met with Hastings-san's two things became frighteningly clear. The boar thought he had control over at least Haru, if not Tally. Second, there could only be one reason he thought he had control. It was a feeling, nothing more, but Haru was certain of it. And when their gazes met, there was a certain understanding flaring in the boar's eyes.

"Satislit Bastille, I suggest you change your tune." Councilman Hastings pulled the hand back.

Haru would not cower in front of him. They refused. "And why is that?"

"Yes, please. I would love to hear why." Agent Firebaugh had hold of the boar's arm, and before the councilman twisted around to face his captor, absolute malice flooded his face. "Councilman Hastings. Why are you intruding on Urusar Bastille's home?"

"Agent Firebaugh!"

"Oof!" For a second, Haru was covered in frightened boar until the agent pulled him off them.

"What are you doing here?"

The wolf stared, looking at Hastings-san if he were an idiot. Haru had to agree. "I am the FBI agent in charge of your Urusar's kidnapping case."

"Oh, yes, of course, yes. I see. And you're right. I've intruded." He picked up the coat and scarf, pulling it on in haste and wrapping himself up. "I'll return another time."

The door slammed shut before Haru had a chance to get a word in edgewise. They looked out the side window thoughtfully and mumbled, "If only I could get him to disappear so quickly every time."

A snort pulled their attention back to Agent Firebaugh.

"So, do you have any idea what that pig wanted?"

Haru slid their eyes to the door. "I think I do."

Agent Firebaugh bent over, pulled one of his ever-present latex gloves from a pocket, and picked an envelope off the floor. "I think you're probably right."

"I want that damnable boar followed."

A little squeak escaped Haru. He hadn't heard Tally approach, or Gunther, who stood at his shoulder — and where had *he* come from?

"Tal, I don't think —"

"*Now*, Gun." Tally's gaze was frigid as he followed Barry's hurried movements to his car. "He could be reporting back to someone."

"All right." Gunther held up a placating hand as he pulled out his phone. "Don't go all ice prince on me, your highness."

While the eagle turned away to make a quick call, Agent Firebaugh raised his eyebrows and leaned around Tally's bulk. "Who's this, Mr. Bastille?"

"Sorry. This is Gunther Curley, acting as my current head of Enforcement." Tally motioned to Firebaugh when Gunther hung up. "Gun, this is Agent Firebaugh, the one assigned to our case."

Gunther clasped hands with the agent, a long, assessing look passing between them. If they shook hands a fraction too long, Haru didn't think anyone was aware of it. Americans could be oddly tone deaf to their own body language, though the wolf's extra sniffing was harder to ignore. *Interesting*.

* * * *

"I just want our babies back," Tally grated out, clutching the edge of his desk to keep from rocking back and forth in frustrated misery. Fur had been in this envelope, along with the note. *Fur* from his little girls. He couldn't even pretend the clumps of gray were fake since his sense of smell cried out with agonizing clarity, *Melia! Livy!*

Behind him, Haru set a hand on his shoulder, fingers kneading his taut-to-breaking muscles. He didn't miss the eyebrow twitch from Firebaugh. Now, what was that about? "What's protocol here? Do we agree to meet? Agree to terms and hope they do the right thing?"

"They've shown more of their hand than they wanted in this last exchange, I think." Firebaugh tapped the edge of the note, still spread out on Tally's desk. "Previously, they've used minions or possibly hired messengers. The vulture, the rat at the rehab center, the skua and so on. This last delivery gives us the identity of the person expected to act as an actual negotiator, I believe."

This note had been addressed to URUSAR BASTILLE—sometimes it had been to Haru, sometimes to Tally. He understood why this one specifically had come to him, though.

Time to start making concessions, the note had read. *Time to come to heel if you want to keep your children safe. You will begin the proceedings for the sale of key Bastille-owned properties, beginning with 2304 Harris Street, 2320 Harris Street, and 4502 Harris Street. You will be contacted by a go-between, someone who has no knowledge of our whereabouts. Be ready.*

"I can't get my head around it." Tally rubbed at the ache in his chest. "We've known Barry's family...well, always. Our families have both lived here for generations. I know we don't agree. On so much. But how could he be involved in *thissss*? Harming children?"

Haru's hand tightened. "Your heart is not like Hastings-san's. Yours is too concerned for others."

"Too naïve," Tally whispered.

"No." Something fierce had crept into his otter's voice. "There is naïve and there is not being able to understand something monstrous. They are different."

"They are." Firebaugh gave them a slow nod. "But we can't jump to conclusions about how far Hastings is involved. He could have just been a messenger, not knowing what he was delivering."

Tally raised an eyebrow at the wolf.

"Fine. I don't believe it either, but instinct is only a directional pointer to evidence, not the other way around."

Somewhere Tally found the patience to ask again. "What do we do?"

"My advice?" Agent Firebaugh edged forward to lean his arms on Tally's desk. "Get paperwork started for the property sales. Meet with this negotiator, whoever it ends up being."

"Anything to get our joeys home." Tally swallowed hard, defeat rising up to devour him.

"I'm not saying you have to sell. But negotiations buy us time we might not have if you refused outright."

Haru stroked a hand through Tally's hair. "You are saying to stall them."

"I am. As much as you can, believably. We'll get another player from the meeting, someone to watch and follow, and the more they talk, the more something might slip." Firebaugh's eyes held a plea. "Can you do it, Urusar Bastille? Play the line out? String them along?"

Tally's wheels began to turn. This was what he did, wasn't it? All the bits and pieces of the deal, keeping everything in play. "I...yes. I think... There are things I can do." He furrowed his brow. "Things that would have to be done. Those properties aren't simple transfers."

"Even better." Firebaugh rose and carefully collected the latest note with its envelope.

A little sound of distress came from Haru when the agent gathered up the bits of fur as well. "Could we not... Could you leave those?"

Firebaugh's voice took on its gentlest tones. "I can't, Uruma Bastille. I'm sorry, but I can't leave evidence."

Chapter Thirteen

Going Home

The contractors had finished — construction, cleaning, plumbing, electrical. It was time. Tally had done a walk-through first to check the work, traversing the floors in a strange, gray haze. The basement at the main house had been gutted. No trace remained of the former rooms, spaces that could only hold memories of violence and anguish for all of them.

It should have been better. He *willed* it to be better. The bland white walls, the bare gray floors, the lack of separate rooms. It was just a basement now. Not a playroom. Not a studio. Just a basement. Even telling himself these things, he'd stood in the center of that echoing, empty space and cried. He could have filled the basement with concrete and still the scurry of small paws and the squeaks and sneezes of playing joeys would have reached him. It was as if his grief always hovered at flood stage, waiting. He could be professional, could hold normal conversations, even smile when he had to, but any piece of memory dropped in that water sent it surging over the banks.

They'd delayed moving back in until they could bring Lahi home at the same time. It wasn't because he was dreading it. This was his childhood home, for all the Gods' sakes, a place he loved. Yes…it was because he was dreading it.

They stood on the drive, Tally and Haru with Lahi between them and Sammy beside them, staring up at the house.

"Everyone ready?" Tally murmured. Stupid thing to say. They were just going home. This was a good thing.

No one answered, showing he was constantly surrounded by smart people. They helped Lahi up the front steps and Tally opened the door with a little ceremonial wave.

"Everything's pretty much back to normal." Tally even tried for a little smile. "I can't wait to show you the new studio out back, Lahi. Soundproofed, state of the art. I think you'll love it."

"But I have to trudge out there in the snow?" Lahi gave him a hard side-eye.

"Nope, there's a hallway so you don't even need shoes if you don't want." Tally gave her a one-armed hug and resisted the urge to pull his baby sister into his arms. Flood surge imminent if he did.

A quick glance at Haru showed a similar struggle. They had on their blank face, but Tally knew by now under what conditions the mask went up like a wall. He — *they* — let a crack show through by holding a hand against their neck, right where the stones from the necklace lay. Holding it together, both of them were doing their best.

"Good choice on the floor, Tal," Sammy said as she slipped off her shoes and did an experimental slide across the new tiles, a shiny, non-porous ceramic that had replaced the previous beige, unsealed stone. It hadn't been a *necessary* renovation, but after all the tromping in and out of various agencies and their snow and mud-covered boots, the front hall floor had started to look shabby.

Just another reminder he had wanted to erase.

"There are little renovations here and there. Things that needed to be done. Better insulation at the front of the house. That sort of thing." Tally led them down the hall and around the main staircase to something definitely new. "Some things are because I do listen. Haru, my love, your elevator."

Haru came forward and ran a hand over the doors with a little squeak. Happy? No, they hadn't made it to happy, but interested at least. "Is it safe?"

"Yes…" Tally asked in confusion. "In what way?"

"For otters. For pups. For snakes." Haru turned to regard Tally sternly. Jasper pushed out of Haru's bun. So that was where he'd been hiding. "For pixies?"

"Ah. I see." Tally pointed to the double set of call buttons, one at human height and one considerably lower. "There are controls for people not humaned. And an electric eye field across the door openings so they won't close on anyone, not matter what size. Should be safe for all of our residents."

Lahi huffed. "Good. I won't have to do stairs. Should've put this in when Hal broke his leg, though."

"None of us were smart enough to think of it," Tally said with a hint of a smile for his husband as he pushed the Up call button. "Our Haru was, though. All right, everyone in. Let's try this out."

Haru frowned hard at the elevator doors. "All of us?"

"It's rated for two thousand pounds." Tally reached across and patted Sammy on the shoulder. "Even with Sam, we still should be well under."

"Hey! No picking on the preggo otter!" Sammy turned a dark scowl his way. "I haven't gained *that* much."

That Sammy was gaining weight now, even slowly, was a relief. The worst of the nausea appeared to have passed and her appetite had roared back with a vengeance. Once they'd all crowded into the car, the elevator doors closed with a soft *huush*. Quiet, as Tally had specified.

"Padding." Haru interrupted Tally's small, satisfied moment.

"Um?"

"There should be padding along the bottom. For bouncy, slidy pups."

"Oh." Tally's tiny bit of smug deflated to a sad pancake. "Of course. I'll take care of it."

Haru darted a sidelong look at him and unexpectedly took his hand. "It is an excellent addition. Thank you."

Once on the second floor, Tally herded his little group to Haru's rooms where the last of the big surprises waited. He hurried them through the bedroom, not wanting to look at the bed where they'd slept with the joeys so many nights, and into the bathroom. With a sweep of his arm, he ushered Haru in without a word.

His little bubble of satisfaction returned as Haru stared, wide-eyed, and actually let out a tiny squeak. Squeak was good, right? One glance at his otter and yes, confirmed. Squeak was good.

He'd taken some square footage from the bedroom next door to expand the bathroom. There was now a separate, multi-head shower stall for when Haru just wanted to get clean. The central attraction, the showpiece, was the tub—the original tub had been removed and replaced by a custom installation, more of a small pool than a tub. Tally had made sure to arrange Haru's stones at the bottom of the tub, four feet deep, lined with colorful tiles. In a basket beside the tub were more river stones of various sizes and colors for additional arranging whenever Haru pleased. On one side of the pool, a slide sat ready for otter tummy-slide entry.

The perfect place for ottering, especially in the winter when the lake was frozen over.

Haru was on their hands and knees at the edge of the empty tub, leaning perilously over the edge. Not a long fall, but Tally still snagged the back of their cardigan to keep them from pitching in headfirst. "Oooh. Pretty stones."

"Do you... Would you want to otter and try it out?"

For a moment Haru's eyes shone with that thought then their gaze flattened out again. "Later, my Argaze. I have... We have guests coming." They stood, fluid and graceful, and leaned in to kiss Tally's cheek. "Thank you. This, all of this, was very thoughtful."

But it'll just be family and a few friends! I can handle things! You should... None of that made it from Tally's brain to his mouth, though. The last thing he wanted was to injure Haru's pride, absolutely the wrong moment for that. "Of course. I'll, ah, take Lahi to see her new studio and meet you in the kitchen in a few."

Lahi made all the appropriate enthusiastic noises about her new studio, and only a few minor criticisms that she would probably fix herself. At the end of the tour, she was obviously at the end of her reserves, too, and Tally installed her on the sofa in the den for a few minutes of quiet rest. It didn't last long. Nan and Addy arrived, demanding to see her, Mom and Dad hard on their heels. Gun came next, subdued and bereft of snark, with Pete and Lily flanking him like his own prairie dog honor guard.

"He okay?" Tally whispered in Pete's ear as they hugged hello.

"Yeah. I think so. I think he might have made decisions? Just a guess."

He let that go and shooed them all toward the kitchen so he could meet Marnie coming up the drive.

No small talk, not Marnie, no platitudes. She gripped his arms and gazed up into his face. "All right, Tal?"

"Managing." Tally even said it without a hitch in his voice. Managing. Because he had no choice. "I am. And...we're home, at least." He stopped and swallowed hard. "Some of us."

"I know, Tal. I'm sorry. Doesn't help. But I am."

He pulled her into a fierce hug and managed to keep the flood from rising too far. "Was I horrible in my last life, do you think?"

"Don't even, Bastille. Don't you dare," she whispered, sharp as her claws. "Because you stand against evil men, you get attacked. Don't read more into it than that."

"I just feel so battered. It's hard not to." Tally dutifully turned at her urging, though, and walked her into the house.

The guests crowded around the food, chatting, catching up. When Hal and Che bounced in a few minutes later, the house seemed almost...normal. Guilt washed over Tally for that thought. It wasn't normal. It wasn't right. It never would be right again, never quite. Even if... No. When. When they got the twins back. He would do everything in his power to make the best home for them, for the pups, for Haru, but it would never be the same.

He found himself drifting away from the comfort of family, wandering to the front parlor for some quiet, and wasn't at all shocked to find Gun there, brooding.

The sofa creaked as he flung himself down next to his friend. He patted Gun's knee. "Something you need to tell me?"

Gun's mouth twisted in an uncomfortable grimace. "I'm staying, Tal."

"I know you are for a... Oh. Staying? Moving back in? As in coming home?"

"Yeah." Gunther nodded slowly, twisting his glass of water in his hands. "I talked to Mom. She agrees. Things aren't *solved* there, but like she says, it's stable for now."

"How stable? Gun..."

"Pike realizes he can't go against the clan's charter without a riot on his hands. Mom stays on the council and he's acknowledged she should. Stable for now. Until Sage's old enough. There'll be trouble later."

Tally wished it weren't so, but Gun's cousin would most likely challenge when he reached his majority. It couldn't end well. "You're here then?"

"I'm here. You're my Urusar. This is my clan. Mom's a short flight away if she really needs me. Right now, I think you need me here, Tal."

"I do. Gods." Tally ran both hands over his face. "If you're sure, I'm grateful."

"I'm sure. Mom's sure. You're stuck with me."

They bumped shoulders and Tally managed a muted chuckle. "More like I'm less exposed with you here. My Lancelot."

"Oh, hell no." Gun reared back in mock horror. "We all know how that turned out."

"Gawain, then. Ever faithful."

"That's better. Whatever you need, Tal. You just point and I'll go."

Tally nodded, still staring at his hands as they leaned together in companionable silence. Small favors. One piece of his life was back where it belonged.

* * * *

"I'd rather you stayed here. Safe." Tally tried not to huff as Haru straightened his already straight tie. "It would make me feel better."

Haru gave a spare shake of their head. "No. We are a united front, you have said. We will present this front to these...*lijun* in all things."

"We're still not sure..."

"But we are nearly so. They want things, my Argaze. Whoever will be at this meeting, they want things."

Tally nodded, translating that as *if they wanted to harm either one of us, they would've tried it by now.* He gave another sharp nod to Gun and Marnie, who would be watching the house while he and Haru were gone, then found himself stopped in the garage by Agent Firebaugh.

"I'd rather have you go in wired, but I understand why not." Firebaugh held up both hands in a placating gesture. Depending on the lijun types present, it was conceivable that one of their enemies might scent or hear something off if they were wired. "Expect a full debrief afterward. Don't try to lead them. Don't try for direct information. Not yet. Let's see what the game is before we start bending rules."

The meeting would be in a room at the community center in town, one that anyone could schedule, provided they didn't need an elaborate tech setup. Neutral ground, had been the admonition from the note writer, nothing Bastille owned. One brief peck on the lips from Haru, reassurance, luck, Tally wasn't certain, and their mask fell back in place, almost with an audible clang. Mask? Haru had full-body armor against the outside world in gestures and posture, every small movement down to the artful tilt of his — *their* — head.

Absolutely breathtaking and heartbreaking to watch.

At the community center, Haru tucked their hand into the crook of Tally's elbow, walking in close proximity but exuding aloof independence. Tally had hoped to arrive first in a need to choose his own ground. Familiar voices already filtered out from the meeting room, though, not the most auspicious beginning, and even though his practical side had insisted that was likely, Tally had still held out hope that this meeting would be with strangers.

"Barry. Dan." At least he'd managed to keep his tone dry and even. "I wish I could be surprised."

Dan rose, apparently caught between aggression and professional greeting. "Just here to do business, Bastille."

"Don't shoot the messenger." Barry had the audacity to grin, all smug satisfaction.

"Hmm. Not my weapon of choice, generally." Tally took the seat opposite Dan, letting Haru choose their ground. They took the head of the table, nearest the door. An interesting symbolic gesture that could've been interpreted as *blocking the exit* or *watching your every move.*

In the chill silence that followed, Tally opened his briefcase and began setting paperwork on the table. "Gentlemen, I think you know what's at stake. This means I have no choice but to work with you on this, but please understand that these aren't simple property transfers."

"In what way?" Dan glowered, first at Tally, then at Barry, whose smile evaporated as he edged away.

"Because of the nature of the Harris Street project, many of the properties involved have severe deed restrictions." Tally handed over a copy of aforesaid restrictions to each of his traitorous council members, nice, fat, multi-page legal documents. He let them leaf through for a moment, his hands folded atop the table, the picture of patience. Hard to stop the stray vindictive thoughts, though, especially when Barry licked his thumb to turn the page. *Too bad we couldn't impregnate the paper with something. A nice case of listeria, maybe. Firebaugh probably wouldn't have approved that.*

"What *is* all this?" Dan snorted, his face growing redder as Barry paled.

"As Urusar Bastille stated, deed restrictions, O'Rourke-san." Haru's answer was soft and polite, their posture a model of serene, proper decorum. "From the city, concerning the types of renters permitted in each property. There is much overlap, but each property has unique strictures."

"This is outrageous." Dan leafed through with ever-increasing speed.

Tally spread his hands in a conciliatory fashion. "I'm terribly sorry this is a surprise. The city's plans have been available for public —"

Dan ignored him to turn on Barry, thrusting his copy in the boar's face. "Did you know about this?"

"I didn't... I..." Barry stumbled in the face of bull moose rage. "It was just supposed to be guidance!"

"You assumed it was." A vein stood out on Dan's forehead.

"Also, in the interest of disclosure" — Tally leaned forward, offering his most serious, sympathetic expression — "the demand that I sell for a token sum is something I can't legally honor. For tax purposes, the property must at least be sold for the current assessment value. You'll find that in the deed as well."

"*Waste* of time!" Dan snarled and surged to his feet, stuffing the documents in his own briefcase. "My attorneys will be combing through these."

Barry stumbled to his feet, his hand on Dan's sleeve. "But we're supposed to —"

"*No!*" The snarl became a floor-shaking bellow. "Don't even *think* about pressuring me into signing now. Next time, you come to me beforehand since you can't bother to prepare."

Dan stomped off, a cowed and anxious Barry hurrying after him.

When the front door to the community center slammed open and shut again, Haru cleared their throat. "You did not say *full disclosure*, my Argaze."

Tally didn't look up from repacking his briefcase. "You're right. I didn't."

A soft "Ha" escaped Haru before they said, "It did not bring our girls back."

"No." Tally's hands froze and he had to swallow hard. "Not yet. But it did give us an interesting piece of information."

"Ah, my clever Argaze caught that." Haru nodded, eyes narrowed. "Yes. It did."

Chapter Fourteen

Moves and Counter-Moves

Each note, each chord struck helped soothe the sting. Logically, Haru knew it would take time to get the girls back. Convincing their heart was another matter. They knew Agent Firebaugh was working, following trails, keeping tabs on Councilmen Hastings and O'Rourke. Everyone hoped they somehow would lead them back to Kaul-san.

But that hope was already dwindling. There was resignation in the agent's eyes. He tried to hide it, but Haru *knew* that look. It was all too achingly familiar. If a trained FBI agent was having doubts, then what did that mean?

A wrong note twinged, the *biwa* making a mournful noise. Haru shook off the thought, tried to focus on the positive. It would be all too easy to fall back into a depressive episode. Humiliation over how they had handled the attack and kidnapping was still close, too raw. As Uruma, Haru should've handled it better. Poor Eberhardt-san had lost so much more than the Bastilles. *As of now.* Circumstances could always change.

It hurt. Tore at their heart they couldn't even give the girls and Jackson a proper farewell yet. The fact their broken bodies were being held as *evidence* and not returned complicated matters. Yes, to the humans they were animals. But they weren't, and they deserved a proper lijun funeral.

Another wrong note. Jasper opened one eye and looked at them, sleep-riddled confusion showing. Poor pixie. Haru shook themself again and began to play, lulling their pixie back to sleep. Hopefully he'd be able to stay asleep for more than a few hours. No nightmares for a while. Good thoughts. Happy thoughts. An image of the girls and Jackson playing in the lake flashed in Haru's mind. A seriously wrong note clanged throughout the studio. Jasper glared then picked up their tiny pillow and fluttered haphazardly out of the studio.

"Sorry," Haru called after him and held the *biwa* tighter. No, they'd get the girls back, they'd have to. Haru wouldn't, couldn't, think of not getting their girls back.

Tally's property sale would take time, give the clan and Agent Firebaugh space to figure out where the girls were, what the danger might be. Would a rescue be possible?

Handing anything over to those…those…*murderers*… curdled Haru's blood. But they would give anything to get Livy and Melia back. Anything. Which would be why Tally was handling the negotiations. Haru breathed in, deciding on a different song. They had to trust their Argaze. Had to.

Negotiations, business dealings, money. Tally lived and breathed the stuff. And he was extremely adept at his job.

The melody of Lahi's song came to mind, and Haru automatically began plucking out the notes with their *bachi*. The sound was different, but then it would be. Guitars and *biwa* were inherently different instruments, despite the similarities, especially in how they were played.

Once they found the correct tempo and equivalent notes, Haru began to play in earnest, humming. The lyrics weren't finished, but Lahi was closer than she had been in rehabilitation. Playing her song for the pups quieted the noise in Haru's heart and head. They let go and tried to find the notes that would complement hers instead of fight with them.

Something cool touched their leg, rubbing against it. Haru opened their eyes, surprised they had closed them. They had been so intent on the song they must've. Oh, dear Gods. Snake! Their movements with the *bachi* stumbled, but then their brain engaged again.

"Lahi," Haru said. They carefully placed the *biwa* and *bachi* on the stand. Last thing they wanted was to startle the extremely large snake in their midst. "Are you... Are you well?"

She had coiled around Haru, holding them, *squeezing*.

Haru expected panic, for their otter to have their back up, but there wasn't any sense of overwhelming fear. Only sadness and affection. When had that changed? When had their otter decided the Bastille uktenas were *safe*? *Family*?

Even when Tally gave the joeys snakeback rides, Haru had needed to push back the fear the humongous predator instilled. They had learned over time the girls and Jackson were safe, but they had to make sure, just in case. Watching all of them play was something Haru had to do.

That feeling was gone.

Lahi lifted her head, her dark gaze burrowing into Haru's heart.

"Maybe when a more dangerous predator came along," they whispered.

Suddenly Lahi lurched, startling Haru, but it wasn't a strike. It was more a gagging motion. It came again.

Could snake's cry? Lahi's mouth opened with the next lurch.

"Oh dear." Haru stood, gathering Lahi's coils, and headed for the bathroom. A shudder ran through her body, the lean muscles jerking under their fingertips. "Hold on. Hold on, little longer."

They threw the toilet lid up just in time.

A horrible gurgling noise came up, followed by whatever Lahi had eaten for lunch. Some kind of soup or stew. The doctors were still limiting what she could eat because of the wound. Smelled awful, but what puke didn't?

"It is okay," they murmured. "Everything is going to be okay. You are okay. Throw everything up. Do not fight it."

Lahi shuddered again, the tremor hard, going head to tail.

More foul-smelling liquid came up.

They stroked down her strong back. Her tail curled around their arm and she leaned heavily against them.

"No more?"

Shake, then Lahi's snout pushed against Haru's neck. They felt the flick of her tongue scenting them. The heavy weight of her center filled their lap. Haru held her close, murmuring encouragement and hoping she wouldn't hack anything else up on them. She must've heard the music. Haru had left the doors open, feeling weird about being cut off from the rest of the house. If something happened, they wouldn't be able to hear it.

Last thing Haru wanted was for Lahi to feel upset because of the song. It was *hers*, and Haru found comfort in the snippets they'd listened to.

"It is a beautiful song. It...it captures our lives. When you finish it, can I be the first to listen?"

Haru found their lap full of a humaned, crying Lahi. "It's my fault." She breathed in, the sound a snotty half-sob. "If-if-if I uktena'd, they-they— I knew something was off when that bastard showed up."

"If you had snaked out, then we might have lost you too." Haru pressed her against them. Nose. Nose. Kiss. Kiss. "Your belly is more vulnerable as an uktena."

"But I have..." Sob. Sniff. Lahi rubbed her nose against their cardigan. "I have my poison."

"You cannot think about what you could not do." Haru stroked her long, flowing hair. Nose. Nose. "You nearly died trying to protect what is ours. Never apologize for Kaul-san's actions. Never."

Lahi lifted her head. The big, brown pools of her eyes reflected so much pain. Yes, everyone had their bad days. Not just Haru. She needed them. Haru gathered her up and stood, despite her protests of being too big.

"I am not exactly small, my dearest sister. Your brother just makes everyone look tiny."

She gave an ungraceful snort. "He so does."

"It is rather...disconcerting."

"Does... Does it bother you?"

Haru gathered a crocheted blanket up and wrapped Lahi in it. They pulled her back into their lap. "What bother me?"

"Tally being...so *Tally*?"

Heh. Yes. That actually did explain *it*. "It is unusual for someone to be bigger than me. I am rather tall for my country."

"Mmm."

"But it has positives."

"Like what?"

"Tally does not seem to mind my appearance. Not all prospective matches were happy about a taller Satislit." Some had been downright furious. "They had certain *expectations*." Some had wanted a more masculine Satislit. Something Haru couldn't deliver despite their size. "It was complicated."

Not to mention Haru had in no way wanted a match. Ever.

Yet here they were. Matched with a snake. His sister — naked — in their lap, crying over pups Haru had campaigned to get adopted. Not that Tally had objected. Life had certainly gone topsy-turvy in the last half-year or so.

Back home they'd be getting their students ready for finals. Waiting on test scores and acceptances from the universities. Planning for the cherry blossom viewings.

A thud echoed through their heart. Jackson would never see the blossoms. Their little family would never be able to go together — whole — and have a viewing. They took a sharp breath in. Now wasn't the time.

Lahi had tilted her head back. She was watching them through knowing eyes.

Nose. Nose. Kiss. Kiss.

Sneaky snake. She really was getting otterisms down.

The two of them cuddled together in silence. The outpouring of her emotions too heavy for any more talk. Taking comfort in holding her, reassuring her, helped Haru too. It gave them someone to focus on besides themself. The lull eventually waned. The heat from her body began to make Haru sleepy. They yawned, jostling Lahi.

"Hey, Haru?"

"Hmmm?"

"Can I ask a question?"

"Of course."

Lahi situated her head against their shoulder, burrowing in the blanket. "Tally said you're enby."

"I am...what?"

"Non-binary, that you prefer they and stuff for your pronouns."

"Oh, I see. I think it depends on how you define it?" Haru rubbed their chin against her head. Like brother, like sister, distracting themselves from all the hurtful things and focusing on Haru. They didn't necessarily like it, but they understood. "I have considered myself agender for a long time. Since I learned about it in high school."

Lahi rubbed her head against their shoulder. "So you *are* agender."

"Yes. I...never felt like I was like the boys, nor did I feel like I was one of the girls."

"Do you think it was because of how you were raised?"

It wasn't a surprising question. Many people made the assumption because of what Satislit were — bridesons. "No, they let us define ourselves. It is actually one of the few things that they do. Prospective partners have different likes and dislikes, after all. If your Satislit is pretending to be something they are not, it can have rather *unfortunate* outcomes. Someone might prefer a more masculine Satislit. Another may want the most feminine partner they could find... I never saw myself in the others."

"Do you not like talking about this?"

Haru glanced down at the concern in her voice. "No. I do not mind. In fact, I was surprised your brother did not ask at the Imsi Tamgradat. It is usually the first question asked. I tended to disappoint because of my presentation and size. Neither one nor the other. Your brother was the only match I met that didn't care to ask."

"Maybe to Tally it didn't matter?"

"Perhaps." Nose. Nose.

"Do— Hmmm. Maybe not the best question." Her nose scrunched.

"Go ahead."

Lahi considered Haru for a moment then shrugged underneath the blanket. "It's personal."

"And that has stopped you before?" They chuckled.

"What do you think of your cock?"

They blinked then blinked again. Lahi's dark russet pinked. They understood what she was trying to ask.

"I shouldn't have asked. Sorry," she mumbled and buried her head.

"No, it is... I understand the curiosity. I would not ask someone else, if I were you. Not unless they say otherwise."

The blanket jostled so they took that as agreement.

"As for *me*, I struggle with... I struggled. Mainly with the terminology."

Lahi's head poked back out, the blanket falling down around her shoulders. "Terminology?"

"It is not the same for everyone. Just like every woman's experience is not yours."

A flash of understanding lit in her eyes.

"For me, the language for our genitalia is divided into male or female words. Since I do not see myself as someone who is either, to have my body defined by someone else's vocabulary caused me to struggle with body issues."

"How so?" She began petting, trying to soothe them.

It was a difficult subject. One Haru struggled to make clear to others.

They pulled her close. "Cock, dick—both masculine descriptors—and those can create a dysphoria when they got applied to me. Breasts are considered feminine. But I have a chest. I have nipples. They are not female. I had to fight for the words that make me comfortable with my body. To be able to keep my sense of self. I have always been told what words were appropriate or not, and they were not what made me feel good about myself or how I saw me."

"That had to be hard." Lahi nuzzled under their jaw.

"It can be, especially when people who do not understand, who are binary, try to force their terms on me."

"Do people do that?"

If only they wouldn't. "Every day."

"I'm sorry."

They shrugged. "It is a fact of life. I may not see myself the way the world does, but there will always be those who try to apply their expectations, their terms, to my life. But now I have my own language to rely on."

"Have you talked to Tally about this?" Instead of looking admonishing, she actually seemed concerned on Haru's behalf, the petting faster.

"No."

"You should. He would want to know. It would... I mean, you should let him know what your terminology preferences are. Oh Gods, have you been having sex all this time with him using cock and dick?"

She looked absolutely affronted on Haru's behalf, though a tiny piece of them went on high alert. Tally and them had not been having any sex.

"Um, I do try. Making up stuff, having fun with the terminology helps me deal. Though not everyone appreciates it. But some lovers have. It is nice when you can have fun together in bed." Not be all serious. *Play. Otters do enjoy their play.* It helped them relax and enjoy what was happening. "Why does everyone have to take sex so serious all the time?" Lahi chuckled and nodded her agreement. The ground felt more level, less shaky after their talk. It had been entirely too focused on Haru, though. "Who doesn't like a humongous snake to snack on in bed?"

For a minute, Lahi looked scandalized. Then a smile formed on her pretty lips. "You did not! Tell me you did not call my brother's dick a *snake*. Wait, what do you use? That was horrible punning."

They shrugged. Lahi snorted then started to giggle.

"Please, when you do, take a picture. Exclude all the bits I don't need to see, but I want to see his face when you do." She began to laugh in earnest. "Poor Tally. Oh Gods. That's good. He-he."

"I will do my best to not send you a penis picture from your brother."

Now Lahi really went off, laughing and protesting in turns. When she finally settled, she was relaxed and warm against them. They petted down her side. So trusting. So at ease. Would Haru ever feel this way? Could Haru ever feel this way with Tally?

Lahi tugged at their cardigan and frowned. They could see the question forming before she even asked.

"Do you have a preference? I mean, you know, as to which way you present yourself."

"Ah, yes, I prefer to look good."

Lahi laughed, which had been the purpose, but she insisted on the question again.

"I prefer my *yukata* over everything else. They are the most genderless out of everything. Though I suppose I favor styles that the Westerns would consider more feminine. But I am the most comfortable with my *yukatas* and *kimonos*."

"You are?" Lahi sounded surprised and pulled away from them. "They're just so...so pretty like the rest of you."

"I suppose you consider my makeup feminine too?"

She nodded. Yes, Haru knew Westerners felt that way. Asian countries weren't so limited, but it shouldn't have been unexpected. Manliness had a definite style and concept here in America. Haru did not fit that image even a little. Not even when they wore pants. Still, it was a blow. Haru did not see eyeshadow or lipstick as inherently woman. Why should the women get all the fun? They liked looking nice. How makeup accentuated their features.

Haru nosed her. "I have to be in a certain mood to wear pants or skirts. I do have some lovely skirts, but they have not felt appropriate for here. They and the pants can mess with my sense of self. I cannot always be the rainbow-suspenders-wearing otter."

She snapped said suspenders. "Just some of the time."

"Yes, well..." The answer was a bit more complicated than that, but Haru wasn't about to correct her.

"I've noticed you've been wearing pants more often."

Because Tally looked so happy when they did, but Haru wasn't going to say that. "It is winter."

"It is." Lahi frowned but didn't call Haru on their lackluster answer. "Did that stop you back in Japan?"

"No."

Lahi pulled on the suspenders again, but thankfully did not snap them. "I haven't seen you wear these in a long time."

"I misplaced them after an outing." More like hid them from their fuming mother after the cake tasting for the wedding. "Then things were so busy with the pups."

That got a nod of understanding. Which meant Haru didn't have to explain they knew how much the suspenders made Tally smile. Why, they didn't know, but it seemed only right they dressed in a way that pleased their Argaze. He was doing so much to get the girls back, had forgiven so much. Haru felt they should try harder to be what made Tally happy.

"But seriously, Haru. Talk to Tally."

Nose. Nose. Kiss. Kiss.

She tugged on their sleeve. "You deserve to be comfortable too."

"Thank you."

Lahi side-eyed them and frowned. "Why have you been wearing all pants lately?"

"Oh, um —" It was like a dog with a bone. Why was she being so insistent?

Probably easier to think of Haru's situation rather than anything else.

"It is fine. Your brother seems pleased with my appearance."

Wrong words. Haru knew the moment they left their mouth. Lahi turned in their lap to face them. "You know Tally thought they were forcing you, right?"

Haru jerked back, startled. They had not thought Tally discussed as much with his family. Friends, yes. Family, no.

"The way you dressed," she continued. "He said you were surprised you'd get to wear pants. Were they? Forcing you, that is."

"Oh, no, not entirely. Though my Argaze gets say as to what I wear—if he wants," they amended quickly. "The Akaike clan seemed to think he was most pleased with my appearance in the *yukata*, so that was *encouraged*." More like regulated beyond belief. "I did not mind. But I do like having the choice."

"Your old clan sounds like it's full of assholes."

Haru barked out a laugh then quickly pushed it away. "Every clan has problems."

There, that was diplomatic. Lahi rolled her eyes. Wasn't convincing, but at least it was diplomatic.

Lahi snorted again and draped against them. "I guess we do, but again, seriously, talk to Tally about what you like to wear and the sex stuff."

Talk about a bone of contention.

"Heeeeey, Haru, Lahi." A cough drew their attention to the door. Tally stood in it, filling the doorway easily. Sammy stood behind him. They jostled together as they came through. "You know, if I keep finding you in women's laps, or naked women in yours, I might start developing a complex."

Everyone laughed, except the laughter didn't reach Tally's eyes. Haru noticed the strain in them. The way the smile was a little too forced. Not that he was wrong exactly. Lahi must've picked up on something because she quickly explained.

"I heard Haru playing my song for the pups... I snaked."

Sammy lifted a pile of clothes. "Which would be why these were in the hall?"

"Yeah, sorry, but I feel better now." Nose. Nose. Kiss. Kiss. "Thanks, Haru."

"Any time."

Tally's gaze slid between Lahi and Haru. "What was this we were hearing about clothes?"

"Nothing," they answered quickly, ignoring Lahi's put-out sigh. "Just that I enjoy seeing your eyes when I wear something you like."

"Ooh, smooth," Lahi teased. They nearly dumped her off their lap.

Tally shook his head and tossed Lahi's shirt, sweater and pants on top of the two of them. "Get changed, before I really do start developing a complex about Haru and naked women."

She threw off the blanket and grabbed the clothing. "All right, all right, but it's not like I do anything for Haru. They have you, after all."

"I prefer women." *Crap.* That had tumbled right out, didn't it?

The room froze for a split second before Lahi gave a nervous laugh. "Lily wasn't yanking my chain?"

"Ah, no, Misaki-san probably told her."

Tally yelped, "Misaki?" Then he cleared his throat. "Why would Misaki tell Lily you're — you're — "

"Bisexual with a preference for women?"

Tally gave a curt nod.

"Probably because she is too. Well, she is demi, and I think she has been dating Lily," they answered, refusing to look up.

"You *think* she's dating Lily?" Tally asked. Oh dear, his eyes were wide, almost panicky.

"She is dating Lily. What? It is not like Lily can get her pregnant, my Argaze."

There was complete silence for about ten seconds before Sammy and Lahi burst out laughing with Tally scowling. "That's not what I was worried about."

Lahi ignored Tally and posed for Haru. "Are you saying if I met you first, I would've had a chance?"

"You are beautiful," they answered.

Tally hissed and Sammy slapped his arm. "Don't get jealous over your sister. You know Haru doesn't think of her like that." But there was also a barely heard 'probably' on the tail end of that. "Stop hissing."

"No, no. I would have admired you for sure, but I am Satislit. I always knew I would end up with a man one way or another."

The bright smile Lahi wore faded a bit.

Haru gave an uncomfortable shrug. "My clan would have never let a progressive clan with a female Urusar marry me."

"But you have Tally," she answered quickly. "You're Em'halafi. I guess it worked out."

Haru met Tally's gaze. "Yes, as you say."

Tally gave Lahi a brotherly shove toward the bathroom. "Get dressed."

"I'm going. I'm going. It's not like you found me wrapped around him."

"Close enough!"

"No, that was just when you were snaked," Haru agreed.

Poor Tally. His head whipped back so fast his spine popped. He was caught somewhere between furious and brotherly affection. "You let her squeeze you?"

"You do have rules about me learning good, platonic touch."

Lahi's laughter as she went to change felt good to hear, though Tally's expression was harder to read. By the time Lahi came back out, cleaned up and dressed, the room had settled into an uncomfortable silence. Haru was left pulling at the hem of their corduroys, Sammy was in a chair rubbing her swollen belly and Tally was looking at the ceiling.

All in all, it was awkward. The most uncomfortable things had been between all them since before...well, *before*.

"Don't tell me you told Haru about Hal's game?" Lahi began to braid up her hair. "You should've let Hal finish it before setting Haru lose on him and Che."

"Is this the game Hal refuses to talk to me about?"

"Oops."

Tally had one hand over his face. "Laaahiii."

Haru stood, eyeing their Argaze. "What did Hal do?"

Lahi's smile went nuclear. "He's made an app, targeted toward children. What was it Mom said?"

"Lahi, don't, please," Tally begged. "Do you want a new guitar? Is this because I didn't get you that Les Paul you wanted for your birthday?"

Of course the begging only made Haru *more* interested.

She tapped her fingers against one of the drums. "Now that you mention it..."

"*Please!*"

"I will play my *biwa* on that song you wanted me to for your new album," Haru countered.

"Any *songs* I want."

"Deal."

"You! You! How could you!" Tally backed up.

"I think Mom said, and I quote, '*It's an educational game where an otter has to collect yummy treats by solving basic puzzles before a snake catches it and eats it'*." Lahi turned toward her brother, smiling blithely. "Was that right?"

"Yeessssssss," Tally groaned out.

That bastard! "You said Hal made this?"

"It's almost done. I know he and Che were discussing contracts." Tally held out his hands. "It really is cute."

"*Cute?*"

Sammy started laughing, setting Lahi off.

"Cute?"

"The snakes don't actually eat the otters. Not anymore. Hal thought it might scare littles, so it hugs the otter until it gives the snake's eggs back."

The tidbit about the eggs threw Haru off. "Eggs?"

"Yesssss, it's protecting its nest. It can be two player where the otter and snake play against each other. The snake has eggs and the otter has pups." But Tally was no longer trying to placate Haru. His lips were twitching.

"And they 'hug' it out?"

"Hal said your table arrangement for that dinner was the inspiration."

"He is a *dead* snake."

Now Tally was laughing too. "Just let me make sure I have my phone out when you go after him."

"I cannot believe that sneaky bastard." Haru growled out and started pacing. What they still couldn't get over was the emphasis on the egg part, though. An unsettling thought had caught on and wouldn't let go.

It was Misaki's fault really. Or rather, all the nure-onna in the Akaike clan. The snakes had always been so private about their pregnancies and births, and she refused to talk about it whenever the two of them did talk. "Do...do you *birth* eggs? I mean, Misaki? The females? Is she laying eggs? Is that actually a thing?"

The room erupted as Haru poked Tally in the chest.

"Do we need to buy incubators?"

The howls got louder.

"I did not think I would need to sit on eggs. I will crush them."

Tally was leaning against the wall, trying to catch his breath.

"Eggs. We are going to have eggs. Not pups. Eggs."

Lahi grabbed their hand. "No, Haru. Gods *no*. Even snakes like us have live births. Snakelets."

* * * *

The picture did not make Haru feel any better. No, not one iota. Yes, the delivery of clothes had gotten to the girls, but there were bags under their eyes, their cheeks were slightly sunken and their eyes were red. Well, Livy's were. She was sitting in her dress, pouting, little lip out dramatically. They had tried to focus on her but hadn't managed to keep Melia opossumed and peeing on the dress out of the picture.

That's my little girl. She must be trying to escape. Melia was the best hider as opossum. Tally's squinty side-eye toward their troublemaker daughter meant he had probably come to the same conclusion.

Agent Firebaugh glanced between the two of them. "Something you want to tell the class?"

Haru tapped the photo. "Our Melia is trying to escape."

"You're joking…"

"You do not know my girl."

"I see." The wolf's eyes narrowed at the picture. "You think she'll find a way out?"

"If anyone can do it, Melia can," Haru replied, skimming their hand over the photo.

Tally pressed against them and gave a nod. "None of the background looks familiar, I'm afraid."

"It was a long shot but worth a try."

"Yes."

Agent Firebaugh sighed as he sat back. His suit was rumpled and his hair wasn't quite as coiffed as it normally was. Exhaustion rolled off him in waves. They nudged Tally with an elbow and gestured with a chin. When their Argaze glanced at the wolf again, he frowned.

"Did you stay up all night blowing up the images?"

"Hm? Oh, yes, but it wasn't me. I was tailing Councilman Hastings. Unfortunately, I lost him, but rest assured, Urusar Bastille, this case is very much a priority." Agent Firebaugh straightened in his chair, putting a smile back in place. "We're doing everything we can to find your girls."

"You're also dead on your feet," Tally responded.

Haru wriggled out of Tally's arms and moved over to the wolf. "How about a hot bath and a nap?"

"Oh, no, I couldn't."

"Yes, you can. We insist." They pulled him up. "You cannot do your job properly if you are about to fall asleep in the chair. Last thing I want is you behind a wheel right now."

"Oh, no—"

A glare shut down his protest.

"You have the mom look down, Uruma Bastille." He chuckled and shook his head. "I suppose getting in the car would be a bad choice right now."

Tally waved the agent toward the door. "Yes. Why don't we wait in the receiving room while Haru gets your bath ready? We have some clothes, don't we?"

"Of course, my Argaze."

As Tally led Agent Firebaugh out of his office, Haru noticed a discreet look in their direction. What was that for? They shook themself and headed to the guest room. Yes, there were spare clothes in the dresser, most likely a result of Gun or one of the brothers crashing at the house often enough to warrant their need. Haru spent a good ten minutes scrubbing out the bath before rinsing and starting the water.

With a satisfied breath, they sat back and surveyed the room. Towels. Check. Toothbrushes. Check. Haru pulled out one in its packaging and left it on the counter next to some toothpaste. Yes, they had shampoo and soap. Ooh, good. New loofahs. They had just reached under the sink to pull one out when they felt a presence. Haru jerked back, hitting their head.

"Ow!" Several choice words came out as they eyed the interloper. "Agent Firebaugh."

"Sorry to, er, surprise you, Uruma Bastille."

"Not at all. I apologize if I was taking too long."

"No, no, I thought I might just crash first, but I heard the water." Agent Firebaugh lifted up one of the pairs of T-shirt and sweats they had left out.

Haru took the proffered hand. "A bath will feel better first. Get the dirt off."

A chuckle left the agent. "You sound like my mother."

"I *am* Uruma. Toothbrush and toothpaste are on the counter. I hope your bath is pleasing." They made to leave, but the wolf blocked them with an arm. A skitter of alarm went down their back but Haru held perfectly still. "Is there something else?"

"Always so helpful. So proper. Though I guess it's not surprising from an Akaike clan trained Satislit."

Ice filled Haru's chest, temporarily striking them numb.

A finger caressed the back of their hand. "They really do know how to pick their Satislits, don't they? You *do* know how beautiful you are, and you use that, don't you? They train all of you so well. It's amazing you stayed unmatched for as long as you did. The Akaike are renowned for their cool-blooded nature, despite being mammals. Must be from aligning with the nure-onna so long ago."

Hearing the words thrown at them—no, not thrown, catapulted—chilled Haru further. They had known Agent Firebaugh had looked into their backgrounds, needing to make sure it wasn't some past association that was in on the murder and kidnapping. To hear the wolf— Haru jolted and shook off his hand. Backing up, they hit the door and grabbed the knob.

Those deep brown eyes were tracking them again.

"Though I do say the lijun community was surprised they let you go to a Bastille." Agent Firebaugh offered a bow of the head. "So properly mannered, despite all the trouble you caused for your clan, so many prospective matches never happening. When did you start behaving like a good little Satislit, Haru? Why did Urusar Akaike hang onto you for so long? More importantly, why did your Urusar really give you to the Bastilles?"

They ruthlessly suppressed a shiver, meeting the agent's eyes. "I assure you, I do not know."

"Something Tally did, perhaps?"

They did not like this line of questioning. Not at all. The wolf crowded them, his breath heavy as he leaned in.

"You were a very high price to pay, my beautiful otter."

They met the wolf's eyes.

"How did he make the Akaike clan Satislit heel?"

Haru turned the knob. "I am Bastille clan, Agent Firebaugh. It would behoove you to remember that."

Running wasn't an option. They wanted. Oh, how desperately did they want to run from that calculating gaze. Years of training helped them bury the urge and they walked away—barely. Maintaining the façade of imperviousness wasn't hard. In fact, it was easy. Every bit of their Satislit training said to show no vulnerability.

What was alarming was how much they wanted Tally. To have him shield Haru from the wolf's assessing manner. They shouldn't need their Argaze so much. Depend on him. When had they decided Tally *could* protect them? The mere thought was dizzying, almost so much they nearly missed the noise from the front of the house.

Voices drifted down the hall. Unexpected voices. Was that Mindy laughing?

They rushed toward the receiving room, their *tabi* masking the thud of their feet against the floorboards. When had she been released from hospital? Though they should be glad she was visiting at all. It had to be hard for her to step back into the house. Haru still wasn't sure how they felt about being back. They hadn't gone down to the empty basement once yet. Not even to see if it had been cleaned properly. Tally hadn't pushed the topic either.

No, that door stayed firmly shut. The void a black hole in their once-happy home.

Happy? Haru nearly tripped over their feet. Had it really been *their* happy home? They stopped in the doorway, thought of Christmas, their joeys, the laughter, so many presents, and then there was the constant chaos of family. For a little while, yes. It had been happy.

But it had been a fake happiness, hadn't it? Tally hadn't known about Haru's pups yet. And Haru had feared the reaction. Was still worried, despite claims Tally wanted the pups. Only when they were born would they know it would be okay.

Maybe.

Then again, Tally had barely stopped to breathe since the murders and kidnapping. He had taken control, was the epitome of the cool and calculating businessman everyone said he was, to find their pups. Their Argaze had pulled in all kinds of favors with other lijun to help resolve their case. There was a kernel of truth to the knowledge that he would do as Haru asked.

Give them Kaul-san's head.

Shouldn't Haru fear that his Argaze would go to such lengths? Be that ruthless, despite it being Haru asking for the Punishment?

Their eyes met Tally's the moment he looked at Haru. A smile, brilliant and open, met them. It was only when the room quieted Haru realized it wasn't just Mindy talking with Tally, though it wasn't surprising. No, that wasn't right. It made perfect sense Justin was escorting

Mindy. What Haru's mind couldn't wrap around was Tyler Hastings being present. Though they kept their expression neutral, they did tilt their head to one side to observe the boy.

Considering his father's involvement, why hadn't Agent Firebaugh warned them?

The answer was obvious when they gave a sideways glance down the hall, catching the agent watching them. Their back went up automatically and their chin lifted a fraction. What game was he playing? In fact, what game was the elder Hastings playing, sending his boy to the house?

A peek down the hall saw the agent gone. Good. Haru wasn't sure how to place him. Friend or foe. Though that was his job, wasn't it?

Haru entered the now-silent room, sure they didn't show any signs of nervousness. They had been playing this kind of game a long time. They knew how to do *this*.

"Mindy." They offered her and the boys a *mokurei*. "Justin. Tyler. It is good see you."

"Uruma!" She struggled to stand, but Tally immediately helped her up. Mindy used her crutches like a pro and threw herself at them. "Uruma!"

Someone as tiny as her was an easy catch. Their arms wrapped around her instinctively. A cast was still around her left leg and a smaller one on her right forearm. Her cheeks weren't the usually rosy color Haru had grown accustomed to. Her body trembled as they pressed her closer, letting her breathe them in.

There was an apology on her lips. They could see it as easily as scent her pain. Should she have left the rehabilitation center yet? Their eyes met Tally's, who gave a small signal to wait. Fine. Not now.

"Look at you! Up and about." Haru drew her back to the couch and sat her down, tucking her next to them. The scandalized expression Tyler wore had Haru narrowing their eyes. Tally caught the look too. "Are you sure you are not pushing yourself too hard?"

Mindy shook her head and burrowed against their side.

"Your strength amazes me every time I see it."

A shudder went through her.

"You have no idea how proud of you I am."

She pressed closer with a whimper. "But—"

"Incredibly proud," they reiterated. Nose. Nose. "You are one of the strongest, kindest people I have ever met."

"Thank you, Uruma."

Mindy settled against them. The boys were watching. Justin had leaned forward and his hands twitched. No doubt he wanted to pull her close like Haru had. Tyler's expression was harder to read. It was confusing. Maybe *he* was confused.

Maybe he's spying for his father.

The room fell into silence, whatever they had been talking about seemingly forgotten. Mindy's breath evened out into a less raspy sound. The boys shared an uncomfortable look between them.

"So, what do I owe the pleasure for this visit? Or were you stopping by for a hello?"

"Oh, um." Justin shifted uncomfortably on his chair. "Councilwoman Pierce wanted us to give Urusar Bastille an update on how the last Evade and Hunt games went."

Too stunned to say anything, Haru listened as the boys rambled over each other during the report. Everyone had come back. In fact, there had been more lijun participating this time than the first games. A show of support, or maybe a worry the clan's kids needed the skills after the attack here at the house. Justin thought it was a little of both. The extra security Gunther and the Enforcers provided had set the clan's minds at ease.

Had it really been more than a month since the games? Had it? Why hadn't they gone to the second ones? Gods, their girls... Melia and Livy had been gone so long. Afraid for so long.

Justin sighed. "Farmer Erikson says we damaged some of his fencing, but I still think it was his cows."

"I can pay for it, don't worry," Tally replied.

Tyler snorted. "Of course you can."

It took a minute to find their voice. "Maybe you shouldn't just offer to pay for the fencing, my Argaze."

"It would be easier than—"

"I know, but you cannot throw money at everything and expect to fix it, my Argaze. Sometimes it only makes things worse. Sometimes it is why people fear you. Sometimes it is why they try to take what they will."

Tyler's face scrunched up and his mouth pulled hard. "Are you going to let your Satislit talk that way to you?"

Their eyes connected with Tally's. Whatever Tally saw, it made him move fast. In seconds he was over by Haru, a hand on their shoulder. He squeezed. "We'll get them back. We will."

Haru nodded, because what else could they say that hadn't been said already?

"Of course you will," Mindy said. She sniffled and sat up. Her eyes were red but no tears broke free.

"Yes." Haru's heart ached.

What kind of Uruma were they if a young peregrine like Mindy thought they needed comfort? She was the one who had been attacked. Tyler must've felt the same way, because he sneered as he stood. It was quickly masked when he saw Haru observing him.

"Mindy, we should go," Justin said, standing as well.

"Not yet. Just a little longer."

Tyler snorted. "Yeah, *you* don't owe Uruma Bastille any more coddling."

Mindy turned her head sharply as she eyed her friend. "Excuse me? Coddling?"

"If anything, Uruma Bastille should be making Reparations to you." Tyler jerked his head, nostrils flaring like the boar he was. "He should be bowing to you."

"They have no reason to be bowing to me. If anything, I failed Uruma!" Mindy had stood up, her chest heaved and her arms shook. Feathers pushed out of the one not covered in a cast. "I failed my sisters—" Her voice caught and she sucked in air, chest puffed up. "I failed Jackson!"

"They?" Tyler writhed in place, nostrils flaring, and latched on to the first part of Mindy's argument. "Who said I blamed Urusar Bastille?" Tyler shouted back, but despite his defiance, his shoulders hunched. "If anything, it's Satislit Bastille's fault for being so fucking needy and demanding. If he hadn't needed all those dates and presents and attention, *you* and *your sisters wouldn't have been here.*"

"I never said Urusar Bastille should bow!"

"But you said—"

Mindy hobbled around Tyler in a circle, her eyes focused solely on him. "I love babysitting the Bastille pups!"

"I know you do!" Tyler stomped and dipped his head. Haru slid closer to Mindy in case they needed to pull her away quickly, noting Tally had moved behind Tyler.

"The fact Uruma Bastille trusted me with their kids means everything to me."

"I know! But—"

A squawk pierced the air. "They keep everyone at arm's length but me, my sisters and the joeys. Do you know how much that means to me?"

"Why do you keep saying they!" Another foot stomp.

Justin tried maneuvering between his two friends. "Wait, Tyler. Don't upset Mindy. She's been through enough!"

"Because of our fucked-up Uruma!"

"They are not fucked-up!" Mindy yelled back, batting at him with her hands. Her nose had sharpened.

"For fuck's sake, I'm not talking about Urusar Bastille! I heard Uruma Bastille ottered out and couldn't human afterwards. Even you could human. What kind of fucked-up Uruma can't be there for the clan! You needed him! You!"

"Uruma Bastille is 'they', you dumbass! They're agender." Mindy tried to take another swipe but Justin caught the cast and twirled her away. He pushed her to Haru.

They wrapped their arms around her as Justin got in Tyler's face.

Mindy protested. "I can fight for myself!"

Justin glanced over his shoulder as he held Tyler back. "I know you can. You totally proved you can. But this isn't just your fight. And you're hurt. You really think Uruma Bastille wants you back in rehabilitation? Or Tyler wants you hurt again?"

"No." She leaned up against them and murmured, "Sorry."

"Both of you, stop!"

"What the fuck is agender? How the fuck does that make Uruma Bastille a 'they'? What kind of fucking gender nonsense is that shit?" Tyler butted against Justin, but the young hawk wrapped his arms around him and—*pulled Tyler into a hug?*

Each question had been a slap in their face. Hard. Unforgiving. The hostility at which they were spat in Haru's direction had been startling. Justin had Tyler pressed against him, rocking the boar, talking to him in hushed tones. Against them, Mindy shook, so they focused on her and petted down her arms.

Nose. Nose. They had to get out of here, before they said something they shouldn't. Tyler was still young. In a bad spot himself. And his fit—his attack—seemed to have more to do with Mindy than with Haru. They doubted Tyler knew how to respond any other way. Not with the way he had grown up.

Carefully, gently, Haru herded Mindy toward the door. "Lahi and Sammy are in the studio. I think Jasper is there too. Want to say hi?"

Shouting started behind them but Haru refused to look back. They were afraid what their face would show. Only a child could hurt them so.

"Oh, should we really interrupt Lahi recording?" Mindy asked, her voice catching.

"I am pretty sure that is what Sammy and Jasper were doing." They smiled and gave Mindy a wink, feeling steadier the farther away from the receiving room the two of them got. "I am also sure Lahi misses her friend."

Mindy nodded, squinting a little. "Yeah, me too."

* * * *

Tally took a step toward the boys, alarmed that Tyler couldn't seem to stop shaking. Unfortunately, Tyler misunderstood. He cringed and cried out, arms going up around his head defensively.

"Okay. It's okay." Tally stopped his forward progress, hands held out in front of him. "Justin, how about you both sit down? I'll be right back."

Good thing Haru kept hot chocolate in the fridge these days. What could be hot chocolate with a quick stir and heating up, anyway. It would have been great if people could be allowed to just be people. But the words people chose for themselves... Those words were important. Even if that included *bi with a preference for women*. Tally squeezed his eyes shut and shook his head. No. This wasn't about him and his insecurities. A preference had nothing to do with the person you finally chose. At least, not necessarily.

With unhurried steps, he returned to the front room with three steaming mugs, pleased that Justin had gotten his friend to sit on the long couch by the window. Tally set the mugs down within reach and took the chair closer to Justin.

"It's all been pretty upsetting, hasn't it?" Tally ventured, keeping his gaze on the contents of his mug.

Justin blew out a hard sigh. "Yeah. But if anyone should be upset..."

"I am." Tally glanced up and sat back slowly. No looming. No threatening motions. "In private. But I have to be focused in a crisis. It's what an Urusar does, even as I blame myself for all of this, too. There's far too much guilt to go around. Someone might drown. Me. Uruma Bastille. Mindy. Lahi."

"Lahi?" Tyler's voice broke and wavered.

Tally nodded. "Yes. She thinks if only she could've uktena'd faster. If only. If only. We could all build houses out of *if only's*." He sipped, staring out the picture window at the snow blanketing the front lawn. "Tyler, I'm not angry at you."

"You're not?"

"No. And I doubt Uruma Bastille is either, though you said some hurtful things."

Tyler cringed again, a smaller one this time, but the reaction set an ache around Tally's heart.

"I would never hit you, you know." Tally kept his posture relaxed, though everything in him screamed to fold this young man in his arms. "My job is to protect clan, to the best of my ability. I'm always aware of what I am. How I look. But I don't strike out in anger."

"Okay." Tyler moved carefully to pick up his mug, keeping a watch on Tally out of the corner of his eye. He sipped and sat hunched over the steam. "Okay. But don't you... I mean..."

"I blame the person who did this. And try to focus on getting my children back. Uruma Bastille... Those joeys were so important to them. They were so devastated. Sometimes letting your other side take over is the only way to deal with a thing without breaking completely." Tally jerked his head toward the back of the house where Haru and Mindy had gone. "You might remember that Mindy's lost both her sisters, too. She needs your support right now."

Tyler nodded at the steam, Justin mirroring the motion, though he stared wide-eyed at Tally.

"And I have homework for you."

Now both boys stared at him, open-mouthed. Justin sputtered, "But...we've got tons of that!"

Tally managed a little smile. "I want you to look up agender and preferred pronouns. It's not something people made up to mess with you."

They sat in relative silence after that while they waited for Mindy, the boys huddled over Justin's phone, hissing and whispering to each other while Tally sipped his hot chocolate and wished that everything would just stop for a bit, just until he could catch his breath.

Chapter Fifteen

Snake in the Snow

"So these were hereditary Hastings' holdings." Tally nodded to the park as they got out of the car.

"You've been saying that a lot during this little tour." Agent Firebaugh raised a dark eyebrow at him over the hood of the car.

Gun let out a sound halfway between a growl and a huff. "Yeah, well, there was a lot of it. Once."

"Once?"

Tally walked toward the nearby gazebo. "The family used to own a substantial percentage of the town. Barry's grandfather started selling parcels off to fund the growing grocery store empire. Smart move, really, having capital to do it instead of taking out loans. Some of the parcels the city bought, like the ones that make up this park. You might still hear Barry refer to this as *his* park."

Firebaugh's eyes narrowed, his thinking expression. "I see."

"I don't," Gun muttered. "Why are we here, Tal?"

"Kennett asked to see any places Barry might frequent."

Gun gave him a look and mouthed *Kennett*? Tally pointedly ignored him.

"Context?" Firebaugh asked as he scribbled in his notebook. Why every law enforcement person Tally knew used notebooks still instead of taking notes on an electronic device, he couldn't fathom.

"Family outings. I've known Barry to have business meetings here over lunch."

They'd reached the gazebo and Tally set a foot on the bottom step, remembering times with his own family in this park. Picnics. Ball games. Him herding his younger siblings away from potential trouble in the guise of large dogs or busy adults.

Growing up part of a big family had been wonderful. It had been--

"What is it?" Firebaugh kept his voice low.

"Hmm?"

"You've gone on alert, Urusar. Share."

So many scents littered the park. Tally opened his mouth, taking air over his tongue. Boar...humans... bear...

"Honey badger," Tally growled and raced off in the direction of the scent.

"Tally, no!" Firebaugh called after him, two sets of boots pounding after his. "Stop! Oh, for fuck's sake. Gunther, do something!"

Tally heard them on the edges of his senses. Whatever they wanted to do didn't concern him. His entire being had tunneled in on that scent, which headed across the park and into the trees. It was *recent*. It was nearly *fresh*. *I will bring you his head. I promised.*

He broke through the underbrush and managed to shed his coat and scarf before he snaked out. Easier to follow the trail on the ground and far easier to navigate through the brambles. Panting and the occasional yelp pursued him, so Firebaugh had wolfed. A raptor's scream from overhead told him where Gun had gone.

Fine. Better with three of them to take this monster down.

The snow raked against his scaled belly, brutally cold, but Tally's fury drove him on. Through the park, across the lane on the other side, out into alfalfa fields slumbering for the winter, and headed toward national forest at the end of the fields. The scent was stronger here away from the confusion of scents in the park, the sharp, aggressive musk of honey badger pounding an infuriating beat against his brain.

Yesssss, they were close. It was a fresh scent. He would trap Kaul in his coils. Squeeze until his ribs creaked, and he would tell Firebaugh where the joeys were. He would...

Why were the next set of trees so far away still? Tally redoubled his efforts, trying to slither faster across the open field. *Trying...trying...suddenly so tired...* Where had the scent gone? Where had the sun gone?

"Oh, Tal," Gun whispered nearby. "You can't do shit like this."

Someone running on four feet pounded past him. Parts of him felt warmer, maybe. The feet came galloping back and Tally thought he saw a handsome gray wolf flop down into the snow beside him. The image lasted only a moment and resolved into Agent Firebaugh, stark naked.

Firebaugh shook his head, rubbing at his side. "It's no good. The trail ends after this stand of trees. Car or something must've been waiting on the next road over."

"We've gotta get Tally back." Gunther's hand stroked Tally's head. "Snake and all that."

"I'll stay with him, you go back for clothes?" Firebaugh's gaze followed Gun as he handed Tally over and rose. "Faster if you fly. Guess we'll have to carry him back."

"Yeah." Gun's voice had a soft, speculative quality to it. Now what was *that* about? "He's not good with humaning when he's too cold."

There were more words, but Tally wasn't wording well any longer. Everything had solidified into a block of white, ice white, frost white, white noise white. Could a snake go snow-blind, even when it was cloudy? Was it cloudy? He tried to curl around the warmth cradling him. Hands seemed to be discouraging that.

"Don't squeeze me to death, Urusar." The words came to him through a strange, echoing tunnel.

Finally, he seemed to be floating, though it was a bumpy, jostling float with lots of curses and grunts. That was all right. He was too tired to care and too disgusted with himself. He'd almost had the bastard. It had been so close.

When Tally came to again, there were muffled voices all around him and arms holding him up.

"Um, yeah. He snaked."

"I can see." Haru's voice was sharp, slicingly so. "Why is he snaked?"

Tally drifted back toward the voices, wondering why Gun sounded so embarrassed.

"Your Argaze caught a scent in the park." Firebaugh's voice was much more assured, but tired, so tired. "He rushed after it before we could intervene."

"More like he wouldn't listen," Gun grumbled.

"*What* scent?"

Tally cringed. That tone was going to leave gashes in people.

Firebaugh answered, his voice barely above a whisper. "Honey badger."

The silence stretched for a long moment, though Tally was certain he was moving again, or rather being moved. He could almost hear Haru *not* saying things.

"Bring him upstairs, please."

More moving, more jostling and finally Tally was on a solid, flat surface, one that was becoming deliciously warm. He nosed against the surface, recognized his own electric blanket, and did his best to coil some of his length in to assist. Hands rearranged him, several pairs, so he couldn't have done a good job.

"You are supposed to protect him," Haru said from somewhere nearby.

Gun snorted. "Some days it's hard to protect him from himself, you know."

"Yes. I suppose so."

Quiet descended after that, so Tally had to assume Gun and Agent Firebaugh had left. Only the soft vibrations of Haru's footsteps remained as they…did things. Tally's eyes still didn't want to open, so he couldn't decipher what. After a few minutes, the mattress depressed and Haru's scent came with the motion.

Maybe it was some strange hypothermia dream, but Tally could have sworn that Haru had snuggled up naked and warm beside his snake. With a gusty sigh,

Tally rested his head on Haru's shoulder. Dream or not, he'd take it.

* * * *

The next day found Tally congested and headache-plagued. Maybe that hadn't been his best idea ever, rushing off into the snow as a giant snake.

I don't want to have a council meeting this evening.

"You have said we must keep everything as normal as possible," Haru said with a frown.

"I said that out loud, I guess." Tally pushed his beans and rice around his plate. "Sorry."

"Are you still cold?"

Tally glanced up to find Haru regarding him with sincere concern. That alone would've warmed him. "I'm doing better. Thank you for the extra socks. It's just residual effects from doing a stupid thing."

Haru reached across the kitchen island where they'd taken to eating their meals since they had no children in the house. "It was not stupid. Perhaps reckless, but it was brave to try to track that...*person.*"

"Thanks, my love. It was still stupid. I should've just pointed it out to Firebaugh and let him do it. The scent just... I was so angry."

"I know." Haru squeezed his hand. "I do know. So. Council meeting?"

Tally nodded and managed a bite of dinner. "Council meeting."

With Haru's expert chivvying and tie wrangling, Tally managed to dress respectably and they arrived at Bastille Arms for the meeting in plenty of time. Tyra hugged them both as they entered the conference room. Hakkon came for hugs as well. Gods, he looked tired, the lines around his eyes and the white hair among the blond at his temples both more pronounced. Even Rose, fidgety, easily spooked Rose, patted Tally's arm.

"Good to have you both back, Urusar, Uruma." Clement managed a friendly smile, and he did seem relieved to see them.

Cora's face was sterner as she said, "Would've been good if you could have made an appearance at the games." Even her features softened as she added, "Though current circumstances…understandable."

Leona Waters and Per Lund had their heads together in the corner and who knew what that meant. Muskrat and wolf respectively, they made an odd alliance of two but were normally so reticent that it was hard to know where they stood.

Maybe Dan and Barry won't show. I could live with that.

But no, that would've been too much to ask. Dan stormed in with two minutes to spare with Barry trailing after him, flushed and flustered. The moose slammed the file he was carrying on the table and took his customary chair with a belligerent glare around the room.

"Appears that Councilman O'Rourke would like to get started, Urusar," Clement drawled, his voice pitched expertly to carry to every corner.

"Everything is well, O'Rourke-san?" Haru inquired, sweet as spun sugar while setting up their own space at the table.

Dan's glower could've stripped the seven layers of wallpaper off Gun's dining room walls, but he didn't bother to answer, having never cared if he acted like an ass when he was angry. Beside him, Barry took his seat at the table cautiously, leaning away from Dan to speak to Cora. The atmosphere was strange—watchful, as if everyone knew where the epicenter of tension lay and were all guessing about the whys.

"Thank you all for coming." Tally planted a kiss atop Haru's head before settling at the table. "I apologize for being less available over the past few weeks —"

"Don't you dare, young man." Tyra cut him off with a little growl, obviously daring anyone to contradict her. "Anyone with half a brain understands."

"And anyone with half a heart," someone muttered. *Rose?* The world was turning inside out.

"Ah, well." Tally ran his worry stone through his fingers before placing it in his jacket pocket and refocusing. "Thank you. It was good to hear that the Evade and Hunt games went well."

Tyra nodded as she shuffled through her notes. "This second one went off without a hitch. Our teenage volunteers have been amazing. We couldn't do this without them. But I would like to propose that we start alternating age groups, starting with next month."

"Age groups?" Cora asked, with a deeper frown than her normal expression.

"Yes. We've had so many lijun families sign up for next month. I don't want this to get so big that we're sacrificing safety." Tyra handed out sheets to everyone that showed all the names of the children broken out by age group. "What we'd like to do is have the games for the littles in the morning, probably age seven and under, and have the older kids in the afternoon. That way we don't overload our volunteers with too many kids."

"Why don't you just add more volunteers?" Barry said with a huff. "It's too much to have it all day, and it'll be confusing."

"It shouldn't be that bad," Hakkon said. "We'll send reminders to each parent group. And we…" His voice caught and hitched. It took a glass of water and several deep breaths before he could say, "We only have so many teenagers and parents willing to volunteer."

Tally put a hand on his shoulder and gave him a squeeze. The council members, for once, had nothing to say to that, every one of them avoiding Hakkon's eyes and shuffling uncomfortably.

"All right, I'm thinking it's a sensible proposal." Tally broke the silence when Hakkon had steadied. "Seconded. Is there need for debate?"

Clement shook his head. "Call it, Urusar."

"Good. All in favor?" To his astonishment, it was nearly unanimous, with only Dan and Barry opposed, probably more out of habit than really opposing Tyra's idea. Small victories, he'd take them as he could.

The rest of the meeting was spent on old business, such as the effort to get some young lijun in the community interested in taking over Melissa Kincaid's vacant spot at the sheriff's department. Considering the deadly way poor Melissa's career had ended, Tally wasn't shocked that they hadn't had any takers.

"Leona, if you wouldn't mind talking to the Blue Hollys?" Tally made a note when the muskrat nodded. "There are so many of them. Good chance *one* of the kids might be intrigued."

Finally, Tally was able to say, with some trepidation, "Any new business?"

"Yes."

Dan. Of course it's Dan. Tally shoved back a sigh. "What do you have for us, Councilman O'Rourke?"

"The restrictions on the properties for the Harris Street project are ridiculous. You need to go to city council and have them changed. Now."

Tally didn't even try to hold back the gusty sigh. "Dan, you know it doesn't work that way. I can give suggested changes to our folks on city council. I can cajole. Pester. But you know how they are. It would take six months for them to get through debate and then they might want a referendum and that takes time and then..."

"But they're so restrictive that they're anti-business! How did you let this happen?" Dan roared and slammed his hand on the table.

Haru clearing their throat broke the shocked silence. "It may be best to table this discussion, Urusar. I believe Eberhardt-san is not well."

Alarmed, Tally twisted in his chair to find Hakkon with his elbows on the table and his face in his hands. "Hak?"

"I'm... It's just a headache."

"Like fun." Tally rose with his hand back on Hakkon's shoulder. "New business is tabled. Meeting adjourned. Hak, you need someone to take you home?"

Hakkon shook his head. He lowered his hands, his eyes glistening with unshed tears. "No. I don't have far to go. I'm sorry, Tal. It just hits hard at the damnedest times."

"We understand," Haru said as they helped Hakkon to stand. Their face was completely neutral and Tally could only imagine the horrible churn of emotions Haru was hiding under that expression. "Perhaps Black-san could drive you home? It would worry me less."

"Happy to, Hak." Clement took Hakkon's arm to steady him. "It's on my way. You can come back for your truck later."

The council members filed out and Tally allowed himself a moment's guilty relief that it was over for another month. Relief that was rudely shattered when Dan and Barry ambushed him and Haru out in the hallway.

"So what are you going to do?" Dan practically bumped chests with Tally, blocking the way. "It's in your best interest here to do something productive. Offer bribes. You can buy their cooperation, like you do for everything else."

Tally raised an eyebrow and loomed. Dan matched him in weight, most likely, but he was still three inches shorter. "I've never bribed city council or any other official, I'll have you know. And changing the rules at this point really would be a process. If you send me specific demands, I'll run it by them, but you *know* it takes time."

While not exactly flustered, Dan did take a step back. "You'll have *specifics* in your email in an hour. I expect to hear progress reports."

"There's another issue," Barry said as a slow, mean smile oozed across his face. "From our mutual acquaintance."

"Oh?" Tally fought to keep his voice calm, the floor tilting under him. *What now?* Haru slipped a hand around his arm, which steadied the floor and lent Tally some courage. "What does he want now?"

"We're without a Sardu, Urusar."

The growl got out before he could stop it. "I can't thank you for reminding me."

"A *proper* Sardu, Bastille," Barry said with a poke to his chest. "People higher up knew that child was *not* and had to be removed."

Tally surged forward, rage hammering in his chest. Haru's arms around his waist couldn't have held him back, but they reminded him of the stupidity of beating Barry senseless. "Jackson's death was *deliberate? Planned?*"

"Let's say it was an optimal outcome." Barry had backpedaled out of reach, but his smarmy smile returned now. "You make sure the next Sardu you declare is a *real* one. A traditional one. Hear me?"

"I hear you. Loud and clear." Tally stopped straining against Haru's hold. "Excuse me. I'm going home."

He waited for them to step out of the way before striding past with Haru on his arm. He shook from head to toe, so hard that he fumbled the key fob twice before he could open the car doors. Once they were both in and alone with the doors shut, Tally leaned his head on the steering wheel to take huge, gasping breaths.

"You did not flatten them, my Argaze. I was certain you would."

"Haru…" Tally groped over the center console to find Haru's hand. "They meant the pups. The otter pups. If one of them is male… Oh Godsss…"

"Yes. I know." Haru's voice was glacial, frightening in its control. "They will not take the pups. Our pups. You will not let them."

Tally sat back and wiped his eyes to find Haru staring at him, their expression fierce and determined. "I won't, my love. I promise. They won't have the pups."

* * * *

"This is where we lost the trail." Tally dismounted from his snowmobile and pointed to the spot beside the trees. The extra six inches of snow the night before had made this expedition impossible for most of their cars, and damn it if those heavy clouds didn't look like more on the way. He shivered and pulled his scarf higher.

"You doing okay, Tal?" Gun asked as he took off his helmet. Damn bird wasn't even wearing a hat.

"Fine. I've got the heated coat on. I'm fine." He waited until his Enforcers had gathered close. Crystal, Deja and Kerns — great-horned owl, coyote and bison, respectively — were nearly all the same age, all in their primes. They'd just needed Gun back to lead them again.

"You want a watch on this spot, Urusar?" Crystal asked, squinting against the snow.

"Yes. Night watch, I think, would be best. I doubt Kaul is meeting someone in the park in broad daylight."

Gun shot him a speculative frown. "Isn't Ken, um, Firebaugh having this location watched?"

"I don't want to take anything from Agent Firebaugh. He's doing all he can with what he's been given. But he doesn't have the resources to cover everything and his agents are human. They'll only follow people in human form. He needs lijun."

"Got it." Gun went to one knee, scooping away snow until he got down to the surface of the one-lane access road. "Don't think a vehicle's been through here in the last day. No tire track or runner track layer until you get down to the bottom."

"Guess he could've been airlifted out. Big enough raptor could lift a honey badger, right?" Kerns gazed at the sky as if such a raptor might appear.

"Maybe." Gun stood, dusting snow off his hands. "Someone like that bastard's not gonna want to give up that much control, though."

"Profiling now, Gun?" Tally managed something close to a smile. "Maybe we should send you to school for that sheriff's department spot."

"Hell, no. I'm not working with Bob Amick every day. We'd kill each other."

"Fair enough." Tally gazed around the semicircle of Enforcers. "Here's what I want. Crystal, night watch here. If Kaul or someone else suspicious shows up, follow discreetly if you can. Do not engage. Deja, I want you on Barry at night. We're pretty sure he's the only direct contact and, yes, Firebaugh has a man on him, but if he boars, it's all you. Kerns, I want you on Dan, in case we're wrong or they change tactics and start contacting him directly."

He waited until he got nods from each Enforcer.

"Gun stays on the house. I need him there. If any of you get visual contact with Kaul, you let Gun know. *Don't* try to be heroes and confront him. We're certain he's Sisum Abser. He's just too good and we've lost too much to him already."

Crystal had paled at this announcement. Deja and Kerns had gone a bit gray. Hadn't Gun told them? Maybe he hadn't wanted to scare them. Too bad. They needed to be scared.

"Questions?" Gun barked out.

"We've got it, boss." Crystal had recovered enough to speak for them. "You can count on us."

Tally hated living in this siege mentality. It was killing him. But it certainly was making it clear whom he could rely on. *Small victories…small victories…*

Chapter Sixteen

Double Trouble

The directions should not have been so hard to follow. Reduce sodium intake. Increase protein. Water. Rest. Like a plant. Except Sammy wasn't a plant. Though focusing on her helped them not to focus on the fact Haru still did not have the twins back. But the majority of what Haru knew how to cook was salty because of the soy sauce. They had bought the low sodium kind, but then the food didn't have the correct taste. Because no salt.

Haru had been struggling with coming up with the correct meals for the past week, ever since the check-up with Tabib Blue Holly-*okaasan*. The one Tally had had to miss because of a meeting with city council members then a follow-up disastrous one with O'Rourke-san and Hastings-san. Their Argaze had come home...*snakish*... so they did not mention the stress the twins were causing on Sammy's body.

She is not *geriatric.* The pre-eclampsia was worrying, but nothing Sammy and Haru couldn't handle with a little care.

Another scorched dinner might not be excusable, though. Haru hadn't even cooked this badly right after *that* night. Cooking without salt shouldn't be so hard. Yet it was in everything.

Eve-ry-thing.

Haru had become convinced food tasted good because of salt.

They sighed as they dug through the cookbook Bastille-*okaasan* had made up for them. Maybe if they adjusted one of these recipes, they could make a suitable meal. They should be trying to make food Tally liked anyway.

"If you just told him, then you wouldn't have to be trying so hard." Sammy's hands rested on their waist. "Do you know how weird it is to see you in pants all the time?"

"Those are two different thoughts," they replied, then sighed again. "And we already talked. My Argaze is under enough strain."

"Quite. Because keeping stuff from Tally worked out so well the first time?" She placed a kiss on their back and rubbed her head against them.

"He almost assaulted those…those…"

"Bastards?"

"Yes." Haru flipped to the salads. How were they even considered appetizing? "He keeps snaking out. Addy found him curled up in his chair at the resort this morning."

"What set him off this time?"

"A lawyer for O'Rourke-san."

Sammy's expression turned curious. "Really?"

"He did *not* eat the lawyer."

"Too bad."

"Yes."

Sammy managed to inch around and put herself between Haru and the counter. Her large belly forced the two of them away from it. Instinctively their hand went to her stomach, needing to protect the twins in some way. Their *boys*.

That was the other reason they had asked Sammy not to say anything.

Tally would... They feared what that outcome would be.

Haru barely had been able to stop touching her belly since the visit. They'd asked because they needed to know what would happen if things were still *unresolved* by the end of June. *Please don't let things be unresolved by then.* Just the idea their pups would be in danger — *taken* — made them sick. Haru pulled Sammy close and sniffed her hair.

"Oh, Haru." Sammy nuzzled against their chest.

If only they hadn't been so needy. Hadn't relied on Sammy and the friendship between them, then none of this would've happened. Jackson. They'd still have their little boy.

Sammy patted them and smiled. "I'm going to put my feet up. Try to get some writing in."

"Okay."

"Some steak with the salad would work."

"You think?"

"Tally gets a salad, I get my protein," she replied as she walked away.

Somehow, they pulled a decent meal together for dinner. No complaints from the Bastilles and Sammy managed to get down the steak before she declared herself full and needing to rest. Tally watched her leave with a frown but said nothing.

Jasper pulled on a chunk of hair and motioned to her.

"Would you?" they asked.

"Stay with Sammy," Jasper replied, fluttering away unevenly. "Stay with pups."

"Do you want your pillow?" Haru called after him.

Jasper nodded and left the dining room in his staggered flight pattern.

"Hasn't his wing healed right?" Che asked, looking through the doorway with concern then asked, "What?" Everyone stared at him. "No, really, what?"

"It's a sensitive topic for pixies. Their wings. You know that." Tally shifted the greens around in his salad bowl. "I've tried getting him to let Ted have another look, but so far he's refused."

Bastille-*otōusan* hissed. "Is he still having nightmares?"

"Yes," Haru answered. "Being trapped in the vents during…during the attack. He nearly tore off his wings trying to get to the pups."

"Yesssss, he nearly did." Tally's hands flattened out, fingers stretching. His forked tongue flicked out. Haru grabbed hold of the closest hand and got a thankful smile in return.

Nan, Lahi, Che, Addy and Hal were having one of those silent sibling conversations, one Haru couldn't follow but knew it was about Tally. When they were finished making faces at one another, Addy stood and grabbed her plate. The others followed suit.

She smiled. "We'll clean up."

"No, you are—" Haru began to protest.

"We grew up here. It's home away from new homes," she replied. "Tally, go to bed. You're beat."

"It's only—"

Bastille-*okaasan* joined her children. "No, you're dead on your feet. Take a bath, relax, get in bed. Haru, the bath?"

"Yes! Of course. I— Of course." Haru scrambled to understand *what* exactly was happening, besides getting volunteered to draw a bath for their Argaze. *Something* happened. Only it was the Bastilles that were in on it.

They still didn't have an answer when Tally found them in their suite, filling the pool.

"Ah, so this is where you are." Tally leaned into the bathroom.

"Where else—oh, your bath. I am—"

"Here is good. Really good. I'm just surprised you're sharing." Tally stepped into the room, picking at his suit jacket. Frowning at Haru.

Did they not please? They had rolled their pants up and tied back their sleeves. Maybe something more suitable?

"I… Let me change and grab my robe. Be right back."

Tally scooted out of the bathroom so fast Haru didn't even get a chance to respond. They had automatically gone to the bath *they* associated with relaxing. Not even the idea of making a bath up in Tally's suite had crossed their mind. It felt like an invasion of privacy.

Not unlike the night they had spent snuggled up to Tally when uktena'd. His Argaze had been at his most vulnerable. Unable to defend himself. Gunther had told them to warm Tally up and they had, holding him close all night against them under an electric blanket and covers. They had sweated so much they had needed a shower first thing to clean up.

"Um, I can, I can take it from here, Haru," Tally murmured as he re-entered, sash tied tightly around his middle. He fidgeted with the candles Haru had lit. "You don't, don't, ah, have to. I can — Why are you sitting like that?"

"I was going to wash your back after you showered off?"

"Excuse me?" Tally actually clutched his bathrobe tighter.

Haru's eyebrows went up, then they glanced between the washcloth and the bucket. Had they misunderstood? It had seemed like the Bastilles wanted Haru to help their Argaze 'relax', so they were trying to do just that. Was this not the correct way to do it?

If they understood Tally better they would know what he needed, but Haru had never asked *those* questions. The flirting, the presents, the talks about the pups, making house, those situations they could handle. Their dreams? Wants? Desires? Those conversations were harder. So many feels. Tally had paid attention. Looked harder than Haru had. The bathroom showed that he did. He had made Haru a *proper* bath suite. Stools and everything to go with the shower and pool — *bathtub*.

More homey. More Japanese. More otterish. Like them.

But is it really me?

Haru frowned, frustration knotting their gut. They didn't used to ask those silly kinds of questions. Only when they'd come here, married Tally, had they really started to look at themself. Haru hated what they saw. Sporadic rebellion and dissent had nothing on years of growing up as a Satislit. Their defiances were only token arguments that gave Haru the illusion of some control and free will.

A hand cupped their jaw. "Haru?"

Tally knelt in front of them, his warm brown eyes crinkled around the edges.

"I can relax in the tub by myself. Mom, Dad, the others, they were *suggesting* help. It wasn't an order, ah, a directive."

"Of course. I apologize." Haru stood, embarrassed, unsure how to retreat.

"Do you *want* to be here?" Tally asked, hand still on Haru's person.

"I want to *help*. Would washing your back not help? I thought you might want someone to *listen* to your day."

"In the bath?"

Haru frowned. "Where else? This is what we do."

"What we — Oooh, oh. Yeah. Okay."

"Would you prefer I undressed too?" They didn't want to. Felt too exposed. Internal laughter rang through their head at the contradiction of the fear being exposed in a bathroom. Their bathroom. Where they had ottered and Tally had watched on. But they would undress, if it helped.

Tally shook his head. "Only if you want to."

"Then if you please, my Argaze."

"Oh, um, right."

There were a couple minutes of awkward silence as Tally washed up in the shower. One hand came out when he was done. Haru handed over a towel, which he wrapped around his waist, then he sat down on the stool, his back so straight they were afraid Tally might actually snap like *higashi*.

Now that wouldn't do.

Carefully, Haru moved behind their Argaze and wiped down his back. The different muscle groups jumped and tensed under their fingertips. Each pass of the washcloth had a whole new ripple effect. Haru moved one hand to Tally's shoulder and pressed a thumb down.

"Ungh." Tally grunted.

The hard planes of his shoulders and back loosened a fraction. Haru dug in deeper.

"*Gods*. Uhn."

Dropping the washcloth, Haru went to work on Tally's neck then up to his temples, taking their Argaze's weight when he leaned back. The moans sent a wave of satisfaction through Haru. They combed their fingers through Tally's wet hair. Another appreciative groan reverberated against Haru's body.

"Would you like the bath?" they whispered.

"Uh?"

"Bath?"

"Oh, um, yes." The relaxed Tally was gone again.

Haru poured warm water down his back to wash the soap off and helped him into the pool. "The towels are here. I will get the bed ready."

"Bed!"

"Yes. For your massage." Haru pulled out a couple fluffy towels. Better not to get the sheets oily. "You need to relax."

"I, you, Haru, you don't have to give me a massage." Tally cupped one hand between his.

"I understand."

"You do?"

"Yes, I am doing this because I want to."

Tally held their hand a moment longer. "If you're sure."

"I am." It was what they were supposed to do after all, and Tally was doing so much to get their girls back. Haru needed to step up their game, or at the very least, show their appreciation.

Waiting for Tally to finish up in the bath was a practice in patience. Something Haru felt they had in excruciatingly small quantities these days. They folded and refolded the towels. They changed into a *yukata* to sleep in. Checked the incense several times. Checked the candles several times. Made sure the new fountain in the room was running properly. White noise made of water certainly helped them when the waves of memories battered up against them.

But the memories in this room were mostly happy ones. With pups. With Tally too, when Haru had let him stay with the family in their bed. It had been a room of laughter.

A creak drew Haru's attention to Tally as he stuck his head into the suite. "Oh, um. So we're doing this?"

Haru bowed and motioned to the bed. "My Argaze. Allow me to pleasure you."

"What?" Tally looked startled, his hands clutching the doorjamb.

"Your massage? Do you not want it?"

"Oh, yes, massage." There was a lot of stiffness in Tally's movement as he walked over. He eyed the towels. "Um."

"Your robe."

"Excuse me?"

Haru held out their hands. "Your robe, my Argaze."

"I was thinking I'd keep it on."

"I assure you it is easier if there is only a towel."

"It's so tiny."

"Towels mean less mess. Unless you do not wish to be undressed? I can get your flannel bottoms?"

"No, um, no. This is, this is good." Tally turned and Haru helped take the robe off, averting their gaze. "Are you sure this one? There are bigger towels."

"Yes, over your bottom. Those are so the oil does not get everywhere." As Haru hung the robe up there were some thumps and a whisper of fabric moving.

"I think I'm decent."

Tally had his arms tucked under the pillow, towel wrapped around his waist, and was watching Haru's every movement. His entire body was taut, coiled hard. Something Haru should fix.

They poured the lavender oil over Tally's back. A shudder went through their Argaze when their palms pressed against his skin. Muscles jumped and jerked under their touch.

"Cold?"

"No, not, not cold."

They'd have to take him at his word.

Slowly, methodically, Haru began to move their hands over Tally. Along the muscles, breaking up the knots best they could. The longer they worked, the more the rigidity fell away, Tally's breathing evened out, lessening the strain carried around his eyes.

"Oh, yeah, right, right. Yes."

Haru pressed the heel of their thumb into a particularly stubborn knot under Tally's left shoulder blade.

"Fuck. Gods."

The deep, rumbling groan made Haru chuckle. "Feel good?"

"If you're asking is the pain worth it, the answer is yes."

"Excellent."

Using their weight, they dug into Tally's lower back. Moans of appreciation met their ears. When they put their hands on their Argaze's hamstrings, the noise got even louder. They were excellent specimens of the perfect legs, if Haru's opinion counted for anything. They loved the way Tally's legs trembled then loosened up under Haru's ministrations.

"You keep that up and I'm going to fall asleep here."

"That..." Would not be so bad. Haru had gotten used to their Argaze sleeping next to them at his parents' house, but the moment they moved home to the estate, Tally had gone back to his room. Instead of answering, Haru moved to the calves.

"Ahh, oooh. Yessssss."

The toes got Tally squirming.

"Because it tickles!" he protested. Though he stopped complaining when Haru set the heel of their hand against his arch.

But when Haru tapped on Tally's hip there was a confused "what?" mumbled. Haru patted again.

"No, really, what? I can't move."

"Roll over so I can massage your thighs."

There was a stretch of silence where the only noise was from the fountain and its motor.

"My Argaze?"

"Did you say roll over?"

"Yes."

Tally had already shifted so one knee came up. "I'm not sure that's a good idea."

"I think the rest of you would say it is."

"Oh, there is definitely one part of me that thinks it's a bad idea."

Haru patted Tally's bum. "Roll over and let me finish. Come on."

"Fine."

"*Oh.*" Yes, well, *that* was a normal hot-blooded male reaction to something like a massage.

Tally had one arm over his face. The darkening hue of complexion definitely betrayed his mood.

Best to ignore the, ahem, growing problem by focusing on Tally's shins. By the time Haru had moved up to quads and other muscle groups on the upper thighs, the towel was slipping. Tally's little snake was definitely not looking so little. He cupped the towel against him with a muffled "Shit."

What should they do next? They were so unsure of what the right thing to do was, and their hands stopped moving. Haru just held on to Tally. Their training said one thing, but Haru most certainly did not want to do *that*. It was one thing to be comfortable touching their Argaze. *That* was another matter entirely. *That* hadn't been the expectation for the evening. Not after Tally assured them it wasn't.

Haru hadn't even thought about *that*. Their body had no interest in the party Tally was offering.

"I think, ah —" The towel jerked, and Haru met Tally's gaze. "I'm gonna shower off. Okay?"

The towel bobbed again.

"A shower. A quick ssshower."

Another bob.

Haru swallowed. Uncertain. Then found themself back on their ass, Tally scrambling off the bed.

"Sss-sshower!" The bathroom door slammed shut. Hard.

They gathered up the towels in a daze, stacking them into the hamper. A haze had clouded their mind. Two halves fighting. Haru hadn't been repulsed touching Tally. Hadn't shied away even a little. It had been nice being close to their Argaze. Training said they should've serviced properly — that thought sent an uncontrollable shudder through them. They hadn't known what to do. How to respond.

Tally must've seen the fight within Haru. Something in the way his gaze had softened before he'd run away. Was he mad? Disappointed? Hurt? Haru checked the sheets before blowing out the candles and sliding into bed.

What was the right answer?

Could Haru think of Tally in a sexual way? Want him *after* — after their disastrous wedding night? After the way he had rejected Haru's Reparations? They snuggled against the body pillow, squeezing hard, stilling when the door creaked.

"Haru?"

The bed dipped.

A hand rubbed their shoulder.

A finger played with a lock of hair.

"The massage was really nice. Thank you."

"My pleasure, Tally."

There was a quick indrawn breath.

"Would you want to stay?" Haru offered, scared of the answer. "The bed is...big."

"For cuddles?" Tally replied after a beat. "Like with the pups?"

The anxious skitter of their heart lessened. "Yes, for cuddles."

Instead of replying, Tally slipped under the covers into bed and pulled Haru against his chest. He tucked Haru against him, holding them gently. One hand trailed up and down their side in slow pets. Tally's breathing slowed with Haru's, and it was hard to keep their eyes open. Not when they felt so relaxed and safe.

* * * *

Darn tie. Of course, if he hadn't overslept, Tally wouldn't have had to rush. He hadn't expected his Em'halafi to ask him to stay the night and he'd been caught without an alarm. Haru had gotten up per usual, but hadn't woken Tally when they'd gotten out of bed. Only when the sheets had chilled had he roused out of otter-filled dreams, then the smell of rice wafted up through the vents had announced breakfast was waiting.

Delaying going into work for another ten minutes shouldn't matter.

Last night had been a gift, and Tally had wanted to linger a little longer. Just to bask in the warmth and uncertain affection Haru had given him. Was it possible the time they spent together at his parents' hadn't been by necessity? Tally wanted to believe it after getting to hold Haru all night.

As Tally walked down the hall, Sammy stepped out of her room. She headed for the stairs, though she wove sleepily and one hand reached for the wall. She shook herself, then huffed.

Tally saw the moment she faltered. Close to the top of the stairs. He yelled and dove for her, catching Sammy before she tumbled. Tally twisted and landed with a thump on his back, breathing hard, mind reeling.

"You okay? Are the pups okay? What happened? Do I need to get the Blue Hollys? What happened?" Tally noticed the dazed expression only when he looked at her, because she hadn't answered his barrage of questions. Sammy's pupils were unfocused and dilated. "What the hell?"

"Sammy!" Loud, heavy footfalls pounded up the stairs. "Gods! Sammy! Why did you not take the elevator like we said? Are you okay? Tally, is she hurt?"

Haru busied himself — *themself* — checking over her and nosing her face, nearly yanking Sammy off Tally's lap. Their hands went to her rounded abdomen in a protective gesture. Like he — *they* — could keep the pups safe if they held on tight enough. She nuzzled back, petting down Haru's sides. What had happened was alarming, but something tugged at Tally's mind. The way neither of the otters seems *surprised* the fall had almost happened wasn't right. Alarmed, yes the two of them were that, but they didn't seem to think it was out of the ordinary.

Since when was Sammy supposed to take the elevator? Why would she have to do that instead of the stairs?

"What haven't you told me?" Tally said finally, when his heart wasn't clenched so hard he thought it would explode. A hiss escaped him, a flare of annoyance burning inside him.

The flick of Sammy's gaze to him and back to Haru meant whatever it was, it was because of his Satislit. Why did Sammy always side with Haru? Not that she hadn't warned Tally she would, but Gods, she'd almost tumbled down the stairs. Tally shuddered at what would've happened if he hadn't caught her.

"Whatever's going on in that head, stop." Tally kept his voice calm and even as he helped Sammy sit up farther. "This is serious. It's about family. And you need to tell me."

"It is not that —" Haru began.

Oh no. They would not put him off like this again. "No! Talk. Now."

There was a full minute of stunned silence, then Sammy began to divulge the details of her last checkup. The further she got, the angrier Tally became. It must've shown. Had to have. Because both Haru and Sammy were looking at the floor and not him and her voice was barely above a whisper.

Tally rubbed at his eyes with the heels of his hands. "And you didn't tell me any of this because…?"

An odd strangled sound came from Haru. "You have been under such stress…"

"No." Tally made sure Sammy was stable before he surged to his feet. "No. No. And more no. We talked about this. About things that are important to family. To health and safety. My Gods! Sammy could've gone headfirst down those stairs. This is *exactly* the sort of thing you *need* to tell me, stress be damned!"

He caught himself before he started truly shouting. Haru was shrinking in on himself — *themself* — and no, no, that wasn't good either.

"Please get Sammy some water." Tally stepped over and around them as he headed for the stairs.

"Tal?" Sammy's voice wavered as she called after him. "Where are you going?"

"To the kitchen. I have some treats to throw out."

He wasn't certain whether the sigh from behind him was upset or relieved. Maybe a little of both. He'd promised, though, and he had to follow through. *For Haru. I'm doing this for Haru, even if it doesn't feel like it.*

This hadn't been how he'd wanted to start his day. He stomped into the kitchen, grateful that no one occupied the chairs or the counter stools, and grabbed one of the smaller trash bags out of the drawer. In went the prawns, the shrimp, the smoked eel, which was indeed a shame, the herring, and finally, and most painful of all, the Alaskan crab legs that Haru loved to crunch and slurp. All of it. Without even bothering to put on shoes, he stomped out to the garage and slammed the bag into the bin for regular garbage.

The headache that stretched from one temple to the other wasn't any better, but he straightened, determined to meet the rest of the day. Rules. Haru needed rules, and if that was what he needed to feel safe and comfortable, by Gods they were going to follow them.

Even if he felt like a tyrant.

What Tally didn't expect to face was a relaxed Haru holding onto Sammy when the two of them got out of the elevator. Haru's head cocked to one side. His otter eyed him speculatively.

"Are the treats in the garbage?"

"They are." Tally was relieved his voice had returned to its normal calm. "Two weeks, my love."

"Absolutely." There was a mournful look toward the garage but when Haru met Tally's eyes, they actually smiled. "You *followed* the rules."

"I did." Tally couldn't help a little frown. "I promised you I would."

Haru plopped Sammy in a chair and came up to Tally. He took a step back, but Haru wrapped their arms around his waist and nosed into his neck. His otter was shaking and murmuring about how Tally had followed the rules. It sounded...happy? And was rather confusing. Tally looked to Sammy for help but she seemed as perplexed as he was.

He stroked Haru's back gently, hoping to calm the shaking. "Didn't you... Didn't you trust me to do as I'd said?"

"How many stones have you given me? How many times should you have been angry and not shown it? My otterness may have loved the gifts, the treats, but did they build the trust I needed to tell you my Kwebabaid was pregnant?" Haru nuzzled closer and let out a shuddering breath. "This is the first time you have shown me you were angry and followed through. And it was not...was not what Akaike-san would have done. You kept your promise, followed the rules you made and threw out the treats."

Hot, sizzling splashes hit Tally's shoulder. He wrapped his arms all the way around Haru, rocking them as his own throat closed over and his eyes welled. "Haru... My Haru... I wish I'd understood sooner. Even a little. I wish you could've told me. I love giving you things. But I want you to feel...right. And safe. And like you *can* trust me."

"I will try, my Argaze. I will try." Haru rubbed their nose against Tally's neck and squeezed harder. Kiss. Kiss.

Tally buried his face against Haru's neck, his breath whooshing out of him in a strangled sob. This, oh, this was so much at once, and so much he'd needed, and he felt like it might take him out at the knees. At the same time, some of the tight ache around his heart loosened. Nothing was really better and wouldn't be until the girls were back home, but somehow he didn't feel quite so alone now.

It wouldn't have been the path he'd chosen to win someone's trust, but he recognized more each day how Haru's...*upbringing* had affected them. If this was how the two of them broke Urusar Akaike's chains, both of them together, then so be it. For his Em'halafi, he would do whatever it took to bring them through. Of course he would. He'd waited for Haru all his life and no one, certainly not a smarmy clan head, would keep him winning through all that weighed Haru's past down.

"Thank you," he whispered. "That's all I ask."

* * * *

The urgent alert came through the business messaging system as Tally was on his way to the office.

Fire at Coraline. First responders alerted.

"Holy fuck." Tally swung into a less-than-legal U-turn to honking horns and sped toward the opposite end of town.

Smaller than Sapphire Lake, and more specialized, the Coraline was a jewel of a resort tucked between hills, inviting smaller gatherings than the enormous Sapphire Lake and boasting a concert hall and a dance studio.

Tally tried not to break more traffic laws as he put the phone on hands-free and called the resort manager. It went to voicemail. "Steven, it's Tally. I'm on my way."

He couldn't even pull into the drive. The fire department had it blocked. The Bentley joined several other vehicles along the roadside and Tally dashed toward the building, only to be stopped by a firefighter.

"Sir, you can't go up there!"

"I'm Tally Bastille. This is my hotel. And I need to know my people are safe."

Wide-eyed recognition bloomed on the young woman's face. "Right. Of course you are. Your folks are over there, sir. You see the group behind the EMTs?"

"Thank you. Is it bad?"

"Not sure yet, Mr. Bastille. We're still assessing the site."

Black smoke poured through what had been a stained-glass rose window above the front doors. The beautiful white stone façade had been soot-blackened. While no flames licked at the windows or shot from the roof, it was impossible to say what might still be burning inside.

"Holly!" Tally jogged to meet the front desk manager as she ran to greet him, slipping precariously on the slush-covered drive. "Everyone all right?"

"Mr. Bastille, thank Gods you're here." Holly reached him, hands on her thighs as she wheezed. "I've done the employee headcount. Everyone's out. Steve's working through the guests. We worked fast, so I think we have everyone."

"How did it start?"

She straightened, shaking her head. "Not sure yet. We saw smoke coming from the bell stand around the corner. Then flames. We hit the alarm and started moving."

"All right. Good work." Tally put an arm around her since she didn't even have a coat on. Beaver lijun, so she was better able to handle it than he was, but she still needed outerwear. "Property damage we can handle, so long as everyone's okay."

Steve was easy to spot, his salt-and-pepper hair nearly a foot above everyone else's. He turned and trotted over when he spotted them, clipboard under one arm, Princess, the hotel's cat, under the other. "You got here fast, sir!"

"Our guests are safe?"

"All out, yes. The brigade captain says they should have things in hand pretty soon." Steve juggled his armloads as Princess clawed her way around so she could put both paws on his bony shoulders, leaving a carpet of white Persian shed on his black jacket.

"Want me to take her?"

"No offense, sir. But you kind of scare her."

Tally tipped his head to acknowledge that. Princess had never become comfortable around large snakes, except Mom, for some reason. The three of them stood shoulder to shoulder in a strange solidarity as the firefighters directed hoses and ran in and out of the building. It wasn't long before some of the hoses were set down and coiled up again. *Couldn't be that bad, right? If they're packing up already?*

He'd just finished thinking that when the fire captain approached, pushing his helmet back. "Mr. Bastille?"

"Yesss?" Tally bit his tongue to stop the involuntary hiss. "Any idea what happened?"

"Not sure yet." He took a long drink from a bottle of water, his voice still hoarse as he went on. "Your lobby's a total loss, Mr. Bastille. I'm sorry about that. All those pretty historical details. My wife and I came out to watch *La Sylphide* not too long ago here."

Tally took a second to recover from that unexpected left turn in conversation. "I'm…ah, thank you, Captain Toulson. Any guesses where it started?"

"First look suggests behind the bell stand." The captain frowned, staring at the front of the building. "I hate to say this Mr. Bastille, but first look also suggests arson."

Blood sang in Tally's ears. He knew people were talking at him, but he couldn't make out what they were saying. They wouldn't have. Would they? He'd been cooperating. Doing the things they'd ordered him to. Why would they have torched his beautiful little hotel?

"Mr. Bastille? Can you hear me?"

He was sitting on the back step of an open ambulance, an EMT shining a light in his eyes. "I'm...yes?"

"You went a little shocky on us there, sir. Can you look at me?"

The usual questions followed, name, location, date. "I just had a dizzy moment. I'm fine. Really."

Captain Toulson crouched beside him. "It'll be a couple of days before we can let anyone inside the front, Mr. Bastille. Not much you can do here."

"There are some things. Yes." Tally shrugged off the EMT's blanket and got back to work. The guests needed to be transported. Housed. Probably clothed if they couldn't recover belongings from some of the rooms. "Steven, hotel shuttles are temporarily rerouted to take guests out to Sapphire Lake. I'll call Addy and make arrangements there. Let's get everyone in out of the snow."

He made inquiries with the fire department as to which parts of the building were safe, then organized a small brigade of bell and housekeeping personnel to go in with firefighter escorts and pack up the rooms they *could* reach. Calls went out to the insurance agent, private security to be sure the site wasn't further damaged and his architect to start gathering research for repairs and restoration. He would have his rose window back. That was non-negotiable.

By the time he made it to his office at Sapphire Lake, he already felt as if he'd been run over by a small herd of cement mixers. Worse still, Addy was waiting for him.

Her face was granite. Their mother's face when she was trying not to let on that she was upset. "Tal, a note came for you."

"A note?" He shuffled in a distracted way through the folders on his desk. *Oh...* "A... *That* kind of note?"

"Firebaugh thinks so. He didn't want to open it without you."

"He's here?"

She raised an eyebrow at him. "Are you going to spend all morning answering my statements with questions?"

At any other time in their lives, Tally would've come up with a smart-ass question for his sister. "Sorry. I'm... Addy, it's been a morning already."

"I know, Tal. I hate hitting you with this now. You want him to come in here?"

"Please." *No. No, I don't. I want to curl into a ball and not deal with anything else quite yet.*

That didn't stop Kennett from sweeping into his office with his latex gloves on and an envelope captured in a plastic bag. He stopped short of the chair across from Tally. "You look terrible. Are you up for this?"

"Thanks. You don't look too perfect yourself." Tally sat forward with a sigh. "Better to not put it off."

With exacting care, Kennett extracted the envelope and used the cap of a ballpoint to retrieve and pry open the note.

Your attitude needs adjustment, Bastille.
Check the news this afternoon.

"I'm so glad that it's so vaguely threatening." Tally ran both hands over his face, wanting to scream. "Are they going to attack another property, do you think? The house?"

"There's no way to guess. I have eyes on all your properties and I'm assuming your own people are on the house?" He waited for Tally's nod. "We can't try to wildly second-guess them right now. Just have to sit tight."

"Sitting tight doesn't...*ssssit* well with me, Kennett."

"I know. Not my favorite way to spend a day either."

The call, when it came, wasn't from one of Tally's properties, but from a frantically tearful Jean Jones.

"It's all going up in flames, Urusar!"

"Jean! Calm down! Did you call the fire department?"

"They're here. It's still burning. I don't know what I'll do."

Agent Firebaugh gave him a long-suffering look when Tally had hung up. "Your car or mine?"

The scene wasn't quite as horrific as Tally had feared. Again, no one had been caught in the blaze. Again the fire department had it under control quickly and prevented the spread to adjacent businesses. Jean, however, was nearly inconsolable as she sobbed in Tally's arms.

"It's all right, Jean. It is." Tally repeated over and over, liberally peppered with, "That's what insurance is for. And what they won't cover, I will. We'll fix this."

"The beautiful new ovens..." she gasped out.

"We'll make sure you get new beautiful new ovens." Tally wasn't entirely sure what he was saying any longer. All of his remaining words deserted him when Agent Firebaugh arrived at his side with another note.

They opened the note in Tally's car before Kennett bagged it, and Tally's stomach felt like someone had dropped an acid-covered ball of lead in it.

You move too slowly

And offer too much resistance.

"Damn it. *Damn it!* What do they expect me to do?"

"Probably play nicer and work faster. Is there anything you *can* do? For their current demands?"

Tally drummed his fingers on the steering wheel. "Possibly. I don't like the way you're saying *current* demands."

"Thought you'd catch that." Kennett tipped the latest note into a bag. "From previous notes, it just feels like there's a resolution still missing on this batch."

"Thanks. The suspense might literally kill me."

* * * *

Spending all day expecting another arson made Tally jumpy and snarly. When Addy appeared in his doorway after three o'clock, he snapped at her before he could stop himself. "What *now*?"

"Don't you growl at me. There's a glass shipment on the loading dock, Tally." Her face was pinched and weary.

"The latest glasses from Gerhard? But that's good news."

Addy shook her head. "You better come look."

That acid ball grew bigger as Tally outpaced his sister to the loading dock where opened crates sat in scattered groups with the tops pried off. He'd been anticipating this shipment eagerly, wanting to see the final product of long negotiations with Gerhard about shape and design of bud vases and martini glasses. His heart sank as he approached the crates.

A sea of glittering shards greeted him as he leaned over the first one. Every compartment in the crate held only shattered glass. The contents of the crate beside it were identical, and the one next to that.

"They're all like that, Tal," Addy said softly. "Every single piece Gerhard sent us. Smashed."

Tally straightened from his horrified perusal of the crates, fingers closing around the worry stone in his pocket. He took a careful breath in and out before he tried to speak. "Is there a note with the crates? Something addressed to me?"

"How did you... Never mind. It's over here. I told everyone not to touch it."

The same cream envelope, the same careful block letters as all the others. Tally sent Agent Firebaugh a quick text to tell him the final terrorist act of the day wasn't arson but property damage, then waited for him to join them by the remains of Gerhard's art.

They spread this third note on the battered metal desk by the bay doors, though Addy stood back, fidgeting, as if she were intruding.

There will be a better show of faith
Stronger positions from the mighty uktena
The famed negotiator

You will announce that no otter will be Urusar.
You will negotiate with the human city council on our behalf.
You will begin work for a buyout of your concerns in Asia.

"They don't want much, do they?" Kennett chewed on his pen cap in a distracted way, *sniffing*. "He's done his best to cover it, but Kaul's scent's on this one. Someone else, too. Ursine? Canine?"

"I couldn't see him dressing the girls himself for those pictures. Makes sense someone else is there."

"You have hotels in Asia?"

Tally shook his head. "Not yet. I have property in Asia on which I'd hoped eventually to build hotels. You have any guidance here? They've proved their point. Slammed it home, really. That they can get to anything of mine, not just family. Property, friends and allies, international commerce. They're saying nothing is safe."

"Really overdoing it." Kennett leaned back against the desk. "Whatever you can reasonably give them, Tally. They hold the cards right now and we don't want them hurting your girls."

"Right. Don't make the psychopaths angry," Tally muttered. "I'll do the best I can. Addy, can we get Gerhard on the phone when it's a decent hour for him? I'm so sorry all his hard work was destroyed like this."

Addy surprised him with a hard side hug. "On it, Tal. Anything I can do, you let me know."

* * * *

Three hours later, Tally finally got home, late for dinner and just...done. He made it into the house from the garage, took his shoes off by the door, shuffled as far as the den and snaked. Maybe it wasn't the most responsible option, but he just couldn't face another thing. Not another question, request, demand, nothing.

He untangled his horns from his dress shirt with some difficulty, left the tie on because he didn't have hands to take it off, and curled up on top of the heat vent by the powder room. It was quiet here and the family would be in the kitchen. This was good. *No more right now.*

The bubble of peace couldn't last long, of course. Tally opened one eye when the vibration of approaching footsteps jarred him from a doze. He flicked his tongue to sample the air. *Ah. Haru.* At least it wasn't Hal or Che or worse, Mom. Haru stopped beside him, cocked their head to the side and crouched down.

"People are worried, my Argaze," Haru said softly. "You may wish to human? Especially since the yellow tie is not a good match for your uktena scales."

Tally lifted his head with a snort and bumped his nose against Haru's knee. His otter twitched but didn't jerk away. *Bump. Bump bump. My otter.* Uktena territorial imperatives notwithstanding, he didn't wrap around Haru like he wanted to. Even snaked, Tally knew that would freak them out. A chime sounded from Tally's jacket pocket. He put his head on Haru's knee, pleased when they stroked his shining forehead scale, trying to ignore the pinging. It didn't stop. *Persistent.*

With a sigh, he slithered to his jacket and nosed around until he got his jaws around his phone and pulled it free. He tapped the screen with his nose and pushed the phone over so Haru could see the screen too, since they'd probably never experienced the family chat.

Mom: Tally where are you? I heard the garage door.
Lahi: Bet he snaked.
Hal: Not taking that bet.
Dad: He could snake and still slither into the dining room to say hello.

Tally heaved another sigh, tapped on the screen and mashed the touch keypad a few times with his nose.

Tally: rvfddfngvkf
Nan: OMG, totally snaked
Mom: Tal-tsu'tsa Bastille! You human this instant and get in here. We are worried about you!
Nan, Addy, Hal, Lahi and Che: Oooh, full name. Tally's in trouble!
Tally: gykujgyjyjvh knhbkjbhgujk
Che: That looks like a no
Hal: That looks like a f--- no
Mom: Language!
Hal: What? I didn't even say it!
Dad: I think Haru went to find him. How about we give Tally some space?
Tally: bkhvmbfgtgjm
Dad: You're welcome, son.

Haru shook their head as they helped Tally shut the chat down. "Your family is so strange." They stroked a finger between Tally's horns and he leaned into the touch with a contented hiss. His otter was definitely getting bolder around snakes. "You must be hungry, though. It was not an easy day for you."

In answer, Tally slithered into the den and up onto the couch.

"Ah. You would like food in here? Where there is quiet, away from all the family?"

He raised the first foot of himself off the couch and bobbed his head in a snake nod. Haru offered a tiny curl of a smile, brought Tally's clothes to him, then walked off toward the kitchen. Easier to stay uktena'd, of course, but then he wouldn't be able to talk to Haru. With a bit of reluctant hissing, Tally melted back into his human form, tugged the tie off and pulled on his boxer briefs and undershirt so Haru wouldn't be uncomfortable when they came back. After a moment, he pulled on his pants and his socks as well. The den was warm. It wasn't *that* warm.

Almost before he'd gotten the second sock pulled up, Haru returned with a big bowl of... Tally flicked his tongue to taste the air. *Mmm. Pumpkin mushroom soup.* And a smaller bowl of red beans and rice.

"Don't tell me Mom got Hal to eat this?"

Haru shook their head. "No. The family had pork chops. Though Sammy also had the beans and rice for extra protein."

"How's our Sammy been today?" Tally broke up the island of sour cream at the center of his soup and took a bite. His stomach rumbled a threat, telling him it *was* hungry, damn it.

The long stare could've meant several things, but Tally suspected it was Haru's *all right, apparently we're not talking about your day* stare. "She has been resting. And not eating potato chips. Sammy's ankles and feet have swollen and she is upset that her new boots will not fit."

"Poor Sams." Tally shook his head. "Telling her it's temporary probably wouldn't be a good idea right now, would it?"

"You might be taking your life into your hands," Haru murmured, fidgeting with the coasters on the coffee table. "My Argaze, you stayed very late at work."

Tally scarfed down some of the beans and rice, fortifying himself, and decided to circumvent Haru's polite skirting of direct questions. "The glass shipment that came in today was completely destroyed. There was a third note. I did text you about the other two?"

"Yes. And that there could be a third." Haru's hands had stilled on the coasters, their expression far too blank.

In calm, measured tones, Tally explained what the note had said, and what Agent Firebaugh had said. "I need to... Because of the joeys, you understand. To..."

"Capitulate." Haru put a hand over his. "This is difficult for you."

"It is. But my ego's not so huge I'd endanger the girls. And why Asia? I don't understand that at all."

Haru had no answer for that, not that Tally expected them to, though he — *they* — stiffened.

"I'll do all I can. There really is only so much I can do quickly."

"Perhaps, my Argaze, they need to be shown that."

He met Haru's eyes and saw the determination there, then leaned his forehead against his otter's as an idea sparked. *My brave Haru.* "You are a genius, you know. Tomorrow, there'll be wheels to set in motion."

Haru tipped his — *their* — head up for a soft kiss, then Tally went back to his dinner, somewhat settled if not feeling precisely better.

Chapter Seventeen

Be Careful What You Ask For

"Tell me why I cannot bite him?" Haru asked again as they straightened their *kimono*. Were the lines properly arranged? They turned. The stones from their pup necklace popped nicely, as did the stones from the betrothal bracelet.

Tally let out a controlled breath. "Because Barry and Kaul still have the girls."

"Just one bite?"

"No, we don't want them retaliating. I — *we* — have more to think about than just the girls."

They knew that, but a bite might be worth the trouble. The latest round of photos showed the girls opossumed, huddled together in their cage. Being opossumed was probably easier at this point. Haru doubted the girls would human unless made to. The world was easier to process as an animal. Less complicated.

"Not the tie," Haru said as Tally draped a lovely silver one around his neck.

"What?"

"No tie."

Tally held on to it. "But we're going to the city council meeting."

"No tie." They smacked Tally's hand and took the tie away, then for good measure flicked open the top two buttons of his shirt. "Absolutely no tie."

Tally's mouth drew shut as he eyed Haru brushing their hair.

"We want your dominating nature on display."

"I don't—"

"You *need* to be imposing. Having presence is not always a bad thing, my Argaze. You will be playing the part they asked for."

There was a sigh, long and heavy, Tally's shoulders drooping momentarily before he straightened again. "I don't like scaring the humans."

"We can send fruit baskets later."

"Food doesn't solve everything."

Haru side-eyed their Argaze. "It certainly solves most of them. And I think most of them will later write off the behavior to our girls being missing. Can you help?"

They had gotten their hair into a ponytail, but the bun wasn't forming properly. It was rebelling and Haru blamed the cold weather, not their fumbling fingers. Tally stepped up behind them and took the brush.

"Let me. Sit." He undid the work Haru had put into the ponytail and smoothed out their hair. Each pull of the brush felt divine. They might have even turned into the touch. Tally tugged on Haru's hair, getting it back up. Jasper fluttered over from a hiding spot and helped their Argaze weave it into something much nicer than Haru had been accomplishing.

Jasper began poking around their jewelry boxes, finding decorations to add to the bun. Pixie and snake working in harmony to make Haru presentable. *Odd*, but not unwanted. It was never something Haru had pictured for themselves, though they had had trouble looking beyond teaching their students. Probably because the prospect of being matched had scared them so much.

"How's that?" Tally asked as he placed the jade hairpiece.

"Perfect. Now let me get my makeup done." They shooed Tally away from their room. "Can you find my *zōri*?"

"Your what?"

"The purple sandals—they look like wedged flip-flops. I think I left them in the hall closet."

"Oh, right. I'll meet you downstairs." Tally stuck his head back in the door. "Won't your feet get cold?"

"Out!"

Tally, thankfully, left Haru alone to finish doing themself up. With Jasper's help they had the precious stones placed and makeup done quicker than normal. They did not, however, offer to shut Jasper in the closet this time. No, no more repeats of that ever again. Of course, Haru realized Jasper probably would've been killed too if he had gotten out of the vents. Instead, Jasper burrowed into their bun again. Hopefully he'd be able to stay warm.

By the time they made it downstairs, Tally was sitting with Gun and a small group of the Enforcers.

"Who is staying?" they asked.

Several hands went up—a young cougar, an ocelot and a fox. Haru glanced over toward their Argaze. These were staying? Then Tally elbowed the wolverine closer to his age and his hand went up. The whole group waited, watching Haru. It took a moment to understand the Enforcers were anticipating their approval.

"Excellent. I do not care how much Lahi and Sammy complain, you do not leave their sides. Do we have aerial support?"

Gunther's eyebrows rose as he cocked his head. "We will?"

"Yes, yes, some of the Sommers are watching the house," Tally replied as he tapped his phone. "And a couple Blue Hollys will be in the woods. I believe Agent Firebaugh has some human eyes on the house too."

"Good. Shall we?"

Tally offered his arm. "We should. You look stunning."

"Thank you, my Argaze." One should always be prepared for war.

The car ride was quiet, filled with anticipation. Walking into city hall was not as easy as it looked. Not with ice on the ground.

Haru hissed as their foot slipped.

"It's not the ground's fault."

"I can blame it if I want to." They glared harder when Tally chuckled.

"Maybe if you wore the boots I suggested," Tally said.

"Boots do not go with a *kimono*."

"You could change them when you got inside. I would gladly be your boot burden beast."

Scandalous. Haru huffed, tried taking another step but slid again. Thankfully, the Bentley was there to catch them.

"Oh for Gods' sakes." Tally wrapped an arm around Haru's waist and *lifted*.

"What are you doing!"

"Trying not to fall." Tally grunted. "Stop wiggling. I'll brain us both."

Another arm had Haru up in a princess hold. "Do you not find this embarrassing?"

"Not yet. Ask me after I maim myself."

Tally carried them into the building. There was a stumble or two where Haru was sure death was imminent, but somehow Tally kept them both upright. The display of strength was...*impressive*. They ran their fingers through their Argaze's tousled hair to help straighten it when he set them down, in the lobby, in front of several stunned onlookers.

"What?" Tally growled in uncharacteristic annoyance at the gawkers. "*Zōri* don't work well on ice."

"My hero." Haru snuggled up close, placed a kiss under his jaw, then straightened and looped their arms together. The blush was adorable. But...

The show has started.

To see Tally shift from protective to business mode was *thrilling*. It shouldn't have been. Not really. Haru felt confused as to why it was. They didn't let that bewilderment show. Oh no. They needed to look the part of doting Uruma—husband—in front of the humans.

The function was planned to be a working dinner. Planners, architects, civil engineers, the city representatives, talking over the steps Wadiswan wanted to take in the town revitalization project. Councilmen O'Rourke and Hastings were present too, invited by Tally on behalf of the Lijun Association. Of course, the real reason they were present was for them to see Tally playing the part of persuasive business leader.

Watching Tally move through the crowd, predatory, capable was different than home. Haru knew Tally did business all the time. It was how they had met. To see him in his element, surrounded by people like him, was *different*.

"Yes, the new roads project was a hefty chunk of change," Tally said, leaning over the plans. "Are we sure about the drainage on the north end? I'm seeing some new sewage installations near the *old* theater house. Do we know if it'll be able to handle that kind of disruption? I seem to remember some concerns about the foundation."

"Oh, yes, Mr. Bastille. We had one assessment done in November, which pointed out worries about the northeast corner and the loading beam," Mayor Burke replied.

"I've sunk a lot of money into this and guaranteed for certain renovations, but I do *not* want to bleed money."

"Oh, no, I don't think they were serious issues, Tally," a lovely redhead replied. She smiled at Haru and gave a tiny wave. "I'm City Manager Jessica Hauptman. We met at the wedding. We appreciate you coming, despite the circumstances. Mayor Burke and I just wanted to say how sorry we are about the Cohen and Eberhardt children. We hope Agent Firebaugh will locate them soon."

"I see. Thank you." Their heart shattered, but Haru managed a *mokurei*. "I am sorry. I could not place you, but I remember the hair."

Jessica winked. "You were occupied with other things during the wedding."

"Yes, he was," Hastings-san replied, edging Haru out of the circle. "But as Tally was saying, that theater already has issues, doesn't it? Is it really worth throwing all that money at it just to have to tear it down if the drainage plans cause problems?"

Mayor Burke and Hauptman-san both scrunched their noses and shared a displeased frown. Good to know the humans didn't like the noisy boar either. Both women seemed reluctant to answer.

"Does the theater have significant historical value?" Haru asked.

"Oh, yes, yes it does," Hauptman-san answered.

"Not if it's falling down," Councilman Hastings interrupted.

Tally straightened up. "I hadn't heard any news the building had fallen into more disrepair."

"It hasn't," the mayor answered. "We have to wait for another assessment when the ground thaws in June, but we expect any repairs needed are within the budget for renovations."

"June?" Hastings-san snorted out.

"June," the ladies replied. Then Mayor Burke turned to their Argaze. "I promise, the fall review was highlighting things we wanted to watch and plan for. We aren't going to look for you to finance a complete rebuild. We're not looking for that and we would never abuse your contributions like that. Trust me, the June assessment should show we're right."

"Why should we wait until June?" Barry asked. "The building has been shuttered for years. It should just be torn down."

"As Mr. Bastille here could tell you, Mr. Hastings, the building has historical protection. The town is legally and financially obligated to repair the building."

"What?"

Tally glared down at Hastings-san's outburst. "Yes, otherwise the land goes back to the *Jennings* family."

The shell-shocked expression on the boar was almost laughable.

"They're quite eager to get their hands on that plot of land, too," Tally added, and shook his head. "They weren't pleased when the matriarch left the theater to the town in her will."

"*Jennings*?" Hastings-san parroted.

"Yes, interesting family," Haru added. A very *human* family. "I believe the youngest son had hopes for a pig farm and butchery? Bacon is quite popular here, is it not?"

"Oh it is," Hauptman-san answered with enthusiasm, her eyes lighting up. "Tristan already has a small farm on the outskirts and just needs a storefront. He's dedicated to the ethical treatment of animals and is breeding rarer types of hogs, before selling locally to the restaurants. But he does keep some back to make some specialty snacks. I hear he's also getting llamas, emus, geese... Weren't you in his class, Tally?"

"Ah, no, he was a year behind me."

Haru hummed. "Does Tristan do the butchering himself?"

"Oh yes," the city manager answered. "He wants to make sure the hogs die as quickly and as humanely as possible."

"Gods." Councilman Hastings had gone a mossy greenish color. "That is— That is barbaric." He stomped away, muttering, "Unbelievable."

Mayor Burke's mouth was pressed together, lips twisting. "Doesn't Barry own a grocery chain?"

"Yes," Haru answered. "You think he would be interested in getting some prize hog meat. He does like his bragging rights."

The ladies nodded.

"Excuse me. I think I will get us some food." Haru left Tally to the city planning committee and wandered over to the buffet table to listen in on the other chatter. Councilman O'Rourke had one of the building inspectors cornered. Poor guy could barely get a word in edgewise, drowned in questions as O'Rourke-san bullied his way forward.

Oooh, treats. They almost grabbed some of the fried shrimp but then remembered they still had time left on their two weeks. Haru sneaked a peek over to Tally — who was watching them. They reached for a plate, added the little quiches, some fruit, then several shrimp.

Tally's gaze narrowed, and his tongue flicked out. Barely perceptible, but he did do it.

Haru cocked their head in the direction of the harried conversation to their right. Just as the conversation escalated, Haru dipped the shrimp and took a big bite. *Oooh, yes, treats.* They might have whimpered. Loudly. Or maybe it was more of a moan. Haru licked their lips and took another bite.

Oooooh, yum.

The booming conversation next to them died. Tally had extracted himself from the mayor and city manager and was crossing the room. When their Argaze took the plate from them Haru barely managed to keep the smile off their face. They looked down at the floor, bowing their head slightly. It allowed them to peek and see the building inspector had put some space between himself and the nasty moose.

O'Rourke-san called over. "Everything all right, Tal?"

"Everything'ssss fine." Tally's eyes slid to the plate then back to Haru. His voice dropped to a whisper. "I thought we talked about this."

"We have, my Argaze."

"You weren't allowed *treats* for two weeks. You broke the rules, remember?"

Haru flicked their eyes up briefly and then returned them to the floor. "I could not help myself. They looked so nicely done."

"Hmmm."

Councilman O'Rourke had edged closer. By now Tally had noticed the two of them had an interloper. There was no way the moose couldn't hear them. The human, no. O'Rourke-san, yes. Tally put the plate down and leaned in, whispering into the ear closest to their enemy.

"This means more Punishment, Haru."

"Yes, my Argaze."

"And what would that be?" O'Rourke-san interrupted, his eyes particularly focused and bright, his eager expression absolutely stomach churning.

The human looked confused and had stopped his progress away from the group. *Stupid human.* Instinct wasn't as strong as it should've been in the older ones. Between the graying hair at his temples and the lines etched into his face, this human had seen plenty of years.

Tally had curled one hand under Haru's elbow. The other had dipped to their ass and patted hard. "I know how to handle the situation. Thank you, Dan."

"Of course. Of course," he replied. O'Rourke-san nodded, a pleased smile on his smarmy face.

"Yes, my Argaze."

The building inspector was still standing there, still a deer-in-headlights expression on his face. Unfortunately, attention went back to him. The councilman shot an unreadable expression to Tally and Haru before latching onto the poor fellow again.

Should've run when you had the chance. And no matter how good the yummy had tasted, it had been a futile attempt to distract the nasty moose. Haru almost let a hiss slip, but they managed to keep it together.

"Tally, I was just discussing the situation with Alfred here about Best Bakery."

"Oh?"

"It seems he thinks the building will be back up to code with a few repairs." O'Rourke-san snorted.

"Yes, it, er." The building inspector shot a concerned glance in the direction of their trio. "There is waterlog from the fire, understandably, er. But the loading beams are sound, as are the other supports. There is a window that needs replacing and some of the kitchen appliances, but overall, insurance should cover it as long as arson wasn't involved."

"Have we heard back on the cause of the fire?" Tally asked.

"No, er, not yet."

"You should really check over the building again," O'Rourke-san insisted. "If there's faulty wiring or something now, it puts the other buildings next to it in danger."

The nonplussed expression from Alfred-san said he felt otherwise.

Tally spoke up. "How about I offer to pay for another inspection? I would hate for anyone to come back and say due diligence wasn't done."

"Well, er, I suppose it wouldn't hurt." There was an annoyed-sounding puff. "But it's gonna take another couple weeks before I can get back to it. I have some other, er, projects I need to go inspect."

"We understand," Haru responded before the moose could barge in with the protest forming on his lips. "What takes you away from us?"

"An apartment complex down south. Might be a couple weeks or more."

"Yes, well, please call us when you get back so we can arrange for a time to have the bakery inspected again."

"Can't we get someone else?" Councilman O'Rourke ground out.

Alfred's dark eyebrows pulled together. "I have a contract with the city, Mr. O'Rourke, because of the size of this project. Unless you want to pay the fine to bring someone else in, I suggest you wait a couple weeks. I'll be back."

"How much is the fine?"

Tally sighed. "The entirety of his contract. In full. Alfred has been a great asset to many projects. His insight is invaluable. The city council wanted the best. *I* gave them the best."

The implied *don't fuck up this business association* was left off.

"Thank you, Mr. Bastille. Er, your praise is always good to hear. I'll, er, give Jessica a call when I get back in."

The human scurried away, diving into the slurry of humans and disappearing.

"Why didn't you stop him?" O'Rourke-san demanded.

"Because Alfred has a lot of influence within his field, and if we hired someone else, the *entire* town development plan could be brought to a *standstill*. No permits. No sign-offs. Do you really want the entire city council fuming at you? Do you think they'd keep banking with you?"

The moose balked.

"Yeah, try to think things through a little more before you open your mouth, Dan."

"Of course, Urusar Bastille. My mistake."

Haru wondered if the moose could turn redder.

"Thank you…for watching out for my *interests*."

Wow. That must have been hard to say. It looked like O'Rourke-san had swallowed a whole humble pie.

Haru put their hand out and squeezed his forearm. "I am sure Alfred-san will not say anything untoward to Mayor Burke or Hauptman-san. Are they still thinking of financing the new town office through your bank? I do not recall."

The two ladies in question were staring right at their group when the three of them looked over. Alfred-san was nowhere in sight, but the timing was rather fortuitous. Seeing the big moose take a step back and let out a muffled bellow had a ring of satisfaction.

"Oh, no, excuse me, Urusar." He rushed off in the mayor's direction.

"My, ever so polite, even when he is stabbing you in the back," Haru observed with a nod.

"Quiet, you," Tally hissed.

"What did I do?"

"You know full well the city council never considered Dan's bank for the town office."

Haru glanced up. "Did I?"

"Yessss." Tally ran his hand down Haru's shoulder. "I am not happy about the shrimp."

"I know."

"No, I mean, that *display* in front of Dan."

Haru snuggled closer and kissed Tally's jaw. "I was trying to let the human escape."

"Oh."

"It backfired."

"Just a bit." Tally nuzzled Haru's ear. "No treats for another month."

Haru choked on their next breath. "What?"

"I mean it."

"But—"

"Nope. You endangered yourself in front of that, that...pompous ass. He was practically licking his chops over you...which... That look was so smarmy. So *vile*." Tally shuddered and held Haru against his chest. "And you cheated with the treats."

"We can agree on the smarmy, but the treats?" Haru nuzzled closer.

"You could have gotten his attention another way. The last thing we need is Dan O'Rourke giving you *that* kind of attention."

"I apologize, my Argaze." Haru bent out of habit, but Tally's hold made it impossible to bow.

"I already said no treats for a month. You don't have to bow."

"Yes, my Argaze." But the compulsion was there, hard to push back. The need to complete their apology was hard to fight against, even with Tally's hands on them. When Tally bent their head back, the soft expression puzzled them.

The kiss was certainly unexpected. They gasped and Tally took advantage, his tongue dipping into Haru's mouth. Quick. Teasing. Snakish. Then he pulled back just as Haru leaned into it.

"Be good," he said then walked away, burying himself in the knot of city council members.

Meanie. That had only been a taste.

Haru glanced around and noticed Hastings-san watching them from outside the circle of movers and shakers. The sneer was quickly replaced by a fake grin. But it had been there long enough for them to see the contempt in the boar's eyes. They lifted their nose and broke out their *akomeogi*, holding the fan in front of their face. Long enough to hide their bared teeth and bow their head respectfully before giving him their back.

Time to take a turn around the room and hear what the people were saying. Moving from one group to another didn't mean Haru couldn't feel Hastings-san's eyes on them, but it gave them a small sliver of satisfaction knowing being ignored was probably irking the tiresome bully. The general chatter was about the different projects, rebuilding, drainage, zoning — mind numbing. But Tally was in the middle of it, talking about costs and lawyers, what would benefit Wadiswan.

They snuck Jasper a bite of cheese, hoping their pixie wouldn't leave a huge mess in their hair. Except the little troublemaker zipped down and buried himself in the folds of Haru's *obi* and *obiage*. Hopefully he'd look like a doll as long as people didn't look too closely. Though he was snug as a bug, so most people probably wouldn't see him. Haru didn't have the heart to tell him to move. The bun couldn't have been overly comfortable. Not to mention it felt good having his little body tucked up against Haru. Made the ache in their heart not flare so bright.

Every time the conversation seemed to go in the direction Councilmen Hastings and O'Rourke wanted, it always toppled down like a house of matches. Deeds. Wills. Complex zoning restrictions. Votes the mayor and city council would have to take. The time for soil assessments and so on.

There was a reason this was year three of a ten-year plan, and when the realization finally hit for Hastings-san and O'Rourke-san, well, Haru had to hide their smile. They had made their way back into the current of humans surrounding their Argaze, jostled a bit here and there before they managed to perch by his arm. Tally barely spared them a glance. Not that they expected him to stop his conversation for their reappearance.

There was sweat building on his chest and brow. *Hmm.* Haru grabbed the corner of their *kimono* sleeve and dabbed. This time Tally did glance down.

"My Argaze."

Tally kissed their temple. "Everything all right, Haru?"

"It is now." They snuggled against his side. "Just a little sleepy."

Everyone glanced up at the clock on the far wall.

Mayor Burke said, "Oh, dear. We've kept everyone past official hours. I am *so* sorry. We should let everyone get back to their families."

Haru let out a gasp and flicked their *akomeogi* up to cover their face. A hand went to their necklace. The sob that followed wasn't even pretend. Their heart couldn't hold back the tide of emotions they'd been holding at bay all evening.

The cacophony of noise was instantly sucked out of the room.

Tally went stiff against Haru and wrapped an arm around their shoulder.

A hand not belonging to their Argaze pulled on their *obi*, followed by Hastings-san saying, "We should get— ouch! What the—"

"Do *not* touch my husssband without their permission."

There was a pinprick of blood forming on the back of Hastings-san hand. *Odd.*

"Haru doessss *not* appreciate being manhandled," Tally continued, getting in Hastings-san's personal space. "Especially since…"

A tear trickled down their face. "Ever since the children were taken." They shuddered against the sudden rush of emotions. "It has been hard to be around strangers at all."

"You just can't help touching what's mine, can you, Barry?"

"I never! I haven't—"

Tally bent close and hissed out, "Don't play ssss-stupid."

Haru gave a respectful-seeming nod to Hastings-san and said in careful, even tones, "*Shi'ne, bakayarou.*"

The humans stared silently as Tally escorted Haru away from the meeting room. Hastings-san stepped forward but O'Rourke-san splayed a hand against his chest and dipped his head. A heated exchange followed, but Haru ignored it as their Argaze hustled them out of the building.

"Did you just say '*die, asshole*' to Barry?" Tally murmured without slowing down.

"Yes?"

"Good."

Once again they were lifted into Tally's embrace as the two of them went to the car. Jasper let out a small squeak and unsquished himself by pulling out of Haru's *obi*. A glint of something metal caught Haru's attention.

"Jasper?"

The pixie glanced up.

"Did you stab Hastings-san with one of my hairpins?"

"Yes." Jasper puffed up, looking cocky.

"*Good.*"

* * * *

Tally had excused himself the moment they'd said goodnight to the extra Enforcers and the house had settled. No, Sammy and Lahi weren't happy with having babysitters when Tally and Haru had to leave the house, but the grumbling was minor and they seemed to have enticed their young wardens into a game of poker for chocolates.

Typical.

Now, alone in his study, he tried to shed layers of unease from the city council dinner. Dan's hungry gaze, Barry's disdain for...everything. He didn't recognize them anymore, these lijun he'd known all his life. Maybe he'd never *liked* them—his father hadn't either—but this rampant, arrogant need to stampede over everyone they perceived to be in their way? This was new.

Encouraged by some outside source? More than possible. Someone or a group of someones who fed those bitter and resentful flames both boar and moose obviously had harbored all those years. Someone was feeding their egos and validating every perceived slight.

There had been little indication of approval this evening, even though Tally had done his best to defend their selfish demands as far as he was able. He'd even won some zoning concessions for one of the properties

Barry *did* own. No note had appeared to say he could come get his girls, though. Not that he'd expected it. There was still too much in play, too many things they wanted.

What was the endgame? That was the question nagging at him. His complete capitulation, something they couldn't realistically expect to have? His resignation as Urusar or his ceding to a challenger? Some sort of merger where he'd be put in a position of uneven power dynamics?

Would they, when they had whatever they wanted, simply murder him and anyone of his family they saw as a threat?

He drummed his fingers on the desk, hating this dearth of information, this inability simply to pick up the phone and issue orders to get everything resolved. On that thought, he picked up the phone.

"Misaki? Yes, I… It's not *that* late." Tally held up a finger and pointed to the armchair in the corner when Gun wandered in. "Sorry. Things are eating at me. Have I provided you with details on the Asian properties yet?"

Gun slouched in the chair, one eyebrow raised, though he kept silent. He knew better than to interrupt a business call.

"I'd like a rundown on how difficult property transfers would be. Yes, China and Japan. Differences between local and foreign buyers. Highest priority." Tally stopped as Misaki listed off her *other* priority work from him and he pinched the bridge of his nose between thumb and forefinger. "New highest priority. Thank you. As soon as you have it."

When he said goodnight to Misaki, Gun was still staring at him. "You're not selling off, are you?"

"Not that the business side of things is strictly your business," Tally said in his flattest, calmest voice. "But I have to appear to be ready to. Right now I don't know what their interest is or why *those* properties in particular. If they wanted properties of mine, either to decrease my holdings or gain a foothold in a specific market, why not something already successful? Something without all the possible international pitfalls? I don't understand it and I *don't* like not understanding. So we start kicking over rocks and see if anything crawls out."

"You're prickly tonight."

"Can you blame me?" Tally surged up to pace, and, though Gun didn't flinch back as someone else might have, he still had a wary glint in his eyes. "Where are we? Anything new?"

Gun shot him a grimace and a sidelong glance. "No. No activity at the site outside the park. No luck trailing Hastings or O'Rourke. I mean, sure, we've followed them all over town during the day. Nothing suspicious about what they're doing. Then as far as we can tell, they go home at night and stay there."

"So what are you doing about it?"

Gun's forehead wrinkled in obvious distress. "I only have so many people, Tal. We're doing the best we can."

"And yet, here we are, with my girls still not home." Tally made a concerted effort to stop grinding his teeth. "We're only assuming activity at night. We've been making assumptions about movements and meetings. I want surveillance around the clock on the targets we discussed before. Maybe there haven't been any meetings in the last few days. We can't take that chance."

"There's not enough... People have to sleep sometime." Gun had risen to face him, a hint of belligerence in his stance.

"You came back home to take this job." Tally stabbed a finger at him. "Are you saying you can't do it now?"

A tiny gasp came from the doorway. Tally spun to find Haru there with a tray clutched in both hands. They'd changed into a more comfortable *yukata* but their hair was still up, making the shock that flickered over their expression easier to spot. "I brought tea, my Argaze."

They maneuvered around Tally and Gun to set the tray on the desk, expression schooled once more, and a wave of shame sloshed over Tally. "Gun, I'm —"

"Don't." Gun held up a hand. "You're doing what you feel you have to do. Guess I'm used to my friend Tally and not Urusar Tally Bastille."

"What does *that* mean?"

"I'll see who I can pull in. Marnie might have some time. Some of the squirrels might be good for certain spots. I'll reshuffle. You're right. It's my job. Better go do it."

Gun walked out, a little too stiff in the shoulders, a little too heavy in his step.

"Perhaps that was not well done," Haru said softly as they poured tea, chamomile by the scent.

"It wasn't, was it?" Tally scrubbed both hands over his face. "I'm sorry you were subjected to that."

Haru tipped their head, both evasion and acknowledgment. "This is part of you."

"Instead of just what I want you to see?" Tally huffed a breath, chest tightening. "Still, that was Gun. I should get him..." He trailed off at Haru's look. "What?"

"Your friend. From childhood. And you wish to buy his forgiveness."

"Oh." Tally sank down into his chair. "Right. I'm... Right."

"Your tea, my Argaze." Haru put the cup in front of him and kissed the top of his head. "To soothe you after a difficult evening."

Tally sipped, letting the steam bathe his face as he blinked back the sting in his eyes. Funny how Haru had gone from *Tally* back to *my Argaze* again these days and Tally had barely noticed, probably because somewhere along the way *my Argaze* had somehow morphed from a formal title to, if he dared think it, a term of endearment. Life did insist on getting stranger all the time.

The next few days didn't bring any flashes of insight or any answers. Tally walked around with shards of glass in his stomach and a squad of jackhammers in his head. Every day was another misery, every night another endless round of anxious fear for his little girls. There had to be a way to them. *Had* to.

Staff scurried out of his way as he stalked through the hotel to his office. For once, he couldn't find the energy to care. *If there has ever been a good time to fear me, it's probably now.* Approvals, inquiries, authorizations—he flew through them that morning, unwilling to second-guess himself, unwilling to wonder if his judgment might be impaired. Then when his emails were cleared, he glowered at his screen as if it had failed him by not providing more to do.

Addy, brave Addy, poked her head into his office. "Tal, just got a call from the airport."

"Misplace a guest, did we?"

Addy gave him a faux shocked face. "As if we would! No. Gerhard's here."

"Gerhard...Klug?" Tally blinked. "Why? Did we know he was coming?"

"Not a peep from him. The last I talked to him, we were discussing getting a replacement shipment done."

"Huh." Tally stood and accompanied Addy out to his admin's desk. "Thanks, Addy. Car sent for him? Room ready?"

"Done."

"Good. Terry, I want to know the moment he arrives."

Terry, one of the few people on staff besides Addy and Nan who weren't intimidated by him, nodded and went back to the computer.

Gerhard was here and the timing was...strange. He knew that Addy sometimes had video conferences with vendors. Phone calls. Emails. Physical samples. All of those options had been enough before, and the current request was to replace an order the Klug factory had already filled.

The visit, without warning, made no sense.

He could either brood here in his lair or go out and face whatever this was. A quick brush through his hair in his private washroom, a straightening of his tie – the tight-patterned maroon and gold floral, *thank you, Haru* – and he retraced his stalk back out to the front lobby. The chandelier needed dusting. The runner in front of the revolving door was crooked. A trash can in the lobby was far too close to full. Tally narrowed his eyes, cataloging. He wouldn't micromanage out here in front of guests, but the staff saw. Housekeeping was getting a call from Addy and everyone would know where it came from.

Within a few minutes, the town car pulled up and the passenger door opened before the driver could run around. Bright-eyed, head swiveling to take in his surroundings, Gerhard Klug stepped from the car, tipped the driver with a charming smile and waved off the bellman trying to take his bags.

Those curious blue eyes seemed to drink in everything around them as Gerhard bustled into the lobby and caught sight of Tally. If he'd had a tail right then, it would've twitched hard, both in recognition and in that instinctive meeting of predators sharing territory. That impression only lasted a moment. Gerhard was far too intelligent to challenge a larger hunter in his own territory, and Tally doubted that was his purpose anyway.

It occurred to Tally as he stepped off to meet the fox halfway that there might be things Herr Klug didn't want to trust to electronic communications of any kind.

He held his hand out and dredged up a smile. "Gerhard! This is a surprise."

"A good one, I hope." Gerhard grinned and put his bag down to take Tally's hand in both of his. "It *is* good to see you, *Herr* Bastille. Even though you are married now."

The tragic sigh was all comic exaggeration and Tally even managed a laugh. "Sorry about that. Do you need some time after your long flight before business?"

"A shower would be wonderful." Gerhard wrinkled his nose. "The airplane air is always so…stale."

"Excellent. Jonas will get you settled and I'll see you in my office around…" Tally checked his watch. "Three?"

"Oh, thank you. You are kindness itself, Herr Bastille."

"Tally. We've been through this. I'll see you in a bit."

* * * *

When Gerhard made his reappearance, he'd obviously had both a shower and a nap. Rested and relatively calm, he'd changed into what must have been casual attire for him with his suit discarded for close-tailored dress pants, dress shirt and cashmere pullover. Neat and trim, every inch of him.

"Thank you." He gave Terry a little bow as he was shown in and stood in the middle of Tally's office, taking in the warm woods and dark fabrics. "Oh, very nice. It does suit you."

"Thank you." Tally waved at the comfortable chairs in front of his desk. "Sit. Please. Something to drink?"

"Water, if you please." Gerhard settled in the left wing chair. "It may be, as they say, five o'clock someplace, but not for me yet."

His soft, melodious voice was as soothing as Tally recalled, a voice that could weave castles for the listener or offer the moon, a voice that made him even more cautious now. He snagged them both sparkling waters from the office fridge and took the other wing chair instead of keeping the desk between them.

"It *is* nice to see you, and I do have to apologize again for the disaster with the shipment..."

Gerhard waved a hand. "Nonsense. It was not your doing. All replaceable, in any case."

"Yesss." Tally sipped. "That was my thought too. Gerhard, I know this will sound blunt, but why are you here?"

"It is blunt." The smile twisted and Gerhard shook his head as he reached across the desk for a pad and pen.

He scribbled quickly in a perfect, bold script, pointed to the walls, and held the pad up to Tally.

ARE WE SAFE TO TALK HERE?

Tally nearly choked on his water. So. This wasn't about glass. "We are. I have people who would either smell or hear surveillance equipment." He took the pad and placed it on the table. "Are you in trouble? In danger?"

"No. I would like to keep it that way." Gerhard's accent had suddenly become more pronounced, his consonants blurring a bit about the *w's* and *th's*. Nerves? Anger? "Tally...your *kinderlein*. Your little ones. I am *so* sorry."

"So this is a sympathy vissit?" Tally winced at the sharp hiss, but how did Gerhard even *know*?

"In part, of course it is." Gerhard reached across cautiously and patted Tally's arm. "I hef...*have* children, too."

"Ah. You give the impression that you're single."

Again that twisting of his mouth, nearly a grimace. "I am. Now. My husband did not, I suppose the most polite word would be *approve*, of my transition. But neither could he be bothered with the little ones, so they live with me."

Tally's face heated, embarrassment nearly choking him because of his assumptions. "I have to apologize. I'm—"

"Water running under the bridge." Gerhard flapped a hand in front of his face. "My point is that I sympathize. Empathize. We heard rumors, rumblings in Germany, that something terrible had happened in Wisconsin. I was concerned, since I know you are here.

My father is council president of the *Bundesland*, the state of Niedersachsen. He made inquiries for me, then made further inquiries."

Tally wanted, hoped, this wasn't going to turn into something sinister, but recent history made him wary still. "Why would he do that?"

"The conservative factions in your country and in some others concern us. This desire to return lijun to a separatist and isolationist way of thinking, of living. They are *fools...*" Gerhard stopped to stare at his shoes and sip his water, perhaps shocked by his own vehemence. "It is far too late to return to the old ways."

"I think they know to some extent," Tally offered. "The world's too small for us to hide in our own villages anymore."

Gerhard tipped his head at that. "True. They would stifle trade with lijun first nonsense. Cripple us and send many into poverty. They are short-sighted and stupid."

Tally leaned forward, locking eyes with his fox guest. "But they're dangerous."

"But they are dangerous." Gerhard leaned forward to match him, taking Tally's hands. "I am here to say... I am *authorized* to say that you are not alone, Tally Bastille. Many of us are watching. Listening. If you need us—for sanctuary, for a voice in the global community—we are with you."

For a long, uncomfortable moment, Tally stared, his brain unable to think in words. Finally, he blurted out, "You came all this way to say *that*?"

"I will leave you specifics, too," Gerhard said with a little bark of laughter. "But yes. We cannot always trust our emails and our phones. It was better, safer, to see you face-to-face. Better for me to come as one of your vendors than someone from the council, too."

"Well…" Tally sat back, willing the sting at the backs of his eyes to go away. "I don't… Thank you. I don't know how or if that can help. But… Thank you."

"Just absorb the thought for now." Gerhard leaped up and clapped his hands together, the bright sheen back in his eyes. "Now. I saw some absolutely glorious chandeliers on my way in. Might we take a look at them?"

Tally rose more slowly, though he did manage a chuckle. Good idea, making sure the business part of the visit would have witnesses. "Of course, of course. If you promise not to be too critical of my poor lighting fixtures, I'll even get you a ladder."

Chapter Eighteen

Pied Piper

An evening at home, a nice restful evening at home, a moment to try not to think about the twins, that was all Tally had wanted. The moment he'd settled on the sofa in the den with Haru, popcorn and a Korean drama Haru wanted to watch, the phone rang.

Of course it did.

Tally thought hard about not answering, but the display showed Linda Sommers, one of his event coordinators at Sapphire Lake. Why would Linda be calling him after hours?

"Linda?"

"Urusar?" The tearful voice on the line was far too young to be Linda's. "It's... It's Carrie."

That explained the caller ID. Carrie must have had her mom's phone. "Carrie? Are you all right?"

"I'm...yes." She heaved a shuddering breath. "No. Urusar, we don't know what to do."

"Are you *safe*? Carrie, where are you?"

"We're okay, me and Mindy, but..." Another hiccupped sob rattled through the line. "Urusar

Bastille, please come. It's Tyler, and I know you'll be mad and everyone will be. We were out. At Figby's. Tyler was... I know we're not supposed to be there."

"It's all right, Carrie. Don't worry about that now. At Figby's, then. Getting drinks you shouldn't be able to."

"Yessir. And Tyler had too much. He... He gets drunk so much these days." Carrie pulled in a deep breath.

Good girl.

"We were leaving. Going to my car. Tyler smacked into a human. They... They started yelling at each other. Then fighting. Then Tyler, he...he...*boared out*! Right in front of the human!"

Holy mother of us all. Tally was up and striding for the garage, stomping into boots as he went, Haru right on his heels since he must've heard both halves of the conversation. "Is the human still there? Was it only one? Where's Tyler now?"

"I don't *know*!" Carrie wailed. "The human's really trashed. He passed out in the parking lot. But Tyler ran off!"

"I'm coming. Stay put." Tally swore as he tore open the garage door and ran to the Bentley. With the phone on hands-free, he told it to call Gun as he backed out with a squeal of tires.

"'Lo? Tally?" Gun had to yell over traffic, most likely on watch at one of their previously discussed guard posts.

"Figby's, Gun. Meet us there sooner than possible. The kids have gotten themselves in trouble."

Gun was cursing up a storm as he hung up. He might be there quicker than Tally could be. Beside him, Haru fidgeted with their seat belt. "You did not bring a coat."

"I didn't..." Tally glanced down at himself and sighed. "I'll manage. We have to make sure this Exposure issue doesn't get any worse."

"Yes." Haru just nodded, expression set and determined. There were children involved, so Haru was in full Uruma mode.

They reached Figby's just as Gun's old Mustang screeched into the parking lot, Crystal in the passenger's seat. The adults converged on the knot of kids in the far corner of the lot. Cody was with them, and Justin now too, though Carrie hadn't mentioned either of them. *Oh, well, safety in numbers, and I'd rather see the youngsters standing with each other than slinking away.*

A human, maybe in his late twenties, sprawled at Cody's feet.

Tally pointed to him first. "Did anyone hit him besides Tyler?"

Four heads shook. Carrie answered. "No, Urusar. Don't think Tyler really did either. Too drunk. He just fell over."

"Which way did Tyler go?"

Justin pointed. "That way, sir. Once the guy dropped, Tyler just charged off, snorting."

Toward the highway. Naturally. "Gun?"

"We're on it. Scent trail is pretty damn ripe."

Tally had to agree as he flicked his tongue to taste the air. Boar and excess alcohol smelled like rotten orange rinds. "Who drove and are you sober?"

Cody raised his hand with a serious nod. "We thought...after New Year's...designated driver and stuff."

At least one of them could learn. Good thing. "Tell one of the employees inside that they have a patron in need of assistance out here, then take everyone home, please."

Haru touched his sleeve, tipping his head toward the scent trail. "Should I...?"

"No. We'll follow by car as best we can."

Crystal crouched behind an SUV at the back of the lot and, a moment later, the soft rustle came of a great horned owl taking flight. Gun snatched up her clothes, tossed them in his car and took off, keeping a precarious eye on the road as he followed her.

"We are not making certain of the human?" Haru asked softly as they got back in the car to pursue.

"This might be one of the only ways it's safe for us to be exposed to humans." Tally snorted. "Not that it's ever *safe*, but that man's so drunk he won't remember, and if he does? No one will believe him because he *was* so drunk."

Haru still frowned, but Tally had always found the less interference in these cases, the better. In past centuries, an Urusar might've slaughtered any human involved in Exposure, or the less bloody-minded might've taken the human to the Shafa to have their memories tampered with. The first wasn't an option, in Tally's opinion. The second would only muddy the waters, since the man's memories would already be, well, muddy.

Following the Mustang's taillights, the triple rectangles, was relatively easy, though Tally hissed at every swerve and sudden lane change Gun made. Tally couldn't see Crystal anymore, but Gun's eyes were far better, even at night. He just wished Gun wouldn't take such fatalistic chances.

Not even a mile from the entrance ramp to the highway, Gun slowed and pulled onto the shoulder, creeping along until he finally braked and burst out of the car. Tally followed his example, still not... *Oh. There.*

Weaving a few steps, running a few steps, stopping every now and then to root in the grass beside the guardrail, an adolescent boar trundled along the road. He lifted his head to snort challenges at passing cars, brush tail whipping madly behind him, but then appeared to forget his aggressive imperatives and go back to exploring the weeds.

Tally snagged Haru's sleeve, then Gun's. "We can't let him dart out into the road. I'll stay behind him. Gun, you and Haru get between him and the traffic lane. Then signal Crystal to herd him from the front."

Gun tipped his head back to the sky and let out a series of short raptor whistles, pointing to the guardrail in front of boar-Tyler. Without a sound, Crystal materialized out of the dark sky to swoop down toward Tyler as Gun and Haru carefully sidled up beside him while faded winter dandelion leaves distracted the boar.

When everyone was in position, Tally called out, "Tyler! It's all right. Come on with me. Let's get you out of traffic."

Tyler turned toward his voice, head weaving from side to side. A snort, a hesitant step toward Tally...

"That's it. Attaboy. Let's get you home."

As soon as the words left his mouth, Tally understood his mistake. At the word *home*, Tyler whirled and tried to bolt. He got perhaps ten yards before Crystal swooped in front of him, flapping her huge wings in his face. Tyler squealed and fell half on his side, scrambling back up to head the other way. He'd obviously forgotten in his fright that Tally was behind him.

Just like scooping up a big football, right? A football with tusks and hooves, at any rate. Tally dove to the side as Tyler charged and caught him around the middle. The boar squealed and squirmed, making it sound like Tally was killing him, but he hung on tight. A tusk ripped through his sleeve before Haru was there to clamp onto Tyler's ears. Between the three of them, they managed to lift Tyler, kicking and grunting.

"Which car, like I have to ask?" Gun *oofed* as a hoof caught him in the stomach.

"Let's put him in the Bentley." Tally took some satisfaction when Gun's mouth dropped open. "Back seat's bigger."

Once they'd wrestled Tyler inside, he quieted and curled up on the leather seat. They all leaned against the side of the car, panting.

"I hate to do this to the kid."

"What is that, my Argaze?"

"Taking him home."

"Hmm."

No one offered an alternative, though, since there was the whole *legal* thing in legal guardian. There was a collective sigh before Tally straightened and held out a hand. "Thanks, Gun, for the quick response time. Sorry to drag you away from things."

Lips pressed together hard, Gun took his hand and stared at him for a moment. "Not a problem, Urusar. My job." Then he shrugged, his expression relaxing a fraction. "Kids have to take priority."

"Right." Tally said it softly, his heart twisting at the forced formality. But he supposed he'd done this to himself. Haru patted his arm and kept their thoughts to themself. Tally appreciated that.

Boar-Tyler had stretched out on the back seat, looking far too comfortable, though the little grunts and snuffles indicated he hadn't fallen asleep.

"Tyler?" Tally glanced in the rearview to see Tyler's ears swiveling toward him. "If there's a reason you don't want to go home... If you don't feel safe there, you have to tell me. We can make other arrangements, but I can't do it on what I think might be the situation."

Maybe Tyler was still too sloshed. He didn't human and gave no indication he'd heard, just set his head on his forelegs with a sigh and closed his eyes.

"It was a good try," Haru whispered and reached across the center console for Tally's hand.

He squeezed it back, grateful for the little bits of affection that kept his spirits from sinking further. When they pulled into the drive of the Hastings' house, Tally groaned inwardly. All the lights were on downstairs. Extra cars were in the drive. Barry and Ada had company. Great.

For a single moment, he debated trying to sneak Tyler in the back, but there were a hundred things that could go wrong with that. "Responsible adult. Yep, that's me."

Tally slid out of the car, pointedly ignoring Haru's snort. He finger-combed his hair back, knowing this was going to look bad. His shirtsleeve was ripped. His hands were probably not the cleanest and he had no coat. Even better. He was going to look like he'd slipped a gear.

Somehow he gathered the courage to ring the doorbell and only rolled his eyes a little when it played Westminster chimes. The *tip-tip-tip* of high heels hurried through the front hall and Ada opened the door with a smile that fell right off her face.

"Urusar." Her hand went to her mouth. "What...?"

"Ada, who is it?" Barry shouted in irritation from the dining room. "If they're selling something, send them away."

When his wife didn't answer, Barry stormed out into the hall and stopped short when he caught sight of Tally. "Bastille. What the hell happened to you?"

"Evening, Ada. Barry. Sorry to intrude on your evening." Tally waved a hand back to his car. "There was an incident this evening. I have Tyler in the car —"

"Tyler!" Now both hands flew to Ada's face. "What did you do to him?"

"Ahem." Tally took a step back so he wasn't looming in the doorway. "He's fine, Ada. Just a bit, ah, tipsy. But the kids were at a human bar and he boared out in the parking lot, you see..."

He trailed off when Barry shoved past him, fists clenched. Tally's heart sank into a deeper pit when he spotted Dan lurking in the dining room doorway, his face growing scarlet, eyes narrowed. *Damn it. The kid didn't need witnesses like this.*

Tally turned and strode after Barry, taking his arm before he could wrench the back door open. "Only one drunk saw him. There's no harm done."

"Hands *off*, you...snake!" Barry shook free and actually shoved Tally away to get to Tyler, seizing him by the ear and dragging him squealing and flailing from the car. Still holding his son by his porcine ear, Barry jabbed a finger at Tally's chest. "*My* son, Urusar. How dare you interfere?"

Trying one last time to be conciliatory, Tally held up both hands. "I only brought him home. He hasn't even humaned since we found him on the highway."

Barry just glared as he dragged Tyler into the house and Tally took in the whole tableau — Ada standing frozen in the doorway with tears in her eyes, Dan lurking behind her like some furious gargoyle.

Oh Gods. I'm sorry, Tyler. I'm so sorry.

He had no proof, nothing to point to law enforcement and say *this child is being abused.* Only his own instincts and all the clues set too plainly out in front of him. "Tyler!" he called after them. "Remember what I said! And stay off the booze!"

When he'd slouched back to the car and slumped in the front seat, Haru leaned over close to his ear. At first, Tally thought Haru would kiss him. Instead he — *they* — whispered, "Are you certain I cannot bite him?"

* * * *

The water was hot. The teapot had been cleaned. The cups shone. They had the snacks arranged on the plates. The tea service was *ready.* Yet Haru hadn't brought it to Tally's office. They stood in the kitchen moving things around, unsure if it was okay to walk in or not. Gunther and Klug-san had holed up with their Argaze hours ago. The guys had to be hungry.

But it *felt* like they shouldn't interrupt.

Tally had had that demeanor. The one he kept carefully under wraps unless he was working. To really see it at home had been enlightening. Haru wasn't sure how it made them feel, but they definitely had feels of some kind or another. However, the safe assumption was, since Gunther had shown up, it had something to do with the twins. *Not* hotel business. Though they weren't sure what Klug-san had to do with clan business.

Which made Haru *want* to interrupt.

Proper protocol said to wait until called for.

But the tea would be better if served felicitously — when ready. Yes, they could warm up fresh water, but Haru had already gotten the treats out. Didn't want them to go stale. That would be rude to the guests.

They adjusted the tray and checked the time. Haru sighed. The cool light from the winter afternoon made everything look so bitter. Frozen. Fine. No more dillying away. They could always leave if Tally sent them out of the office. Haru balanced the tray and made their way down the hall. The murmur of voices didn't make it out of the room. Not even through the door. Haru had already checked. Ear and everything. Not a word made sense.

Knocking on the door halted the conversation. Then Tally's voiced boomed out a "Come!"

"My Argaze." Haru entered, sliding their gaze momentarily over to Klug-san and Gunther. "I have prepared tea and snacks for you and your guests."

"Yes, thank you. Um."

They settled next to the table, tied back their *yukata* sleeves, and began making up the tea. The men moved over to the table, Klug-san walking closely to Tally and leaning in to say something Haru couldn't quite catch.

"I thought some *gyokuro* might be in order, and it should suit your sweeter tooth, my Argaze."

Tally picked up one of the *joyo* and plopped it in his mouth. "Yeah?"

Oof. Well, he did not know better. Haru smiled. "When the spring comes, the sakura tea may be pleasurable to your palate as well, my Argaze."

"I'll make sure to get an order in when I order more of your favorites and the *sake* you wanted."

"Thank you."

They placed the tea in front of everyone and offered the plates with the *joyo* to Gunther and Klug-san. Their fox guest used the cutlery and divided up the treat. Someone had manners. Haru smiled and got a wink. Well, now. Flirty fox. Klug-san's grinned widened.

The fox cleared his throat. "So you are Akaike."

"*Was,*" Haru answered immediately.

Tally, for some reason, brightened. His expression lost the tension he had held around the eyes.

Klug-san hummed. "I see. Tally said you are one of their trained Satislit."

"Yes."

Maybe coming in wasn't a good idea.

"Is there a reason you ask?" they inquired after several beats.

"These requests, about the Asian properties, they seem *different.*" The fox rolled his shoulders.

"What requests?" Haru eyed their Argaze.

"To sell off the holdings I have to certain interested buyers." Tally hissed. "I have Misaki making it look like I am doing so. I just don't understand why."

"Where is my contract?"

Klug-san nodded.

Tally frowned, but rose from his seat and went over to a row of bookcases, which were actually filing cabinets if one looked closely. He pulled out a file and came back to the table. The cover sheet of the contract looked so *normal.* But inside it held Haru's existence. One, whether Tally had understood at the time or not, that determined their lot in life.

"What does it say about Absolution?"

"Absolution!" Tally's neck snapped as he turned toward Haru.

"How much did your parents handle the negotiations?" they asked.

"Mom and Dad got a lawyer in Japan. I told them to make sure the Akaike clan couldn't refuse…"

Klug-san sighed. "Which meant concessions."

Tally's expression darkened. "Which meant concessions. It's not like we interacted with Urusar Akaike a whole lot."

"And if your parents told the lawyer to make him happy, then whatever lawyer helped with the contract didn't necessarily point out every detail," Haru said softly.

"Or we didn't think something so antiquated would actually be invoked."

"Contracts have items included for a reason, my Argaze."

Tally sighed. "I know… I do *know*. For me it was just a formality to have my Em'halafi."

Gunther had been flipping through the pages, the sharp features of his face pulling tighter as he read through it. "What the fuck is this shit?"

"A contract, I'm guessing a Traditional contract — yes? Thank you — for a Satislit," Klug-san replied. "You Americans don't really know what you're getting into sometimes, which is a gift and an Achilles heel rolled all in one. Has Agent Firebaugh seen this?"

"No, I don't think so," Tally answered. He moved his worry stone between his fingers. "Though he seems to know about the Akaike."

"Most lijun outside of the US do," the fox replied. "They're a small, but *old* Traditional clan with influence and connections. Little short of cash these days. Not anymore, thanks to this contract, it seems."

Tally slumped down in his chair. "Everyone kept trying to tell me, at the hotel, to make me understand, but..."

"You wanted your Em'halafi," Klug-san finished.

"*Yessssssss.*"

"You Americans need to pay more attention to clans outside of the US."

Tally frowned, but Klug-san wasn't wrong. The Americans rarely paid attention to clans outside of themselves or the Western countries. Their self-importance was infuriating sometimes.

Gunther had stopped flipping, looking with a fierce intensity at one of the pages. He must've gotten to the relationships page. "Why are there separate sections for divorce and Absolution?"

"Because they are different things, Curley-san."

"Does this really say you'd be banished from all clans if Tally *returned* you?" Gunther squinted. "Like no one could take you in? What are you? Defective merchandise?"

"Yes," Haru answered, surprised by the echo from Klug-san.

The fox rolled his shoulders. "I do not agree with the practice, but I know what it is. Though that condition seems harsher than most. Urusar Akaike...did not like your behavior?"

"I rebelled, tried to, at times," Haru answered, holding the tray in front of them. The questions were becoming too personal. Too close. "Just because it was the life decided for me, does not mean I could always accept it. There were times I was angry over the choices taken from me."

"Why didn't you leave?" Tally asked.

Klug-san snorted. "It is easier said than done for a Satislit, especially ones like your beautiful Haru here, to leave."

"Fuck me." Gunther was still reading. His sharp gaze going over the lines again and again. "Tally, the Akaike get those land holdings if the marriage is Absolved."

"What are the conditions for Absolution?" Klug-san asked.

"There are a few: Endangerment, Inability to Provide Financially, Inability to Provide Security, Impairment—physical or mental—where the Argaze can no longer perform his duties and hold up his end of the bargain... What the fuck are these? They are, are—" Gunther's face flushed. "What is this, this?"

"Archaic?" Haru offered.

"Yeah, yeah they are... They treat you like a commodity."

"But that is what a Satislit is, Curley-san."

Klug-san was right alongside Haru, nodding, also ignoring the stunned expressions Tally and Gunther wore. "The Americans are so fun, are they not, Uruma?"

"Their innocence has a refreshing taste, not unlike the tea."

The fox laughed, though Tally and Gunther were still silent.

Their Argaze shook himself. "So the Akaike, and through them the Traditionalists, are going to make a play at my holdings through the pups and Haru?"

"Yes," Haru and Klug-san answered. It took a moment, but they centered themself and let out a breath. "It looks like it. But since Melia and Livy are not a direct line—"

"The Traditionalists don't care about them," Tally finished.

"Yes, the announcement, with Sammy. That is…" Haru shuffled back.

"There was a conversation, not long after that," Tally said, watching them carefully. "Was it your parents? Or Urusar Akaike?"

"Akaike-san. He thought you would be asking for Dissolution. He was not happy the return fee would not be higher, due to my negligence."

"Why didn't— No, no, I do get why you didn't say anything." Tally sipped the tea and made a face. "That explains a lot. Yeah."

Gunther cleared his throat. "So we have to figure out their next move."

That was when the phone rang. All of them looked over at the desk.

Klug-san's accent thickened as he asked, "Does anyone else not like the timing of that call?"

Tally and Gunther raised their hands.

Their Argaze got up, scowled when he read the ID. "Rory? What's— No, I have a minute. Uh-huh." A scowl wove deep wedges along his mouth. "Uh-huh. When?" Then an exasperated huff followed. "Why wasn't I notified? No, yeah, but still, there's an order to these things. No, I appreciate the heads-up, but the timing is shit. Yeah. No, thanks. I'll let you know what happens. Okay. No, yeah, bye."

The silence was deafening. Tally's humongous frame had coiled tight. Haru could almost see the serpent underneath. None of them instigated a conversation. Waiting.

Finally Tally turned back around. "Dan, Councilman O'Rourke, has brought Exposure charges against Tyler Hastings."

Haru grabbed his arm. "Has the human talked?"

"No, the human hasn't said a word."

"But why is MacLean-san from State calling?"

Tally's expression soured further, his pupils turning to slits, and he let out a hiss. "Because Dan asked State to approve the Punishment since I hadn't given one, proof that I'm being derelict in my duties."

"State is still supposed to follow up with you first," Haru insisted.

"Yes, they should," Klug-san agreed. "Unless someone at State is playing games too."

Tally pulled on his braid. "Yes, but I guess we know what play the Traditionalists are making for Absolution. Dan has always been the sneakier one in that unholy pairing."

"So when is the meeting?" Gunther asked.

"Tomorrow," Tally answered with a huff. "The meeting is tomorrow."

"Then we need a plan," Klug-san said. Gunther nodded in agreement. "We should probably call your Agent Firebaugh with the update?"

"Yes, we need logistics. A plan and counterplan. I am not dancing to their tune anymore. How dare that bully of a moose drag another kid into this."

Fury, tight and hot, rolled off Tally. The cold, calculated look was new. Their Argaze was ready for battle.

But, for Haru, tomorrow would come too soon.

Chapter Nineteen

To the Pain

Absolute torture. Nothing else could describe the utter chill in the air. Normally the Oak Room's dark-paneled walls gave the meeting place a warm, cozy feeling. Not today. Bastille Arms, while a treasure for its architecture and old-world class, was beginning to hold a lot of unpleasant memories for Haru. Like New Year's Eve. Things had been finally going right, or as right as they could have been, then they'd gone sideways, hurtling them in directions Haru didn't know how to handle.

But then, Haru had been oscillating between sheer panic and anger to snippets of happiness to frustration and confusion since the Global Lijun Alliance conference. Their life had certainly changed quite a bit in the last half a year plus. One minute their biggest concern had been the welfare of their students and whether or not they could escape a match. The next it was trying to understand an Urusar who didn't follow the rules and taking care of frightened pups. They dipped their head and followed their Argaze's movements out of the corners of their eyes.

Tally cut a fine figure in his suit. It was once again one of his custom suits which probably cost an arm and a leg, not that all the *kimonos* and *yukatas* he let Haru buy were cheap. Their clothing definitely cost more than the suits, but one must look the part of a wealthy Urusar's spouse. Their Argaze had positioned himself between the pale, shell-shocked Tyler and the council. The State council member had chosen a place behind Councilmen Hastings and O'Rourke. She had been introduced as State Representative Bancroft.

Almost everyone in audience had given a discreet sniff.

Haru had detested the woman on sight. Her smug expression brought out all kinds of feels and they weren't sure they wouldn't bite her. Bastille-*okaasan's* hand on their arm was the only thing keeping Haru from confronting the little weasel.

One thing was obvious — they expected Tally to lose.

And that was the one thing the Bastilles could not allow. Tally, Agent Firebaugh, Gunther and Klug-san had stayed up late trying to think of possibilities and how to counter them.

"As I said, we are living in the twenty-first century. We can*not* simply kill humans who see us." Tally drew in a breath, making his large frame even more formidable. "I followed general council rules for the Exposure."

O'Rourke-san leaned forward in his chair, tenting his hands together. "You did not bring in a Shafa to make sure the memories were fixed."

"The human was so drunk they passed out. His memories of the event were already questionable. Why send a Shafa in to find the memories and risk making them clearer by finding them?" There was a beat of silence before Tally continued, "The law says to make sure the human's memories cannot recall the Exposure, and that use of a Shafa or *other means* are acceptable."

State Representative Bancroft growled out, "State has already agreed these were special circumstances, since the location was in such a public place."

"Then why didn't State contact me?" Tally hissed.

Oooh. The muscles under his suit rippled. Power rolled off Tally, a bit of his serpent coming to the forefront. Poor Councilwoman Howe shook and her nose and ears twitched. Haru sincerely hoped she did not rabbit. It looked like it would be a close thing, though.

It was Hastings-san who replied to their Argaze. "Because you were derelict in your duties by not assigning a Punishment to my son, Urusar Bastille. Now he faces Exposure because of you!"

"You had said you'd handle it," Tally shot back. "As Urusar, I trusted you would act appropriately. You did not come to me or Uruma Bastille for Judgment."

The boar snorted, red-faced, but instead of looking upset, he came off as angry. Like the Punishment was an embarrassment. Not very fatherly. No Usar should reject their child in such a public fashion. Not even the mom had stood up in his defense. She sat to one side, quiet and focused on her husband. Tyler hadn't even looked at either of his parents since being paraded into the Oak Room.

Bancroft-san slithered forward. "Be that as it may, was Tyler not one of the youths drunk at the New Year's Eve banquet?"

"He was."

"If the children involved had been punished then—"

"They had community ssssservice," Tally hissed out.

"The Punishment did not fit the crimes then," the weasel answered, baring her teeth slightly. "Because young Tyler Hastings did *not* learn his lesson. It needs to be something more appropriate."

"I can have him working at the morgue then, see the results of drunk driving."

Ah. One of the counters they had come up with. A murmur went through the small crowd.

State Representative Bancroft shook her head. "We at State feel the measures taken need to fit the crime, and that you as Urusar are compromised, due to current circumstances. We have already approved Punishment."

Tally hissed, his chest puffing. "That ssssstill ssshould have been disssssscusssed with me."

"We at State feel differently," she answered dismissively.

Wrong move.

Their Argaze stalked forward, moving with a graceful beauty Haru had only seen in ballet dancers. "Is that the argument you're really going with? Do you think I don't have friends at State? Or the National Assembly? Or Global?"

For the first time since the closed meeting had begun, the weasel's confidence visibly wavered.

"What issss the Punisssshment?" Tally hissed out.

The narrowed, smug expressed fell back into place for Bancroft-san. "Yeakib Kasab."

Haru gasped and at the same time Klug-san shouted, "No!"

Out of everyone in the crowd, the two of them were the only ones who had reacted. The grin on O'Rourke's face was almost frightening. The glower Hastings-san wore wasn't any comfort. Not when most everyone was looking at Haru and Klug-san with varying expressions of confusion. Poor Tyler had lost several shades of color and was doing an impersonation of a snowdrift—white, drifting and frozen—his gaze solely focused on the weasel and what she leaned on. The boy had figured it out. Haru's heart ached. No one should ever have to experience such a cruel torture.

Klug-san recovered first. "I am here on behalf of the council president of Niedersachsen and must object in his place. How can Americans have something so barbaric still on the rule books?"

"Barbaric?" Tally swiveled toward the fox. "What do you mean barbaric?"

"It is an older, more *traditional* Punishment that fits the crime," State Representative Bancroft answered. She had moved out in front of the desk. When the audience's gaze moved to her, more gasps and murmurs moved through the crowd.

Haru found themself on their feet and only a couple meters from their Argaze. Nausea rolled through their stomach. How? How could these people be so cruel? They saw the exact moment his gaze landed on the cane.

"What isssss thissssss?" Tally's humongous frame loomed over the floor.

"How we mete out the Yeakib Kasab, Urusar Bastille." The weasel had the audacity to smile and offer their Argaze the cane. "And since it would be cruel for an Usar to have to do harm to their own child, we at State feel the Punishment should be handled by the clan father."

"What?" Tally snapped, and for a full measure, Haru thought he'd uktena out.

"It would be cruel for Councilman Hastings to have to strike his own son," State Representative Bancroft repeated.

"You cannot think I want to strike one of my clan?" Tally protested.

Haru glanced at the crowd—noting the alarmed expressions among the lijun present. The Punishment certainly had come as a surprise to the sleepy clan. Despite the Traditionalists in plain view, this was something *new* to them. A Punishment they hadn't seen before.

This is how they plan to beat Tally. Because the maneuver would have him beat. It would fulfill the image of the huge, powerful, cruel uktena in front of the clan, the last thing Tally needed.

It was the perfect way to undermine their Argaze *and* allow Urusar Akaike to use the Absolution clause.

White-hot rage stormed through Haru.

How dare they! How dare these cruel men inflict such pain on everyone! For what? Control? Power? Petty revenge? To throw another innocent pup in the middle of it made it ten times worse. How could Hastings-san allow this to happen to his own child? Was he really so blinded by that much hate?

Tally was still protesting, arguing, fighting a losing battle. The words slid over Haru. They cast about, searching for Misaki. They found her, seated next to Sammy and Lily, with a wary sheen to her eyes. She must've seen something on Haru's face, because her cool mask flickered for a moment, then she nodded.

Between Tally taking a breath and a pause from the State representative, Haru spoke up. "I invoke Dahia."

Tally spun to them, his expression halfway between confusion and horror. "Mother's sake, what the hell now?"

Misaki stood. "I second Uruma Bastille's Dahia."

"What the hell is Dahia?" Tally asked again. "Misaki?"

She only inclined her head, her eyes darting toward the weasel, who admittedly looked confused as well. Oh, the representative understood what Haru had asked for, but Bancroft-san apparently didn't know Haru as well as their Argaze. They were a mystery player to her. The representative seemed to be at a loss as to why Haru would invoke Dahia. She was seeking guidance from Councilmen Hastings and O'Rourke, but both of them appeared to be happy with how the game was playing out.

Bakayarou.

Tally had moved to stand over Tyler—exuding a startling presence of protection over the boy.

Haru came up next to Tally, laying their hand on his arm. "Trust me."

Their Argaze moved his mouth next to their ear and whispered, "What are you doing?"

"Hastings-san still has our girls. This, this will please him. Those bastards may have hurt our family, but I refuse to let them continue hurting children. No more." Haru stole Tally's hand and gave it a kiss.

"Haru." There was a warning in Tally's voice.

"I will not let them hurt Tyler. It is my right as Uruma to guide and protect the children of this clan."

"But what is Dahia?"

"A rule as old as the Punishment," Haru answered. They gave Tally's hand one last kiss then turned to the Bastilles. "Someone is going to need to hold him."

"Dahia has not been confirmed," the weasel protested.

Haru met Klug-san's bright gaze. He shuddered, then said, "I confirm."

Councilman O'Rourke grinned and waved a hand toward the weasel. "It has been decided."

The crowd had gone eerily silent. The clan might not understand what they were watching, but they *felt* something. Tally's worried brown gaze had settled on Haru. They grabbed the end of their *obidomo* and pulled it. Then their *obijime.* The *obi* pooled on the floor next.

"Make sure the fifty strikes count, Urusar Bastille."

"What!" A wave of power nearly sent Haru to their knees. Their Argaze was close to uktenaing out.

That needed to be stopped. Haru shook their head. "You are forgetting, Councilman O'Rourke. It is Hastings-san and you who will, as Bancroft-san said, mete out the Punishment. One cannot expect a loved one to be able to deliver it without bias. We are Em'halafi, after all."

A wave of murmurs went through the crowd. Councilman Black shushed the lijun.

"Is this really what you want, Uruma?"

Haru refused to look at Tally. They were afraid, so very afraid. "Yes. We cannot have our young ones showing up to school with bruises they cannot explain. It risks us all. The humans would talk."

His calculating gaze became resigned. "Then so be it."

They were still unraveling themself, trying to get as many layers tied off as they could without undressing completely. Tally could've protested, brought the issue back to State, but in the meantime, the girls would be in danger and his reputation attacked relentlessly by the Traditionalists. This was the quickest way to resolve the problem, and hopefully, bring the ball back into their court. Tally was protesting again, but Bastille-*otōusan* had moved in front of him, a hand pressed to their Argaze's chest. Finally Haru had enough of the *kimono* taken apart, their back was exposed.

"This isn't right, Dan! Barry! You *know* it isn't!" Tally bellowed.

Haru snuck a look toward the crowd. They had been fixated on the council and the sinister little weasel before, but now they were watching Tally — and the looks were mostly thoughtful. Like they hadn't expected him to be so upset. He was no longer the big, cold serpent in their eyes.

Maybe this was exactly what needed to happen.

Haru caught Tally's gaze and mouthed 'trust me' again. They weren't naïve. It was going to hurt. They knew *exactly* how much it hurt. What they hadn't expected was the outrage they felt. How could such a rule exist, here of all places, in Wisconsin. They mouthed one more thing — 'make it right' — before turning back to the council.

"Councilmen O'Rourke and Hastings."

The weasel frowned. "I'm surprised you chose the back."

Because I was taught to, so I could still sit in seiza. "Where would you like me?"

"This is archaic!" Tally shouted.

The boar grinned, cane in hand, and pointed to the wall. They carefully positioned themself with their hands, leaning forward. Haru snuck another look at their Argaze. His pupils were slitted.

Gunther, Che, Hal and Bastille-*otōusan* all had a hold on Tally. His chest heaved, puffing up like a predator ready to strike.

"This kind of corporal punishment is not what we are!"

Bastille-*okaasan* moved in front of Tally, blocking the view.

The boar leaned over them and whispered into their ear, "I promise this will hurt."

The first stroke cut hard. Heat blossomed quickly and spread out. It banked the anger Haru had been holding in their chest. Somewhere, during all the things that had occurred since the wedding, Haru had stopped thinking something like this could happen to them again. Each stroke inflamed their outrage more. They heard Tally arguing, the hissing, the rustles of cloth indicating hard struggles — despite the *rule*, the allowance for this kind of brutality, their Argaze refused it.

"I will take this to State, Barry! Dan! Don't you think I won't!" Tally shouted. "This isn't right!"

Another slash burned into their back.

"How can you jussssssstify thissss kind of treatment?" Tally yelled.

Haru almost laughed at the question. The boar had the rules on his side. Another slash burned across their back. They were barely able to keep the gasp inside. Some of it must have escaped because Tally's shouting grew as the room grew quieter. Gunther, Che and Hal were arguing.

"Hastingsssss!"

Each strike hurt more than the last. How soft had they gone, for it to hurt so quickly?

"If I have to take on Sssssssstate, the National Assssssembly, I will." Tally hissed. A crackle of electricity tinged the air in the room. "I will not tolerate this-thissssss barbarisssssssm."

373

There was a pause, allowing Haru a respite. Had that been twenty-five? They chanced a gander over the Oak Room. Their clan's attention fluctuated between horror when the lijun looked at Haru to relief when they focused on Tally.

Another body leaned in close, the scent of bull moose heavy and stomach-churning. A hand went over the cuts, burning Haru's skin. *Pervert.* They gasped. In turn, O'Rourke-san chuckled and said, "Count, otter."

The boar had nothing on Councilman O'Rourke. The sheer pain when the next stroke hit was numbing.

"Twenty-six."

Soft.

"Twenty-seven."

I had allowed myself to believe, to think, I wouldn't be harmed.

"Twenty-ah-ah-eight! Ah!" But it wasn't their Argaze who was hurting them. *Despite* the rules, he rejected status quo and was challenging them. Making promises about State. How he would change it all.

And for the first time since Haru had landed in America, they believed their Argaze. Wholeheartedly believed their serpent would do anything to protect them. It was taking four grown men and his mother to hold him back after all.

"Ugh! Ha! Ah! Ah!"

"Count!"

Haru fell to their knees, silver and black dots swarming in front of their eyes. The strokes did not yield. More than anything, Haru wanted to otter. Run away. But then, they couldn't. Each hit of the cane kept them in their place. Each cut faster, harder than the next.

The hits did not stop until everything went black.

Chapter Twenty

Not His Father's Son

Tally paced the length of the sofa in the front parlor. The floor shook with each step and he didn't care — didn't care that he was probably frightening the two people effectively trapped on the sofa, didn't care who else in the house might hear.

"I don't *care* if that's what Haru wanted! How could you *do* that to them! Knowing exactly what was about to happen without explaining it to me, I might add! How *could* you!" Yes, he was bellowing, his voice shaking the walls now even as his feet made answering tremors in the floor.

The whole world could shake apart for all he cared. His fury had gotten away from him in that room and he couldn't seem to call it back.

"Tal," Gunther broke in softly from the corner. "You might wanna bring it down a notch. Calm down."

"Calm down? Calm *down*!" Tally rushed him, pointing a finger in Gun's face. "My Haru is lying upstairs with his back sliced to ribbons. My beautiful otter, who's seen more than enough abuse for seven lifetimes. Who I swore to protect. Who *you* held me back from saving. And you want me to calm down?"

Gun swallowed hard but stood his ground. "I had to, Tal. We all did. I'm sorry."

"Think of the alternative, Urusar." Misaki's smooth, cool voice made Tally whirl on her. "A child, beaten by your own hand. Think, Urusar. Call upon your serpent and find that colder center."

"I can't! Gods!" Tally gripped his hair in both hands, nearly bent double over his knees. "All I can see are those stripes being laid across their back. The blood. I can't."

Gentle hands took his arm. "T-Tal. You h-h-have to sit d...down. Come on." Lily tugged on him until she got him over to the big armchair on one end of the coffee table. "You'll b-blow a g-g-gasket or something."

She stayed with a hand on his shoulder while people talked softly around him. When he looked up again, Pete was there with a glass of water, both twins watching him with concern. Not fear. Concern. Tally's rage nearly dissolved into tears. It was a close thing.

"Tally, if I may?" Gerhard spoke up from the sofa, his voice a mere ghost of its normal chipper tenor.

"I'd rather you didn't." Tally waved a hand, his head still pounding but his brains no longer threatening to pour out of his ears.

"Yes. I don't blame you." Gerhard heaved a shaky sigh. "But I am a persistent little fox and will have my say."

Tally sank farther into the chair with a grunt, not trusting himself to speak.

"Everyone here agrees, you agree, that beating a child bloody would have been wrong."

"Yesssss."

"I think we can also agree that protests filed with State and National take time. They would have been too late."

"I still could have—"

"Short of brute force, there was nothing you could have done." Gerhard's words clipped out now, sharper as he wound himself up. "They had everything pre-arranged. Either you beat Tyler as they asked, and look like a monster, and ruin the trust and confidence you have built in the community and give that greedy *Hurensohn* Akaike the excuse to call for Absolution of your marriage. Or you attack your council members with much the same result, showing yourself as the deadly, dangerous snake some have always believed you might be."

"Look, Tal." Gun came and perched on the arm of his chair. "You know I've had problems with Haru. But what they did today was brave. That was a true Uruma in that room today. And if you go around making it seem like there was another good choice, or that they did something wrong, it's like you're trying to make that courageous thing they did...well, invalid."

Was that what he was doing? Tally sipped his water, trying to make sense of things, wanting to storm upstairs to see Haru, even though Ted Blue Holly and Shafa Lamar had told him to stay downstairs until they called.

"I can't feel good about this. You can't expect me to."

"N-no one does, Tal." Lily stroked his shoulder. "No one c-could."

Gun gripped his other shoulder, as if they were trying to hold him together. "Haru made a strategic decision. It was the best solution in a room full of bad choices.

The only one that didn't tear everything you worked so hard for apart."

With a shuddering breath, Tally felt more in control. Not any better, Gods no, but less like he was going to lose himself in a destructive rage. He pointed at the two people on the sofa. "You two. Out. I understand, intellectually, what you both did. But I can't look at you right now."

"Of course. Perfectly understandable, Urusar." Misaki stood, smoothing the front of her suit jacket. "Herr Klug, I'll give you a ride to the hotel. Lily?"

Maybe it hurt a little that Lily deserted him to go with Misaki, but it wasn't something he had any business complaining about. Misaki's Lexus purred off down the drive and Tally squinted against the winter landscape, certain he'd seen the flash of another car passing it on the way up. He didn't have time to find out, since Ted picked that moment to clomp down the stairs.

"You can go up, Tally. They'll be sleepy if you try to talk to them. Pain meds are on the side table by the bed if they need more. Keep everything clean and unwrapped for now. Only reason to wrap things up is if Haru wants to get up and put clothes on." Ted shook his head as he snapped his bag shut. "Bastards. Awful excuses for lijun."

Tally wobbled a little as he rose. "Thanks, Ted. I'm… Thanks."

"And you…" Ted pointed at him. "Make it an early night, Urusar. Get some sleep. You look like hell."

Tally murmured goodbyes and more thank you's as Shafa Lamar came down, and he saw everyone out the door except Gun, who was on house duty.

"Tal, do you want—?"

"No, no, I'll be all right." Tally waved Gun off as he trudged up the stairs. Things weren't right between them, not at all, but at least they'd gone back to *Tal* instead of that cold, bitten-off *Urusar* that Gun had been using.

Haru lay face down on the bed, covered to the waist, the angry red stripes on their back gleaming with salve. Before he eased onto the mattress beside Haru, Tally took stock of the supplies on the nightstand. Pain meds, mild and more serious, more of the salve that smelled of comfrey and...hemp? Maybe. Bandaging and tape for later.

"Haru? Love?" Tally teased a few strands of hair from Haru's face. "How are you feeling?"

"Hhrmph."

"Yeah, I get that." Tally kept stroking when Haru leaned into the touch. "I want to yell at you and hug you and then yell at you some more."

"Do not yell, *anata*. The boy, Tyler, he is well?" Haru slithered a hand to his and squeezed.

"As far as I know." Tally heaved another breath that stuck in his lungs. "No, I don't know. He went with his mother. His father may not have been satisfied with one act of cruelty in a day."

"Mmmm. He is not safe then." Haru tried to push up, but Tally laid a hand against their shoulder.

"Stay down. Enough heroics from you. I'll send someone by the—"

"Tal?" Lahi stuck her head in the door, carefully not looking at the bed. "Someone's here to see you."

"Now? I don't think I can manage seeing anyone this afternoon. Can it wait?"

Lahi chewed on her bottom lip. "It's Tyler."

"Oh." Tally blinked. "Oh, I see. Tell him to come up."

"Sure, Tal." Lahi disappeared out of the doorway.

Haru grabbed onto a lock of hair, carefully pulling Tally down to eye level. They placed a gentle kiss on his cheek, then one on his lips. "Do not scare the boy, *anata.*"

"Promise. I think he just about died of fright in that meeting room."

A soft knock sounded on the door and Tyler slipped in at Tally's *come in.* The kid looked shocky still, too pale, eyes nearly popping out of his head, and a gasp came from him as he caught sight of Haru. "Uruma... Shit. I'm so sorry."

"Don't be sorry, Tyler." Tally tipped a head toward the chair by the bed. "Yes, you did a dumb thing, but you're not responsible for some grown-ups being sadistic."

"I...I guess." He twisted his beanie in both hands. "My fault though. So stupid."

"Tyler, are you all right? Did your dad... Was he angry at you afterwards?"

Haru snorted. "Sometimes one must say it, my Argaze. Did he hit you?"

Tyler shook his head hard enough to dislodge the bit of snow there. "No. He was way too happy. It was so gross."

"Has he hit you?" Haru pressed, letting out a small groan of discomfort as they shifted in bed.

"He..." Tyler stared at the floor. "Yeah. He has. He does. He... He hits Mom too."

"Now can I bite him, my Argaze?"

"No, you can't bite him. I don't want you near enough to him ever again. So no biting." Tally patted Haru's arm, though he focused on Tyler. "I don't want you going back there. You're not safe in his house, Tyler. One of these days, he'll take things too far."

"But Mom —"

"Is an adult. But I'll try to get some help to her, too. You're welcome to stay here if you like. Until we can make arrangements?"

Tyler shook his head again. "No, um. I mean, thanks. But Justin drove me. I'm... I have some stuff. I'll stay with his folks."

"Good choice. The Tripps are good people." Tally watched the beanie twisting for a moment longer. "So what can we help you with? Or was this just an apology visit?"

Now Tyler began to rock, tears tracking down his cheeks. "I should've...but he said I couldn't. But I don't care anymore. He's *awful*."

"Tyler?" Tally reached out, concerned, but withdrew the moment Tyler flinched. "What's this about?"

"Your little girls...your joeys..."

Tally stilled, hardly daring to breathe.

"My dad... I know he's helping the kidnapper. There's...under our house...there's an old escape tunnel. From back when sometimes...you know...humans."

Tally nodded carefully when Tyler looked up at him.

"Dad goes down to the basement every night. And he uses that tunnel. It goes under the street and into the woods. Way back. And I know what's at the other end, Urusar."

Tally let him rock for a moment more before handing him the tissue box. "What's at the other end?"

"There's..." Tyler blew his nose with a honk and wiped the tears from his face. "It's a cabin. Really old Hastings place. Family hasn't used it, oh, probably since Grandpa was little. That's where he *goes* every night, Urusar. And if it's not to meet with people hiding something terrible, then why would he *do* that?"

"Hey." Tally crouched in front of him, even though he wanted to rush out to this cabin right that second. "You did the right thing. The brave thing. Coming to me with this. Can you do me a favor and go down and talk to Mr. Curley? Tell him, show him on a map if you can, exactly where this tunnel comes out and where this cabin is. I'll be right down."

With a sharp nod, Tyler gathered himself up, sidling toward the door. "Uruma Bastille, you...you wanted to... I never had anyone do something like that for me." Beet red, the poor kid rushed out.

Tally took off his suit jacket and stared out the window, cracking his knuckles.

"What are you thinking?" Haru whispered.

"That tonight, I may get to keep my promise to you."

* * * *

"Explains why we never caught him leaving the damn house," Gun grumbled after Tally had related the new intelligence to his gathered Enforcers and Agent Firebaugh.

"Not something you could've anticipated." Firebaugh reached over and actually patted Gun's knee.

Tally tried not to stare. Was he seeing what he thought he was seeing? And did he... He wasn't sure he approved. He shook himself. Not a time to get distracted. "Right. So the old Hastings cabin is *here*." He pointed to the spot two miles into the woods. "It's not that we didn't *know* about it, but as kids we all tell each other it's haunted and then we grow up and don't think about it."

"Again." Firebaugh shook his head. "Not something you could've anticipated. The last thing I would've thought Hastings would do is risk himself so blatantly by using one of his own properties."

"And everyone's a profiler now," Tally muttered. "Obviously the girls are the priority, so what are your thoughts, Kennett?"

"That you let the professionals handle this."

"And how long would it take you to gather a team of lijun agents?"

Firebaugh puffed out his cheeks and blew out a breath. "No, I get it. After today's events, they're going to conclude you're not really playing ball. Because you aren't and now it's clear. So the danger to the kids increases."

He glanced around the room, seeming to take each person's measure individually. Crystal, capable, experienced. Harry, their wolverine, not often called upon but fierce. Deja and Kerns, young, untried, but dedicated. Gun, of course, always watching, always aware. And Tally.

"And I bet if I tell your Urusar to sit this out, he's going to deck me, isn't he?"

"After the day he's had?" Gunther edged away as if to distance himself from the thought. "Not taking that bet."

"Good enough. We'll need stealth, then muscle." Kennett tapped the X indicating the cabin. "So I'll get us a way in, then Crystal and Tally in animal forms go for the kids. In and out. Once the little ones are safe, we can swarm the place and secure whoever's there. I suggest as many of us stay humaned as possible, and if there are gunshots, for all the Gods' sakes, don't play *Mission Impossible*. Get down and stay down. That's what I'm there for."

"We're all qualified—" Deja started but Firebaugh cut her off with a sharp gesture.

"Qualified on the range is not qualified to take on a career assassin. Until he's secured, stay alert, and if you don't know *exactly* where he is, be worried." Firebaugh rolled his shoulders and cracked his neck. "Tally, if you're in a bad spot where you have to use your natural weapons, please be cognizant of who else is nearby."

"Of course."

"All right. I'm taking a quick nap. We'll reconvene in about an hour and head out. The Hastings kid said his dad always left the house around ten, so we wait by the tunnel exit for the boar to come out. Better if he's caught red-hoofed here."

"You better actually sleep and not work." Gun pointed at the agent. "Starting to think you forgot how."

Firebaugh offered a smile so brief and incandescent it was like a flashbulb. "I sleep between cases. It's the only way."

* * * *

Several hours later saw them scattered throughout the trees near the tunnel exit, waiting for Barry to emerge. Marnie had joined them, because Gun must've said something to her and because she was Marnie. All of them had been doused in chemicals Firebaugh had pulled from his truck to mask their scents, since the porcine sense of smell was far too keen.

Barry's night vision, however, didn't extend far, allowing them to create a tight enough semicircle behind the entrance that their nocturnal predators would still be able to communicate in hand signals. No light shone from the cabin up ahead, but the scents of opossum and honey badger lay thick on the air, mixed with at least two other large predators. The place wasn't empty. Kaul had just blocked the windows to prevent light escaping.

It couldn't have been more than five minutes after ten when a sizable boar burst from the tunnel entrance, grunting and snuffling about in the snow. He turned and stuck his head back underground to pull a gym bag out with his teeth. The boar humaned — the sight of Barry naked was *not* something Tally had needed to see — and dressed quickly before trudging to the cabin. A spear of light answered Barry's knock as the cabin door creaked open, confirming occupation, then Barry hurried inside and the dark healed itself.

Firebaugh signaled everyone to hold positions while he slipped forward through the trees and vanished around the corner of the cabin. They'd expected a wait while he did his reconnaissance, but the wolf was back in under a minute. *Something's gone wrong...*

But his grin rivaled the snow's brightness as he whispered, "They're screaming at each other. Couldn't be more perfect. I have the bathroom window open. Better hurry."

"Any idea where the girls are?"

"No." Firebaugh grabbed Tally's arm. "If it's too dicey to retrieve them, you come right back out. Do you hear me, Urusar?"

Tally nodded, though his brain was on fire with the thought of being so close — *so close* — to being able to get to his girls. No, he shouldn't take stupid chances, but if he saw them... He kept his mouth shut so he wouldn't have to lie to the nice FBI agent.

Crouching low in the winter-denuded brush, he followed Crystal around to the side of the house Firebaugh had indicated. That the cabin had a bathroom was a surprise, though not a shock. There's wasn't an outhouse in sight and a lot of these places outside town had put in septic tanks and dug wells decades ago.

He pointed to himself, *I'll go first*, and Crystal gave him a sharp nod. The window was small, though not small enough to be a challenge to his snake form, except for his horns. Tally stripped quickly, teeth chattering as he stood in nothing but his boots and socks and stuck his head inside the window. When he uktena'd, his horns were already inside, allowing the rest of him to slither in easily. His tail made a small thump when it landed on the bathroom floor, but Firebaugh was right. There was a lot of yelling going on, some of it loud enough to vibrate through the floor.

Crystal fluttered up to the windowsill in owl form and squeezed through to land silently on the bathmat. Owls were better at the whole silent thing. She hopped toward the doorway where light filtered from somewhere nearby, though not enough to dispel the shadows in the bathroom. Good. That meant the building had more than two rooms.

When Tally stuck his head out, he found himself in a dim hallway. The room with the lights on was down on the end to the left. He flicked his tongue, tasting particulates. Melia and Livy suffused the air, had probably been in every part of the cabin by now, but their scents were stronger...

Tally swayed his head back and forth, making certain before he slithered toward the darkened doorway immediately to the right. They were here. His girls were *here*. His heart stuttered and galloped within his serpentine skin as he hurried into the room. It took a moment for his eyes to adjust. Floor-level views could be tricky. He raised his first few feet off the floor to take in the layout as Crystal walked carefully past him.

A bed sat along the far wall. Empty. It certainly would've been big enough for two preschool girls, but they weren't in it. A sharp sneeze pulled Tally's attention around. There. Up on a ratty, wobbly dresser sat a wire cage and inside the cage were two little opossums. *His* little opossums. He reared up farther, resting his head atop the dresser. Livy squeaked, but Melia put a paw over her mouth and they both scampered to him, quiet, so quiet. Nose kisses. Desperate huffs of breath. He could almost hear them. *Usar! Usar! You're finally here!*

More nose kisses. Crystal landed atop the cage and the joeys shrank into the farthest corner, so Tally strained to lift up a bit more. Nose the owl. *Look, it's okay. Owl is with me.* Crystal allowed it, thank the Gods, and the joeys settled.

Now the priority was getting the girls out. The lock on the cage was serious. Wait, no, there were two. Melia had probably figured a way around just one. The bathroom window was far too small. Even if Tally humaned and used his hands, there was no way to either quietly rip open the cage or to shove it outside through the bathroom. This room... Did this room have a window? Tally uncoiled far enough to reach across the room and drape over the bed, nosing at the space above it. Ah, yes. There was something soft tacked up here. Blackout curtains, probably.

He turned carefully, gestured with his head to the cage, then the window. Crystal positioned herself dead center atop the bars, opening and closing her wings. She understood. This wouldn't be quiet. They would have to be fast.

For a moment, he considered humaning and warning the girls, but he discarded that. No need to be the person in the action movie that takes too long to explain things and runs out of time. He turned back to the window, hooked his right horn under the fabric and ripped it aside. Without stopping to check if anyone had heard, he repositioned, swung his head hard and let his horns crack the glass.

Thud.

"What was that?"

Thud.

"Damn it, that's the brats' room!"

Thud. Ccsssshhhhh.

Glass cascaded around Tally as he ducked, his heart exulting as Crystal lifted the cage and soared out the shattered window with a few strokes of her wings. The moment of triumph was short-lived. He didn't even have time for a Dorothy-esque 'They got away, the kids got away' before menacing figures burst into the room.

Firebaugh had told him to rescue the joeys if he could and get out. Right. Except it was more important to give them extra time to get safe. Also, there was Kaul, in the very biteable flesh. Tally wasn't about to make a dive for the window now.

He reared up, puffing himself to match their menace with his own, tongue flicking for a quick assessment. Kaul, yes, gun pointed at Tally. Barry, gaping like a dying fish beside him. A bear lijun of some sort with a huge knife in her hand. Another lijun Tally couldn't identify beyond *canine*.

"Brainless moron." Kaul backhanded Barry without taking his eyes off Tally. "First you make a martyr of that simpering, mincing *otter*. And now you lead Bastille here." He waved a hand at his minions. "Get the kids. His accomplice can't be far."

Tally hissed, swaying, *looming*.

"Try to use your scale flash or your poison, Urusar, and I will shoot you in the eye," Kaul stated calmly. "It probably won't kill you, but it will be excruciating. I have orders not to kill you, but I might still. The chaos of your death would be more than useful, since you have no named Sardu and neither of your brothers are fit to be Urusar."

Another angry hiss tried to get out as the minions raced back down the hall, but Kaul didn't get any more taunts in as a splintering crash came from the front of the cabin, one that sounded suspiciously like a door being forced open.

"FBI! Drop your weapons! Hands on your heads!"

Naturally, Agent Firebaugh's commands were met with gunfire. Kaul merely shifted to a two-handed firing stance, his gaze not even twitching from Tally's. *I might just be able to do this. Maybe.* Tally tightened the forehead muscles around his shining diamond scale, preparing for the quick contraction that would set off the blinding uktena flash. He feinted left, then dodged right as he squeezed, his pupils automatically narrowing to thread-width slits to minimize the effect.

Kaul snarled, but still fired several shots blind. Flat on the floor, Tally tried to make himself as small a target as possible, difficult when he was such a large snake.

Pain lanced along his left side and near the end of his tail. *Not in either eye though, so ha! Take that Mr. Professional Assassin.*

Bedlam reigned in the front room of the cabin — gunshots, screams, snarls, howls and raptor shrieks all combining into an unholy battering of sound. The near silence in the back bedroom was deadly calm by comparison.

Still blinking furiously, Kaul tossed his handgun and melted into honey badger. Tally had just enough time to brace before Kaul erupted from his pile of clothes in a whirlwind of teeth and claws. Tally's horns fouled on a wicker-seated chair by the dresser as he tried to meet the attack. Kaul launched and Tally barely twisted around in time for the claws to puncture the scales along his back instead of into his throat.

Tally hissed, twisting furiously to try to dislodge Kaul and to try to sink his teeth into the honey badger's back. The angle was bad, too close to Tally's head, and he could only rear and plunge as razor-sharp teeth tore into him, aiming to sever his backbone.

The pain became a brush fire sweeping through him, threatening to engulf his sentience and leave only animal fury behind. He thrashed, hoping to get in a slash with his horns, but couldn't bend far enough.

An enraged raptor scream echoed in the hall and suddenly the room seemed filled with eagle wings. A hard hit to Kaul's side knocked Tally flat and horrible tearing sounds came from behind him as Kaul first dug in his claws, then suddenly released, screaming in rage. A ball of tumbling, slashing fur and feathers, talons and claws, went careening into the corner of the room, allowing Tally a precious moment to regroup. Blood ran over his scales in rivulets, but he could still move, spine intact.

In the corner, Kaul had Gun on his back, wings beating feebly, and the sight made Tally rear up, hissing in rage. *Not Gun! You're not taking Gun from me!* He coiled back and struck with all the force of his huge serpentine body, latching onto Kaul's face with his teeth and yanking him off Gun.

Kaul still fought, twisting and snarling, trying to claw at Tally's head to get him off. But the angle was bad for him now and Tally extended his jaws to take more of the honey badger's head in his mouth. When he had a firm grip, he hauled the struggling predator up onto the bed and dangled him out of the window. *Not safe to do it inside. Not with Gun right there.*

Another tightening of muscles, this group the small ones just behind the hinge of his jaws, and he released the poison gas from the sacs in his mouth, breathing out so Kaul would get the full effect. The honey badger let out a shriek, claws flying in a last desperate attempt to break free. His struggles slowed, becoming feeble twitches, until finally he stilled.

Tally spat him out on the bed and humaned. The fire along his back and his cheekbone only grew worse, and damn it, Kaul's tail shot had gone through his feet, but he'd survived. He poked at Kaul. Shoved him off the bed. Kicked him into a corner. Jason Kaul had not been as lucky.

Just in case, Tally lifted the dresser and planted one leg in the middle of Kaul's back. If he had some miraculous recovery, he wasn't going to be able to sneak away. One thing down. Tally dropped to his knees and crawled over to the heap of feathers on the floor that was Gun.

"Hey." Tally leaned over Gun, stroking his head feathers. "Don't be dead, Gun. Please."

Gun managed a barely audible, "Rrrrra."

"Okay. That's a start. Unless you're zombie Gun. That wouldn't be good either." Tally managed a crooked smile when Gun pecked at his hand. "Lemme see. Don't...geez. Don't try to get up. Just...um...just stay still."

One wing had been bitten through, the joint barely holding together. The other appeared only broken. Sharp claws had slashed his abdomen, the blood making it difficult for Tally to see how badly. Tally lay down beside him, letting Gun close his talons around Tally's fingers. It was the closest to holding his hand Tally could get.

"Don't die, Gun. We'll get help. Don't die on me."

"Rrrrr."

Booted footsteps ran down the hallway. Naked and exhausted as he was, Tally levered himself up on one elbow to meet the new assault.

"Oh Gods!" Crystal skidded to a stop in the doorway, humaned and fully dressed. "Kennett! *Kennett!*"

Agent Firebaugh arrived in nearly identical fashion, boots pounding down the hall, skid, careen into doorframe. He had his phone tucked up between his ear and his left shoulder and his right arm held close to his chest. After a single moan of, *"Gods...Gun"*, he pulled himself together. "And I need a medivac chopper. Two serious casualties, one...ah..."

He stared down at Kaul's body and Tally mouthed, 'dead'.

"And one fatality." Firebaugh listened for a moment. "Straight to Wadiswan General. Alert whichever Tabib

Blue Holly you can raise." Another pause. "No, Urusar Bastille isn't dead, but he could be if you don't move!"

Firebaugh flopped gracelessly onto the floor and Tally eased away to give them room.

"Gun. Shit. Why didn't you wait for me?"

"Rrrr."

"It's all right. You can tell me later." Firebaugh took over stroking Gun's head feathers, confirming what Tally had suspected for some time.

"Crystal?" Tally tried to look up at her and couldn't move his head that way. "The joeys?"

"With Marnie and Deja." Crystal dragged the quilt off the bed to cover him. "Deja's figuring out how to get the cage open. The girls look unharmed..." She frowned when Tally made a wounded sound. "*Physically* unharmed. They're safe, Urusar."

"I promised..." Tally murmured as the room began to spin. "Promised Haru that monster's head."

"We'll make sure they see the body. Before it gets carted away." Firebaugh's voice trembled. This was worse than Tally had thought.

"Barry?"

"Ha!" Crystal's eyes gleamed with unholy glee. "Kerns is sitting on him. Literally."

"Is he...?"

"Bisoned? Yes. And not getting up, no matter how much Barry cusses."

"Good. That's good." Tally sighed, trying to ignore the blood dripping on the floorboards. "Haru's going to be so annoyed with me..."

Chapter Twenty-One

Family

A noise caught Haru's less-than-stellar attention. They glanced down. Livy's little opossum nose and eyes poked out of their *kimono*. She shook her head then burrowed back down between the layers. Ah, it would be Melia. They had zoned out, so it hadn't been clear.

No sleep made for a tired Uma.

"Yes, little girl?"

Their left side bun wriggled.

"Hungry?"

The wriggling increased.

"Apple or cheese?"

One chirp.

Haru cut up the apple into smaller pieces then lifted them toward the bun. One piece was yanked from between their fingertips, as were the next two pieces.

Their slightly smaller but puffed-up right bun wriggled moments later, so Haru silently cut more apple and some cheese and lifted the pieces up. A paw came out of their *kimono*.

Good. Livy had decided she was hungry too.

"Is no one else seeing this?" Gunther asked the table of sleepy-eyed adults.

Haru handed up another piece of apple to Melia.

"No, really, anyone? Anyone seeing this or is it the drugs?" Gunther yawned and shifted in his chair. Both his arms were in slings and strapped against his chest at different angles. "Ted gave me some wicked strong painkillers."

Agent Firebaugh, who had been spooning oatmeal into Gunther's mouth, stopped and looked over just as there was a yanking motion on Haru's right side. He blinked a few times then smiled.

"See what?"

They lifted up another piece of cheese. Maybe some Cheerios would be a good idea, then Haru thought of all the crumbs. A shudder passed through them before Haru could stop it.

Maybe not.

Gunther groaned. "No fucking with the broken eagle."

Haru smiled. "Temporarily grounded eagle."

"Fine, grounded, but my argument still stands. No fucking with the grounded eagle who happens to be a guest at your house."

"Your arms need time to heal. It is better if you do somewhere comfortable."

"Comfort is debatable, Haru." Gunther scooted in his chair, his razor-sharp gaze on Haru's head. "There were definitely paws and hands coming out of your buns."

The wolf guffawed, but Haru managed to keep their cool and not laugh. It was too fun not to. A few of the other adults snickered, but most looked studiously elsewhere when Gunther's sharp eyes fell on them.

Another chirp made a demand. Haru dutifully handed their daughter another bit of apple. They could wash their hair later. Like right after breakfast.

"Are Melia and Jasper in your buns?"

"Yes," Haru replied and sent up a small piece of bacon.

That got appreciative squeaks from both sides, and Livy nosed her way out of the *kimono* again. She took a larger piece then disappeared again. Haru looked back up to find Gunther staring.

"Yes, Curley-chan?"

Said eagle frowned. "Chan? Isn't that for little girls? Or girls?"

"Usually, but not always." Haru got a tug on the left ear. "Patience, little girl."

They sent up a combo of cheese, bacon and apple. If opossums could moan, the sniffles and chirps were it. Gunter was still watching their interaction with the twins and Jasper.

"So the weird buns are because you have a pixie and opossum bunkering down in them?"

"Yes."

"Why two? It's kind of a Pri— Ouch!" Gunther turned his affronted gaze on Agent Firebaugh. "What?"

"Because, apparently, when it comes to buns, there can be only one." Haru had lost some hair in that battle. The other pixies had been all too happy about it too. Little pests.

Gunther sat a minute before nodding. "Makes sense."

It would to him.

"But the food. You're always pree—"

Haru narrowed their eyes.

"Clean," Gunther finished in a lame attempt to cover what he'd been thinking.

Tally chuckled, reached for a piece of cheese and popped it in his mouth, causing protests to erupt from both buns.

He smiled — the slippery snake — and said, "Showers. There are lots more showers. Or at least hair-rinsing periodically through the day."

"Ewwww."

Agent Firebaugh barked out a laugh but quickly focused on the oatmeal when Haru gave him the death stare of all Urumas. Gunther wasn't nearly as quick to stifle himself. So dead.

"I am not the one who looks like a *shibari* experiment gone wrong."

That set the table off. Every single person, including Bastille-*okaasan*, laughed. Gunther was busy squawking with indignation and a little bit of pain as Agent Firebaugh laughed and tried to clean up the oatmeal that had spilled onto him. Livy poked her head out of the *kimono* and the two buns shook, the balance changing. The troublesome duo must've decided to see what the ruckus was all about.

One paw touched their shoulder the same time two tiny pixie feet did. One pair of paws held onto their left ear while one small hand held onto their right. Gunther's irritation faded when he noticed the new table guests.

"Hey, Melia. How are you feeling?"

She squeaked but didn't move.

Tally brightened, adjusting in his chair with slow, stiff movements. He really shouldn't have been up, but it was his first breakfast home since being released from the hospital and he had insisted. Melia must have noticed his groan of pain because Haru felt a twitch, a jerk forward. She didn't let go of them, though. Tally's eyes dulled a little.

"It's okay, little girl. I'm okay," he said. "Just trying to get comfy."

Melia let out a mournful sneeze-chirp.

Maybe it wasn't that she didn't want to go to him. It was the distance. Tally wasn't in his usual chair because being seated at the other end meant less movement for him, therefore less stress on his injuries. The last three weeks had been hard on everyone. They hadn't gotten to see their Argaze much, relying on the rest of the Bastilles to pitch in. The pups had needed constant attention after their ordeal, and Melia had spent most of her recovery in Haru's hair. She only came out at certain times—like when Dr. Stix showed up for the therapy sessions, or bedtime.

They saw the longing on Tally's face and decided it might be worth a try. Haru slowly backed up the chair then went to their Argaze.

Within a foot of him, Melia tensed, then launched herself. Tally had just enough time to put his hands up to catch her—just like a football—before tucking her against his chest. Both Usar and joey sighed, snuggling. Tally kissed her head.

"Hey, little girl," he murmured. "Missed you too."

Two little paws cupped his jaw as she sniffed and left kisses.

Haru returned to their seat, inquiring if anyone else needed anything before sitting.

Agent Firebaugh's phone went off, the now familiar ring of State—*Doom and Gloom*—summoning him. "Be right back."

"Take it in the office," Tally said.

"Thanks."

Tally began to feed Melia scraps off his plate, and Jasper decided he wanted to snuggle with Livy in Haru's *kimono*. It felt good to have the whole fami—a twinge went through their heart. No, they weren't whole. Jackson wasn't at the table watching over his sisters, trying to boss them around. Haru had to take a deep, deep breath in. Then another. Livy and Jasper glanced up.

"More bacon?" they offered.

Excited squeaks and grabby hands and paws stole away the treats. When Haru was able to look back up, everyone was watching them, especially Tally. They waved a hand and went back to feeding their pup and pixie. For once the family was at the table together. Haru would be grateful for who they had here.

Noises picked back up as the others began to dig in again. Addy was discussing her upcoming visit with Klug-san and looking rather excited about the prospect. *Hmmm.* Che and Hal fought over sausages, taking much too long because Meli swept in and stole them. The brothers didn't even notice. Meli winked at Haru. They inclined their head. It was nice having her there, because she seemed to hold *almost* as much sway as Tally. Her husband and kids were still back in Chicago, but she had been right not to bring them up yet. Too much too soon after everything.

Agent Firebaugh stalked back into the dining room. All conversation dropped off again. It had to do with the expression he wore. Angry. Resigned. He dropped into his seat next to Gunther.

"Problem, Firebaugh?" Tally asked.

"No, no." He tilted his head back and forth, his shoulders swaying with him. "I have *news.*"

The agent did not elaborate.

"I see." Tally frowned. "Should we take this back to the office?"

"Probably for the best."

Tally pressed Amelia against his throat as she nuzzled. It was obvious he wanted to stay with her, but since there was news, it would be better not to let delicate ears hear it. What to do? Haru pressed a hand against the lump in their *kimono*. They could tell Tally briefly — very briefly — considered asking Haru to take their little girl. The smart serpent prevailed.

"Lahi," they suggested.

"Right."

Panic erupted all over her face before Sammy and Bastille-*okaasan* said they would help. Tension bled away from her shoulders, though they stayed tight. It took a few minutes of convincing, lots of loud chirping, but the twins and Jasper went with Lahi to play up in Haru's suite. The devastation on the Bastille family's faces was clear as day. Their hearts breaking with every little sniff and sneeze the girls made.

"How is it going with them?" Gunther asked.

Haru frowned, picking their words. "The therapist, Dr. Stix, says it will take *time*. It helps they stayed opossumed for most of the captivity, since our animals process differently, but still time. They have sessions on their own, together, with Lahi. She still has her own. Sometimes Mindy comes. We're doing what we can. The separation anxiety is expected. They still... They look for Jackson. Mindy's sisters. At their age, we don't know how much they will remember, or what."

Several people nodded, the table quiet again.

Agent Firebaugh stood, helping Gunther steady himself as he did as well. "Come on, we don't want the twins accidentally hearing this then."

The walk down the hall took too long. Waiting for everyone to settle was excruciating. Agent Firebaugh looked as though he'd rather *not* be there. Haru tucked a blanket around Tally then glared when he tried to protest.

"You are not even supposed to be up, my Argaze. You. Must. Sit." They licked Tally's lip and left a quick kiss before settling on his lap. Something told Haru a good offense was the best defense in this situation.

Tally froze underneath Haru. They dared their audience to say anything by turning their best Uruma stare on the room. Bastille-*otōusan* had the nerve to chuckle, but he covered it up with a cough. Good snake.

Haru pulled Tally's arms around them then leaned back, letting out a long exhale. "Agent Firebaugh. Your news."

"Yes, right, that. News." The wolf blinked away a confused squint. "First, let's start with the bad news. State will not be prosecuting Representative Bancroft. Not enough evidence."

Tally hissed and nearly knocked Haru off his lap. They held on harder and sniffled. Their Argaze's action immediately went to comfort, Tally hugging them close. It worked. The anger coiled inside their serpent lessened.

"I promise, Urusar Bastille, there will be an investigative team keeping an eye on her. Unfortunately, Tyler's Punishment was all sanctioned, so State's hands are tied there. Everything that happened *here* since, since—"

"The intrusion," Tally supplied.

Agent Firebaugh nodded. "Yes. It's not something State or National can ignore. Her part has raised flags, so no one is stupid enough to just let her walk away."

"Good," Haru said.

"Yes, quite." Agent Firebaugh growled and crossed his arms. "Jason Kaul's accomplices are copping to plea deals, but so far their statements haven't been worth much. It may take time."

Gunther clucked. "Break and tear apart *their* arms."

"You know we can't."

Haru agreed with Gunther. Bastards deserved everything coming to them. They hissed, earning several impressed smiles from the Bastilles. They even felt one from Tally against their neck.

"It's getting snakier, Haru," Che teased. Bastille-*otōusan* cuffed him upside the head.

"They know *things*," Haru said.

Agent Firebaugh sighed. "We know. We're working on it, but our main culprit happens to be dead."

"I am not sorry for that," Haru replied.

"Neither am I," Tally said.

The wolf hung his head for a minute. He looked in desperate need of some coffee. Well, more coffee. "In good news, I have convinced the coroner to release Jackson's, Morgan's and Mason's remains back to you, Urusar."

Haru's heart struck out, tearing in two. There was a nod against their head before they managed a rough, "Thank you."

"Least I could do."

Tally gave Haru a squeeze. "What about Dan and Barry?"

"Councilman Hastings is an easy arrest, but he's been trying to bargain. Still working on it. Dan is harder. So far the boar hasn't turned on him, and Dan is claiming he didn't know anything. He was only working a business deal."

"Figures," Tally replied.

"We're working on Mrs. Hastings."

"Ah, that. You're not going too hard on her, I hope? She was probably abused as much as Tyler," Tally answered. The hurt in Haru's chest eased a fraction at the concern they heard in his voice.

"We're walking the line."

"Thanks, Kennett. I suppose the next step is to plan the burials. We've got the Blue Holly's reports made up for the children."

There was a lull, everyone processing the news. The air felt dense and heavy. Tally held Haru close, rubbing his chin against their neck. Then something occurred to Haru.

"If the coroner is releasing my boy, then is Kaul-san being released as well?"

"Yes, State is having him—"

"I want him stuffed, *anata*."

"Uruma Bastille—"

They slid to the right so they could face Tally. "I know the perfect place to put the bastard on display, *anata*."

"Haru, I don't think—"

"I *want* him stuffed. You promised me his head, *anata*."

Tally puffed up a little. "That's not fair. Using *anata*. Sitting on my lap."

"You finally figured it out?" Haru smiled.

"Misaki told me."

They sniffed. "A *traitor* and a *cheat*. That is what you two are."

"Uruma Bastille," the wolf tried again, but they ignored him. They would not allow State to take their prize.

"I *need* the badger stuffed, *anata*. You defeated him in combat. It is only fair we get his remains. There *is* a rule. And there is another about bringing defeated foes in front of the council."

The wolf's groans were only slightly louder than Tally's. Agent Firebaugh mumbled something about using traditional rules for convenience. Haru ignored the complaints. The threat against their family was out there, and they fully intended to let everyone know where things stood when lijun chose to go against the Bastille clan.

"Please, *anata*. Bring me his head."

* * * *

The funeral for their boy hurt more than anything Haru had ever experienced. Watching Eberhardt-san and his wife let go of their two girls was a close second. As soon as the procession had started, Haru had wanted to cry and rage against the world, but instead they had to comfort the twins, who finally understood their brother was *not* coming back.

"I have you, little girl." Haru kissed Melia's head and smelled in her fresh toddler scent.

The girls were minature clones of them. Both had their dark brown hair pulled back into a bun like theirs. Though neither had a pixie riding along like Haru did. They all had the same design for their *kimonos*. They were blood red with flowers cascading over them, a stark contrast against the white snow covering the ground. Melia had done the talking for both of them when chosing their funeral attire. Livy had only pointed and nodded. What passed as the usual since the *intrusion*, pointing, no talking. Dr. Stix said the speech would come back in time. They were only three — a blessing and a curse. There would be progress and remission. Their job was to listen and support best they could.

Today was harder than others, though. Haru hurt, too, but couldn't show it. Holding Livy and Melia close helped ease the pain. Made it easier to pretend they were all right. The clan had come to say their goodbyes, so they all would.

Haru focused on the pyre in front of them, carried by Lahi, with her guitar slung over her shoulder, and Mindy. Shafa Lamar a few steps in front of them. It was so small. Too small. Haru held the girls a little tighter.

The immediate Bastille family, Sammy and Misaki walked in front of Jackson's pyre while Tally and his friends walked behind Haru. Then the rest of the clan followed behind in a long procession. A guard for their boy against the dark. The clan, their new family, coming together for their Urusar and Uruma.

They walked around the lake, back to near their den, to a large clearing in the forest. A stone amphitheater with lamps lit all around it. An old gathering place for the clan. An extremely symbolic choice by their Argaze. This was a pyre for the son, the former Sardu, of the Bastille clan. *All* the lijun needed to remember that.

The clan fanned out, taking their places among the gray, cold stones. The Bastilles and Haru circled the pyre and Shafa Lamar stood next to it with Lahi and Mindy. The two held hands as they looked ahead. They had been so insistent about being the guard to carry him, Haru hadn't had the heart to say no.

Now they were glad they had said yes. The worry about letting the two of them perform the task washed away as they noticed the expressions Lahi and Mindy wore. The two of them needed this as much as Haru and Tally. Now they could all say goodbye properly.

"Welcome, Bastille Clan," Shafa Lamar said in her melodic voice. "Today we gather to give our farewells to Sardu Jackson Cohen-*Bastille*. A small but mighty lijun who died defending his sisters against the worst of lijuns."

The twins pressed against Haru. Their little bodies trembled, but the girls did not cry. Haru wasn't sure that was a good thing or not.

"On this day, we give our thanks for his too-short life and return his body to the Mother and give his spirit to the stars."

Lahi came forward, her guitar in hand. Her eyes sought Haru's. They gave a head bob of encouragement. She settled, breathing in, then widened her stance as she began to play Jackson's song — *Break of Day*.

Her long, nimble fingers moved over the stings. Her voice rose and carried throughout the entire amphitheater. Lahi's use of syncopation, the carefully constructed melodic tension complementing her rough voice, vulnerable and emotional, built the song up, her soft words soaring into a crescendo.

The break in her voice, her heartbreak, laid bare to everyone.

Livy and Melia buried their faces against Haru's neck. Wet drops fell against their skin. Maybe they shouldn't have let the girls come, but Dr. Stix had advised it could help the twins process Jackson's death. To expect some regression. A hand took hold of the back of Haru's neck. Tally's. Large. Cool but not cold. Grounding.

The bubble burst. A hum of chords in the air, but Lahi no longer playing. Only her voice, strong and loving, filled the clan's stone circle. And when her voice dipped. The crack. Gods. Haru leaned against Tally.

A sweet, melodious end. Lahi's bittersweet hum echoed through the amphitheater. And only then Haru could catch their breath, could anyone, the exhale synchronous. As one.

Shafa Lamar stepped forward, a lit torch in her hand. The fire glowed blue and white. Sparks danced around the flames. The lamps dimmed. Stars twinkled overhead. Tally took the torch and limped to the tiny pyre, cane in his other hand. He used his full height, large and imposing. *Humongous*. His pupils were slits, forked tongue tasting the air. There went the horns. Uktena, all powerful, on full display.

"Jackson Cohen-Bastille had a heart too large for his small body." Tally's voice cracked and faltered, then gathered strength again. "At an age when he should have been thinking of play, or learning about the world, he worried about others—his sisters, his Uma, his grandparents...me. His last act was to put himself between his baby sisters and a predator far too old, far too large and strong for him to face. Courage and compassion. He would have been the *besssst* of Urusars."

Tally took a huge breath, the chest expansion threatening to rip his dress shirt as he gathered himself. Then he bent toward the pyre and with tears beginning to track down his face, touched flame to kindling. The dry moss and twigs caught and Tally placed the torch at the foot of the pyre before he stepped back.

The flames traveled quick as lightning and leaped into the air, consuming the pyre. Those blue-white tendrils reached for the sky. The sparks twirled and danced in the wind. Only the crackle of the kindling filled the stone circle.

Their Argaze limped back over to Haru. He gathered them and the twins up in his arms.

"Goodbye, my little man," Haru whispered and snuggled the twins a little tighter. "May the stars be filled with your light."

Chapter Twenty-Two

Taxidermy and Repercussions

"What's that?" Justin pointed to the glass case outside the Oak Room, his eyes wide in youthful, horror-laced curiosity.

Tally had to do a slow turn on his cane to come about. It was a nice one, people kept giving him pretty ones as gifts, and this one had a gold-painted dragon's-head handle, but he hated the damn things. Ted had warned him that the foot might never heal correctly and that he might need them for the foreseeable future. Tally hated that, too. Small price to pay to have his girls safe, though.

"Ah. That." Tally cleared his throat and raised an eyebrow as Haru sailed past him into the conference room. "*That* is a show of strength. A warning. A trophy of war."

The taxidermist had done an outstanding job with Kaul, mounting him on a miniature hill of granite and posing him so he looked as if he'd been perpetually trapped in a frustrated snarl. At first, Tally had been surprised at Haru's somewhat bloodthirsty request.

Only at first — it was an appropriate end for a heartless monster.

Justin rolled his eyes. "I know that. But what *is* it? I mean, it kinda looks like a wolverine, attitude and stuff."

"Oh. Honey badger. May we never have another come visit." Tally waved Justin and Tyler into the room. "Come on, boys. Let's get settled."

Haru already had their seat at the table, the little lift of chin indicating the otter was pleased with themself. This wouldn't be full council. Agent Firebaugh had advised against it. Only Hakkon sat beside Haru, his right as an injured party, and Tyler was there as witness. Tally had allowed Justin's presence as a steadying influence for him.

"We have to keep this brief, Tal." Hakkon leaned around Haru. "Firebaugh can't have too much of a time gap in transporting them."

"I'm hoping..." Tally tapped out a quick text. "It doesn't take more than a few minutes."

Multiple sets of footsteps echoed down the hall, some the steady tramp of martial boots, others more hesitant and wavering. Agent Firebaugh led the procession, followed by three of his largest lijun agents with prisoners in custody — Barry, Dan and Ada Hastings. These weren't the agents who had helped on the case. They didn't want humans escorting pissed-off lijun. A couple favors had managed to get them in for transport.

Barry shook his guard off with a snarl while Dan had the audacity to look smug. Ada shrank back against her assigned agent, pale and trembling.

"Mom..." Tyler got out in a choked whisper.

Tally held up a hand. "You can talk to your mom in a bit, as long as we get this resolved quickly."

"If you're just going to murder us, *snake*, better do it fast so your goons can cover it up before too many people know we're here," Barry spat out.

A sigh of exasperation was the only concession Tally allowed his boiling rage. "If I wanted you dead, you would've died at that cabin, Hastings. But, whether you believe it or not, I still believe in due process."

"Then why the hell are we here?"

A soft rustling of fabric heralded Haru shifting in their seat to speak. "There is human law, Hastings-san. And there is lijun law."

Tally gave a nod and continued. "Regardless of the outcome of your trials, there are consequences to be met. Barry Hastings and Daniel O'Rourke, before these witnesses, as is my right as Urusar, I declare you exiled. Cast out. You are no longer clan."

"This is outrageous! My family's been here as long as yours! We *built* this clan—we are this clan! How dare you...you upstart, jumped-up business school—"

Tally ignored the tirade and turned to Mrs. Hastings, who looked like she might fall if the agent let go of her elbow. To her he spoke softly, "Ada, I don't want to exile you if I can help it. It's possible that you'll see some jail time for hiding what you know, and I want to assure you that Tyler will be safe, protected and cared for in the heart of the clan. None of this was his fault."

With a hiccupping breath, Ada buried her face in her hands and burst into tears.

"Stop blubbering, you stupid bitch!" Barry yelled, fighting the hold of his handlers. "*Your* traitor son turned on us or we wouldn't be here! No son of mine would be that weak!"

A huffing snuffle came from Tally's right, and he turned to find Tyler with his tusks growing, perilously close to boaring out. His eyes shimmered with unshed tears and he was blinking rapidly to try to keep them back. Poor kid. Still worried about looking weak in front of his jackass father.

"Perhaps this is a time when anger is warranted, my Argaze," Haru murmured, eyes on the table.

Tally tapped his pen against the wood, glaring as he thought that over. *No. No more thinking. When the otter's right, they're right.* He rose slowly, allowing his full bulk to unfurl from behind the table, then approached Barry with deliberate, heavy thumps of his cane. He slid out of his suit jacket and handed it off to Agent Firebaugh.

"You know, Barry, there's something I've wanted to say to you for a long time." Tally pulled back his fist, Barry's eyes going wide when he realized he'd have no time to duck, and punched that smarmy, self-righteous face right in the nose. Barry only kept his feet because of the hands on him, and Tally shook his fingers out. "You, sir, are an asshole."

He ignored the sputtering and the blood dripping from Barry's face as he continued down the line to Ada. "I don't hold you blameless, Ada, but I think you were in a place where you didn't feel safe speaking up. With Barry in custody, he can't reach you. And he will go to jail. There are too many witnesses from that night."

She wiped at her face and gave a little, hesitant nod.

"You were present when Barry and Dan met, I'd bet. Probably lots of times. You know things that would put them both away for a very long time."

Something gleamed in her eyes. Hope? Anger? She straightened up and regarded him face-to-face.

"Turn state's witness, Ada. Agent Firebaugh will help you. Testify, tell all you know and your own sentence will be decreased. Afterward, you can come home. The clan will be here for you. But you have to say it. You have to ask for help."

Ada swallowed hard and snuck a quick look at her mess of a husband. In a voice that shook but was audible and clear, she said, "I'll do it. Yes. I'll testify. Both of them."

Both Dan and Barry erupted in shrieking epithets, but Tally had the feeling Ada had withstood those and worse over the years. She stood firm, head up.

"Thank you, Ada." Tally patted her arm. "You're very brave."

"Do you have all you needed, Urusar?" Agent Firebaugh called over the din.

Tally nodded and stepped back. "Thank you, Kennett. Yes."

The agents led their prisoners out, though Firebaugh stayed behind and waited until they'd cleared the doorway. "Just a heads-up, though you would've known soon. I'm being reassigned here for now."

"Here?"

Firebaugh checked his phone while he answered. "Yes. We have rogue elements at State still at large. You're not out of the woods yet, and the powers that be feel it's best if I stay here since I'm familiar with the principles and the area."

"And this has nothing to do with a certain mangled eagle?" Tally leaned in to ask.

"Ha. No. That is…" The corners of Firebaugh's eyes crinkled and his gaze found Haru's for a beat. The two dipped their heads to each other. Tally had a brief flare of *'Now what?'* before the wolf brought his attention back. "I may have made a suggestion or two. But I'm serious, Tally. You need me here."

"We're glad to have you. In whatever capacity." Tally held out a hand. "Thank you, Kennett, and we'll see you back here soon."

Agent Firebaugh tossed Tally his jacket and gave the room a jaunty wave as he strode out. That left only the five of them in a suddenly silent room. Tyler shifted uncomfortably, fully humaned again. Justin cleared his throat.

"So." Tally limped his way back to the table and leaned hipshot against the edge. "Tyler, I know you've been living with the Tripps, and that's very kind of them. But I know that house has to be crowded. I'd like to request temporary custo—"

Haru made an odd bark sound and Hakkon tapped the table for Tally's attention.

"What?"

"Tal, you've got pups on the way," Hakkon began slowly.

"Yes?"

"And you can't keep taking in every lost child in the community..."

"I can't?"

Haru patted his knee. "Listen to Eberhardt-san, please."

"I...ah..." Hakkon swallowed hard. "Else and I have plenty of room. Maybe too much." He grimaced and caught himself. "Tyler, I'd be pleased if you'd come stay with us. Mindy'd be happy to have you."

Oh. Oh, I am clueless sometimes. Tally sat stunned for half a breath. "That sounds ideal. What do you think, Tyler?"

"I'd like that, sir. It's... We're over there a lot already."

"Settled, then." Tally clapped Tyler on the shoulder, patting him more gently when he nearly knocked the boy over. "Thanks, Hak."

They sent Tyler out to go say goodbye to his mom and Haru grumbled about getting ice for Tally's hand. With a sigh, Tally rose from his perch and started to limp back out of the conference room.

"You realize, Tal," Hakkon said as he fell into step beside him, "that we have a couple of council seats open now."

"Can we please put off fresh hells until another day, Hak?"

Haru leaned up to kiss his cheek. "Perhaps, at least until after dinner."

* * * *

"Where are the girls? Why aren't you ottered?"

Haru lifted their head from tub ledge. Their surprise was mirrored in Tally's face. He had on swim trunks and a rather large rubber duckie tucked against his side. Not to mention their Argaze's hair had been braided back. Both his eyebrows were up and his mouth gaped a bit.

"The girls are with Lahi and Sammy."

"Really?" Tally looked as though he wasn't sure whether he should stay or if he should go.

"Sammy convinced the twins Uma needed a break. Some *alone* time." Haru sighed. "And to let me clean my hair."

"Jasper?"

"With the girls." Haru slid down into the tub a little farther and batted at the bubbles. "They are cuddled up in Sammy's bed."

"Oh. Ah." Tally stared down at his feet. "I should leave you to that, then."

"Wait!" Haru reached without thinking. Not sure what to do once they were hanging over the side of the tub, buck naked, slipping off Tally's arm. "Floor!"

And head met floor.

Though it could've been worse. Maybe. Tally actually caught them, so they didn't hit as hard as they could've. Haru also found themself eye to eye with the duckie.

"Where do you even find one this big?" they asked.

"Internet."

Yes, that made sense.

Tally maneuvered Haru upright, *and* in his lap. Probably the only way he could've without braining them. They stared, unsure what to say. Haru *knew* letting Tally walk out would have been the wrong thing, though. Probably. Now that they'd stopped him, they had no idea what to say. It was the first time since...since *that night* the two of them were alone and not worrying over the twins, or mourning Jackson or worried about another attack.

The small threats locally had gotten resolved, but bigger ones loomed. At State, not to mention the property grabs by Akaike-san. But those problems were in the distant future. More immediately they'd have to deal with Agent Firebaugh and his sniffing around. Haru knew the wolf was suspicous of them, not that they really blamed him, considering where they came from. What a mess. No, not something Haru could do anything about now.

What they needed was their hair clean, a bath and a good night's sleep.

Haru also needed to talk with Tally. Things had changed. The relationship between them had changed.

The doubt, the confusion as to what that was, unfurled through their chest. They did not have the words, the English words, to explain their befuddlement right then.

They should've let him walk away. Haru couldn't give Tally any answers. But...

"I believe you," Haru said, followed by a gulp. "I mean..." They gulped again. Their chest felt so tight. "I believe that you will not hurt me. Not on purpose."

Tally sat back, both arms wrapped loosely around their waist. He combed his fingers through Haru's hair then made a face. He pulled his hand out and waved it back and forth. A bit of something went flying.

"Ewww," Haru said, unable to repress a shudder. "I thought I found everything."

"No, it seems not." Tally offered them a soft smile.

Again, the mood was not something Haru understood. What should they do next? It went from absurd to fumbling awkwardness.

"How about..." Tally's lips came together, then his tongue flicked out. "I could wash it for you? Make sure all the food is out?"

Haru almost let a moan escape right then. "Yes."

Their scalp hadn't felt clean since Jasper and Melia had moved in. Tally's brows shot up. Okay, so maybe some of the moan had come out. Their Argaze's surprise was followed by another of those bashful smiles and a chuckle.

"Here, sit on the stool."

"But—"

"There are more. I hadn't brought them in yet." There was a catch in his voice.

Ah. So he'd made a set for the family. The ache in their heart blossomed bright for a moment.

Haru reached out and pressed their palm against Tally's broad chest. Right over his heart. He cupped their hand, the sad smile twisting something inside Haru. Their Argaze's hurt plain as day. No, not hurt. This was different than what he showed the others. The clan had seen his pain, his rage, but this was something much more vulnerable and precious. It was his heart. Open and vulnerable.

That knocked them for a loop.

"I'll be right back." Tally settled Haru on the stool and hightailed it out of the bathroom. The bedchamber echoed his limp, but also a procession of, "Oh shit! Oh shit! Oh shit!"

Did he think Haru was going to say no?

Ohh, yes, he probably did. Was Tally expecting *more*? Haru's heart ratcheted up to an allegro.

The kisses were one thing. The cuddling another. Haru looked down at their nakedness and suddenly felt overexposed. Their behavior certainly would seem to indicate Haru wanted more. They curled their arms around their abdomen, their heart thudding decidedly harder.

"Hey."

Haru looked up at Tally's soft hello.

Again with the smile. He held up a larger stool. One that fit him much better than Haru's. While their heights weren't too dissimilar, the mass was another matter. Tally settled the stool behind Haru then reached for the bucket. He tested the water.

"Still warm," he murmured. "Good. Close your eyes."

Tally poured the water over Haru, it slid down their front and back. Almost like a kiss.

"Lean back."

They obeyed as Tally ran a comb through their hair. There were a couple plops. "Gods."

Tally's deep chuckle rebounded in the bath and he leaned over and chucked something in the bin. "You're tired. Very, very tired, my love."

"A bit."

"Let me, yes, here we go." The scent of lilac and lavender surrounded the two of them.

"What is that?"

"Something I asked Shafa Lamar for. I told her about your predicament and she said this would help with any follicle damage."

Strong fingers dug into their scalp. "Oooohhh. Yes."

"Feel good?" Tally asked.

"So gooood." Each little dig, each press, each time Tally ran his fingers through Haru's scalp and hair felt miraculous. Then he started with the comb. Haru whimpered.

"Maybe we should encourage the twins and Jasper to the table for eating and snacks?" The question was right next to their ear. Tally's scent close, his strong chest against their back. "You're changing multiple times a day. Your hair, well, yes."

"But—"

"Just to the table or counter. Bacon treats look promising." Tally's thumb pressed into the bottom of their skull, right at the back. "Dr. Stix says to encourage independence when and where we can. Eating at or on the table seems like a good place to start."

"Fiiine. Just do not stop."

"Close your eyes."

They might have whimpered in protest, but did as requested. Once again warm water flowed over them, wrapping around them like a familiar friend. The comb. A rinse. The comb again — each pull through sent a wave of serenity through them. Their breathing slowed, becoming rhythmic and sleepy. Another rinse.

"Want back in the bath?" Tally's voice was low and close. So was his cool body.

"Yes, please."

"Can— Can I get in with you?" The question was barely audible. So hesitant.

"That would be nice."

Tally lifted them. There was a grunt. Haru didn't dare look at him. No need to bruise their Argaze's ego. The two of them managed to make it into the bath with no incident, no bumps or bruises. He even ditched the swimsuit after Haru complained about it rubbing against their skin.

"This all right?"

"Yes."

"Good."

They lay together in the quiet of the bath. Tally held Haru close with those gentle arms of his. He periodically rubbed his cheek against Haru's and sighed. A squeeze would follow every time. This was what contentment felt like. Had to be. Haru had never felt this safe before. Hopeful.

The two of them floated in the bath — which really *was* more of a pool. Both of their breathing slowed, becoming synchronous. Hypnotic in its rhythm. Haru could lose themself in a moment like this. Safe in the water. A fire burning, stoking the once dormant embers in their chest. A hand holding theirs. One that wouldn't let go no matter what. A hand that would never let go in a storm. A hand that would lead them home if they had the strength to reach out and take it.

"Haru, my love. I hate to say this, but how about we get out?"

Haru grunted a refusal.

"The water is getting a bit cold."

Yes, quite. For Tally it would be. Like his serpent, Tally was susceptible to the cold. "Of course, *anata*."

Haru got out of the bath and greeted their Argaze with a towel, wrapping Tally up then using another to dry him off. They shot down protests with a simple, "I do not get cold like you do." They wiped themself down, Tally watching, waiting on his stool. The look of uncertainty was back.

"Do you want me to go?" he asked.

"No," Haru answered. "But..."

"What *do* you want?"

"I do not know."

The soft, warm smile returned. No harsh judgment. No disappointment. "You know why I'm asking, right?"

"Because you did not before."

"No, no I made assumptions," Tally answered. He reached out, trailed his fingertips along Haru's arm. "Didn't see the power I wielded. And the assumptions I made about what we both would want, those hurt my Em'halafi and me."

They twitched, couldn't help it. Their eyes went to the floor, staring at Tally's feet. What kind of answer was expected of them?

"It's okay, my love," Tally said quietly.

"What is?" Haru lifted their gaze to meet Tally's.

"That you don't believe in Em'halafi. It's okay for you not to believe and for me to believe." Tally offered the smile again. It was so bright and open. "It's part of who you are. I would never blame you for that. Just as I hope you can accept that I do."

"I can do that."

"Thank you, my love." Tally stood and kissed Haru's temple. "But maybe it would be best... How about we say goodnight?"

"Okay." But it was tinged with disappointment on Haru's side.

They walked out into the cool bedroom chamber with their Argaze. Uncertain. The bath had been so good, so nice. Like home. It had been a shame to end it. But...

"Wait!" they called as Tally opened the door. "*Anata*."

Their Argaze closed the door and studied Haru. Really examined them hard. Not leering. No, he had one hand on the towel and the other tugging on his braid. After a minute he went over to the wood stove and chucked a few more logs in, stoking the burning embers back to life.

Tally went over to the dresser and rooted around for a minute, humming triumphantly when he pulled out some flannel bottoms. "I knew some still had to be in here."

Haru had climbed in bed and watched him as he moved around. Assured. With a limp. All Tally. He checked the stove one more time, turned off the lights and tossed the towel in the bath. Then he crawled under the covers with Haru. There was a pillow adjustment for his foot. Then again when he decided he wanted to be on his side.

It took several minutes before Tally settled.

When he finally did, Haru let a breath and relaxed. But it felt odd. Haru on one side of the bed, Tally on the other. They reached out and placed a hand on their Argaze's chest, that hand quickly enveloped by Tally's.

No, this wasn't it. Wasn't what Haru needed. They snuggled closer. Then again. Not close enough.

Tally chuckled. "You're being a wriggle worm."

"Am not."

"Are too. Now we know where Melia gets it from."

Haru huffed but let the argument drop. They pushed closer.

"Love?"

"*Anata.*"

"Do you want me to hold you?" Tally asked.

"Yes, I do." Excruciatingly so.

"Come here." Tally rolled to his back, swearing as his foot got tangled with the pillow and he had to deal with that. "That wasn't smooth at all."

"Nope." Haru laughed.

"Shush."

At once Haru was engulfed in Tally's embrace. It felt *secure.* Loving. Not suffocating or overwhelming. Not like before. It was a place for Haru to belong. They pressed their head under Tally's chin and took a breath in. Yes. This was it. What they needed after everything.

A hand traced up and down their back, slowly lulling them to sleep. It was tender and cool against their hotter body temperature. Tally nudged their head, making them move it so they were face-to-face, Haru practically draped on top of him.

"I know there are things that still need to get done, to be fixed, issues bigger than the both of us that are looming overhead, but Haru, I will be here every step of the way."

"I know."

Tally sighed and squeezed. "Good."

"Is this all right? Laying here like this? Nothing else?"

Tally pressed a kiss against their mouth. Just a quick peck. Innocent. "This is perfect, my love."

"Are you sure?"

Tally squeezed them, inhaled their scent and placed a kiss by their temple. "It's absolutely perfect, you know why?"

Haru wrinkled their nose.

"Because for the first time since I saw you in those rainbow suspenders, I know with absolute certainty you *want* me to hold you. You *want* to be in my arms. So, my love, this *is* perfect."

Glossary

Lijun terms:

Abay/Abago: grandmother/grandfather
Akka: daughter
Argaze: husband
Atigislit: dowry
Awi Tamgradat: matchmaker (literally: brings together before the wedding)
Dahia: the Uruma's perogative of sacrifice. Uruma may offer themself in the place of a clan member about to be punished, often used where children and physical punishment are involved.
Em'halafi: destined match
Idinen: spirit
Imsi Tamgradat: matchmaking dinner
Kwebabiad: birther/carrier — person who carries child of same-sex couple ("egg carrier")
Lijun: dual-natured (a being who has both a human and an animal spirit)
Ruh: ghost
Sa: son
Sa-awi Tamgradat: matchmaking
Sahnkes: shift (to change, to swap)
Sardu: heir to the Urusar (gender neutral)
Satislit ("the bride-son"): son raised to be "bride"
Shafa: witch
Sisum abser: (the silent knife) a lijun government assassin - mostly used as enforcement now.
Tabib: medicine man
Tamgrakwal: betrothal contract
T-asna: clan

Tislit: wife (also betrothed)
Uma: mother
Urusar: village father
Uruma: village mother
Usar: father
Xatiba: betrothed/fiancé (male)
Xus or Tarir: possessed spirit (male and female)
Yeakib Kasab: caning, punishment usually reserved for infractions that endanger the community

Organization: GLA — Global Lijun Alliance

Japanese terms:

Akomeogi: a folding hand fan, originally used by Japanese courtesans then by the general population
Anata: means "you" and is typically considered rude to use, but between couples it is a term of endearment often translated to "darling" in English
Arigatou: thank you
Bachi: straight, wooden sticks used to play Japanese *taiko* drums, or the plectrum for stringed instruments such as the *shamisen* and *biwa*
Bakayarou: stupid/idiot, often translated into English as *asshole*
Biwa: a Japanese short-necked fretted lute
Dogeza: kneeling directly on the ground and bowing to prostrate oneself while touching one's head to the floor
Dōitashimashite: you're welcome
Eshaku: a brief courtesy bow between acquaintances or equals
Furisode: the most formal style of *kimono* worn by unmarried women, brightly colored with long, hanging sleeves

Futsuurei: a more formal bow offered out of respect to an elder or someone of higher social standing

Geisha: one who is trained as an entertainer, with specific training in music, dance, and the art of conversation

Geta: a wooden-soled, elevated sandal with a thong that passes between the big toe and the second toe

Gomen'nasai: I'm sorry

Gyokuro: type of tea from Japan that is grown under the shade

Hakama: loose, pleated trousers with many pleats in the front—part of Japanese formal dress for men

Higashi: is a type of *wagashi*, a traditional Japanese confection often served with tea, which is dry and has little moisture

Irouchikake: a brightly colored bridal *kimono*, often worn untied and over the *kakeshita*

Itadakimasu: a phrase said before eating, meaning "I humbly receive," or in less literal terms, "thank you for the food"

Joyo: a traditional fresh sweet served with tea. The dough made from Japanese yam combined with either rice or wheat flour and covers a small bean ball

Kakeshita: a bridal *kimono* worn under the *uchikake*, usually tied with an *obi*

Kawauso: a river otter (can also refer to otters of folklore)

Kimono: a long, loose robe with wide sleeves often tied with a sash

Kinchaku: a traditional Japanese drawstring pouch for personal items, similar to a handbag

Koropokkuru: the little people of Ainu folklore

Koshi himo: a thin belt used to hold *kimono* or *yukata* material in place before the *obi* is tied over it

Maiko: an apprentice geisha

Montsuki hakama: the most formal *hakama*, worn by bridegrooms

Moshi moshi: a telephone greeting used in certain situations that translates to "I'm going to talk", but is often translated to "hello" in English

Nagajuban: a simple *kimono*-shaped under-robe worn under the *kimono*

Obi: a broad sash worn around the waist of a *kimono*

Obiage: a smaller sash worn between the top of the *obi* and the *kimono*

Obijime: a thin decorative cord worn around the center of the *obi*

Okaasan: mother

Otōusan: father

Saikeirei: a reverent bow, deeper than the *futsuurei*

Sakazuki: a ritual exchange of *sake* cups

San-san-ku-do: three-three-nine times, the wedding drink from ever larger *sake* cups binding the bride and groom

Seiza: an upright kneeling position sitting back on one's feet

Shi'ne: a Japanese curse, meaning, literally, "die"

Shinzen kekkon: a Shinto purification ritual

Shiromuku: a white wedding *kimono*, sometimes worn under a more colorful one

Suminasen: excuse me, or I'm sorry

Tabi: traditional Japanese ankle socks that have separate section for the big toe (often worn with *geta* or other similar footwear)

Takoyaki: is a Japanese snack made with special molded pan so they are in the shape of a ball, typically filled with octopus

Uchikake: (see *irouchikake*)

Wagasa: a traditional bamboo and paper parasol—ones used to escort the bride in weddings are often larger

Wataboshi: a traditional bridal *kimono* hood
Yukata: a casual, light summer *kimono*
Zōri: flat, thonged Japanese sandals similar to flip-flops are made out of a variety of materials

Want to see more from Angel Martinez? Here's a taster for you to enjoy!

Endangered Fae: Diego
Angel Martinez

Excerpt

"Don't go." Finn glowered down from his lofty height, arms crossed over his bare chest. "I forbid you to go."

"You…what?" Diego blinked at him in shock. "Since when did you decide you wanted to play lord of the manor? You can't 'forbid' anything."

Finn slumped against the wall and slid down until he sat on the floor. "Apparently not. I thought I might try it once. Would begging and pleading alter your ill-conceived decision, then?"

Diego crouched down to take Finn's long-fingered hand between his. "*Cariño*, what is all this? I'll only be gone a week. You left me once for five days and told me it wasn't long at all."

"But I wasn't doing the waiting, now, was I?" Finn said with a sharp bark of laughter. "Oh, love, I can't explain it. I have an ice spear lodged in my spine, and I don't know why."

"Please don't tell me you've got a bad feeling about this." Diego rolled his eyes. When he had first mentioned the trip to New York, Finn hadn't protested. Now, when it was too late to cancel his plans, his impending absence caused Finn such anguish.

"But I do. Have a bad feeling." Finn put his forehead on his knees, long blue-black hair falling forward to hide his face.

"So come with me."

"No."

"We could take a train. I don't have to fly. Or you could become an eagle or a peregrine and meet me there."

"I won't go back to the poisoned lands. Not even for you."

"I'm sorry. I shouldn't ask you to." Diego leaned in to nuzzle at Finn's jaw. "Are you afraid I won't come back? That I'm leaving you for good?"

Finn opened his arms and pulled him close with a gusty sigh. "It's not that sort of feeling, my love. It's more as if this journey of yours will act as a...catalyst. That we are at some strange turning point I cannot see beyond."

"Even you can't see into the future..." Diego stroked a hand over Finn's hard-packed chest. "Can you?"

"No. No, I can't. Frustrating sometimes."

"Whatever it is, *mi amor*, we'll work through it. Don't worry so."

* * * *

Finn stared out of the bedroom window at the larches. Tamaracks, they called them here. The soft burst of gold as they prepared to shed their summer needles amidst the dark green of the pines should have made his heart sing. They only made him think of Diego's golden skin against the dark sheets and compounded his misery.

"Bloody, blithering fool," he muttered at himself.

Diego would return in another three days, a blink of an eye for someone who had lived for thousands of years. The thought didn't help. He yearned for his love with every scrap of his being, hating the emptiness of his arms and the empty spot in his mind where Diego's presence usually nestled. He was so cursed lonely without him, which was what made falling in love so gods-be-damned stupid in the first place. Only someone in love truly felt this consuming, hollow pain.

"I need to go out," he told the pillow he held, the one where Diego's scent still lingered. While he liked the new house nestled in the Montana forest, close to the wilderness for him but not too far from the little town for Diego, he had never spent five days sequestered inside a building of his own free will.

There, that was it. He was depressed because of confinement and lack of food. Not that the larder was empty. He just hadn't felt like eating. A nice fat trout sounded good, or perhaps whitefish, cold and shining.

He would swim, feed, and return by nightfall, when Diego might call. Good. Perfect. He hurried down the stairs, poked his head out of the back door and lifted his face to the breeze. No humans lurked nearby to see, so he stepped onto the wooden porch and wriggled out of his jeans. Clothes were fine now and then, and he wore them to satisfy Diego's sense of modesty, but the best part about putting them on was shedding them again.

The sun caressed his bare shoulders. The cool grass kissed his feet. He spread his arms to the breeze and closed his eyes. A faint blue glow danced over his skin as his body melted, his form condensing, his hair shortening and spreading to cover him in sleek black fur. A river otter soon stood where Finn had been.

Otter Finn galloped for the river, his heart singing as the tumult of its rush and tumble reached him. He stumbled and stopped as another noise drifted over the roar of the rapids — a scream, inaudible but in his mind. Terrible fear knifed through him — the cold panic of a human in mortal danger.

This is none of my business. I should not involve myself...

What would he say to Diego, though, if he came back and found out someone had died on the river? "Oh, yes, my love, I heard them dying. I simply decided not to act."

He cringed. Diego would disapprove in the worst way, and perhaps this was someone else's beloved, someone whose absence would cause terrible pain.

He shifted to hawk form and took flight. His powerful wings arrowed over the river, sharp eyes searching the water. *There.* A little bean-pod-shaped coracle rode the rapids, upside-down and unmanned. Not far behind, its former occupant struggled, head tugged under the whitewater again and again despite the orange vest humans wore to help them float.

Hawk Finn folded his wings and plummeted on an unerring course to intercept. The moment before he hit the raging rapids, he shifted again, his body elongating to a scaled, sinuous form. Dragon Finn caught hold of the unconscious human's collar with his teeth and knifed through the water to shore.

"Probably best not to have you see a dragon first thing," Finn muttered, and shifted back to his own shape. He sat panting a moment. All the swift and sudden shifts had taken a frightening amount of effort.

He cocked his head to the side to regard his odd catch. The scent was female and she still breathed. Her skin was fish-cold, though. Not normal for a human.

He shook her gently. "Do you hear me? Do you have companions nearby?" No response and, as he sifted through all the sounds his ears could reach, no companions either. *Dagda's balls.* He simply wasn't any good at dealing with ailing humans. *What would Diego advise?*

"Most likely to get her warm, you dunderhead," he muttered. With a sigh, he slid his arms under her and carried her back to the house.

The strap under her chin frustrated him, but he finally found the little catch to the clasp to remove her helmet. He supposed if one were to go boating in the rapids, which struck him as a supremely unwise idea, a helmet would be prudent. The wet clothes only pulled more warmth from her, so he removed those as well.

Pity, really. He traced a finger over the dark bruise forming on her perfect jaw. Such a beautiful human girl, full-hipped and plump-breasted. He would have liked… No, Diego put such stock in exclusive pairings, like swans did. For Diego, he would refrain.

He frowned. The girl still wasn't any warmer. Bed. Diego had a blanket that warmed itself. It should help. He carried her up and wrapped her in the magic blanket, then stared at the white box with the buttons that told it what to do. Which button did one push? The one with the red circle looked threatening so he chose the yellow as a happier color.

She remained stubbornly unconscious. He sat beside her and stroked the dark tendrils of damp hair from her face. Such soft hair, he fought the temptation to bury his fingers in it. *Still so cold. Damn and damn again.*

He would simply have to warm her himself.

Finn lifted the blanket and slid underneath with her. He pressed his skin to hers, wrapped his limbs around her and pulled warmth from the surrounding air.

Slowly, her body temperature began to rise, and he smiled, pleased at his success. Of course, something else began to rise, as well, but he steadfastly ignored the erection pressed against her lovely bottom. He was no brainless slave to his mating urges. He could control them, despite what some might say.

* * * *

"No, really, Miriam, I don't mind," Diego said into his cell. The plane eased up alongside the gate, thumps and thuds coming from outside the door. "It's just one book signing. There are bound to be cancellations here and there, right?"

Miriam's snort was neither ladylike nor polite. "You just want to get home to that handsome beefcake of yours so you can screw like bunnies."

"I won't say the thought didn't cross my mind." Diego laughed as she swore softly. "But seriously, one promo event canceled in a dozen? I'd say that was pretty good."

"All right. But when you're bigger than Michener, those idiots'll regret canceling on you."

"Maybe. Thanks, though, for setting all that up in the same week."

"All to make me more money, hon. Don't ever think it's anything else," Miriam growled. Then her voice softened. "You done good, Sandoval. Though I always knew you would. When's my next book coming?"

"*Dios*. Don't I get some time off?"

"No. Not at the snail's pace you write. Tell me you've started the sequel."

"Started, yes." Diego shifted to pull his laptop from under the seat in front of him. "But finished is still months off."

"Get cracking, then. You tell that man of yours to take care of you so you can work."

"He watches out for me. I haven't had an episode since Canada." Diego cringed. Bringing up the seizure that had landed him in the hospital for two weeks was a bad idea.

Miriam only snorted her disbelief. "All right, kiddo. Talk to you soon. Kiss Finn for me."

Diego smiled, knowing she would have much rather claimed the honor herself. He said goodbye to the flight attendants, one of whom blushed, clutching her newly signed copy of *A Pooka's Life* to her chest. The notion of fans still amazed him, people who gushed and stammered upon meeting him and said absurd things such as 'you're so much cuter in person'. Officially, the events in New York had all been for the *Dragon Rites* release but many of his readers had fixated on his first book. One girl at a book signing had had tears in her eyes when she'd confessed she wished the pooka was real.

If only she knew.

He had given Finn a pseudonym, Thistle, for the book, but all the material came from recorded interviews about Finn's life, and the artist had used photographs of him for the illustrations. More than one plea had come in from agencies and advertisers for the model's name and phone number. Miriam said it added to the book's mystique when Diego steadfastly refused to divulge any information, and though Finn would never reveal himself to the world, he found the whole thing incredibly funny.

A spring in his step, he hurried to the parking garage, eager to get through the three-hour drive home. Finn had been so despondent over his departure; he hoped the surprise of coming home early would make up for any heartache.

* * * *

The girl struggled toward waking. Her thoughts took form as she fought clear of her dreams. Mother of waters, though, she was loud. Finn's forehead creased as another mental shout battered the shield he had thrown up against her psychic noise. The birds singing outside were drowned out by her.

Of course, some humans were naturally loud, like mental blue jays, but some only reacted to trauma this way and fought their way back screaming. She would most likely quiet when she woke. He hoped. Diego was never this loud, not even in his moments of greatest anguish.

"Fire and storm, Diego," he muttered. "Why did you choose this week to leave me on my own?"

* * * *

The house was still standing. Good. Finn hadn't had any major battles with household appliances. Diego pulled the truck into the freestanding garage at the back of the house. He smiled as he caught sight of the black jeans discarded in an untidy pile on the back porch. Finn was out, then, swimming and hunting.

A terrible thought had struck him on his way home. What if Finn had truly been pining, neglecting himself? He had sounded cheerful enough when Diego called each night, but he was a practiced liar and could have been covering up to keep Diego from worrying. A Beauty and the Beast scenario had crept into his thoughts, where he would come home to find Finn stretched out in the garden, dying. Stupid, of course, since Finn could go years without food, but knowing that he was doing what came naturally and not sitting inside sulking lifted a shadow from his heart.

He picked up the jeans and draped them over the porch railing. Finn might want them when he came back. "All right, *cariño,* you've had to wait days for me. I can wait a few hours while you're fishing."

The house was in order, no mess, no plates of half-eaten chicken strewn about and no oil paints smeared on the living room rug. A completed canvas leaned against the wall, a new one. Diego frowned at it, head cocked to one side. Predominantly black and gray, with anguished streaks of red and yellow, it screamed emotional distress. *Perhaps not doing so well after all.*

He climbed the stairs to take his bag to their bedroom and stopped cold in the doorway. A young woman lay in his bed, wrapped in his electric blanket and in his Finn's arms. As he watched, she turned with a little cooing sound and nuzzled at Finn's throat.

"Holy. Shit."

Finn's head jerked up, expression frozen in horror. "My love, I didn't hear you arrive —"

"I guess not," Diego said softly. "You're a jackass." He dropped his bag, hurried down the stairs and out of the back door.

"Diego, wait!" The anguished wail followed him but he didn't stop until he hit the gravel drive.

Finn shot through the door, stark naked, still half-erect. *Great, wonderful, go ahead and throw it in my face.*

"Diego, please." Finn spread his hands, looked down at himself, and at least mustered the sense to reach for his jeans draped on the rail. "Let me —"

438

"No. Don't." Diego held up a hand to stop him. "I don't want to hear your excuses, your justifications. Not just now."

Finn's mind reached for him, a soft, tentative touch, while he took a step closer, holding a hand out to him.

"No, damn it!" Diego flung up the mental wall to keep him out and backpedaled three steps. "You need to leave me alone right now. I came home early. I was worried about you. Stupid me."

"But I—"

"I don't care why you took her to bed! I don't want to hear what happened!" He ran his hands over his face, chest constricting with anger and pain. "I knew. I *knew* what you were when I fell in love with you. A liar and a satyric who's let his dick lead him around for centuries. But why make me promises you knew you couldn't keep? *Dios...* Finn..."

"My love—"

"Leave me be for a few! Let me think without you hammering to get in!"

He spun away and strode off into the woods.

* * * *

Finn shivered in the wake of Diego's fury and yanked the jeans on, marking the path of his retreat. Diego was so hurt, so angry, Finn could sense the lightning beginning to spark in his head. If he let it go too far, he would have an attack of the falling sickness. Out there in the woods. Alone.

Of course, if Diego was angry enough, he might turn the lightning on Finn.

He chewed his bottom lip and came to a decision, taking the steps two at a time to race back to the bedroom. The girl was just sitting up, befuddled and groggy. She looked up as he skidded to a stop in the doorway.

"You were drowning. I pulled you out. There's a phone beside you. Call someone to collect you. You are in a house at Box 22 on Old Route 249. They should find it by that."

He didn't stop to see if his rapid-fire instructions were heard or followed. Heart pounding against his ribs, he flung himself back down the stairs and after Diego. The trail was as much physical scent as thought scent. Diego's anguish could have been heard for miles by any creature not head-blind and the little sparks of magic leaping from him crackled more and more loudly.

"Don't turn me into fried pooka, love, please, please," Finn muttered as he ran. Diego had never been able to use his enormous potential while fully awake, but once he seized, the unleashing of his mental lightning was daunting.

The hairs on the back of his neck stood straight up, the sudden pull on the flows of surrounding magic nearly sucking all the air from the woods. Finn broke into a full-out sprint.

"Diego! Diego, no!"

A wall of force slammed into him and hurled him through the air. His back smashed into something with a sickening crack. The sun went dark.

Sign up for our newsletter and find out about all our romance book releases, eBook sales and promotions, sneak peeks and FREE romance eBooks!

https://totallyentwinedgroup.us7.list-manage.com/subscribe/post

About the Authors

Angel Martinez

The unlikely black sheep of an ivory tower intellectual family, Angel Martinez has managed to make her way through life reasonably unscathed. Despite a wildly misspent youth, she snagged a degree in English Lit, married once and did it right the first time, (same husband for almost twenty-four years) gave birth to one amazing son, (now in college) and realized at some point that she could get paid for writing.

Published since 2006, Angel's cynical heart cloaks a desperate romantic. You'll find drama and humor given equal weight in her writing and don't expect sad endings. Life is sad enough.

She currently lives in Delaware in a drinking town with a college problem and writes Science Fiction and Fantasy centered around gay heroes.

Freddy MacKay

Freddy is a bisexual, biromantic, genderfluid nerd and geek who grew up in the Midwest playing soccer, diving, swimming and doing gymnastics, along with running around outside as much as possible— preferably spending that time in swamps and hiking through forests. The haphazard escapades have not changed, except some of them have been replaced with a healthy geocaching addiction and a love for Science Fiction and Fantasy. This love of SFF developed into a writing passion and has led to several awards in the gay science fiction and fantasy categories. Freddy likes worms, dancing and being outside…and toll passes, but you'll have to ask on that one. (They/Them/Their pronouns.)

Angel and Freddy love to hear from readers. You can find their contact information, website details and author profile page at http://www.pride-publishing.com

www.ingramcontent.com/pod-product-compliance
Lightning Source LLC
Chambersburg PA
CBHW030750030726
47497CB00001B/220